GEORGIANA DARCY

A SEQUEL TO

JANE AUSTEN'S *PRIDE AND PREJUDICE*

BY

ALICE ISAKOVA

ISBN-13: 978-0-6483808-0-1

TABLE OF CONTENTS

CHAPTER 1

A young woman is never so beautiful, charming, or accomplished as when she also possesses a large fortune to add to her other attractions. If a suitor does not consider riches to be an indispensable virtue, his family certainly does, and woe to him who does not choose his wife accordingly. The lady's relations, being no more ignorant of these facts than the suitor's family, guard their beloved daughter, sister, or niece all the more closely lest such a treasure should fall into the wrong hands.

"My dear, there is something I must discuss with you," said Mr. Darcy to his wife one fine day in October.

"Yes, what is it?" replied Elizabeth.

"Lately, I have been thinking of my sister. As you are aware, in less than a year she will be eighteen, and perhaps it is therefore time to give consideration to her future. Ordinarily, that is a task that falls on the parents, but since my mother and father are no longer living, I believe it becomes our duty to guide Georgiana in society and help her make a good match."

"Do you have any candidates in mind?"

"No, not as yet," answered Mr. Darcy, "but whoever is chosen in the end, my chief concern is for Georgiana to be happy. I wish for my sister to discover the same felicity in marriage that you and I have found together." After a slight pause, he added, "Yet, at the same time, I would not want for her to marry into poverty, for I hardly see how a sharp decline in her style of living could contribute to her happiness."

Elizabeth remarked, "With her fortune of thirty thousand pounds, I doubt that she will ever know true poverty no matter whom she marries."

"Perhaps," said Darcy, "but I believe that as regards unequal marriages, it is far more perilous for a wealthy woman to descend into the valley of poverty for a husband, than it is for a wealthy man to come down for a wife. She is much less able to raise her partner in life to her level than he is. Moreover, the size of my sister's fortune is precisely what concerns me. Many a fortune-hunter will find the sum of thirty thousand pounds a very attractive inducement, indeed; above all else, I fear that some greedy, heartless rogue will insinuate himself so far into Georgiana's good graces as to persuade her to marry him, and that afterwards she will live a life of misery while he spends her fortune to the last farthing. I hardly need remind you of how close she came to that fate not so very long ago with Mr. Wickham."

Here Elizabeth stopped her husband to point out that his sister was a sensible, virtuous young woman, and although Georgiana had once made the error of contemplating an elopement, she had been only fifteen years old at the time. Did her brother now think that she would repeat her former folly?

"I suppose not," conceded Darcy, "but still, we must be cautious."

"And so we shall be! But for the present, had we not better turn our minds to how best to help your sister find a husband who *will* be suitable? Spending a season in London is the established way, I believe. At one of the balls and parties in town, she may perhaps make the acquaintance of a worthy, young man with whom she can be happy."

Mr. Darcy had no objection to going to town for the season except one: he would soon be much occupied with business matters relating to his recent purchase of an estate in Scotland, and therefore, he could not be certain whether it would be possible for him to take his family to London at all that year. The newly-bought estate was a very promising one, with some of the most fertile land in Scotland, but its former owner had allowed the property to fall into a state of neglect in the last years. It would be necessary to find a new land agent since the current one had shown himself to be abominably remiss in the execution of his duties. For this task and others needed to bring about substantial improvements on the estate, Darcy intended to leave for Scotland in the latter part of October, and after a week or two, he would rejoin Elizabeth and Georgiana in England to visit their family and friends. Afterwards, he planned to take both ladies with him to Scotland in December, where they would remain for at least a month, but possibly all winter.

Elizabeth agreed that this was a good plan, though it would be a pity if Georgiana missed the London season, especially when the maiden had just come into full bloom.

"Yes, my sister has improved markedly in the last year," said Darcy, "and it is all on account of your influence, my dear. She no longer has that painful shyness which characterised her manners in the past; you have softened her diffidence into modesty, and your good example has brought out a playfulness of spirit in Georgiana that I have not seen in a long time—not since the death of my father, in fact."

"I will not deny having had some influence," returned his wife, "but neither do I think I can justly claim all credit; it is natural for a girl who is nearing eighteen to shake off much of the awkward diffidence of youth even without assistance."

Still determined to find a way for her sister-in-law to go out into society during the fashionable season, Elizabeth paused to contemplate the problem, and then said suddenly:

"What do you think if, instead of coming to Scotland with us, Georgiana goes to Bath in December with my sister Jane and her husband? It is not the equal of London, I know, but Mr. Bingley has a wide acquaintance there, and it would be in his power to introduce your sister into the circles of elegant society in Bath."

"Do you think they will want to take her with them?"

"I am sure of it! Jane is very fond of Georgiana and has more than once expressed a wish to see her more often, and your sister and Mr. Bingley have always been good friends. I will write to the Bingleys and ask them, of course, but I feel certain they will be very glad for her to accompany them when they go to Bath this winter."

Mr. Darcy was pleased with the idea. He would still endeavour to conclude his affairs in time to go to London in January, said he, but it would only be of benefit for Georgiana to make as many new acquaintances as possible, in Bath as well as London.

"But what about your sister Catherine?" asked he. "We have never discussed her future. She, too, is of marriageable age, and since she is living with us, should we perhaps be helping her to make a good match as well?"

"In time, yes," answered Elizabeth, "but I think it is yet too early to trust Kitty to behave properly in society. Though she has improved to some extent of late, she still forgets herself sometimes. I would hate for her to embarrass Georgiana in some way and thereby harm her chances. For the present, I believe Kitty will do better simply to continue her education. Marriage can wait."

Following this conversation, Elizabeth wrote to Jane, who lived in the neighbouring county with her husband. The reply she received was exactly the one she had hoped for; the Bingleys were delighted at the idea of taking Mr. Darcy's sister with them to Bath, and so it was settled. Georgiana and Elizabeth would first travel into Kent later that month, while Catherine Bennet would go to Mr. and Mrs. Bingley. In late November, Miss Bennet and the Bingleys would then journey into Hertfordshire to visit their family at Longbourn, where the Darcys would join them soon afterwards. From there, Elizabeth and Mr. Darcy were to continue on to Scotland, while Georgiana would set out for Bath with Jane and Mr. Bingley. Kitty was to remain with the Bennets at Longbourn for the winter.

It was a very pleasant surprise for Georgiana to hear that she would be accompanying the Bingleys to Bath. She had never been to that city before and was all excitement and anticipation to go. The prospect of visiting friends and family in Kent beforehand also occasioned much enthusiasm. When travelling into that county in the past, Georgiana had always stayed with her aunt and cousin at Rosings Park, but this time, the Darcys would instead be staying at Kleistringham House, the home of the Townsend family in the same neighbourhood. Mr. Townsend and Mr. Darcy were very good friends and had been so since making each other's acquaintance at Cambridge.

The Darcy family had a good reason for avoiding Rosings. Lady Catherine de Bourgh, Mr. Darcy's aunt and the mistress of Rosings Park, had severely disapproved of the marriage between Elizabeth and her nephew.

The bride's lack of wealth and a grand family name was strongly objectionable to her ladyship, and although a reconciliation had eventually been achieved, relations between Lady Catherine and Mr. and Mrs. Darcy were still quite strained. Staying at Rosings during their sojourn in Kent was therefore out of the question.

Family difficulties aside, the next several months promised to be as interesting and agreeable as any young lady could wish for, at least in Georgiana's estimation. Elizabeth's younger sister, however, had a very different opinion. She was anything but pleased by her family's travel plans for the following months and was particularly resentful to learn that rather than going to town, she was to sit at home in the country, first with the Bingleys and then with the Bennets, where she would have no adventure at all! Kitty had long been looking forward to spending a season in London and had dreamed of going to countless balls and dancing with dozens of handsome young men. Was she now instead to languish in the country, while Georgiana partook of all the pleasures that would be denied to her? It was all her sister's doing, Kitty was sure of it! Mr. Darcy could never have suggested such an arrangement; he would not have wished to seem unkind by excluding her and giving preference to his own sister. Where was Elizabeth's loyalty? Where was her sisterly affection?

It was with the greatest bitterness that Kitty complained, and all the worst of her peevishness, which Mrs. Darcy had spent the last months trying to eradicate, was now on full display. All day long, Catherine could talk of nothing but the unfair treatment to which she was being subjected, and even in the evening, while the family were on their way to a ball, she continued her protests. Elizabeth endeavoured to reason with her:

"We may perhaps all go to town next year," said she, "and do you not want to visit Papa and Mama and your sister Mary? It must be nearly a year since you last saw them."

"I am not so anxious to visit my family as to wish to forego Bath and London! Why is it that Georgiana gets to spend her winter attending balls and parties while I must be exiled to Longbourn?!"

"There will be dances at Meryton, I am sure."

"And what of it? Since the regiment went away from Meryton, there is no one left within thirty miles of the place who is worth dancing with. It will be the same plain, dull fellows every time, some of them nearly old enough to be my father! And I am sure that the men at tonight's ball will be little better!"

Mr. Darcy maintained a grim silence and kept his gaze fixed on the view from the carriage window. It was only for his wife's sake that he had allowed Catherine to live with them at Pemberley, and at times like these he almost regretted the decision. How grating to the ear was her petulant whining!

When they arrived at the ball, Mr. and Mrs. Darcy's attention was soon distracted by one of their neighbours, who approached to share some new bit of gossip. Georgiana and Kitty meanwhile continued on in the direction of where the dancing was to take place. As they walked, Kitty was saying something about how her sister likely wished for her to become an old maid, when suddenly, the tone of her voice altered, and in the sweetest, most agreeable accent imaginable, she began praising the room and remarking on how much she was looking forward to dancing that evening.

Astonished by this sudden change, Georgiana turned to look at her companion. Kitty's face was the picture of good humour, the cause of which soon became obvious: coming in their general direction was a tall, handsome gentleman whom neither Miss Darcy nor Miss Bennet had ever seen before. He was finely-proportioned and tastefully attired, and in his air there was a certain dashing quality that never failed to draw the attention of the fair sex.

When he was nearly upon them, Kitty's reticule unexpectedly fell from her hand and landed with a faint thump on the floor. Georgiana perceived it at once and could scarcely believe that its owner did not, but Catherine Bennet walked on as if nothing had happened.

"Kitty, wait!" exclaimed Georgiana. However, before she could point out the fallen article to her friend, the man lifted it from the ground and addressed Miss Bennet with:

"I beg your pardon, Madam. I believe you dropped this."

Kitty rewarded him with a radiant smile, and taking back her reticule she replied, "How very careless of me! I thank you, Sir, for your trouble."

Georgiana blushed with shame on Catherine's account. When the man had moved some distance away, she said, "Kitty, you should not have done that. It was most indelicate of you!"

"What is so indelicate about accidentally dropping a reticule?"

"If only it were an accident! But you and I both know that it was not, and worse, I think that gentleman knows it too. You are not even acquainted with him!"

"I am sure it will not be long before we *are* introduced, and now that he has noticed me, perhaps he will even seek out an introduction."

The unknown gentleman did indeed return a few minutes later alongside Mr. Newnham, the master of the house. Mr. Newnham presented the handsome stranger to the ladies as his step-son, Mr. Morgan, who had completed his education at Cambridge that year and had now come to live in Derbyshire. To Kitty's delight, the young man requested the honour of her hand for the first two dances.

A minute or two later, Georgiana was herself asked to stand up for a set, and soon she and her partner were weaving with sprightly step through the mazes of a country dance. As they did so, she could not help noticing the way in which Kitty and Mr. Morgan were dancing together, and in particular, her friend's coquettish manner, the enticing glances she threw at the gentleman, and the flirtatious snippets of conversation that passed between them.

In the interim following the opening dance, Georgiana whispered to Kitty that she should not be so forward, but her friend would not hear reason.

"La! You are starting to sound just like Elizabeth!" exclaimed Catherine with some annoyance and then returned to frolic with Mr. Morgan in the next jig.

Georgiana was much admired at the ball and could scarcely finish treading one measure before some gallant spark invited her to join him in another. She had many agreeable partners that evening and was enjoying herself so much that she soon forgot all about Kitty and did not even notice when for two consecutive dances, her friend did not take part, and neither was she among the ladies sitting on the side waiting to be asked.

At the end of a quadrille, Mrs. Darcy came to Georgiana and inquired whether she knew where her sister had gone. Georgiana answered that she had no notion of Kitty's having quitted the room at all. After a moment's pause she added that perhaps Kitty had gone to the refreshments room. Elizabeth replied that it was the first place she had looked, and there was no sign of Catherine there, nor anywhere else one might reasonably expect to find her.

Knowing it would be in vain, the Darcy ladies nevertheless again went to the refreshments room in search of her and even looked behind a screen that was stationed there, but to no avail; she was nowhere to be found. As the ladies were returning, both with concerned countenances, they suddenly heard the sound of soft, girlish laughter coming from Mr. Newnham's library. Georgiana and Elizabeth exchanged a look—that must be her!

As they approached the library doors, which were nearly closed, the ladies heard a man's deep voice speaking in lowered tones, and then the sound of Kitty purring something in reply. Opening the doors, Elizabeth beheld her sister seated quite close to Mr. Morgan on a sofa in the dimly-lit room. With a look of alarm, Catherine leaped to her feet and declared in a quivering voice that she and Mr. Morgan had merely been getting better acquainted.

"I can see that," answered Elizabeth curtly, and then turning to the gentleman, she asked in a calm, yet stony voice whether she might have a word alone with her sister.

"Certainly, Mrs. Darcy."

Looking simultaneously sheepish and amused, he left the library. Once Elizabeth was sure that no one else could hear, she demanded, "Would you like to explain what the two of you were doing here all by yourselves?"

"There is nothing to explain!" returned Kitty defensively. "We were just talking—it is not as if we were kissing or anything!"

This answer did little to pacify Elizabeth, who proceeded to scold her younger sister in the most earnest terms:

"Kitty, you stole away to be in a room alone with a man you hardly know, and when I found you here, you were sitting immodestly close to him. Suppose that someone else had walked in and seen you together? Are you not aware of how quickly gossip spreads and how little it takes to harm a woman's reputation?"

Kitty did not contradict Elizabeth, but neither did she appear to be in the least remorseful. On the contrary, there was something of defiance in her countenance. Mrs. Darcy saw that her words were making little if any impression on her sister's mind, and therefore she needed no more proof that it would indeed be unwise to let Catherine go to Bath or London that year; if her conduct at the Newnhams' ball was any indication, nothing good would come of taking her to town.

CHAPTER 2

Shortly before breakfast the next morning, a footman brought the Pemberley ladies their letters. There was one for Kitty from Lydia Wickham, her younger sister, and another for Georgiana from her cousin Anne de Bourgh. As Georgiana was opening her letter, Elizabeth observed, "You always seem so pleased to hear from Miss de Bourgh and appear to enjoy reading her letters. Are you so very fond of your cousin, then?"

"I am, indeed... You look surprised."

"I must admit that I am surprised; you and Miss de Bourgh do not seem at all alike," answered Elizabeth.

"In what way would you say we are different?"

"Well, my impression of her was that she is very proud, like her mother, and if I am to speak plainly, I also found her to be rather uninteresting. The first time I dined at Rosings, she did not speak to me at the table even once, though we were seated right beside each other."

"I do not recall speaking very much to you when we were first introduced," remarked Georgiana.

"That was different—you were shy."

"And Anne is not?"

"I do not think so; to me, it appeared that pride was the source of her reticence... The first time I ever laid eyes on her was when she drove by in her phaeton a day or two after I arrived in Kent to visit my good friend

Charlotte and her husband, Mr. Collins. Miss de Bourgh stopped at the parsonage-house to invite us to dine at Rosings, but she would not come in and instead kept Charlotte out in the cold wind while they talked, and she looked rather cross, besides."

"Knowing Anne, I do not at all wonder at her having been so out of spirits," said Georgiana. "She dislikes driving in windy weather, but my aunt insists that she must go outdoors every day except if it rains. 'Fresh air is good for the lungs,' my aunt often says."

"But if not for reasons of self-importance, why would Miss de Bourgh not come inside the parsonage-house then, if only to escape the cold wind?"

"Anne feels very ill at ease in company and rarely calls on anyone except the very closest friends, other than when she makes charitable visits to poor families in her parish, of course."

"But why should that be? Lady Catherine de Bourgh and her daughter are among the wealthiest and most respected ladies in England. Why should Miss de Bourgh be ill at ease in society?"

"I believe Anne's upbringing is at fault for her timidity," replied Georgiana. "My aunt can be very overbearing, and even though her daughter is full-grown, she still directs every particular of her life. My cousin cannot so much as choose the colour of a gown without her mother's interference."

"That I can well believe!" laughed Elizabeth. "You should have heard the officious manner in which Lady Catherine instructed Charlotte as to the care of her chickens!"

Smiling, Georgiana answered, "Though Anne is timid and very unsure of herself, she has a gentle nature and a good heart. I am certain that when you have become better acquainted with her, you will love her as much as I do."

Kitty, who had just finished reading Lydia's letter, interrupted the conversation to say that her sister had invited her to stay at her home in Newcastle and wondered whether she might go. Mrs. Darcy, however, would not hear of it and reminded her that their father had expressly forbidden any scheme of the kind. Kitty exclaimed that it was not fair—why was it that she was to be banished to Longbourn on the pretext of visiting her family (while Georgiana would be enjoying herself in town!), and yet she was not allowed to see her own sister?!

"You know why," returned Elizabeth. "Considering your and Lydia's past behaviour, it is lucky for you that Papa did not send you off to a nunnery!"

In reply, Kitty only complained all the more vehemently. Lydia's letter had contained a particularly lively account of the last ball she attended, as well as a promise to introduce all the young, handsome officers in her husband's regiment to her. The idea of being forcibly kept away while Georgiana would in the meantime be dancing with all the dashing gallants of Bath and London filled her with the deepest indignation. What injustice! What cruel usage!

Not for a minute did Elizabeth consider capitulating to her sister's demands. On the contrary, Kitty's eagerness to be reunited with her errant younger sister only strengthened her conviction that she should be kept as far away from town as possible that winter. After much petulant protesta-tion, Kitty at last relinquished the hope of convincing Elizabeth to let her go, and afterwards she moved some distance away to pout resentfully on a sofa.

With the storm over, Georgiana was finally able to read her own letter. Anne had written the following:

"My dear Cousin,

"I have just received your letter, which I found very entertaining indeed. I wish I could make a proper return with a story equally amusing, but unfortunately, little has happened here since I last wrote, and nothing at all that would make you laugh. My only news is that our parson, Mr. Collins, died of a severe chill on Friday, of which occurrence I thought you might wish to be informed since he is Mrs. Darcy's cousin.

"About a week before his demise, Mr. Collins awoke with a sore throat and a slight headache. Rather than stay home to nurse his cold, he insisted on going out for his morning walk as usual, for my mother had often spoken to him of the great benefit to health that must arise from walking every morning. With her words in mind, he ventured out. For perhaps half an hour he pursued this exercise, but just as he was about to turn back, it started to rain heavily. He had no choice but to walk home in the downpour, and by the time Mr. Collins reached his house, his clothing was completely soaked, and he felt feverish. His wife urged him to seek the assistance of a physician, but he was adamant in his refusal and consented to be seen only by Mr. Leech, the apothecary, because he did not wish to risk my mother's displeasure. Mr. Collins clearly remembered Mama's instructions that an apothecary would be perfectly adequate for his family's needs, and if she should hear that he had used the services of any but Mr. Leech, she would be highly disobliged. My mother being Mr. Collins' patroness, he was always unfailingly attentive to her wishes, and this time was no exception.

"The apothecary came, but the draught he gave his patient produced no beneficial effect. Mr. Collins' condition deteriorated rapidly, and before a week had passed, he met his end. Mama was at first very displeased when she heard of his death, both because she dislikes the inconvenience of now having to find a replacement for him, and because she feels his untimely death could have been prevented; she believes he was very careless to go walking when ominous rain clouds had clearly been gathering in the sky that morning, and he knew that he was already ill. However, Mama is in better spirits now; she busies herself with giving Mrs. Collins instructions on every detail of the funeral arrangements and mourning: 'a widow must wear black crape and bombazine; no jewellery except a mourning ring or brooch, and perhaps jet beads; black gloves and scarves to be given to the mourners for the ceremony,' and so on. I am sure Mama means to be helpful, but Mrs. Collins looks a little exasperated at times by all the advice, notwithstanding that she is a very patient woman in general.

"As a consequence of Mr. Collins' death, the living of Hunsford is now vacant. Mama wishes her nephew William de Bourgh to have it, but since it will be some years before little William is old enough to take the living, a curate will be employed until my cousin is ordained. Mama has chosen a gentleman by the name of Mr. Grey for the post, though nothing has been finally settled yet. She will make her decision after he comes to visit us on Friday, and she has had the opportunity to speak to him further. Though Mr. Grey lives in the same county, I have never met him; he comes from the eastern part of Kent, near Canterbury. There is nothing else I know about him except that he is a well-educated young man of good family, but that he and his nearest relations now find themselves in reduced circumstances following the death of his father.

"I had better leave off here, for if I do not seal and put away the letter now, Mama will almost certainly wish to hear what I have written when she comes into the sitting room, and she is likely also to desire the addition of a postscript with various directives for you. No doubt that is something you could do without.

"Yours affectionately, Anne"

Looking up from her letter, Georgiana said, "Lizzy, Anne has written here about your cousin Mr. Collins."

"I am all eagerness to hear it! Has he gone to Rosings again to pay homage to Lady Catherine and her daughter?" asked Mrs. Darcy mirthfully.

"No, nothing like that. I think I had better read it to you."

Finding the pertinent passage, Georgiana proceeded to read the letter aloud. When she had finished, Elizabeth exclaimed, "How unexpected is my cousin's death! I am very sorry for it, particularly as regards his wife. Poor Charlotte! I can imagine her distress! And I am sure it does not help matters that Lady Catherine finds it necessary to provide so much unasked guidance on everything... But at least it may be some comfort to Charlotte to know that Mr. Collins would not have had it otherwise. During his lifetime, he was always profoundly grateful for Lady Catherine's advice on everything concerning his private affairs, and no doubt he would be pleased that her ladyship now takes such an active role in supervising his passage into the next world."

Forgetting her own troubles for a moment, Kitty asked, "But if Mr. Collins is dead, who will inherit Longbourn? Will Papa's estate come back to us?"

"No, Kitty, that is not how an entail works. None of Papa's daughters can inherit Longbourn. The estate must go to a male heir."

"But who will that be?"

"I have no idea," said Elizabeth, "but I am sure we will find out soon enough."

CHAPTER 3

O n the morrow, Anne spent the early part of the afternoon in the main drawing room with her mother and her companion, Mrs. Jenkinson. The morning had been an unusually cold one, and although the maids heaped wood on the fire, the ferocious blaze could not seem to get the better of the chill that seeped in through the walls and windows. Lady Catherine had a hardy constitution and did not mind, but Anne could not seem to get warm; her shawl proved quite inadequate, which compelled Mrs. Jenkinson to fetch her a warmer one.

It was nearly time for that day's first callers to arrive. The two ladies whom they were expecting, Lady Catherine informed her daughter, were from a family that had recently settled in the neighbourhood at Belargent Hall, only a few miles away from Rosings. The family's name was Villiers. What a relief it was, proclaimed Lady Catherine, to finally have a fine, old family of Norman stock settle on that estate, and what a welcome change from Belargent's former occupants—an upstart family but one generation removed from trade.

Although Lady Villiers and her daughter had called at Rosings once before, Anne had been unable to make their acquaintance on account of having to spend the whole week in bed with a severe cold. She was suffi-ciently recovered today to see them, but the thought of meeting her new neighbours at last filled Anne with apprehension rather than eager anticipation. Oh, how she dreaded making new acquaintances! It could not be helped, however, as here was the Villiers' carriage coming now. Watching its progress through a window, Anne observed that it was an exceptionally elegant coach drawn by four magnificent Arabian grey horses. Completing the handsome equipage were the coachman and footman, both of whom were attired in splendid livery.

Sitting comfortably inside the coach were the two Villiers ladies, who were deeply engrossed in earnest conversation:

"Now, Mama, it would be best if you were to speak as little as possible while we are at Rosings. In society you often say more than is prudent," said Priscilla Villiers to her mother.

"Well, I cannot sit there in complete silence. I will have to say something," came the reply.

"Mama, I daresay Lady Catherine will do most of the talking as she did on our previous visit to Rosings. If you must speak, try to keep to harmless topics such as the weather. You would not wish Lady Catherine to think us gauche, especially if we are to accomplish a marriage between John and Miss de Bourgh."

"Ah, what a fine match that would be," replied Lady Villiers with enthusiasm. "To think, my own son marrying the granddaughter of an earl, and one with a princely fortune too!"

Given Lady Villiers' descent, such a hope for her child's future was indeed an extraordinary one. Lady Villiers was the daughter of Benjamin Taylor, a London shop owner whose insignificant business barely managed to remain solvent. His only daughter, Penelope, was not clever, and with no money or connections she would have been unlikely to make a good match. Yet, Penelope Taylor had the good fortune to be extremely beautiful and turned heads wherever she went. At sixteen years old she caught the eye of Edward Villiers, a young man of modest means who nevertheless could claim the honour of being a direct descendant of Sir George Villiers, the great sixteenth century representative of the illustrious Villiers family. Although Sir George himself began as merely a sheep farmer, he received a knighthood, and many of his descendants went on to become dukes, earls, prime ministers, and even kings' favourites.

Edward Villiers' branch of that great family tree was much less prosperous. For several generations, his family had been in trade, and his own father kept a shop. After marrying Penelope Taylor, Edward Villiers took over his father's business and through a series of shrewd decisions transformed it into one of the most successful shops in London's fashionable Bond Street. Not long afterwards, he was made a baronet. The day he became *Sir* Edward was the happiest of his wife's life as she would henceforth be addressed as Lady Villiers. All that remained for Sir Edward to do to become a true member of the gentry was to live a life of idleness on a large estate in the country, which he promptly achieved by moving his whole family to a fine property in Kent.

The arrival of the Villiers' coach at Rosings put an end to the passengers' discourse. After they stepped out of the carriage, their thoughts were occupied solely by the magnificence before them. The house was every bit as grand as they remembered it, and as the butler led them through to the drawing room, Priscilla Villiers and her mother turned their heads in all directions and cast their eyes on everything with covetous delight. Once they had entered the drawing room, they admired more discreetly, though with no less awe than before. The guests took in every detail of their surroundings: the Chippendale bookcase, the chairs upholstered with blue damask silk, the great fireplace. The carpet, Miss Villiers observed, was undoubtedly an Axminster. Hand-knotted and worth a fortune, it was no less a work of art than the Thomas Lawrence painting on the wall. "All this may be John's someday!" Lady Villiers thought with pleasure.

For her part, Anne observed the newly-arrived guests with as much interest as that with which they surveyed the room. Both of them were very richly dressed, but Anne's eyes fell first on Lady Villiers, who, despite her matronly years, never failed to draw the attention of all who beheld her. The other lady looked to be approximately seventeen or eighteen, and though not her mother's equal in beauty, she was nevertheless very handsome. Miss Villiers' most striking feature was her red-gold hair, which was arranged to its best advantage in a very becoming manner. Her face was quite attractive, though perhaps somewhat lacking in that delicacy and refinement which one might expect in a woman of elevated birth. Similarly, her figure was pleasing and shapely, but of rather robust build. The young lady's manners and countenance were very self-assured almost to the point of haughtiness, and although Anne was close to a decade older, she felt herself shrink beneath her young guest's appraising gaze.

Once the necessary introductions had been made and all the ladies were seated, Lady Catherine began the conversation:

"How are you settling into your new home, Lady Villiers?"

"Very well, thank you. Everything quite exceeds our expectations, although I do sometimes miss London and our house in Park Lane."

Priscilla Villiers nodded approvingly. She was pleased to hear her mother mention their residence in that most fashionable street in Mayfair, so highly sought-after among England's wealthy.

"I was especially fond of our daily walks in Hyde Park," continued her mother.

"You are fond of walking? I am glad to hear it. There is no exercise more beneficial than walking, and I find that the best time of day to engage in such exertion is early in the morning. I hope you are an early riser, Lady Villiers?"

"I confess I am not. I rarely rise before half past nine, but often I stay in bed until after ten."

"Till after ten?! Not up until such an indecent hour? Why, Lady Villiers, how can you expect to keep a well-managed household if you spend the best part of the day in bed?"

"The housekeeper and the butler see to it that everything is managed properly, and all our servants are up at six to do their work. I hardly see how it would make much difference if I were to rise early."

"The mistress sets the tone for the whole household," came the reply. "If she remains in bed until a late hour, the servants will acquire some of her ways and become lazy in their tasks. Moreover, waking early in the morning is not only a question of household management but of Christian duty; the Bible commands us to rise early."

"It does?"

"Of course! Have you forgotten the passage in Proverbs about the virtuous woman, who eats not the bread of idleness but rises while it is yet night to tend to her home and family? I have no doubt that Jesus himself woke early in the morning to secure time and solitude for prayer to his Holy Father. We must spare no effort to follow our Saviour's good example!"

Not relishing the idea of spending early mornings in useful activity, Lady Villiers hastened to change the subject:

"What splendid weather we have had these last few days. What a welcome change from that dreadful rain a fortnight ago."

Lady Catherine answered, "You may have heard that Mr. Collins fell ill while walking in that thunderstorm and died as a result."

"Oh yes, it was most unfortunate news. Such a dreadful story! As a young girl in London, I once got caught in just such a thunderstorm. I was carrying large baskets of fish and vegetables from the market when a heavy rain began to pour most unexpectedly. I was soaked to the skin by the time I returned home."

"Baskets of fish and vegetables?! Where were the servants?" cried Lady Catherine in astonishment.

"What Mama means is that she was taking baskets of food to the poor. Is that not so, Mama?" Priscilla Villiers added hurriedly.

"Oh, yes, yes of course," replied her mother.

"Mama got wet in the rain when going to and from her carriage."

"It must have been a heavy rain indeed," remarked Lady Catherine.

"It was, Madam."

Miss Villiers searched desperately for a change of topic:

"What a splendid room you have here, Lady Catherine! How elegantly and tastefully furnished, and what a magnificent pianoforte! Do you play, Miss de Bourgh?"

"I..." Anne started to reply, but Lady Catherine cut in:

"My daughter's talent for music is nothing short of prodigious, but sadly, her delicate health has prevented her from realising her true potential."

Miss Villiers smiled knowingly but made no reply. Her mother had more to say on the subject:

"What a pity, for Miss de Bourgh's hands look as if they were designed for the pianoforte! She has the long, slender fingers of a virtuoso."

Anne looked down at her hands in surprise, for she had never perceived anything remarkable about them, but Lady Catherine appeared very pleased to hear such praise, and turning to the younger of her two guests, she asked, "Do you play, Miss Villiers?"

"I am very fond of music and take great pleasure in playing on the pianoforte."

"Priscilla had the best teachers that could be found," added the girl's mother.

"Is that so? Well, let us hear you then, Miss Villiers. Play me something by Mozart."

Glad of a chance to display her talents, the young lady glided elegantly to the pianoforte and began to play. As the music started, Lady Villiers puffed up with pride at the thought of how very accomplished her daughter was, and how superior to other young ladies. She thought, also, what a fine thing it was that Lady Catherine and her daughter, ladies of great consequence, could hear her daughter play. Anne also listened with admiration; she herself could not execute any of Mozart's compositions with as much technical skill, and she respected such musical abilities in others.

No one could deny that Miss Villiers was well-trained, and yet, there was something wanting in her execution; it lacked that quality that separates a great performance from an ordinary one. She played the tune with her hands and not her heart, and as a consequence, her rendition of Mozart's piece lacked any real depth of feeling. Lady Catherine could sense that something was amiss but could not identify what it was.

When her ladyship decided she had heard enough, she made a sign for Miss Villiers to stop and then said, "You play tolerably well, but I think you performed that piece rather too quickly. I do not believe that Mozart intended it to be executed at quite that speed."

"She will practice some more at home, won't you, Priscilla?" said Lady Villiers in a very obliging tone of voice.

"Yes, Mama."

In the carriage on the way home, Miss Villiers was much less submissive:

"Mama, you almost gave us all away with your talk of carrying baskets of food in the rain."

"I tried to speak about the weather as you said I should," her mother protested.

"Yes, Mama, the *weather*, not stories of your girlhood days in Cheapside! As for Lady Catherine, the woman is insufferable. To say that I played Mozart too quickly! I played the music at exactly the pace that was required. It was Lady Catherine's ears that could not keep up! And for all that she is a fine lady, the lace on my gown was superior to what her daughter had on hers."

Lady Villiers answered, "I thought Miss de Bourgh's lace was very fine."

"Perhaps it was, but mine was finer. The pattern was more intricate. And the colour of her gown—such a hideous shade of purple! It does not become her complexion in the least!"

Without stopping to draw breath, the young lady continued, "I doubt that Miss de Bourgh knows any languages besides English, and we know she cannot sing or play the pianoforte. I am sure she cannot even draw! Miss de Bourgh lacks every refinement of a true lady!"

During the whole ride back to Belargent Hall, Priscilla Villiers had no shortage of things to say or grievances to air, and so she continued to fill her mother's ears without intermission.

CHAPTER 4

In the afternoon of the following day, Anne descended the stairs to the blue drawing room, where she found one of the maids hurrying to finish dusting before the arrival of Mr. Grey, who was expected at Rosings shortly. Lady Catherine had been displeased with how the room was dusted that morning, and, her ladyship having given the order to do it again, the maid now worked at lightning speed to complete the task in time. Seeing Anne come in, the servant said, "I beg your pardon, Miss de Bourgh. I shall be gone in an instant."

"That is fine, Hannah. Please feel free to finish your work."

Anne chose a comfortable chair nearest the fire, while the maid flew about the room with her dust cloth. Lady Catherine was to enter at any moment, and Hannah was anxious to finish in time to avoid her mistress' scolding tongue. In her haste, she knocked a vase off of a table, and despite her best efforts to catch it before it fell, the vase came crashing to the floor. For a few seconds, the maid stared in disbelief at the pieces of porcelain before her.

"Oh, no! What have I done?!" cried she. Kneeling to the floor, the servant began picking up the shards. "No, no," she moaned, as if willing the vase to reassemble itself back to its former condition. "It is worth more money than I will see in a lifetime. Her ladyship will surely dismiss me from the household when she discovers what I have done!"

"Oh, Hannah! Do not cry," Anne entreated. "Perhaps it will not come to that."

Half-blinded by her tears, Hannah could hardly see what she was doing, and not surprisingly, she cut her hand on a fragment of porcelain. The wretched girl began sobbing in earnest as drops of scarlet began trickling down her palm.

"There, there, Hannah. Calm yourself," said Anne as she produced a handkerchief and proceeded to tie it around the wound. Just then, Lady Catherine walked into the room.

"What is all this?" her ladyship demanded. Then, perceiving the broken pottery strewn on the floor, she cried, "My favourite Sèvres vase! How did this happen?!"

Hannah opened her mouth as if to speak, but no words emerged, and all she could do was stare in terror at her mistress.

"I broke the vase, Mama," said Anne. "I... I stumbled and accidentally knocked the vase off the table. Hannah was collecting the pieces, and she has cut her hand, you see."

The maid at first looked astonished at these words, but then her expression turned to profound gratitude and relief at having escaped her ladyship's fury.

"Anne, it does not do to always be stumbling about and knocking into things," Lady Catherine chastised her daughter. "You must endeavour to move with more grace. And straighten your shoulders! If you continue hunching them in that manner, you will soon have a permanent hump in your back."

Anne bore her mother's scolding patiently and silently except for the occasional "Yes, Mama." While Hannah collected the vase fragments, Lady Catherine upbraided her daughter and would have continued to do so at length if she had not been interrupted by the arrival of Mr. Grey.

The gentleman who entered the drawing room was uncommonly good-looking; he had flaxen hair, a warm smile, and beautiful, blue eyes full of merriment—he was one of the handsomest young men Anne had ever seen. She coloured at the sight of him and knew not where to direct her gaze but became suddenly self-conscious about her appearance. Oh, why had she not chosen a prettier dress that day! The one she had on was one of her plainest and least becoming gowns. But it could not be helped now! The best Anne could do was to arrange her shawl in a more attractive manner around her shoulders.

Lady Catherine, on the other hand, looked as grand and imposing as ever, or perhaps even a little more so than usual, as she cast a scrutinising eye over her visitor. Yet, although Mr. Grey conducted himself with respect towards her ladyship, he did not at all seem to be awed or intimidated by her presence, not even when she began her interrogation:

"Mr. Grey, you attended Oxford, I believe?"

"Yes, that is correct."

"And how did you make use of your time there?"

"Use, Madam? I am not sure I comprehend your meaning."

"Then I will speak plainly—the universities of England were once fine educational institutions, but over time they have become more akin to seminaries of vice rather than learning. Many a promising young man has descended into dissipation after commencing his studies. Free from restraint, he adopts the drunken habits of his new acquaintances and spends less time reading books than gambling, fox hunting, and visiting houses of ill repute. Is that how you spent your years at Oxford?"

Looking a little surprised but at the same time amused, Mr. Grey replied:

"No, not at all. While it is true that some students hardly attended their lectures and led lives of dissipation, I was never one of them. Although I made many new friends at Oxford, the greater part of my time I spent in study, and those with whom I chose to spend my leisure hours were fine gentlemen of sense and good character."

"What about your academic results? Did you take honours?"

"I did, my lady."

"In classics or in mathematics?"

"In both. I received a double first."

"A double first class degree! That is a fine distinction, indeed!" her ladyship exclaimed.

Anne was no less impressed and could not help but regard Mr. Grey with admiration. Not only was he extremely handsome, with pleasant and engaging manners, but also he was clearly an intelligent man, a scholar. Had he also been rich, Mr. Grey would have had no equal among men. However, his lack of a fortune did not prevent Anne from taking a keen interest in his response to Lady Catherine's next question:

"Mr. Grey, marriage is a fine institution. Have you considered getting married?"

Somewhat taken aback by the directness of her question, he answered, "I... well... yes, I have, my lady," to which she replied:

"I firmly believe that an unmarried man more easily falls into temptation and every form of vice, and marriage is therefore the natural remedy against such evil. A clergyman must lead by example and get married as soon as may be. You are of the same opinion, I hope, Mr. Grey?"

"The institution of marriage is indeed a fine thing," answered Mr. Grey thoughtfully. "If a man is so fortunate as to find a woman with whom he can share his life, then I suppose there is no reason for delay."

"Good. I am pleased to hear it. The late rector of Hunsford, Mr. Collins, found himself a wife not long after I advised him to do so. He chose a very sensible, useful woman as his wife. I hope that you will follow Mr. Collins' good example?"

"Madam, I thank you for your concern regarding my future, but much as I might wish to find a good wife sooner rather than later, I think we must await God's will in the matter."

"Mr. Grey, with a little effort, it cannot be difficult to find such a wife. In the village there are a number of fine young ladies of the same station as yourself. Surely you can find one among them who is suitable."

Lady Catherine proceeded to question the gentleman about his family and his upbringing, as well as to inquire who had paid for his education (since his family was in reduced circumstances), what sort of sermons he might give, and so on. Finally, she completed her interrogation with the following:

"In your position as a curate, you will doubtless encounter some foolish young couple who wish to elope and attempt to involve the clergyman in their scandalous plot. You seem to be a worthy young man, and I am sure I need not ask, but would you consent to perform the marriage ceremony in such a case?"

"I could not even if I wished to, Madam. Lord Hardwicke's Marriage

Act requires that if either the bride or the groom be aged under one-and-twenty, the parties cannot be married unless there is paternal consent. Moreover, in marriages by licence, at least one of the parties to be married in a parish church must have lived in that parish for at least four weeks before any marriage licence can be granted."

"Well, that is the answer I wished to hear," said Lady Catherine, "but I believe the law does not go far enough! Where family fortunes and the family name are at stake, the law should require the bride and groom to seek paternal consent in all cases, even where both parties are of age, and if the father is no longer living, then the parties' nearest relations should be consulted and give their approval before the marriage can take place."

Mr. Grey thought it absurd that full-grown men and women should be prohibited from marrying whom they choose simply because their families disapprove, but out of respect for Lady Catherine's rank, he did not say so. When his eye chanced to fall on Anne, however, he observed that though she sat quietly and looked at her hands, her countenance betrayed something other than enthusiastic agreement with her mother's views. For a moment, Anne looked up to meet his gaze, and though no words were spoken, she and Mr. Grey understood each other.

"Miss de Bourgh," the gentleman said suddenly. "What is your opinion on the matter?"

Before her daughter could utter a syllable, Lady Catherine exclaimed, "Why, her opinion is the same as mine, of course! Can there be any other view on the subject?"

Mr. Grey smiled and said, "It is merely that Miss de Bourgh looks as if she has something she wishes to contribute to the discussion. I would very much like to hear her thoughts."

Anne hesitated to speak, but drawing courage from Mr. Grey's reassuring smile, she replied, "I... I do not question that a child has a duty to respect his mother and father's wishes, and yet, there must come a time when a person is deemed old enough to make his own decisions, especially those that so greatly influence his future happiness."

"Anne, I am surprised at you!" cried Lady Catherine. "Considering the pains I have taken with your education and upbringing, I never thought to hear such words from your lips! When I was your age, young people deferred to the superior judgment of their elders; my generation knew the value of the Lord's commandment: 'Honour thy father and thy mother'. But now, everywhere one looks, one encounters rebelliousness and disdain for paternal wisdom!"

So vehement was Lady Catherine's disapproval of the views her daughter had had the temerity to express, that even after Mr. Grey had gone, her ladyship could talk of nothing else:

"How could you even think such things, Anne? I could not mention it in Mr. Grey's hearing, but need I remind you of the harm that has resulted to our own family from filial disobedience? My nephew Fitzwilliam Darcy ought to have married you. He knew full well that it was his late mother's wish as well as mine! But what did he do instead? He married an impertinent, artful woman with a disgraceful family and no fortune. That such a woman should now take my daughter's rightful place as the mistress of Pemberley! Oh, it is intolerable!"

Anne listened without protest to everything her mother had to say and regretted having spoken her mind so freely. It would have been much better to have kept her thoughts to herself. Lady Catherine's next words further heightened Anne's disquietude:

"If only your cousin had done his duty! But now, his ungrateful, impetuous behaviour compels me to commence a search for a suitable husband for you."

Though stunned by her mother's admission, Anne dared do nothing more than ask a few tentative questions about Lady Catherine's plans for her future. Her ladyship replied that while she had not yet made a final decision, she had several suitable candidates in mind and was making the necessary inquiries in the matter.

Her mind in turmoil, Anne left the drawing room as soon as she could and ascended to her bedchamber. In that unhappy moment, she wished desperately to see Georgiana, but being many miles away from her cousin, Anne could seek relief only in writing to her, which she proceeded to do directly.

Anne's letter was delivered shortly before Georgiana set out on her journey into Kent with Mrs. Darcy. As they were walking towards the chaise, the young lady said, "How fortunate that we did not leave home as early as we had planned. Otherwise, I would have missed Anne's letter."

Inside the carriage, she unfolded the page and began to read its contents silently:

"My dear Cousin,

"Much has happened since my last letter. Yesterday, we had a visit from Lady Villiers and her daughter, our new neighbours who have settled at Belargent Hall, but I have yet to meet the gentlemen of the family. John Villiers, the only son, is currently in London but is expected to come down to the family estate next week. Lady Villiers is most eager for Mama and me to meet him and assures us that he is a brilliant scholar.

"This afternoon I also made the acquaintance of Mr. Grey, whom, if you remember, Mama was considering installing as the curate of Hunsford parish. He came today, and my mother was pleased with both his answers and his manners. Therefore, he will take over the late Mr. Collins' duties in the parish until our cousin William is ordained. I must admit that I myself have formed a high opinion of Mr. Grey and look forward to introducing him to you when you arrive in Kent.

"After Mr. Grey left Rosings, I received some news that caused me a great deal of apprehension, and I am sure you will feel as much concern when you read it. In short, Mama has informed me that she intends to find me a husband, and as always, she did not think it necessary to consult my wishes in the matter. I know not what sort of man she will choose for me, except that he will almost certainly be very wealthy and come from an old, well-respected family.

"As you already know, it is not pomp or riches that I want but a man I can love and esteem, who will be as fond of me as I am of him. What I fear most is being connected for life with a man whom I cannot like, and who himself cares nothing for me except for the wealth and connections I will bring him. Sometimes I feel like a sparrow inside a golden cage. Though trembling at the thought that it is soon to have a new keeper, the little bird is powerless to escape; it knows only that its future master is likely to value the cage more than its contents, for who would want a plain, little sparrow?

"Forgive me if I pain you with such melancholy thoughts. Nothing will

cheer my spirits as much as seeing you at Rosings soon.
"Yours affectionately, Anne"

CHAPTER 5

The long, tedious journey from Pemberley to Kent was wearying to the limbs and fatiguing to the mind, so when at last Kleistringham House came into view, Georgiana and Elizabeth found it a very welcome sight. Mrs. Townsend must have seen their carriage from a window, for as the chaise neared the house, the Darcy ladies observed that she had already stationed herself outside to receive them.

The mistress of the house welcomed both ladies with all possible affability and kindness and then urged them indoors saying, "It is far too windy today to remain outside with any degree of pleasure. But the men do not seem to mind; they have gone out shooting." While leading her friends into the entrance hall, she added, "Among the shooting party is a gentleman from Cheshire who has only recently become known to our family. His name is Sir Matthew Leigh; he is a distant kinsman of Mr. Townsend. My husband met him by chance through a mutual acquaintance on his last trip to London, and since then they have become good friends. Sir Matthew joined us here at Kleistringham earlier this month, and he will continue to stay with us for the next few weeks."

When Mrs. Townsend had shown the Darcy ladies their rooms, Georgiana asked their hostess, "May I play some music on your pianoforte? It seems like ages since the last time I played."

"Certainly, if you wish, but you have only just arrived! Would you not prefer to rest after your long journey and take some refreshment?"

"I assure you, Mrs. Townsend, that nothing will revive my energies better than to play some tunes. As I recall, you have a very fine instrument in your drawing room."

"Yes; I do not play myself, but you may remember that Maria, my sister-in-law, has talent for music and used to practice a great deal before she married. Please feel free to use the pianoforte as much as you like, Miss Darcy. I should be delighted to have music at Kleistringham again."

While Elizabeth remained upstairs to get settled, Georgiana promptly went down to the drawing room. Chatting pleasantly with her guest, Mrs. Townsend took up some embroidery to work on, while the young lady arranged her music sheets on the pianoforte. Meanwhile, the gentlemen who had been out shooting were returning to the house. One of the party, Mr. Meggott, remarked to the others, "That last pheasant was a particularly wily one!"

"Oh yes, a wily pheasant indeed! If Sir Matthew were not such a good shot, it would surely have gotten away!" exclaimed Mr. Townsend.

Walking just behind the rest was a young gentleman no older than perhaps five-and-twenty. He was rather handsome with dark eyes; a well-chiselled jaw; and thick, dark brown hair that flowed in loose waves. As he and his companions reached the staircase that led to their bedchambers, the first notes of Beethoven's piano sonata *Quasi una fantasia* emanated from the drawing room. The music began softly, and since the men were much absorbed in conversation about that day's sport, most of them hardly noticed the sound. The young, handsome gentleman, however, perceived it and consequently paused at the bottom of the stairs. Instead of continuing up with the rest of the party, he turned around and began to move towards the source of the music. With almost no conscious thought on his part, he crossed the floor in the direction of the drawing room as if impelled thither by an invisible force.

Although the young man was familiar with Beethoven's famous sonata and had heard it performed on previous occasions, never before had the piece affected him so powerfully. Never before had he heard the music played with so much emotion and so much beauty as he did in that moment. He felt an irresistible curiosity to discover what sort of being was producing that heavenly sound. As the gentleman neared the entrance, he half-expected to see a fairy or some celestial spirit within. The reality was not far removed from what he imagined, for seated at the pianoforte he found a lovely young lady of nymph-like beauty.

So absorbed was she in playing the music that at first the handsome stranger standing in the doorway completely escaped her notice. Perhaps a minute passed before Georgiana finally looked up, and when she did, the music stopped abruptly. For several seconds, neither of them spoke or moved; the gentleman and Miss Darcy only gazed at one another in silence.

Wondering what was the matter, Mrs. Townsend lifted her eyes from her embroidery, and, perceiving the newcomer, she exclaimed, "Sir Matthew, you have returned! I was so occupied with my needlework that I did not see you come in." Then, turning to the young lady, she said, "Miss Darcy, allow me to present Sir Matthew Leigh, Mr. Townsend's cousin. Sir Matthew, this is Miss Darcy. She has only just arrived from Derbyshire."

The gentleman bowed, and Georgiana curtsied.

"Miss Darcy, you played that tune most beautifully. I do not exaggerate when I say that it was the most moving performance of Beethoven's composition that I have ever heard," said he.

"You flatter me, Sir Matthew."

"It is no flattery, Miss Darcy. I speak sincerely. I have heard that piece played numerous times before, but never with so much feeling as you did just now."

"Then, Sir, I thank you for your kind words."

"And shall I hear you play again this evening?"

"Yes, of course, if you wish."

"It would give me great pleasure."

As it was nearly time for dinner, there was only a sufficient interval to exchange a few more phrases. The young man inquired about whether Georgiana had had a pleasant journey, whether she had been to Kent before, and so on. In short, nothing more of consequence was said, but both the gentleman and Miss Darcy left the room with a strong desire to become better acquainted.

In her own chamber, Georgiana urged her maid to help her dress as quickly as possible, and then she hurried back downstairs to the drawing room. The butler soon announced that dinner was served, after which everyone proceeded to the dining room. At the table, Miss Darcy and Sir Matthew were seated farther away from one another than either would have liked, but from the furtive glances she occasionally cast in his direction, Georgiana could see that the young gentleman's eyes were often upon her.

After the meal had been eaten and the men had consumed their port, the two young people at last had an opportunity to deepen their acquaintance. Sir Matthew took a chair next to Georgiana in the drawing room and then tried to engage her in conversation, but the maiden spoke little and blushed more. She was, however, very interested to hear about his life and family in Cheshire. He told her that his mother and father were both dead, but he had a younger sister.

"How old is she?" asked Georgiana.

"Adelaide is thirteen."

"Is Miss Leigh in school, or does she have a governess?"

Sir Matthew started back a little at this question before answering:

"She has—that is to say—my sister *had* a governess... but some circumstances arose... it became necessary for the governess to leave, but a new one will be found in due course..."

After a momentary silence, he asked, "Miss Darcy, will you play something for us? I have been looking forward all evening to hearing you again." Georgiana agreed, and Sir Matthew offered to turn the pages of the music for her while she played. In reply, she smiled bashfully, clearly pleased by the attention.

Georgiana performed several lively tunes, to which everyone (and Sir Matthew in particular) listened with great enjoyment. From his position right beside her, he had the additional advantage of being able to admire her lovely form at close proximity. His eyes first rested on her swan neck, then moved down to her graceful shoulders, and then to her sylphlike arms, before finally stopping at her delicate hands. No less attractive than her person and talents was Georgiana's manner. Hers was not the demeanour of a bold, self-assured temptress. Instead, she captivated with a different kind of charm, one that Sir Matthew found even more alluring. Far from discouraging him, her shy silences and modest ways only added to the enjoyment of pursuit.

As Georgiana's fingers danced over the pianoforte keys, she was acutely conscious of her admirer's presence next to her, to the point that she could hardly keep her mind on the music she was playing; and whenever he offered some gratifying little remark or attention in between songs, she received it with the greatest pleasure. Sir Matthew was like nobody she had met before. It was not that the gentleman's conversation was unusually witty or profound—but rather, he possessed a magnetic energy and a liveliness of spirit that drew everyone to him. His laugh was infectious, and there was something in his countenance, his mien, and his expressive eyes that Miss Darcy could not name, but which she found fascinating. To her, it seemed impossible that Sir Matthew could ever say or do anything dull.

When everyone had retired to bed that night, Georgiana came to Elizabeth's room. Too excited to sleep, she instead preferred a tête-à-tête with her sister-in-law, and after first touching on other subjects, she at last gathered the courage to ask, "Lizzy, what did you think of Sir Matthew?" Elizabeth smiled at this query; she had not failed to notice the gentleman's partiality for Georgiana, but though Mrs. Darcy did not view the young people's interest in one another with disapproval, she was somewhat reserved in her reply:

"Well, he appears to be a gentlemanlike man with cheerful manners, and he is by no means lacking in personal attractions, but it would be difficult to say more until we know him better."

"What about the Townsends? Did they say anything about him?" pressed Georgiana.

"Mrs. Townsend did tell me that his estate brings in eight thousand a year, which is certainly no inconsiderable sum, and both she and Mr. Townsend seem to like Sir Matthew. But Georgiana, though these circumstances all appear in his favour, I still feel it is my duty to caution you not to be too hasty in giving your heart."

"I will try, Lizzy," came the earnest answer. "And, one thing I can promise you is that I will never do anything to grieve my brother, nor anything to be ashamed of. Be assured, I have learned my lesson on that score."

CHAPTER 6

The following day, Anne de Bourgh called on the ladies at Kleistring-ham. She and Georgiana greeted each other with all the warmth and exuberance attendant on a much-awaited reunion after a long separation. Observing them from the side, Elizabeth was struck by the pronounced differences between the cousins. Georgiana was tall, with a well-shaped, graceful form and lovely features. Miss de Bourgh, on the other hand, was much smaller with a thin, peaked little face and an awkward manner. Apart from her pleasing, grey eyes, she was almost plain. Elizabeth did, however, perceive a gentleness in the lady's air that had not brought itself to her notice before.

Far from being jealous of her pretty cousin, Anne loved her like a sister and was never happier and more self-assured than in her company. Yet, in the presence of the other two ladies, Anne was a rather silent visitor. It was only with considerable effort that Mrs. Townsend was able to keep the conversation going, and between her and Georgiana, with an occasional addition from Elizabeth, they were able to coax a few phrases out of Miss de Bourgh.

It was the proximity to Mrs. Darcy, in particular, that brought on Anne's reticence. She felt awkward to be near her, not only because of the tense relations subsisting between Elizabeth Darcy and Lady Catherine de Bourgh, but also because Anne had long sensed that Mrs. Darcy did not have a very high opinion of her. Though Anne did not share her mother's hostility towards Mr. Darcy's wife, neither could she feel comfortable in her presence or enjoy her society.

Miss de Bourgh did not stay long. She had been on her way to visit a poor family in the parish, and she stopped at Kleistringham mainly to invite her cousin to come with her. Georgiana readily agreed, and soon the two of them set out in the de Bourgh coach. In the absence of Mrs. Darcy and Mrs. Townsend, Anne now spoke freely, and the dialogue became as lively as any to be heard between two carefree young ladies in England.

Before long, they came to the subject of Sir Matthew Leigh, of whom Georgiana was curious to learn as much as possible. When she asked her cousin what she thought of the gentleman, Anne replied, "I cannot say—I hardly know him. We were introduced last Sunday at church, but then we seemed to find little to say to each other. Of course, as you know, I have no great talent for speaking with new acquaintances, and Sir Matthew did appear to be an amusing, interesting sort of man when he was with others. There is certainly nothing I can say against him."

While this was not exactly praise from Anne, it was at least better than the reverse. Georgiana sighed. She had hoped to receive some guidance from her cousin but now saw that she would just have to rely on her own opinion of Sir Matthew. Anne, who herself had a certain gentleman on her mind, soon brought up the subject of Mr. Grey. His conversation and manners, she said, were very different from those of Mr. Collins, the late rector of Hunsford.

"Different? In what way?" asked Georgiana.

"Well, though Mr. Collins was very courteous, very attentive, and always spoke with great deference to my mother and me, I often wondered whether his behaviour towards us would have been the same if Mama were not Lady Catherine de Bourgh, mistress of Rosings Park, and I her daughter. Would he still have been so eager to agree with everything Mama said, and would he have been as generous in his praise of us? Mr. Grey is also very polite, but there is also sincerity in all he says. He never flatters either Mama or me, and he always has something interesting to say. I was surprised to discover that he even writes his own sermons. Would you not agree that it is admirable? I think it shows a dedication to his vocation and a love for his work that is rare these days among clergymen."

"A curate writing his own sermons? That *is* singular!" remarked Georgiana. "Mr. Owens, our parish vicar, almost never does. He normally just reads some other clergyman's sermons out of a book."

"So did Mr. Ross, who used to be the rector of Hunsford, though Mr. Collins after him did write his own sermons."

"But you prefer those of Mr. Grey?"

"Yes. Mr. Collins did try, but the sermons he wrote were somewhat tedious, and he often preached on subjects such as the duties of servants to their masters, or the importance of accepting the station in life in which God places us. Mr. Grey's sermons, on the other hand, are inspiring and also very heartfelt; one leaves church afterwards feeling a genuine desire to do good and become a better person."

Ahead of their charitable visit, Anne told her cousin a little about the poor family to whose cottage they were travelling. There were five living in the house: a widow named Mrs. Fisher and her four youngest children. The past years had not been kind to them; like many others in the parish, they were reduced to severe poverty by a combination of high food prices and low wages. Before Mr. Fisher was killed in an accident, he had struggled to support his family on what he earned as a farm labourer. With wages for farm work very low, the man sent his eldest son to serve as an apprentice to his uncle, a wool cropper in Yorkshire, as soon as the boy was old enough. Croppers being among the best paid of the textile workers, his parents thought the lad would have a better future if he learned that trade, and for a time, they were right. After Mr. Fisher's death, the widow and her children were able to live mainly on the money the eldest son sent home to his family.

"But then," said Anne, "the family suffered another misfortune."

"Why, what happened?" asked Georgiana.

"It was some trouble involving Mrs. Fisher's son, the one who completed an apprenticeship in Yorkshire. Two inventions—the gig mill and the shearing frame—came into widespread use and began putting wool croppers out of work. The machines could finish more wool in less time and with fewer workers than is possible using traditional methods. The men who were losing their livelihoods to these inventions brought their grievances to the mill owners and at first made some attempt to reach a peaceful solution, but the owners were unwilling to make concessions. The croppers grew angry, and a number of them rioted, breaking the machines that were putting them out of work. Naturally, the owners tried to protect their property, with the resulting conflict leading to bloodshed on both sides. Some of the croppers who took part in the revolt were arrested, Mrs. Fisher's son among them. Though he was not hanged, unlike several of the other rioters, his punishment was not a light one: he was sentenced to transportation to Australia."

"Oh, how awful!" exclaimed Georgiana.

Anne continued, "Without the money he used to send home, his family is now destitute. The four youngest children are not yet old enough to work, and the other two, both girls, are in service; one is a laundry maid, and the other a scullery maid, but neither earns enough to be of much help to the family. Mrs. Fisher takes in washing to feed herself and the children, but the money does not go very far."

The carriage soon brought the ladies to the Fisher family's cottage. It was a small, poor hut, pitiably in need of repair. A man's hand to put things right again was clearly lacking. Miserable as the house looked, however, its appearance was made more cheerful by the presence of a tidy, little garden composed of neat rows of carefully-tended vegetables.

When Anne came into the cottage, to her great surprise she found Mr. Grey inside with the family. He was seated at the table, apparently teaching one of the children to read, but when the ladies entered, he rose to his feet. On perceiving him, Anne reddened considerably and stammered through the introductions. Yet, he scarcely noticed, for he was too much struck by the loveliness of her young cousin. It was not only Miss Darcy's beauty that drew his attention, but also the sweetness of her manner, the grace with which she moved, and the lively cheerfulness of her countenance. There was intelligence in her eyes and an endearing modesty in her demeanour, which likewise attracted his admiration. The gentleman tried not to betray what he felt, though he was so taken with Miss Darcy's charms that he hardly knew what he uttered following their introduction.

Georgiana, however, was completely unaware of her conquest, and after making the clergyman's acquaintance, she turned her attention back to the

Fishers and the cottage in which they lived. The family's clothing, she observed, was faded and patched over several times; their garments were ill-fitting and threadbare, and the younger children looked to be clothed in what the older ones had grown out of. The house they inhabited was very dim inside with only the bare ground for a floor. What little furniture they had could hardly be called such—the table, for instance, was merely some old boards nailed together crudely. Although it was cold in the room, there was no fire, nor any firewood in sight. Yet, despite these numerous deficiencies, the children had smiling, carefree faces. Still too young to fully grasp the grim reality of their circumstances, the little ones thought only of what was passing before them and of the entertainment furnished by the arrival of visitors.

The gifts the ladies brought with them also occasioned much excitement. There were eggs, cheese, wild duck, a large hare, and a goodly quantity of apples and pears. Anne also told Mrs. Fisher that she would arrange to have some firewood delivered to the cottage.

While the others were talking, Georgiana suddenly felt a faint pull on her shawl. Looking down, she saw Mrs. Fisher's young daughter, a child of perhaps six years old, stroking the soft cloth and admiring it with wide-eyed awe. The shawl was a truly beautiful one. The colour of ripe cherries, and decorated with a paisley border, it looked particularly striking against Georgiana's white muslin dress and dark-coloured spencer.

"Do you like it?" asked the lady.

The little girl nodded silently in reply. For an instant, Georgiana hesitated; it was her favourite shawl, woven from genuine Indian Cashmere; but then she thought of how cold the small child must feel in her threadbare clothing, and how little the whole family had to live on. Without another thought, she removed the shawl, and draping it around the girl's shoulders, she said, "It is yours, then... Look how pretty you are!"

"Oh no, Miss Darcy. We could not accept such a gift!" protested Mrs. Fisher, but Georgiana was determined. "I insist," said she. "This is not my only shawl; I have plenty more at home, and it would give me great pleasure to know that your daughter has it."

Prompted by her mother, the child thanked Miss Darcy and then danced about the room in her new finery, with an occasional pause to lovingly stroke the fabric.

Mr. Grey was very touched by the scene and by Miss Darcy's generosity. Not every young lady would let even her own sister *borrow* such a splendid shawl, much less give it away to someone else's child. Charmed as he already was by Georgiana's person and manner, he now looked at her with a new sort of regard; in her actions he had glimpsed an open-hearted nature and a degree of kindness that was rarely to be found.

After stepping out of the house, the visitors lingered a little by the de Bourgh carriage. Mr. Grey addressed Georgiana and her cousin with:

"You do a great deal of good, ladies, with your visits to families such as the Fishers."

"How could we do otherwise but help them, when they are in difficult circumstances and we are blessed with good fortune ourselves?" returned Anne, and then added, "I cannot imagine what Mrs. Fisher must have suffered in losing her husband, and then, so shortly afterwards, having her eldest son transported to Australia. If only he had not taken part in the machine-breaking riot!"

In reply, the gentleman said, "While I cannot support the croppers' violent methods, I understand their plight and their desperation. Technological progress, while benefiting the nation as a whole, is harming many textile workers, and not just the croppers. Stockingers, cotton weavers, and others are similarly seeing their skills being made obsolete by new inventions. They are losing employment and being pushed into poverty. The reality is not easy to accept or to adjust to, and some of them see no other way to remedy their situation except through riotous protest and destroying machinery, or even setting fire to factories to draw attention to their cause."

"But what good can possibly come from all this violence?" asked Georgiana. "Mrs. Fisher's son, for instance, is even worse off now than he was before the riots. I do sympathise with those who are losing their livelihoods to new technology, but what has been invented cannot be uninvented. Would it even be wise to deliberately choose the less gainful way and produce less cloth using slower and costlier methods? Might it not be better for the displaced workers to instead learn a new trade and find work doing something else?"

"It is unfortunately not that simple," answered Mr. Grey. "Learning a trade takes time and effort—years, in fact. The problem arises of what the labourers' families are to live on while they are acquiring new skills. At present, neither the government nor the factory owners appear willing to provide them with any compensation or assistance."

"I had not thought of it that way, but of course you are right," said Georgiana, "and I suppose, after they finish their second apprenticeship, some new machine might be invented and take away that trade also."

Mr. Grey remarked, "They could always do unskilled work instead, possibly in the factories that supplanted them, but the wages are lower, and the working conditions are harsh and often dangerous."

The clergyman would gladly have remained longer with the ladies, and with Miss Darcy in particular, but having more than one important matter to attend to before the close of the day, he was obliged to take leave. Before he did so, he asked them whether they had any plans to attend the assembly that was to be held on Friday. Without hesitation, Anne replied that she would be sure to come. Georgiana was quite surprised by her cousin's answer, and by how emphatic it had been. Suppressing a smile, she voiced her own intentions to attend. The gentleman brightened and answered that he looked forward to seeing them both at the dance.

They then said their goodbyes and parted, and once the ladies had set forth in the carriage, Georgiana asked, "Could we stop in the village on the way home? I need to buy some hairpins. My maid forgot to pack them at Pemberley, so now the only pins I have are those that you see on my head."

"Yes, of course. I have some things I would like to purchase as well."

After a slight pause, Georgiana said, "Anne, I had no idea that you wished to go to the assembly on Friday, nor have I ever seen you so eager to dance before. Might Mr. Grey's plans to be there have anything to do with your decision to attend?"

"Cousin, I beg you would not ask me; I should blush to answer truthfully... But tell me, what did you think of Mr. Grey? Did you like him?"

"I thought him a very sensible, good-humoured gentleman, and he *is* remarkably handsome. I can see why you have a high opinion of him, but Anne, have you thought things through? You know I am the last person in the world who would wish to discourage you, but I cannot imagine that

Aunt would ever countenance a match between you and a country curate."

"No, I am sure she would not," returned Anne, "but it has not yet come to that and probably never will. For the present, I intend merely to enjoy Mr. Grey's company, and there is no harm in going to a dance, is there?"

"No, I suppose not. On the contrary, it would make me very happy to see you dance, but will Aunt let you go?"

"I doubt it. Mama would most likely say that in my delicate state of health, I ought not to contemplate dancing, and perhaps she is right, but I am determined. Fortunately, she has gone to London for several days, and therefore she cannot prevent me from going. Mrs. Jenkinson has gone to town with her, but perhaps Mrs. Harding can accompany me as my chaperone instead."

By now their carriage had arrived at the shop. The ladies stepped out of the coach and went inside the building, where they found the shopkeeper much occupied with serving two of his customers. The third, a gentleman, was at that moment facing away from Anne and Georgiana as he looked at some items in the shop. With his back turned towards the entrance, the young man did not see the ladies come in, but he overheard their conversation.

"When will my aunt return from London?" asked one of them.

The other, who had a very pleasant, though somewhat quiet, voice answered, "She is expected back next Monday. While Mama is away, I want to take advantage of the opportunity to call in a physician to see Betty, one of the maids in our household."

"Why must your mother be absent in order for you to call in a physician?"

"Mama always sends for an apothecary if one of the servants is ill, but Betty really ought to see a physician. She has been coughing a great deal, and the medicine Mr. Leech gave her provided no relief. I am concerned that she could have something more serious, such as consumption of the lungs."

"Does my aunt object to the cost of her being treated by a physician?"

"Yes, but it is not only the cost that she opposes. I intend to pay the physician myself, out of my own allowance, so Mama can have no objection on that account. Still, she would strongly disapprove if she knew. She thinks that employing a physician for servants encourages them to think themselves above their station, which is why she insists that only an apothecary should tend to the servants no matter how ill they may be."

As she was finishing speaking, the young gentleman turned around and saw that the soft, pleasant voice belonged to the elder of the two ladies. She was small and somewhat pale, and not what others might consider beautiful, but still, he liked her face; it was a kind, gentle face. Her eyes settled on him for a brief moment, but then she looked away, and she and her companion walked on towards the just-vacated counter. After making their purchases, the ladies immediately left the shop.

The gentleman had never seen either of them in the village before, and neither did he know their names. Watching them leave, he wondered about the one who had caught his interest, but presently, the shopkeeper's voice broke through his thoughts:

"Mr. Brooke... Mr. Brooke, may I help you, Sir?"

Awakened back to the present, the gentleman approached the counter to purchase a substantial quantity of letter-paper and some ink.

"I see you must be pining for home already," said the shopkeeper. "Why, with so much letter-paper, you will keep your whole family well-supplied with letters! Or do I mistake your purpose, and you intend instead to shower some young lady with love letters?"

"Neither, I am afraid, Mr. Gibbs," laughed Mr. Brooke. "There is no young lady at present, and after only one week in Kent, I think it is yet too early for me to feel homesick. But you are right; it is a fair amount of paper, though I expect much of it will be used for my work. I do intend to write to my family often, but also I correspond a great deal with other members of my profession."

"Do not think that I mean to complain, Mr. Brooke; I am always glad to have more custom, and there is plenty more paper in the shop if you need it, as well as some excellent candles for all those late nights when you will be writing to your physician-friends."

"Thank you, but I do not need any more candles at present," was Mr. Brooke's reply. Then, looking a little bashful, he asked:

"Mr. Gibbs, who were those two ladies who just left the shop?"

"Oh, I see you waste no time, Mr. Brooke! Good, good—that is just how a young man ought to be! The younger of the two ladies was Miss Darcy. She lives in Derbyshire but travels into Kent now and then to visit her aunt and cousin."

"And the elder?"

"The elder lady was Miss de Bourgh, the only daughter of Lady Catherine de Bourgh of Rosings Park."

"Ah, I see," replied Mr. Brooke with a little regret in his voice.

The shopkeeper may as well have said that she was the Queen of England. Mr. Brooke had heard of the de Bourghs and knew that they were the foremost family in the neighbourhood. Lady Catherine was one of the wealthiest women in Kent, and as her heiress, Miss de Bourgh likely already had a number of eminent suitors for her hand. Being merely a country physician, Mr. Brooke knew he had little chance with her; it was no use thinking of Miss de Bourgh any further. With a sigh, he gathered up his purchases and quitted the shop.

CHAPTER 7

Like many a public ball in England, Friday's assembly brought together a medley of various types: persons with birth, wealth and position, and persons without; those who loved dancing, and those who had neither a liking nor talent for it; dancers and chaperones, the young and the old, the plain and the beautiful. Regardless of their differences, they all came, united by one interest and one purpose—marriage.

Much may be accomplished during a ball. For instance, a romantic attachment may be formed, or an existing one deepened, and more than a little information of a man's preference may be gleaned from his choice of dancing partners. Many a dance has led to a proposal of marriage, which, in turn, often determines the course of one's entire life with respect to fortune, station in life, and hope of future happiness. A ball is therefore not so much a pleasant diversion as a game of dancer's chess. The ultimate aim, of course, is to capture a king or queen, along with a castle. This may be accomplished by taking a direct path, though oftentimes a more circuitous manoeuvre, in the manner of a knight, may be required. A pawn, being lower even than a bishop, is worth little and desired by few. Yet, it is unwise to underestimate a pawn since, as anyone familiar with the game knows, in time the humble pawn may become a much larger chess piece.

"Miss Darcy, if you are not otherwise engaged, may I have the honour of your hand for the first two dances?" asked Mr. Grey. Georgiana replied that she was already engaged to dance the first set with Sir Matthew. The clergyman would have liked to inquire about the following dance, but any possibility of further discourse was interrupted by the stately arrival of the Villiers family, which drew the attention of every eye in the room. There was Sir Edward Villiers, the head of the family, imposing and dignified; his son John, a very stout gentleman with fiery red hair; and the two Villiers ladies. The latter were bedecked in such resplendent finery as to eclipse every female in the room, and were adorned in as much jewellery as it was possible for a lady to wear while still appearing fashionable rather than gaudy. Their coiffures were likewise very elaborate; some poor maid must have spent an eternity arranging their hair so. Most striking of all, however, was their grand, self-important air.

The Villiers ladies, with Sir Edward's approval, had contrived a simple but ambitious plan for the evening. John Villiers had until the last few days been visiting friends in London, but now that he had rejoined the rest of the family on their estate, he was to be introduced to Anne de Bourgh at the ball and then dance with her at the earliest opportunity. He was also expected to spend the rest of the evening wooing Miss de Bourgh, and if all went well, Mr. Villiers would not long remain a bachelor.

To the disappointment of the Villiers ladies, Anne had not yet arrived, which left John Villiers at liberty to enjoy himself for awhile. It was not long before he noticed Georgiana and asked to be introduced to her. The gentleman then spent a pleasant ten minutes or so chatting with the young lady and Sir Matthew, and afterwards Mr. Villiers withdrew to the refreshments room for a glass of wine.

After having made his fortune in trade, Sir Edward Villiers had wished for his son to obtain a good education to fit him for the society of those with whom his wealth would allow him to associate. Young John Villiers was therefore sent to Eton and then went on to study at Oxford. His parents hoped he would distinguish himself by taking honours, but after two years of study, Mr. Villiers was plucked for failing at his responsions. Thrice he attempted the preliminary examination but was unsuccessful each time, and so he was disqualified from further pursuing his education at Oxford. Yet, the ignominy of leaving the university without a degree did nothing to dim Mr. Villiers' enthusiasm for great literature, for he considered education to be the mark of a true gentleman. For this reason, he owned a large collection of books. It must be admitted that the number of volumes in his collection rather exceeded his understanding of their contents, but the gentleman nevertheless took great pleasure in showing his library to visitors.

In the refreshments room, Mr. Villiers spoke to his mother with great animation about the mutton they had enjoyed for dinner the previous day, but when he observed Miss Darcy approaching, the discussion turned to loftier subjects.

"Mother, have I ever told you about Aristotle's concept of arete, the means by which mankind may achieve true happiness?"

Unfortunately, such elevated discourse on ancient Greek philosophy went unappreciated as Miss Darcy simply walked past for a glass of lemonade, and a minute or two later, Mr. Villiers' sister came and quelled her brother's conversation altogether.

"Here is our chance!" said she excitedly, taking care to keep her voice down. "Miss de Bourgh has just arrived. Make haste, John! I shall take you to her now and introduce you."

"Must it be now, Priscilla? I was just telling Mother about Aristotle's writings on ethics."

"Aristotle can wait until we get home, and then you can philosophise all you want, but now let us not delay any longer, or someone else will occupy Miss de Bourgh's attention."

Knowing that arguing would accomplish nothing, Mr. Villiers sighed and followed his sister in unwilling obedience.

After a brief introduction, Miss Villiers left her brother alone with Anne so that they might become better acquainted. Although Anne was not fond of Priscilla Villiers' company, in this instance she would have preferred for her to stay, for she was at a loss of what to say to the new acquaintance standing before her. Anne knew she ought to ask a polite question or make some clever remark but could think of nothing to say. To her relief, the gentleman spoke first.

"Miss de Bourgh, do you read much?"

"I read a little."

"And do you enjoy Shakespeare?"

"I confess I take little pleasure in reading his plays."

"Not enjoy Shakespeare! You cannot be in earnest! Surely, you cannot dispute that works such as *Julius Caesar* and *Othello* are among the greatest ever written not only in England but in the whole world."

"It is true that Shakespeare was a master of his craft and wrote with great skill," the lady replied, "but his tragedies put me in a melancholy mood, and I cannot read them with enjoyment. *Othello*, for instance, is about a man who unjustly suspects his wife of adultery and then murders her, after which he kills himself."

"Yes, but before Othello takes his own life, he utters one of the greatest phrases in all literature," remarked Mr. Villiers reverently, turning his gaze up to heaven, his face the picture of exultation. "'To be, or not to be,' said Othello, 'that is the question.' So few words... yet, so much meaning."

Anne was perplexed. "I may be mistaken," she replied, "but was not that speech from *Hamlet* rather than *Othello*?"

"Oh, yes, *Hamlet*, of course! That is what I meant."

An awkward pause followed, and Mr. Villiers looked somewhat uncomfortable. "There is my sister Priscilla," he finally exclaimed, "She looks as if she wishes to speak to me. Please excuse me."

While Mr. Villiers was making his escape, an attorney by the name of Mr. Peter Jouras came towards Mr. Grey.

"I see you looking at Miss Darcy a great deal this evening, Mr. Grey," said he.

"She is a lovely young woman. I do not think that anyone could look upon her with indifference."

"I cannot disagree with you there," said Mr. Jouras, "but if you wish to marry a lady of large fortune, you will never succeed with Miss Darcy. With her beauty and accomplishments, not to mention her wealth and connections, you will see that she will dance every dance this evening, and with men who are not merely curates... or attorneys."

"What makes you think that my aim is to marry a woman with a large fortune?"

"Is it not the aim of every man in our situation? Every sensible man, at least? For if that be the case, you would do much better to ask someone like Miss Meggott, or better yet, Miss de Bourgh."

"Whatever do you mean?"

"Oh come, man. Is it for Miss de Bourgh's beauty, or accomplishments, or her conversation that men such as Mr. Villiers pay her any notice? If she were not a wealthy heiress, she might sit in that chair the whole evening without once being asked to dance."

Mr. Grey was appalled at the man's words. He did not know which was worse—Mr. Jouras' shamelessly mercenary views or the disdainful, ungentlemanlike way in which he spoke of Miss de Bourgh.

"I do not share your opinion," replied Mr. Grey. "I have spoken with Miss de Bourgh and find her to be a pleasant young woman, although perhaps quite shy. *I* will ask her to dance, Mr. Jouras, but for the reason that she is an amiable young lady and not because I have any design on her hand or her fortune."

John Villiers, who himself had just left Anne's side, was sadly mistaken if he expected a warm welcome from his sister.

"Why have you returned so soon?" Priscilla Villiers hissed. "You have scarcely spent two minutes with Miss de Bourgh! Did you ask her to dance?"

"No, and I beg you would not importune me on the subject. Her conversation was so dull, I could not bear to stay in her company another moment. Do you know she said she does not like Shakespeare?! I fear that her education was neglected most abominably!"

"What nonsense! Miss de Bourgh is perfectly lovely. John, you must go back and ask her to dance!"

"But she is several years older than I am, and in any case, I would much rather ask Miss Darcy," protested Mr. Villiers, but his sister was unyielding:

"I have never before heard such foolishness in my life! What is a few years' difference? There is no equal in the room to Miss de Bourgh."

"In wealth, perhaps, but in every other respect, she is in no way suitable to be the future Lady Villiers."

"Why must you be so obstinate?" Miss Villiers cried in whisper. "Look over there—Mr. Grey is drawing near to Miss de Bourgh... now he is speaking to her, no doubt asking her to dance at this very moment. Just look what you have done! If you continue in this fashion, a curate will be the master of Rosings and not you!"

"Well, he is welcome to Anne de Bourgh and to Rosings! As for myself, I think I shall try some of those delicious-looking biscuits in the refreshments room, for I am famished."

Miss Villiers would have preferred to continue remonstrating with her brother, but not wishing to draw attention to what was becoming a very heated discussion, she instead resolved to continue her haranguing at home. There was little she could do, therefore, other than look on in vexation as Miss de Bourgh danced with the clergyman.

Georgiana, on the other hand, was delighted to see her cousin dancing with Mr. Grey. Anne's face, normally pale, now had a little colour, and her eyes were bright and full of life. Her radiant smile transformed her features so that she looked almost pretty, and Georgiana did not know when she had ever seen her cousin look so well or so happy. Indeed, Anne's outer appearance was very much a faithful reflection of her state of mind. She had not expected Mr. Grey to solicit her hand for the first dance, and the compliment of having been singled out by him filled her with hope and tremendous joy. It only added to her pleasure that the gentleman was an excellent dancer.

Mr. Grey in no way neglected to pay the polite attentions of a partner, and yet throughout the dance, he found his eyes returning often to Miss Darcy—and who could help it! She danced through the maze of figures with unrivalled musicality and grace, and her movements had the ease and lightness of a gazelle. Every tilt of her head, every elegant sweep of her slender arms was perfection! Most captivating of all, however, was Georgiana's lively, exuberant spirit during the whole performance. In short, Miss Darcy was enchanting!

Much as Anne would have liked to dance the whole set, the exertion of unaccustomed exercise proved too much for her, and she was obliged to sit down after only one dance. Mr. Grey accompanied her to a chair, and when she had regained her breath, Anne ventured to ask, "Mr. Grey, do you think it is wrong not to like Shakespeare?"

"I have never heard of any harm resulting from a disinclination for his plays," the clergyman replied, smiling.

"But you like Shakespeare, do you not?"

"I do, but that does not mean that you must. Life is more interesting when there is a difference of opinion. Think how dull it would be if everyone always thought the same and agreed on everything."

Anne was not fully convinced and protested that it was not only Shakespeare, but also a number of other works considered great literature that she did not care for either.

"Read what stirs your heart, Miss de Bourgh. If you force yourself to read something you find tedious, most likely you will gain little from it and forget most of it the moment you close the book. I myself cannot bear poetry, though others cannot imagine life without it and would almost consider it blasphemy to dislike it."

Anne smiled.

"But Miss de Bourgh, if you would like to make a more serious study of Shakespeare, perhaps you might enjoy one of his comedies? Tragedy is generally considered the superior form of art, but I believe one can learn as much from a well-written comedy as from a tragedy. *As You Like It* is one of my favourite of Shakespeare's plays; I think you might find it entertaining."

Anne was surprised by how much less timid than usual she felt in Mr. Grey's presence and how much they found to talk about; with others, she could hardly summon the courage to utter a syllable. The more time she spent with the gentleman, the more she was drawn to his cheerful manner and his lively conversation.

John Villiers was Georgiana's partner for the third dance, and while they were thus engaged, Sir Matthew could not help noticing the sharp contrast between Anne de Bourgh and Georgiana, the latter dancing with spirit and energy, while the former, lacklustre and sickly, sat in a chair. How plain, how awkward Anne de Bourgh looked in comparison with her cousin! Sir Matthew could not comprehend how Georgiana could speak of her with affection. If only Miss Darcy, and not Miss de Bourgh, were the heiress to Rosings, he thought wistfully. Ah, but how rarely one obtains everything one might wish for!

While Sir Matthew was thus absorbed with his musings, he was completely oblivious to the fact that he himself was the subject of another's observation. Priscilla Villiers was at that moment studying the gentleman intently out of the corner of her eye, while pretending not to notice him, of course. He had not yet asked her to dance and had spoken to her but little even though she looked especially handsome in her peacock-blue gown and had exerted her powers of pleasing to the utmost that evening. Even more vexing, Sir Matthew seemed to have eyes for none but Miss Darcy. Lady Villiers tried to reassure her daughter in that regard:

"Miss Darcy may be a pretty, sweet thing," said she, "but Priscilla, my dear, you should not let it trouble you. She is a very different sort of girl from you, and Sir Matthew Leigh cannot help but see your superior qualities."

"No doubt you are right, Mama. Still, I think it would be wise not to underestimate a rival, especially since we know little of her as yet... Do you remember that poem[1] we read about coquettes? The part about the nymph, in particular."

"Only vaguely."

"I remember it well. It went like this:"

The languid nymph enslaves with softer art,
With sweet neglect she steals into the heart;
Slowly she moves her swimming eyes around,
Conceals her shaft, but meditates the wound;
Her gentle languishments the gazers move,
Her voice is music, and her looks are love.

Lady Villiers considered that there was sense in what her daughter said, but before Miss Villiers could ruminate much further on the subject of Miss Darcy, her mother alerted her to a new botheration:

"Priscilla, Mr. Grey is looking at you. I believe he comes this way to ask you to dance."

"Do not be anxious on my account, Mama," was the reply. "I would no sooner dance with an impoverished curate than I would with a farmer. I will think of some excuse."

However, to the ladies' surprise, the clergyman walked past them towards Georgiana, who, after finishing dancing with John Villiers, had promenaded with the gentleman across the room and stopped not far behind the Villiers ladies. Mr. Grey had no intention of asking Priscilla

Villiers to dance and desired only Miss Darcy as a dancing partner. Yet, while Georgiana had no objections to dancing with the curate, she declined his invitation since she was already engaged to dance the next with Sir Matthew. Indeed, only a few seconds later, the latter came to claim his partner's hand for the dance. Mr. Grey's eyes followed them as they walked away and took their places in the set.

Mrs. Townsend was very pleased to see how well things were progressing between her husband's kinsman and Miss Darcy, but she was also somewhat concerned by Mr. Grey's evident interest in the same lady. As Mrs. Townsend entertained high hopes that Sir Matthew and Georgiana might be united in marriage in the near future—an event that would forge a closer connection between the Darcy family and her own—she felt it her duty to remove even the slightest obstacle in the path of the desired union.

With these considerations in mind, Mrs. Townsend joined Mr. Grey and said to him, "They make a charming couple, do they not? It is such a joy to watch them together! It will not be long now, I believe, before an engagement is announced." The clergyman made no reply, but his dismay was plain to see. Satisfied that her remark had produced the intended effect, Mrs. Townsend left his side, all the while congratulating herself on having spoken thus. There was, of course, little cause for concern since the curate's income was too low to enable him to marry well. However, as Mr. Grey was a very handsome man of considerable merit, it would be prudent to leave nothing to chance. This was a critical time in the acquaintance between Sir Matthew and Georgiana Darcy, and the fewer young men to interfere in a potential match between them, the better.

CHAPTER 8

Not yet ready to sleep on their return to Kleistringham after the ball, Elizabeth and Georgiana stayed up to talk over their impressions of all they had seen and heard that evening.

"Oh, it was such a delightful dance!" exclaimed Georgiana. "I do not know when I have ever enjoyed an assembly more!"

"I can easily believe it!" laughed Elizabeth. "Especially considering that there was no shortage of agreeable partners tonight, and all of them wanted to dance with you... one of them, perhaps, rather more even than the rest?"

Seeing that her sister-in-law smiled bashfully and lowered her eyes at this mention of Sir Matthew's attentions, Mrs. Darcy reassured her, "But I will not tease you on that subject. Let us talk of something else... What did you think of the Villiers ladies?"

"They both looked beautiful and were sumptuously dressed, but I cannot say that I liked them," was the answer.

"Lady Villiers seemed civil enough," said Mrs. Darcy, "particularly when she discovered that I am married to Lady Catherine's nephew. She was then all pleasantness and smiles and proceeded to tell me of her eminent family connections, from the Right Honourable John C. Villiers to George Villiers, the Earl of Jersey. I think she must have listed nearly every member of Sir Edward's family tree!"

Georgiana smiled in amusement, but remembering Lady Villiers' daughter, her countenance clouded a little.

"Miss Villiers did not seem to like me. Her manner towards me bordered on incivility," said she.

"Do not take it too close to heart, Georgiana. I think the cause of her ill manners has more to do with Sir Matthew Leigh than with you."

"You think she admires him?"

"Unquestionably so! Miss Villiers was very charming to him at the ball and flirted shamelessly, but I would not have you make yourself uneasy on that account. Sir Matthew hardly seemed to notice her all evening, and though he danced with her once, it was only after she hinted at it so strongly that not to have asked her to dance would have been impolite."

"I do not doubt Sir Matthew's constancy," replied Georgiana, "but it surprises me that Miss Villiers is so determined to have him. They are such very different people! He is affable and courteous to all whom he meets, while she is just the opposite."

"Priscilla Villiers *is* capable of pleasing when she wishes to," said Mrs. Darcy. "The trouble is, she often does not wish to. At the assembly, I noticed that she was well-mannered to those of rank and fortune, but anyone of more modest means she treated with disdain. Imagine how she must treat her servants!"

"I did, in fact, hear Miss Villiers mention something of her servants," said Georgiana. "She said that at Belargent Hall, rather than learning the names of new servants who come into their household, she and her family instead give the newcomers the names of their predecessors. For instance, their former housekeeper was named Mrs. Harrison, and when she left, they renamed the woman who replaced her Mrs. Harrison as well. Miss Villiers said that not only does this practice save the trouble of learning new names, but also it keeps the servants in their place."

"How dreadful!" exclaimed Mrs. Darcy. "Now, I do not claim to know the name of every servant at Pemberley—there are simply too many to remember them all, and most of the servants, such as the laundry maids and the kitchen maids, we never even see—but at least we allow them all to keep their names. I would not dream of doing otherwise!"

"At Rosings, my aunt and cousin do not change their servants' names either, although Aunt does insist on using a different form of the same name for those that sound too grand. For example, a maid named Elizabeth might become Betty or Betsy. Anne thinks it unnecessary, but it is her mother who decides."

After a moment's pause, Mrs. Darcy said, "I had an opportunity to speak with Miss de Bourgh this evening, and you were right; I misjudged her, just as I misjudged your brother when I first met him."

"You liked her, then?"

"Yes, very much. Miss de Bourgh is neither dull nor proud, as I first thought, but only very shy. We had a good conversation. She said very little at first, and I was obliged to do most of the talking, but when we spoke further, I found her to be very amiable. And, remarkably, she seemed to bear me no ill will for having married Mr. Darcy."

"Indeed, I have heard Anne say that she wishes you both happiness."

"That is kind of her. I hope we shall become good friends in time."

"I was very pleased to see Anne dance tonight. She looked well, did she not?" asked Georgiana.

"Yes, remarkably so, though it surprised me exceedingly that she joined in the dancing. When she stood up with Mr. Grey, I could hardly believe my eyes. I did not realise that Miss de Bourgh dances."

"She almost never does, which is why it gave me much joy to see her do so at the assembly... And her partner in the first dance, Mr. Grey, how did you like him?"

"Much more than I thought I would," came Elizabeth's reply. "I fully expected him to be another Mr. Collins, although perhaps a handsomer version, but I was pleasantly surprised. Mr. Grey is a sensible man and at the same time very amusing and gentlemanlike. Lady Catherine showed good judgment in choosing him."

"Yes; Anne thinks well of him too."

"Miss Villiers, I fear, does not share our good opinion of that gentleman," said Elizabeth. "I do not recall her exact words, but they were something to the effect of how a curate would never have been allowed to dance at Almack's, and if that sort is to be permitted at country assemblies, why not servants too?"

"Oh no, how unkind!" laughed Georgiana. "It is a pity that Mr. Grey has no benefice; not only would having a church living remove the opportunity for Miss Villiers to belittle him, but also I think he deserves more than what he is currently paid. Mr. Grey performs all the same duties that Mr. Collins did, but he receives much less for his efforts."

"And, compared to a beneficed clergyman, Mr. Grey has much less chance of marrying well," noted Elizabeth. "A curate's salary is hardly enough for one man to live on, let alone a whole family. But," she added mirthfully, "even had Mr. Grey been the rector of Hunsford, I still doubt whether he would be in any danger of becoming Lady Villiers' son-in-law, however handsome and deserving he might be; no less than a wealthy baronet will do for her daughter!"

"Yet, Mr. Grey is still young," returned Georgiana. "He may in time obtain a benefice, and although he is not to Miss Villiers' taste, perhaps, he may succeed with another."

CHAPTER 9

On Sunday after divine service, as Georgiana and Anne were stepping out of the church, they were joined by their friend Miss Lawson, a young lady of fifteen years old. The three of them stopped a short distance away from the building for a little conversation. Georgiana began by observing, "What a thought-provoking sermon we heard today! I wish the church services back at home were half as interesting. What did you think of it, Miss Lawson?"

"I do not know," the girl answered sheepishly. Then, lowering her voice, she added with a giggle, "To tell the truth, I did not hear half the sermon. Perhaps if Mr. Grey were not quite so handsome, I might have benefited more from his preaching."

"God must truly have smiled upon this parish to have sent such a clergyman to Hunsford," laughed Georgiana.

The three ladies continued their cheerful discourse until Miss Lawson was called away by her father, who was most anxious to return home as soon as possible so that he might have some luncheon.

Once they were alone, Anne said to her cousin:

"My thoughts have often returned to Friday's assembly, and to Mr. Grey in particular. You know, he sought my hand for the first dance, and afterwards, he did not dance again for the rest of the evening even though he admitted to being very fond of the pastime. Instead, he kept me company for quite some time; you may remember that I was obliged to rest after the fist dance and did not have the strength to tread another measure until the end of the evening in the Boulanger. That Mr. Grey should have danced with me alone at the ball awakened a hope that he may perhaps regard me as more than just the daughter of his employer."

"Anne, he did ask me to stand up with him, but I declined because I was already engaged to dance with Sir Matthew."

Observing that her cousin looked quite downcast at this admission, Georgiana hastened to reassure her:

"But Anne, his asking me to dance does not mean that he prefers my company. Mr. Grey hardly spoke to me all evening, whereas I observed that he conversed at length with you."

"Yes, that is true," Anne brightened. "If only I had more opportunities to talk to him! Other than in church or occasionally at Rosings, I never see him, and when I do, Mama is always with me, so I hardly dare speak at all."

"Well, that does present a difficulty, but it is one that can be overcome with a little effort," said Georgiana. "Why do we not invite Mr. Grey to go for a walk with us this afternoon? Sir Matthew and I thought to take a stroll in the forest today after church, but we had to put off the plan because Elizabeth wants to call on Mrs. Collins instead, and so she cannot chaperone us. But now you and Mr. Grey could accompany us instead!"

Anne was delighted at the idea. In a burst of uncharacteristic boldness, Georgiana approached the curate, and with Anne standing quietly beside her, she invited the gentleman to join them on their walk. However, in her eagerness to arrange the outing, Georgiana forgot to mention that Sir Matthew would be with them also, and the clergyman therefore formed the erroneous impression that he alone would accompany the ladies on their forest walk.

Mr. Grey was very surprised to receive Georgiana's invitation. Indeed, he could not account for the unexpected attention. Perhaps Miss Darcy wished to discuss religion during the walk? But then, she had made no mention of spiritual matters. A thought came into his mind, and was bolstered by Georgiana's warm smile, that maybe Mrs. Townsend was mistaken as to the degree of regard that Miss Darcy and Sir Matthew had for each other. Perhaps the imminent union between them was nothing but idle gossip? Needless to say, Mr. Grey received a rude shock when, arriving at the appointed hour, he discovered that Sir Matthew Leigh was one of the party. Still, the clergyman determined not to be too hasty in making unpleasant conclusions.

Anne could hardly believe that she had taken the daring step of seeking out Mr. Grey's society. Suddenly overcome with shyness, however, she could not bring herself even to look at him but instead stayed doggedly and silently by her cousin's side. Awkward and diffident though she felt, Anne was filled with anticipation and excitement and would not have given up this opportunity for the world.

At the outset, the path was just wide enough for four, and so the young people began their stroll walking side by side. Miss de Bourgh said almost nothing at first. Perceiving her timidity, Mr. Grey spoke to Anne kindly and made a special effort to include her in the conversation. Georgiana noticed this attention to her cousin and smiled inwardly to see the trans-formative effect that his efforts had on Anne; she gradually began to appear more sure of herself, and now and then Miss de Bourgh even ventured to make some little remark or observation in contribution to the discourse. Together, the four of them ambled through the magnificent woods and enjoyed the pleasures of conversation and good company.

To Anne, the forest had never looked so beautiful as it did on that October day. The trees wore ornaments of fiery orange, scarlet, and gold, which appeared all the more stunning in the warm glow of the sunlight. Every so often, the crows' harsh cries of "Caw! caw!" would ring out through the air; in concert with the voices of other birds and woodland creatures, as well as the rustling of fallen leaves beneath the walkers' shoes, their discordant accents produced a pleasing forest cacophony. Listening to these sounds and admiring the picturesque scenery around her, Anne could imagine nothing more perfect than this lovely stroll with Mr. Grey next to her on one side and her cousin on the other.

As they came to a clearing, Sir Matthew remarked, "It was an excellent sermon you delivered this morning, Mr. Grey. I consider that any man who can preach without putting a single member of the congregation to sleep during the service must be a genius."

"Thank you, Sir Matthew, but it was not such a very great accomplishment. I find that when one speaks from the heart, people are interested to listen."

"You are too modest, Mr. Grey. I think you are a very gifted speaker," interjected Anne and then blushed deeply as soon as she had uttered the words.

The curate thanked her for the compliment, and Sir Matthew continued, "I have great respect for the cloth, but I could never have become a clergyman myself."

"Why not?" asked Mr. Grey.

"It is not in my nature; the duties of a parson would soon grow tedious for me, and I must have excitement. To add to that, a clergyman preaches every Sunday against sin, and if one is to avoid becoming a hypocrite, it becomes necessary to make a scrupulous study of avoiding sin. Striving to improve oneself daily is certainly admirable, but the discipline of watching my every action would be more than I could bear. I believe that whatever a man says or does, his heart ought to be in it."

"Oh, yes," cried Georgiana. "Nothing is worse than hypocrisy!"

"Sir Matthew, striving to do what is right is not such a great burden as you imagine," said Mr. Grey. "When one considers the harm and pain caused to another by doing wrong, sin loses much of its temptation. But let us not speak of such weighty matters. I am sure you have all had enough of preaching in church this morning."

With a laughing smile, Georgiana said, "All this talk of sermon-making reminds me of a rather memorable service I attended in Derbyshire last winter. It was very cold that day. We came to church to find that the vicar was ill and could not come, but luckily a galloper had been found in time to take his place. He was a very young clergyman who looked as if he had only just been ordained. With him he brought a book of sermons—I think it was one by Hugh Blair. The galloper chose a sermon from the book and read it aloud with good elocution, although perhaps without much spirit.

"Part of the way through the service, when trying to turn the page, he grasped two leaves instead of one. Then, trying to turn back again, he went a page too far. At first, the man was calm, but after several failed attempts to find the correct page, his consternation mounted, and his face grew quite red with fury. Back and forth flew the pages with a loud rustling sound, much to the amusement of the congregation. At last, he came to a stop and began to read again, but after a few lines, it became clear that it was not the same sermon; previously he had been speaking on the duties of the young, whereas now he was on the subject of devotion. Whether the galloper really thought that he had reached the right place in the book, or whether he had merely chosen a page at random in the hope that no one would notice, I do not know, but he preached with as much solemnity and dignity as before until someone at the back called out, 'I think you are in the wrong place! We heard that sermon last Sunday.' With evident vexation, the galloper replied, 'Did you?' and then resumed flipping the pages side to side.

"At last despairing of ever finding the right page again, he slammed the book shut and said that the service was over, and we could all go home. But the parishioners did not seem to mind; it was such a teeth-chatteringly cold morning that we were all eager to return to our fireplaces, though I think not as eager as the galloper was to escape the pulpit."

"Poor fellow!" laughed Mr. Grey. "I can imagine his mortification. At least he did not have to face that same congregation the following Sunday."

"True," returned Georgiana. "We certainly never saw him again."

The young people wandered alongside each other a little longer, talking and laughing merrily, until the path narrowed enough that the party was obliged to break into pairs. Sir Matthew and Georgiana walked on a little ahead, while the other two followed behind. As Anne was by now a little tired, she moved more slowly than she had done before, and so the distance between the two couples gradually lengthened.

Mr. Grey observed that Sir Matthew bent down to whisper something to Miss Darcy, and she laughed softly in reply. Their preference for each other was obvious. As the curate watched them together, he could scarcely keep his mind on what Miss de Bourgh was saying, and though he maintained the conversation, his replies were a little distracted. Anne, however, did not notice. As frequently happens in such cases, she saw only those signs that seemed to indicate Mr. Grey might have a partiality in her favour. For the present, at least, she was blissfully happy.

The company strolled for a considerable length of time, and though Anne was reluctant to admit it even to herself, she grew very tired during the walk and struggled to keep pace with the others. Mr. Grey observed her fatigue and suggested a stop so that she could rest. Not wishing to spoil their outing, Anne at first protested, but at everyone's concerned insistence, she finally agreed and sat down on a fallen tree.

Sir Matthew noted that twilight was already upon them, and as any further exertion might prove too much for Miss de Bourgh, perhaps it would be best to ride the rest of the way home in a carriage. "Oh yes," said Georgiana, "the days are shorter now, and if we do not hurry back to Kleistringham, the darkness will overtake us. Mr. Grey, if you could stay here with my cousin, Sir Matthew and I will walk quickly back to the house and return for you in a carriage. It is not far, and we should be back in no time." The clergyman agreed, and Anne herself was far from protesting at the prospect of spending a little time alone with the man she so admired.

As the couple was hastening away in the direction of the house, Mr. Grey looked after them wistfully. Feeling painfully shy again, Anne did not speak and instead waited for the clergyman to say something first. When he did, it was only to remark on how pleasant the weather had been for their walk. Then, after a brief pause, he said hesitantly, "Miss de Bourgh, at Friday's assembly, I heard it mentioned that Miss Darcy and Sir Matthew may soon be married. Do you happen to know whether they really are engaged?" The tone of his voice betrayed that he had a more than ordinary degree of interest in the answer.

"I do not know," replied Anne, "but as they have not been acquainted for long, I doubt that they would be engaged as yet. My cousin has never said a word to me about the existence of an understanding between them."

"Miss Darcy seems to enjoy his company a great deal, though, does she not?" said the gentleman, a note of bitterness in his voice. "What was I thinking coming here? My presence is superfluous when she already finds herself in such agreeable society."

He then directed his eyes back to Georgiana and Sir Matthew, who by now appeared quite small in the distance. So preoccupied was Mr. Grey with his thoughts that he did not notice the effect his words produced on Anne, and she herself did her best to hide her feelings from him. The lady turned her face away so that he would not see the tears that had welled up in her eyes. Everything had suddenly become clear: Mr. Grey was in love with Georgiana, and it tormented him to see her friendship with Sir

Matthew blossoming into something more. Overcome with the anguish brought on by this realisation, Anne braced her hand against the fallen tree she was sitting on to steady herself. Notwithstanding that she did her utmost to suppress them, her feelings soon got the better of her, and a sob burst forth from her throat. Mistaking the sound for a cough, Mr. Grey turned his attention back to the lady and was startled to see that she was trembling. Anne clasped her hands together and pressed them to her heart, and there was such an expression of pain in her countenance that Mr. Grey became truly alarmed.

"Miss de Bourgh! ... Miss de Bourgh, are you ill?!" cried he.

The only reply he received was another sob, followed by a torrent of tears. Mr. Grey tried to calm her, but to no avail. At a loss of what to do, he looked desperately in the direction of the road and prayed that the carriage would come soon. Though it seemed like an eternity, the wait was in fact not long. One of the carriages was fortunately able to set out at once since Mrs. Townsend had just returned home in it from the Beauchamps' house. Before long, the coach came rumbling towards the woods. When it finally arrived and its occupants alighted, Georgiana was dismayed at the condition in which she found her cousin.

"Anne... Anne, what is the matter? What has happened?!" However, Miss de Bourgh was in such a wretched state that she could make no answer. Mr. Grey spoke for her:

"It all happened so suddenly. One moment we were talking, and the next, Miss de Bourgh was struggling for breath and fell into a fit of coughing. I think she must be in some pain—you see, she is crying."

"We must get Anne to the house at once!" cried Georgiana. "She needs a physician; we will need to send for Mr. Wise directly!"

"That will not be possible," replied Mr. Grey as he and Sir Matthew were helping Miss de Bourgh into the carriage. "Mr. Wise has gone to London and will not be back for several days."

"Then there is no one except the apothecary!" exclaimed Georgiana in dismay, but Mr. Grey reassured her: "There is another physician—a Mr. Brooke who has recently settled in the neighbourhood. We can send for him instead."

Anne continued weeping during the short drive back to Kleistringham.

When they reached the house, she was immediately taken to a room upstairs, and Georgiana stayed with her while they waited for the physician. Miss Darcy was relieved when she finally heard him arrive, but when she saw him, she felt less certain. Mr. Brooke was considerably younger than she had expected—he was surely not yet thirty. Georgiana would have preferred a much older physician, and if he had a gold-headed cane, so much the better. A cane always gave a physician a certain air of solidity and inspired confidence in his abilities, but Mr. Brooke unfortunately had neither years nor a cane to recommend him, and therefore Georgiana was somewhat dubious about leaving her dear cousin in the hands of a young physician who likely had only limited medical experience.

Anne was also taken aback when she saw Mr. Brooke, albeit for a different reason. Though the gentleman was not exactly handsome, he nevertheless had a pleasant appearance, and Anne felt a little bashful at the thought of being alone in a room with a man scarcely older than herself. Yet, Mr. Brooke had such a kind, reassuring manner that she soon felt relatively at ease in his presence.

Although Anne was by now somewhat calmer than she had been in the woods, Mr. Brooke perceived that her tears still flowed freely, and her delicate frame quivered with emotion. Seeing her like this evoked his tenderest feelings of compassion. He wished to give relief, but it was not yet clear how to proceed since his initial attempts to determine what ailed Miss de Bourgh met with little success. Nothing creates more difficulties for a physician than a patient who gives little away; in response to his inquires, the gentleman received more sobs and shakes of the head than answers.

Sighing, Mr. Brooke walked once around the room and tried to decide what to do next. He then approached the fire and stirred it about aimlessly. Having been made only recently, it was still weak—a shortcoming the physician remedied by adding more wood to the flames. Returning to the bedside, he offered Anne a glass of water—it seemed to compose her a little. Afterwards, he arranged the pillows so as to make her more comfortable. Then, drawing up a chair next to the bed, Mr. Brooke seated himself and asked of Anne:

"Miss de Bourgh, when you awoke this morning, how did you feel?"

"I felt fine—no different than usual," came the tearful reply.

"And when I saw you in church today, you seemed to be in good health then also."

"Yes, there was nothing the matter with me then."

"When did you begin to feel unwell?" asked the gentleman kindly.

"While in the forest," said Anne. "We walked for a long time, and I became very tired. Towards the end, I had to sit down and rest."

"But apart from that feeling of fatigue, was there anything else the matter? Did you, for example, feel pain anywhere?" asked Mr. Brooke.

"No."

"What happened after you sat down to rest?"

"Sir Matthew Leigh and Georgiana returned to Kleistringham for the carriage. We had reached the edge of the woods, and the carriage was to take me the rest of the way back to the house."

"And when your friends departed, were you in the state of distress in which I find you now?"

"No," Anne replied cautiously.

"Were you left to wait in the forest all alone?"

"No, Mr. Grey remained with me."

After a few moments' silence, Mr. Brooke said softly, "Miss de Bourgh, what happened in that period of time before Sir Matthew and your cousin returned with the carriage? What was it that caused you so much anguish?"

"I am not sure what you mean," came Anne's guarded answer.

"Did Mr. Grey say something that unsettled you, perhaps?"

The tears flowed from Anne's eyes with renewed force as she answered, "Mr. Grey did nothing to offend me—it is I who have been foolish... Oh, Mr. Brooke, please do not make me say any more. I cannot bear it."

He did not press the issue further. Indeed, there was no need to; the strength of feeling in her last words convinced him that he had come very close to the heart of the matter already, and he guessed enough of the rest to see that only the passage of time could offer Anne relief. Still, he must endeavour to help her in some way, but what is there that a physician can do in such cases?

Furrowing his brow, Mr. Brooke tried to think of something that might be of use. At last he rose, and opening his medical bag, he said, "Miss Darcy mentioned that when she returned for you in the woods, you were coughing a great deal."

"Well, 'coughing' is perhaps not exactly the right way to describe it," protested Anne.

"Nevertheless, Miss de Bourgh, it would do no harm to take a precaution."

Finding what he needed inside the bag, the physician brought out some tablets. They were large, light-coloured squares that looked to have a soft, spongy texture. He held them out to his patient and invited her to take one. A little hesitantly, Anne inquired what they were.

"These are marshmallow root lozenges. They are an excellent remedy for coughs, but I find that they are also very useful for lifting low spirits."

Anne took one of the tablets from his outstretched hand and placed it into her mouth. The taste of its puffy sweetness brought a faint smile to her face. After chewing for a few seconds, she remarked, "I wish that any of the medicine my regular physician prescribes were as nice. These lozenges taste more like confectionery! Are they really medicine?"

"You may depend upon it, Miss de Bourgh! Marshmallow root has been used since the time of the ancient Egyptians, and the Greeks have long appreciated its medicinal properties. But I agree with you—they are rather like sweetmeats. In fact, the confectioner at Gunter's Tea Shop in Berkeley Square sells something very similar under the name of 'guimauves'. All these lozenges are is some marshmallow root syrup and honey beaten together, and then boiled down to a paste and allowed to dry."

The physician urged her to have another one, after which they talked a little longer. Mr. Brooke was then obliged to leave. As he came downstairs, he was met by Georgiana, who had anxiously been awaiting his verdict on her cousin's condition. He assured her that there was nothing seriously the matter with Anne—nothing that rest, time, and the kind attention of her friends could not cure.

"Oh, I am so glad!" exclaimed Georgiana. "You cannot imagine how relieved I am to hear that she is not gravely ill. And yet, I cannot help feeling that this is all my fault. It was my idea for Anne to go walking with us today, and at the very least, I should not have been so thoughtless as to choose the longer way through the woods."

"You must not blame yourself, Miss Darcy. The long walk may have made Miss de Bourgh a little tired, yes, but I believe her distress was caused by something else, and there is little you could have done to prevent what happened."

After Mr. Brooke left the house, memories of Miss de Bourgh's gentle, grey eyes overflowing with tears occupied his mind for the rest of the evening. He remembered, also, the first time that he saw Anne in the village shop. Her kindness and her concern for the well-being of others had made a lasting impression on him, and it did not seem right that such a sweet young lady should now be suffering.

Mr. Brooke felt increasingly drawn to Anne and was desirous of becoming better acquainted with her, but at the same time, he wondered whether any such effort would only be in vain. After all, what chance had he of succeeding with her? Wealthy ladies of Miss de Bourgh's station were accustomed to marrying within their own sphere, but even if she could overlook his lack of rank and fortune, he was sure that Lady Catherine would not. Moreover, he had some reason to believe that Anne's affections might already be engaged elsewhere. What she had told him of the forest walk, and also the way in which he had seen her look at Mr. Grey in church, both confirmed this conjecture. Any attempt to pay his addresses to Miss de Bourgh, therefore, would likely only leave him broken-hearted. Yet, unattainable though she was, Mr. Brooke could not help thinking of her.

CHAPTER 10

The following day, Anne was anxious to return to Rosings Park as soon as possible. Lady Catherine was expected back from London in the late afternoon, and her daughter wished for some quiet and repose at home ahead of the inquisition that would inevitably ensue. Her ladyship would, as always, wish to know every particular of how Anne had spent the last several days and also to mete out admonishments where she thought necessary. Anne could not yet trust herself to answer her mother's questions composedly and feared, above all, that her sad secret would be discovered. She did, however, confide in her cousin.

During the carriage drive home, she told Georgiana the whole story of what had occasioned her misery the previous evening. "Oh, Georgiana! Mr. Grey cares nothing for me," said she. "It was you he preferred all along!" Even after the ladies had arrived at Rosings and were seated in the yellow drawing room, Anne could talk of nothing else. Georgiana attempted to comfort her, but without success; her cousin was inconsolable. Trying to think of something that might brighten Anne's spirits, Georgiana suggested, "Cousin, why do we not go outdoors into the flower garden? It is warm and beautiful today, and I am sure the fresh air and sunshine will do you good."

Alas, the change of scene did little to lighten the mood of the conversation:

"No one will ever love me for myself. I am so plain and awkward that only my wealth could tempt anyone to marry me!"

"Anne, you must not be so harsh upon yourself—I would not call you plain."

"But neither am I beautiful; men only wish to marry beautiful women and take no interest in the homely ones."

"That is not true, I am sure. You know that good sense and virtue count for more than beauty."

"Do they? It is perhaps what we are taught in church, but no one seems to believe it, except perhaps older maiden ladies, who comfort themselves with the idea whenever they are reminded of still being unmarried."

"Anne, it is not like you to be so bitter."

"I cannot help it, not after yesterday! Oh, how I wish I were lovely, that all might look upon me in awe and admiration! Then I would have no difficulty in making men fall in love with me, and I could marry anyone I wished. If only I were like Helen of Troy, whose face 'launch'd a thousand ships'[2]; with my ordinary face, I doubt whether even a rickety, old fishing boat would have set sail in my honour!"

Georgiana replied with:

"You have given me one example of a highly-admired woman, but I have for you another—think of Cleopatra. Plutarch wrote that contrary to what has been reported, she was no extraordinary beauty,[3] and yet people remember her as if she were; and Julius Caesar and Marcus Antonius, two of the most prominent men in history, both found her irresistible. Why is that?"

In between sniffles, Anne admitted that she had no idea.

"It is because there is more to beauty than having a pretty face," said Georgiana. "Cleopatra possessed an alluring grace in her movements and sweetness in her manner. Her voice was incomparably harmonious, and her conversation captivating. Her charms were such that all who came into her presence were stung to the soul, Plutarch tells us. You see, she had something other than physical beauty to offer. It was her mind, her manner, and her grace that Caesar and Antonius fell in love with, much more than with her appearance."

"Cousin, surely you can see that I have none of those allurements myself," protested Anne. "I have neither conversation, nor grace, nor a charming manner."

"But you are clever, and you can learn!"

"Oh, I doubt it. How does one even go about being irresistibly charming? I would not know where to begin."

"But I have some idea of it, and I can teach you," said Georgiana. "The skill of moving lightly and gracefully is perhaps the simplest one to acquire. We may start there."

Anne argued that she had little talent for graceful movement. Could they instead begin with something else? Was an elegant bearing even so very important? Georgiana insisted that it was.

"Consider the different ways in which a lady might walk," said she. "An awkward gait and heavy step do attract attention, but for the wrong reasons. An ordinary manner of walking is better, but still it does nothing to stir the heart. However, when a woman steps into a room with elegance and dignity, she excites the admiration and delight of all who behold her."

Anne was still reluctant and pointed out that her mother had once already tried, unsuccessfully, to teach her how to walk properly. "When I was quite young, she made me promenade back and forth with a stack of books atop my head, and yet I remained as ungainly as ever. I think I must be incapable of improvement."

Smiling, Georgiana answered, "Nonsense, Anne! You had a poor teacher, that is all. I am not surprised that you should have had so little success; the book method only works if you wish to look as if you had swallowed a broomstick—the resulting gait is stiff and unnatural. A lady's walk should instead be light and effortless. Here, let me show you."

Georgiana rose from her bench and demonstrated the correct way. Her step as she traversed the lawn was delicate and almost balletic.

"Now you try," she urged.

Anne obediently followed suit with a genuine effort, though a somewhat clumsy result.

"No, no, Anne. That is not quite it. At the moment, your walk is more like that of a stork. You must *extend* your leg on each step like this, and try to *glide* as you walk. Picture a swan floating on a lake. And also, it is important not to hunch your shoulders forward or to jut out your head.

The neck must always be vertical, and the head should align with the rest of the body."

After a few unsuccessful attempts, Anne cried out in exasperation that she would never manage it, but Georgiana persisted and would not allow her to be defeated. She encouraged her cousin by telling her that one of her own governesses had made her practice walking gracefully every day for a whole year until she mastered it.

"I did not even put in very much effort at first because I thought it silly," said she. "With determination and diligence, I am sure you will not take half as long to learn."

The ladies had their backs to the path leading to the house, and so pre-occupied were they with their lesson that they did not notice Mr. Brooke coming up the path. He perceived that they were doing something very strange; Miss de Bourgh was making some sort of exaggerated motions, and Miss Darcy was gesticulating and correcting her cousin. While approaching, the physician had an ample view of the goings-on: the swan gliding on the lawn, and the stork striding beside her.

It was Georgiana who saw him first. As she and Anne swung around to face in the opposite direction, Mr. Brooke came into her line of vision. Realising, to her horror, that he had just witnessed the walking lesson, the lady halted suddenly. A stunned silence followed, but knowing there was nothing else to be done, she at last acknowledged the visitor in as calm and dignified a manner as she could muster. Feeling mortified, Anne echoed her cousin and then hastily retreated to a nearby bench.

"What is it that you ladies were doing just now?" asked Mr. Brooke in amusement. Anne blushed to a deep crimson and knew not how to reply, while Georgiana answered somewhat sheepishly that they had merely been taking a turn about the garden in the fresh air. The gentleman did not pursue the subject further and said instead that he had come to inquire about Miss de Bourgh's health, and that he was delighted to see her looking much better.

Mr. Brooke had brought something for Anne—it was some dried fruit of the wild rose, which he recommended consuming in the form of a tea. The physician had great respect for the medicinal properties of the wild briar, it being one of the best plants to use in preventing infections and strengthening the overall health of the body. In fact, he often recommended it to sailors as an excellent preventive against scurvy on their voyages.

Anne thanked him for his gift and said she would speak to the head gardener at Rosings about planting several wild rose bushes in the walled garden.

"Why not instead plant them here with the other roses?" asked Georgiana.

"No, I think the kitchen garden would be a better place for them," replied her cousin. "The wild briar would be lost here amid the showy flowers of the decorative roses, but in the walled garden, among the vegetables and potherbs, the beauty of its simple flowers would be more appreciated. When I am in the garden, I will enjoy looking at the blossoms in summer, and the medicinal fruit can be harvested and put to good use in autumn."

In the future, Anne further said, she planned to create a physic garden full of curative herbs such as St. John's wort and wormwood. She would model it after the physic gardens grown in monasteries during the middle ages, and wild roses would be a valuable addition.

"Do you take an interest in gardening then, Miss de Bourgh?" asked Mr. Brooke.

"Oh, yes. I am never so happy as when working in the garden," was the answer.

"What is it that draws you to the pursuit?"

"I do not know, exactly, though I suppose I enjoy the sunshine and having the birds singing around me, and I always feel at peace when tending to the vegetable and herb beds. It also adds to my pleasure to know that my efforts serve a useful purpose—the kitchen garden keeps the house well-supplied with fresh vegetables, and there is always a large surplus to take to the poor families in the parish."

Georgiana added, "Anne has done a great deal to the walled garden at Rosings. She designed most of it herself and spends at least a little time each day working in it."

His interest piqued, Mr. Brooke asked whether he might see Miss de Bourgh's creation. Anne could not very well refuse, and so she led the way, but as they walked, she inwardly scolded herself for having spoken so much and for revealing her thoughts and feelings to such an extent. Whatever had come over her? Determining to be more reserved, she came closer to her cousin's side and kept her gaze on the ground as they proceeded to the walled garden.

Although the gentleman did not doubt that the potager would be a fine one, he expected to see merely a larger, grander version of the kind of vegetable gardens to be found everywhere in England. What greeted his eyes instead was a colourful mosaic of vegetables and herbs, carefully laid out in decorative geometric shapes. There were no purely ornamental plants in sight, and yet the garden was no less interesting than if it *had* been composed of flowers. All the crops were thoughtfully arranged into attractive blocks of colour. The lettuce, for instance, was planted in a chessboard pattern of green and red varieties. Not far away was a bed of cabbages, where purple heads made a striking contrast to white ones in the triangle and rhomboid-shaped patches they inhabited. In a similar fashion, the entire potager was lovingly designed to combine beauty and utility.

"It is extraordinary, Miss de Bourgh! And you designed all this by yourself?!" exclaimed Mr. Brooke.

"Most of it, yes, though I did consult with the head gardener on some aspects of it," said Anne, adding that the geometric style had been inspired by the work of André Le Nôtre, the famous gardener of King Louis XIV. "And of course, I cannot claim to have planted everything myself," said she. "The estate gardeners do most of the work. I merely help a little."

"Nevertheless, what you have created here is very impressive," said the gentleman.

Following this exchange, Anne fell silent again. As they walked through the potager, she said almost nothing, except when replying to a direct query, but Mr. Brooke was very kind and appeared undiscouraged by her laconism. On the contrary, he seemed genuinely curious about her work and asked her various questions about the garden. With his and Georgiana's encouragement, she began to speak a little more freely, and when the gentleman asked Anne whether she also designed the flower gardens at Rosings, she relinquished her reticence enough to answer, in lieu of a monosyllabic reply, "No, I leave that entirely to our gardeners; fruit, vegetables, and herbs hold far more interest for me. Mama prefers the flowers, but to me, the most beautiful plants are those that are also useful."

Passing a large bed of celery plants, Mr. Brooke remarked, "What a vast quantity of celery! Are you very fond of the vegetable, Miss de Bourgh?"

"No, not particularly, and Mama positively dislikes it."

"Why grow so much of it then?"

"Well, to speak the truth, I would prefer not to cultivate celery at all; it occupies far more space in the garden than it deserves, and it is laborious to grow the species in our climate, but my mother insists upon it. Being a rare and expensive vegetable, celery always has a place of honour on our table, and Mama says that no great house should be without it. In consequence, our celery vase is never allowed to stand empty."

While they strolled along the paths, Mr. Brooke often found his eyes wandering from the plants to Anne herself. She had a very timid air as she showed him around the garden, but where others might have seen awkwardness, he saw manners that were endearingly shy and unassuming. Additionally, in her answers he perceived intelligence and a keen interest in plants and nature. It was clear that Miss de Bourgh had much to say, but that she was often too afraid to say it.

When the party came to a good-sized strawberry bed, Anne pointed out her favourite variety. "It is a very special one from South America," said she. "The berries are cream-coloured at full ripeness and very sweet. It is a pity you cannot taste them—the season for these strawberries has long passed... But there should be some fruit on the strawberry tree. You may try it if you wish."

"You have strawberries that grow on trees, Miss de Bourgh?" asked Mr. Brooke in amused astonishment.

"Well, no, not exactly. The tree is a different species—Arbutus unedo— which is completely unrelated to the garden strawberry, but it is often called the strawberry tree, perhaps because of the red colour of its berries."

They went to the tree and plucked its cherry-sized fruit. The prickly-looking surface of the arbutus berries made them appear like tiny, red hedgehogs, with lemony sweetness inside. Whereas the skin was a little gritty, the flesh was very soft and made for pleasant eating, though it was not the sort of fruit that could be enjoyed in quantity. In any case, Mr. Brooke was unable to stay much longer—he had already lingered more than he intended. While wandering with the ladies through the garden, he had quite lost track of the time, but at last the position of the sun in the sky alerted the gentleman to his lateness, and so he was obliged to make a hasty departure.

When he was gone, Georgiana observed, "It was very kind and thoughtful of Mr. Brooke to call on you so soon," and then added playfully, "He even brought you roses, albeit in dried form."

"Cousin, you make it sound like more than it was; I doubt that he had any intention of giving me flowers, and what he brought was the dried fruit of the rose, not the blossoms."

"Still, one could argue that it is a bouquet of sorts, and he *was* very attentive to you during his visit."

"Georgiana, although it was kind of Mr. Brooke to call and inquire after my health today, he was only doing his duty as a physician."

"Only his duty? Well, he must be a conscientious physician, indeed!"

"You must not tease me, Cousin. I am sure that Mr. Brooke can have no interest in me other than as a patient."

"Well, we shall see," replied Georgiana with a significant smile.

On her return to Kleistringham that afternoon, she went walking with Sir Matthew and Elizabeth before dinner and gladdened them both with news that Anne seemed to be on the mend. As the three of them walked over the grounds together and talked upon various entertaining subjects, Elizabeth took delight in observing Sir Matthew's affectionate manner towards her sister-in-law and seeing how happy she appeared to be in his company. With some pleasure, Mrs. Darcy indulged the thought that if things continued to progress in the same way, a season in Bath and London might not be of any practical use to Georgiana after all.

CHAPTER 11

Hearing Georgiana practicing on the pianoforte, Sir Matthew Leigh smiled to himself, and with a book in hand, he followed the sound to the drawing room.

"I hope I am not disturbing you, Miss Darcy," said he upon entering.

"No, not in the least. I am practicing some new music, that is all. It is a difficult piece, and I have not yet mastered it, but if you do not mind hearing my mistakes, you are welcome to stay."

"I am always glad of an opportunity to hear you play, Miss Darcy—even your mistakes are charming."

Sir Matthew settled into a chair and opened his book, but it is doubtful whether he profited at all from the volume, for half the time his eyes were directed at Georgiana rather than at the page before him.

At last, the gentleman dropped all pretence of reading and came towards the pianoforte. Leaning his elbows on the instrument, he looked into Georgiana's eyes deeply until she cast them down shyly to the keys below. Yet, the slight smile on her lips gave proof that she did not find these attentions displeasing.

"What are you thinking of now, Miss Darcy?" asked Sir Matthew softly.

"I was just remembering the ball we attended on Friday... the dancing—it was such a happy evening."

"And you would like to dance again now, perhaps?"

"Well, yes—only, of course, the next ball will not be for some time," came Georgiana's answer.

"Must we really wait that long? We could dance here, right now."

"What, just you and I, right now?"

"Yes, why not?"

"But Sir Matthew, consider," laughed Georgiana, "What kind of dance will it be with just two people? The English country dance and the quadrille are designed to be performed by several couples at once. It will not be the same with only one couple."

"Perhaps if the English country dance or the quadrille is what you have in mind, but we could try something else instead, such as... Miss Darcy, do you know the waltz?"

"I have heard it mentioned—it is popular in Germany, I believe."

"It originated in Germany, yes, but the waltz has since spread to other parts of Europe, and recently it was introduced in England. The advantage of the waltz is that it can be performed as successfully by one couple as by several together. When I was last in London, I learned the steps of the French waltz—I could teach you if you like."

"Oh no, I think it would be better if you did not. Though I know little of the waltz, I have heard that it is not a very proper dance."

Raising himself back up to a standing position, Sir Matthew answered, "Doubtless, that is the opinion of some stuffy, old clergyman of the Puritan persuasion. When the dance is better known in England, I am certain that it will become widely accepted. Miss Darcy, I have seen the waltz, and I can assure you that it is a very beautiful dance—here, if you will stand up, I can show you."

Somewhat reluctantly, Georgiana obeyed. As the gentleman led her across the floor to the centre of the room, he explained:

"The dance begins with a short march, which leads into the first part— the slow waltz. The next part is the sauteuse, which is faster and consists of a series of springs and leaps. Last of all is the jetté, which is faster still. Would you like me to show you the march steps first, Miss Darcy?"

"Yes, I suppose."

"Then let us begin. Instead of facing each other, we start with standing side by side, and we face in the same direction, like this. Now, I will reach my arm across behind you and place my hand on the back of your shoulder—and you do the same."

The next thing Georgiana felt was the electric sensation of Sir Matthew's arm encircling her shoulders. Hesitantly, she followed suit by lifting her own arm and placing it on the back part of his shoulder.

"Now, Miss Darcy, we must bring the outer arm around to the front so that we may join hands."

Georgiana obediently but tremulously placed her hand in his.

"Next, we take four steps forward: one... two... three... four."

Georgiana had always considered dancing, regardless of what kind, to be a romantic, exciting amusement, but neither the English country dance, nor the Scotch reel, nor the quadrille was anything like this. With Sir Matthew's arm on her shoulder, and her arm on his, they were essentially in an embrace. She had never danced so close to a man before—he was so near, in fact, that she could hear his breathing and feel his warmth. All this was somewhat foreign to her sense of female delicacy, but she had no wish to pull away, although the thought kept returning to her mind that perhaps she should.

He, in turn, was thinking of how exceedingly gracefully Georgiana executed even those first few simple steps of the dance. Her dainty, slippered feet pointed beautifully and landed lightly, as if stepping on a cloud. Positioned so close to her, the gentleman was better able to observe, in minute detail, the perfection of Georgiana's person: her delicate, rose-coloured mouth; her soft, satiny curls framing a lovely face; her flawless, glowing complexion, made more enchanting by her modest blushes. He felt himself grow more enamoured of her with every moment. Holding her little hand in his, he said:

"Now I make a half-turn to face you, and then we step so that we are again positioned side by side, only this time, we will be facing in opposite directions. From here, we encircle each other's waists from the front with one arm, and with the other, we join our hands above our heads in the form of an arc."

Sir Matthew spoke gently and looked at Georgiana tenderly, his eyes seeming to caress her. Feeling as if in a haze, she managed to summon just enough presence of mind to inquire, "And our feet? What do we do with them?"

"With our feet, we perform the pas de bourrée step, and at the same time, we turn together in a circle. But even more important is what we do with our eyes; in the waltz, while revolving about their own axis, the partners must look into each other's eyes without breaking the gaze."

Georgina did her best to comply, but at last she could bear it no longer, and laughing softly, she turned her face away.

"No, no, Miss Darcy, do not look away! We must dance the waltz properly!"

The maiden forced her clear orbs back to his, and with their eyes thus fixed on each other, they turned slowly in a rotating embrace. Although there was no music to accompany their dance, both felt then, and remembered their time together afterwards, almost as if there really had been music; the moment was perfect as it was.

After completing several revolutions, the young man began to lean a little closer to Georgiana, whereupon a thousand thoughts raced through her head: would he try to kiss her? Should she allow him to? It would of course be very improper, but with her feelings overpowering every prudent objection, she was not sure she cared. Before Georgiana could decide what to do, or even be sure of what the gentleman's intentions were, she suddenly heard the faint sound of footsteps on the stairs. Startled back to reason, she pulled away from him.

"Miss Darcy, what is the matter?"

"I hear someone coming!"

"You must be mistaken. I do not hear anyone."

"No, I am certain I heard something!" she insisted and immediately fled to the safety of the pianoforte. Sure enough, a few moments later, Mrs. Townsend entered the drawing room. Catching sight of Georgiana's crimson face, she asked with concern:

"Miss Darcy, are you ill? Your face is flushed, and your eyes look almost feverish!"

"I assure you that I am well. Perhaps I have stayed too long near the fire. The room has grown quite hot."

"Now you really make me anxious, Miss Darcy. Why, the room is not hot at all! I was going to tell one of the servants to put more wood on the fire," said Mrs. Townsend. "I fear that you have caught a fever. Let me send for a physician."

"Truly, I am perfectly well. Pray do not call in a physician. Perhaps I just need a little rest and calm in solitude," replied Georgiana. Still feeling a little giddy from the dance, she then quitted the room in embarrassed haste.

CHAPTER 12

A little over a week after their arrival in Kent, Elizabeth and Georgiana received word from Mr. Darcy that he would be delayed in joining them at Kleistringham. His newly-purchased estate in Scotland, he wrote, had been mismanaged to a greater degree than he had first thought, and there were a number of pressing matters to attend to, which could not be concluded for at least an additional week. He would write again when his plans were more settled, and for the time being, he desired his wife and sister to convey his sincere apologies to the Townsends for being obliged to prolong his absence.

Georgiana and Elizabeth were both disappointed by the news, but there was nothing to be done about it except to wait. Yet, though the ladies were to be deprived of Darcy's company for some time longer, the present was not without its enjoyments. Their many friends in Kent occupied much of their time; Elizabeth was especially glad of Charlotte Collins' society, while Georgiana had many opportunities to see her dear cousin Anne. That very same day, in fact, the two of them met to visit a book shop in the village.

On the way there in the carriage, Anne said, "In case I forget, remind me to buy a book called *The Whole Duty of Man.*[4] I must not leave the shop without purchasing it."

"What is so very remarkable about the book? It sounds frightfully dull," answered Georgiana.

"It *is* dull. The late rector Mr. Collins read it to us at Rosings one evening, and I could barely stay awake while listening."

"Why on earth buy it then?"

"Mama insists that I should. She thinks that I would benefit from reading it, especially one particular section on the duty of obedience that children owe to their parents. She also wants me to study the portion on the wife's duty to obey her husband."

"Must you really buy the book if you dislike it?"

"Yes, of course; I dare not disobey Mama's orders. But once the book is purchased, I will not so much as open it. Let it collect dust on a shelf!"

The carriage soon came to a stop, and as the ladies were alighting, Anne continued, "The part about obeying one's husband I particularly object to. For a small child, whose mind is yet unformed, to obey a parent is one thing, but absolute obedience to a husband is another matter entirely."

Inside the shop, Anne found the odious book she was to buy, and pointing to one of its pages, she said, "Here is the section on children. Some of what the author writes about filial duty to parents has some merit, I suppose, but then look here at what he goes on to say about marriage:"

of all the acts of disobedience, that of marrying against the consent of the parent is one of the highest. Children are so much the goods, the posses- sions of their parents, that they cannot, without a kind of theft, give away themselves without the allowance of those that have the right in them

"I can see why Aunt would approve of these writings!" exclaimed Georgiana. "You surely remember how furious she was when my brother married Elizabeth, and how she considered that he had broken every duty, though he was not even her son but her nephew, and of age too!"

Anne then flipped the pages of the book until she found the passage dis- cussing wifely obedience. Showing it to her cousin, she said, "I hardly know which I dislike more, this part or what we just read. The writer here poses the question: how must a wife conduct herself if her husband commands her to do something that, though not unlawful, is yet inconvenient or imprudent? Should she obey or refuse? All the author believes God permits the woman to do is to 'calmly and mildly' attempt:"

to persuade him to retract that command: But in case she cannot win him to it by fair entreaties, she must neither try sharp language, nor yet finally refuse to obey; nothing but the unlawfulness of the command being sufficient warrant for that

"In other words, she must obey him no matter what."

"Let us hope the husband has not been drinking when he decides to give commands, and that he is a sensible man in general!" returned Georgiana.

"As to that, there may be little choice in the matter, for if one is to do as the book says, a woman must cede the final decision regarding the selection of a husband to her father and mother; and after the parents have handed their daughter, or perhaps I should say their *possession*, over to a son-in-law of their choosing, she is to spend the rest of her days bowing meekly to her husband's every order, however unreasonable the man may be. What a dismal prospect! It depresses one's spirits to read such a thing."

"But Anne, this book was written decades ago, and I would not be surprised if the author was already an old man when he penned it. Public opinion has changed since his day; we live in a more liberal age now."

Anne was not convinced. "Do you think even modern men would be opposed to the idea of an obedient wife?" she asked.

Just then, Mr. Brooke unexpectedly entered the book store. He had ordered a medical book the previous week, and today he decided to stop by to inquire after it on the way home from visiting a patient. How pleasantly surprised was he to discover the ladies inside the shop! Even if the book had not come yet, what did it matter? Encountering Miss de Bourgh was a sufficient reward for the trouble of taking a slight detour.

After the gentleman had exchanged greetings with Anne and her cousin, Georgiana said to him, "Mr. Brooke, we need a man's opinion. Would you read this passage and tell us what you think of it?"

He complied with the request, and when he had finished the paragraph that Anne and Georgiana had just been perusing, he replied, "I cannot say that I agree with such a strict interpretation of a wife's duty. A marriage in which the husband commands and the wife obeys is more akin to the relationship between master and servant than to a union of two free beings, bound by mutual love and respect for each other."

"Then you do not relish the thought of a scrupulously obedient wife?"

"No; in fact, I would prefer to see the word 'obey' omitted from marriage vows altogether."

The shopkeeper, who had just finished serving a customer, called out, "Ah, Mr. Brooke, the book you wanted me to order from London, *A System of Surgery* by Benjamin Bell, arrived for you this morning."

"Thank you, Mr. Wilson. I will pay for it before I leave."

"Are you interested in surgery, Mr. Brooke?" asked Anne in surprise.

The gentleman replied in the affirmative, adding, "You may not know this, Miss de Bourgh, but before studying Physic at Cambridge, I was apprenticed to a surgeon, and now I practice as both a physician and a surgeon."

"You do not also happen to work as an apothecary in secret, do you, Mr. Brooke?" asked Georgiana jokingly.

"No, Miss Darcy," he replied, smiling, "though I would not object to knowing more of the apothecary's craft. I believe that the separation between these three branches of medicine is a rather artificial one; in my opinion, a practitioner is much better able to help his patients if he has some knowledge of all the areas of medical science."

Following these words, Anne viewed Mr. Brooke with a new-found respect. He had considerably more years of training and education than any medical man she had ever met—certainly more than her own physician, the venerable Mr. Wise; but even more estimable, in her view, was the apparent diligence with which Mr. Brooke persisted in furthering his knowledge.

"I think that of all the professions, Physic is the most difficult and requires a man to possess a certain degree of natural genius if he is to succeed in his vocation," said she.

The gentleman answered, "Much as I would like to own to possessing natural genius, I think you might discover, Miss de Bourgh, that Law and Divinity are also not without their challenges, both in their study and their practice, and likewise, I would not wish to exaggerate my healing powers. In some respects, I agree with Voltaire that, 'The art of medicine consists in amusing the patient while nature cures the disease.'"

"And how many patients have you entertained into good health?" asked

Georgiana with amusement.

"Not so many as to give occasion for alarm, but there are times when I feel even entertainment would be preferable to administering a treatment with uncertain benefits but the potential to do harm. Take leeches, for example. In the medical profession they are widely regarded as being safe and effective for treating a variety of ailments, and when I first began my training, I dutifully learned all I could about using them in medicine: the proper method of applying leeches to a patient, in what circumstances they should be employed, how to coax reluctant leeches to bite, and so on; but when I began applying the knowledge to my practice, I found that leeching seemed to bring no real advantage to my patients. On the contrary, it tended to weaken them. So disappointed was I with this form of treatment that I rarely use leeches anymore. At times I face the dilemma of whether to adhere to widely accepted methods against my own judgment, or instead to depart from the established way and try something else, or perhaps not intervene at all if there is no good alternative available. There is much about the human body and its diseases that is still unknown. Neither I, nor any other physician, for that matter, can cure every illness, and until such a thing is possible, there will always be room for humility and restraint in the profession."

Mr. Brooke spoke with feeling and conviction, and Anne listened to him with interest, but at the end of his speech, the physician seemed almost as if he were a little embarrassed, and afterwards he hastened to change the subject. After taking leave of the ladies some time later, Mr. Brooke thought back with mortification to his discourse inside the shop. Leeches! Of all things! When there were so many other, much more elegant topics of conversation, what on earth had possessed him to choose such a repugnant subject to discuss with the lady he admired?! The gentleman shook his head in disbelief and self-reproach.

If only he knew how far Anne was from disapproving of him or his conversation! In fact, she was at that very moment remarking to her cousin how thoughtful and knowledgeable a physician Mr. Brooke appeared to be, and how commendable it was that he continued to expand his under-standing of even those areas of medical science that other physicians might consider it beneath their dignity to make much study of.

"The work of a surgeon requires as much skill and knowledge as that of a physician, surely," said Anne. "Why is it, then, that society holds surgeons in less esteem? Men in that vocation would not generally be introduced to persons of high rank, and unlike physicians, their daughters certainly cannot be presented at court."

Georgiana answered, "I suppose it may partly have something to do with surgeons' former connection to barbers, or perhaps the nature of their work, which requires them to touch wounds and injuries that others find distasteful."

"I think it is unfortunate," said Anne, "that any honest employment which is useful to the world should be held in disregard. A farmer, for instance, is far from being considered the equal of a barrister, and yet, if one considers the relative importance of their occupations, I think few would dispute that people have a greater need for food than for legal representation. Does not growing the crops and raising the livestock that feed mankind deserve at least as much respect as practicing the law?"

"And how much less even are barristers esteemed than those who have sufficient wealth that they need not work at all!" exclaimed Georgiana. After a thoughtful pause, she added quietly, "Sometimes I wonder whether the lives of ordinary labourers are perhaps worth more than those of the wealthy, if not in the eyes of fashionable society, then at least in the sight of God. I wonder how He views the idle rich... I wonder how He views us."

"Georgiana, though we have both been blessed with good fortune, that does not mean our existence must necessarily be one of uselessness and idleness. There is more than one way of contributing to the world, you know."

"Do you mean charity work?"

"Relieving the poor is indeed a laudable way of employing one's time, but so is developing one's talents and putting them to good use—and I know of no young lady who devotes more time each day to such pursuits than you do."

"I am not sure that my talents are of use to anybody," protested Georgiana. "What difference does it make if I can play a pretty tune, or write a poem, or embroider a cushion? Who is fed or clothed thereby?"

In reply, Anne said, "Well, by that reasoning, Mozart and Beethoven; da

Vinci and Michelangelo; Chaucer and Cowper would all be considered the worst sort of idlers, for whom have they ever fed or clothed with their endeavours?"

"I hardly think that my talents, such as they are, qualify me to rank among those great artists," answered her cousin.

"Perhaps not," returned Anne, "but with your music, you bring joy to all who hear you. And even embroidery, of which you speak so lightly, in my opinion has more value than you have ascribed to it. Think of the Bayeux Tapestry, for instance. Queen Matilda, who was merely an accomplished lady much like yourself, created a wondrous embroidery with her ladies-in-waiting that is not only admired as an object of beauty, but also serves as an interesting historical record of the Battle of Hastings. As I see it, if a task brings happiness to others, surely it is worth something, even if it has no practical purpose and creates no wealth for anyone."

CHAPTER 13

On Thursday, the de Bourgh ladies settled in for a quiet evening at home. They had had no guests to dinner that day, and after the meal, Lady Catherine bade Anne's companion, Mrs. Jenkinson, to read aloud to them to relieve the tedium. The woman would have preferred to retire early to her room on account of a bad headache, but as she would not dream of opposing her ladyship's wishes, Mrs. Jenkinson instead took some medicine for her headache and then returned to Lady Catherine and her daughter in the main drawing room, where both ladies were drinking tea.

On entering the room, Mrs. Jenkinson found the book she needed, Homer's *The Odyssey*,⁵ and sitting down in a chair, she waited for Lady Catherine to finish her conversation with Miss de Bourgh. Feeling somewhat drowsy, she began to doze but was startled back to wakefulness by Lady Catherine's voice, which demanded that she "begin reading from the same place we stopped yesterday". Suppressing a yawn, Mrs. Jenkinson answered, "I am afraid my mind is not very clear tonight. Where did we leave off yesterday evening?"

"It was the portion in which Ulysses' ship reaches the land of the Lotophagi," came the reply, "the part where Ulysses sends some of his sailors to discover what sort of people live on the island, and then the Lotophagi offer those men some lotus fruit to eat."

"Lotophagi—what a peculiar name for a people!" remarked Anne.

"Why, what is peculiar about it?" asked her mother. "On the contrary, it is a very rational name for them; 'phagi' comes from the Greek 'phago', which means 'eating', and 'Loto' refers to the lotus, which is the only food that the Lotophagi eat. In other words, they are lotus-eaters."

Anne made no protest to this line of reasoning, and Lady Catherine continued, "But how a people could have subsisted on lotus alone defies comprehension! Lotus, lotus, and more lotus from morning to night; even setting aside the monotony of the unvarying fare, such a limited diet could have done nothing to promote good health!"

"But Mama," Anne countered, "What about the Israelites, who ate nothing but manna from heaven. It did them no harm."

"You are comparing two completely different things," returned her ladyship. "One is the nectar of God, and the other is, well, the food of the devil, most likely."

By now Mrs. Jenkinson had found the right passage and began to read aloud:

The lotus; of which fruit what man soe'er
Once tasted, no desire felt he to come
With tidings back, or seek his country more,
But rather wish'd to feed on lotus still
With the Lotophagi, and to renounce
All thoughts of home. Them, therefore, I constrain'd
Weeping on board, and dragging each beneath
The benches, bound him there. Then, all in haste,
I urged my people to ascend again
Their hollow barks, lest others also, fed
With fruit of lotus, should forget their home.
They quick embark'd, and on...

The sound of Mrs. Jenkinson's voice ceased unexpectedly, and the book she was holding fell to the floor.

Lady Catherine looked up from her tea and exclaimed, "Have a care, Mrs. Jenkinson!" However, no sooner had the words been uttered, than Mrs. Jenkinson herself, after swaying for a moment in her chair, came tumbling to the ground.

"Mrs. Jenkinson, are you alright?" cried Anne and hurriedly knelt to the floor beside her. Strangely, Anne's companion appeared to be asleep. In reply to Miss de Bourgh's question, she only half-opened her eyes and murmured, "Please do not eat my lotus. I want some more."

"What is this nonsense?! Mrs. Jenkinson, recollect yourself!" exclaimed Lady Catherine.

"Mama, I think she has fallen ill!"

Anne shook the sufferer's shoulder desperately—"Mrs. Jenkinson, please wake up!"

"No... let me sleep," came the drawled answer.

"I think we ought to send for Mr. Leech," said her ladyship.

"No Mama, an apothecary will not do. You must see that she needs a physician."

"Mrs. Jenkinson to be seen by Mr. Wise?! Our own physician!"

"I was not thinking of Mr. Wise. I wanted to send for Mr. Brooke, the new physician."

To have the patient receive treatment from a young, little-known medical practitioner did seem like less of an affront to her ladyship's rank and dignity than to commit her to the care of the eminent Mr. Wise, and as the present case seemed rather urgent, Lady Catherine reluctantly agreed.

While the physician was being fetched, a strong-armed servant carried the half-sleeping woman to her room and carefully placed her on the bed. Miss de Bourgh stayed with her companion and endeavoured, as well as she could, to keep her awake.

Before long, Mr. Brooke came. When Anne heard his voice below, she hurried downstairs to meet him, and while they were walking to Mrs. Jenkinson's room, she related the events of that evening. The physician inquired what the patient had had to eat and drink that day.

"Nothing remarkable," was the answer. "We all ate the same dinner together. I should mention, however, that after dinner Mrs. Jenkinson complained of a headache. She went to her room to take some medicine before joining us for tea."

"Do you know what sort of medicine?"

"I cannot be sure, but it may have been laudanum. There is a bottle of it standing on a table near her bed."

When the two of them entered the patient's room, Mrs. Jenkinson was in a stupor, and her complexion had grown very pale. Examining her eyes, Mr. Brooke observed that the pupils were constricted. He noted, also, that her pulse was slow and full, and her breathing was prolonged, though not stertorous.

"The signs all point to laudanum poisoning," said he.

Anne, her eyes wide with alarm, asked fearfully, "She will not die of it, will she?"

"That depends on how large a dose she has taken and how much of it has been absorbed, but based on her current condition, I believe she can be saved. I will do all I can."

While the physician was searching through his medical bag, Anne entreated her companion, "Mrs. Jenkinson, please try to stay awake. I know it is difficult, but do try." Finding what he needed, Mr. Brooke said, "I must give her sulphate of zinc; it is an emetic." He then administered the substance, which soon induced the patient to expel the contents of her stomach. A disagreeable odour instantly filled the air. The smell was strongly reminiscent of laudanum mixed with an unsavoury medley of that day's dinner.

Repulsed, Lady Catherine covered her nose and mouth with a handkerchief and turned away. "I cannot stay any longer," said she. "If you should need me, Mr. Brooke, I will be in the blue drawing room." She started to leave, but stopping in the doorway, her ladyship called out, "Anne, are you coming?"

"No, Mama. I will stay here with Mrs. Jenkinson."

"If that is what you wish," replied Lady Catherine before disappearing from the room.

After she had gone, the physician was obliged to provoke vomiting in the patient a few more times. When he was satisfied that her stomach had fully discharged its poisonous burden, Mr. Brooke next administered a purgative, while a servant was sent down to the kitchen with instructions to bring back some strong coffee.

Though still drowsy, Mrs. Jenkinson appeared to be significantly better, which gave Anne much relief. She held her companion's hand and tried to comfort her with soothing words. Meanwhile, the gentleman again felt the old lady's pulse and checked the state of her pupils.

The servant presently returned with the coffee, which Mr. Brooke prevailed upon Mrs. Jenkinson to drink. "Its stimulating effect will help to counteract the laudanum," he explained. While the convalescent was sipping the beverage, Anne inquired, "Mr. Brooke, what is laudanum, exactly?"

"It is a tincture—an alcoholic preparation—of opium," was his reply. "In ancient Mesopotamia, the opium poppy was called 'the joy plant', but in my opinion, it is a very dangerous sort of joy. When a person first starts using laudanum or any other form of opium, he finds that physical and mental anguish are greatly reduced thereby. The substance soothes his pain, it raises his spirits, it helps him sleep, and when dispatching business, the person finds that opium gives him alacrity and promptitude. As he continues taking it, however, and its use becomes habitual, despondency and lethargy creep in whenever the effects of the opium wear off. His disposition becomes dull and mopish. Yet, if he attempts to abruptly leave off taking it after long and slavish use, strange agonies and intolerable distresses beset him. After a few days, even death may follow unless he takes opium again."

In reply, Anne observed, "So many people take laudanum daily. Why is it that no one ever warns of its dangers?"

"That I cannot answer," returned Mr. Brooke. "Considering how long it has been known that opium and its derivatives have harmful effects when used for prolonged periods, I am surprised that laudanum is still prescribed so indiscriminately."

Since Mrs. Jenkinson's condition appeared to have improved, and there seemed to be no need for any further interference, the physician gathered up his things and said that he had to leave to see his next patient. Before quitting the room, he gave instructions for the sick lady's care. Someone must stay and keep watch over her, he said, and if there were any signs of a decline, he should be called again. "Mrs. Jenkinson should have only light, nourishing foods at first," he added. "Raw milk fresh from the cow would be best, as well as arrowroot and broths."

Miss de Bourgh accompanied Mr. Brooke downstairs. They descended slowly, both quietly glad to be in each other's company, and wishing to prolong the rare moment alone together as long as possible. Anne found herself admiring the gentleman; he somehow seemed considerably more handsome now than he had ever appeared to her before.

As the pair was nearing the bottom of the stairs, the young lady expressed how grateful she was to him for having saved her companion. "Mrs. Jenkinson is a very dear friend to me," said Anne. "She has been with us for some years, and I have grown very attached to her. Mrs. Jenkinson is one of the few people in the world, and certainly the only one at Rosings, with whom I need not be guarded, and to whom I can speak openly without fear."

"There is no need to thank me, Miss de Bourgh, and I hope I may convince you that you may rely on me as well. If you should ever need help, or just need someone to talk to, you will always have a friend in me. I want you to know that."

"Thank you, Mr. Brooke. You are very kind," said Anne softly.

By now, they had reached the doorway of the blue drawing room. Lady Catherine's demand of, "Anne, is that you?" rang out from within.

"Yes, Mama," her daughter answered with a sigh.

Unwilling to part, the couple stood together quietly for another second, and then Mr. Brooke went inside the room to take leave of her ladyship. A polite exchange followed, after which the gentleman departed into the night.

Anne stayed awake nearly until dawn to care for her friend, but when she felt herself unable to hold her eyes open any longer, the housekeeper took her place by the bedside. As soon as she rose in the morning after a scanty sleep, Anne returned to her sick companion's room. "How are you feeling today, Mrs. Jenkinson?" asked she upon entering.

"Somewhat better, Miss de Bourgh, thank you, though I have a terrible headache."

Anne poured a glass of water from the pitcher and offered it to the convalescent. Mrs. Jenkinson accepted it gratefully, but after taking a few sips, she protested, "I should be the one taking care of you, and here I am, lying idly."

"No one has looked after me all these years better than you, Mrs. Jenkinson, and maybe it would even do me good to be more self-sufficient for a little while. For now, you must think only of resting and getting well."

Half-rising anxiously from her pillow, the sick lady answered, "It is very gracious of you to say so, but if I am ill, who will be your chaperone when you go out?"

"I could always go with Mama instead," came the reassuring reply.

"But who will arrange your footstool? Who will make sure that you are warm and comfortable?"

"I will be perfectly well for the next several days; I am not as delicate as you think. Besides, one of the servants can help me if I need anything."

Not fully convinced, the old lady lamented, "If only I had not been so careless with the laudanum! I have only myself to blame for what happened."

"You should not be so hard upon yourself," said Anne. "There is not a single person on this earth who has gone through life without making any mistakes."

Mrs. Jenkinson smiled sadly. "Can you believe, Miss de Bourgh, there was a time when I did not take laudanum at all; when I did not feel I needed it—a time when I was not in its clutches. It was after my husband's death that I first took the sweet poison. You see, when Mr. Jenkinson passed away, he left me with hardly any money. In addition to the immense sorrow I felt to have lost my husband, the dearest being on this earth to me, I became overwhelmed with anxiety when contemplating what I would live on and how I would survive. Headaches tormented me, and sleep became all but impossible. Able to bear the misery no longer, I went to the apothecary's shop and obtained some laudanum from Mr. Leech.

"The medicine relieved the pain and helped me sleep, but more than that, it changed how I felt. It lifted my spirits and gave me courage and a new-found vigour, making the daily tasks of life seem easier and less burdensome. Laudanum became to me like a trusted friend, enveloping me in its comfort and soothing my anxieties.

"Unfortunately, these pleasing effects lasted only while the medicine was in operation. At other times, I became increasingly listless, irritable, and fidgety, and I was plagued by excessive perspiration and itching. These changes alarmed me, and I tried to stop taking the laudanum, but in consequence, I became so unwell as to be obliged to resume drinking it. What was once a source of comfort and relief became a captor; the laudanum would not relinquish its hold on me. And last night, it nearly killed me."

CHAPTER 14

Some days later at Belargent Hall, the Villiers family was assembled at dinner in the evening, and while they ate, the footmen hurried up and down the stairs with steaming platters of food. By the dessert course, one of the servants felt himself in need of a little sustenance. Therefore, as he came up the stairs from the kitchen, the footman chose the choicest morsel from his tray of sweetmeats and popped the delicacy into his mouth. Chewing as hastily as possible, he nearly choked in the process, but recovering himself, he entered the dining room as solemnly as he could and began serving.

John Villiers was very fond of dessert, and consequently it was with some indignation that, towards the end of the meal, he cried, "Priscilla, must you take the last slice of cake again? I had meant to have that piece. Why do you never think of anyone but yourself?"

"For heaven's sake, John, it is not the only dessert on the table," his father returned sharply. "Eat something else!"

Lady Villiers remarked, "I really must speak to the new cook about the size of her cakes—this one is far too small. One would think she was baking for only two people rather than a whole family... But John, dear, just this once, why do you not have the barberry ice instead, or perhaps a little marmalade?"

"I have already eaten some barberry ice, and I do not want marmalade. I wanted another piece of cake! But Priscilla has taken it for herself, as she does all too often."

"Perhaps it is as well that I did, for the physician says you are too stout and should not eat so many sweets," came Priscilla's answer.

"Well, cake does nothing to improve your figure, either. Maybe if you ate less cake, Sir Matthew would not have come to prefer Georgiana Darcy's society to your own."

"Pray, do not mention Sir Matthew," lamented Lady Villiers. "How unfortunate that Miss Darcy should have come into the neighbourhood at the time that she did. Another fortnight, and Sir Matthew would have made Priscilla an offer, I am sure. He had paid her such marked attentions!"

"But now he has quite forgotten the way to Belargent Hall and hardly notices my sister," laughed Mr. Villiers.

"Instead of talking of matters that do not concern you, John, why do you not instead think of Anne de Bourgh and do your duty in marrying her?" retorted his sister.

"Oh no, not that subject again!"

"Besides, as concerns Sir Matthew and Miss Darcy, his foolish passion for her cannot last. She should enjoy his attentions while she can, for he will never make her an offer. How can he when he has beheld a far superior woman?"

"Yourself, you mean?"

"And why not? What is she compared to me?"

"Yes, what is an angel compared to a shrew?" Mr. Villiers muttered under his breath.

"What was that you said, Brother?"

Louder, the gentleman replied, "I meant to say that Miss Darcy is a very fine young woman. I can see why Sir Matthew likes her, and I would marry her myself if I had the chance."

"Then you will have made a very bad trade, indeed. Miss Darcy is worth only thirty thousand pounds, while Anne de Bourgh will inherit Rosings Park and a large fortune besides."

After a momentary pause, Miss Villiers continued, "But now that we are on the subject of Georgiana Darcy, there is another matter that I wish to discuss. I have heard that she plays the harp. Why did I never receive harp lessons, Mama? How could you have neglected my education so?"

"Of course you shall have harp lessons, my dear. We can inquire about a teacher tomorrow."

Satisfied with this answer, the young lady remarked, "I daresay I will master it quickly, and I shall soon play the harp better than Georgiana Darcy just as I perform better on the pianoforte."

"Sister, I have heard Miss Darcy on the pianoforte, and although you play well, your execution does not compare with hers."

"That shows how little taste you have, John. Your understanding of music is on the same level as your understanding of Shakespeare."

"What is that supposed to mean?"

"Enough!" bellowed Sir Edward.

The young people kept silent but glared at each other across the table.

"Priscilla, my dear, perhaps it is time we withdrew to the drawing room," suggested Lady Villiers.

"Nothing would please me better," came her daughter's peevish reply. Miss Villiers then rose from her chair and flounced out of the dining room with her mother trailing close behind.

When the two footmen who had been serving at dinner at last descended the stairs to the kitchen, one of them said to the other:

"Wipe your face; your mouth is covered in crumbs!"

"Good Lord! Did I look like this the entire time?"

"I am afraid you did, my friend. I would have told you sooner, but there was no opportunity while we were serving. It is lucky for you that they were all too busy arguing to notice. Otherwise, the red-haired Medusa would have caught you for sure, and then you would have gotten the boot out of the household—without a reference too! You should be more careful; I always wipe my mouth thoroughly before entering the dining room." With these words, the footman took a swig of the wine he was carrying, and then both of them continued down the stairs together.

CHAPTER 15

Little did Priscilla Villiers know that only two days after she had pronounced it to be impossible, Sir Matthew Leigh made Georgiana an offer of marriage. Almost since the first day of their acquaintance, he had entertained thoughts of making Georgiana his wife, and after they waltzed together, she was all he could think of. Miss Darcy was as close to perfection as one could find in a woman. The more he knew her, the more convinced he became that he could find none better, and after much reflection, he determined to make her an offer.

Having formed the resolution, a new quandary now entered his mind: how best to go about the business? He had never before proposed marriage to a lady, nor even contemplated it seriously, and now he was uncertain how to proceed. What should he say? How even to broach the subject?

Sir Matthew remained awake until a late hour to plan his speech and rehearse the words in his mind. He rose early, hoping to solicit a private audience with Georgiana before breakfast, but no such opportunity presented itself, as the object of his love awoke later than usual and did not come downstairs until everyone was already at breakfast. The anticipation of speaking with her was agonising. During the repast, Georgiana's suitor hardly noticed what he ate and was impatient for the meal to end, inwardly willing everyone to eat faster.

At long last, the breakfasters' appetites were satisfied, and the company began to separate. Mr. Townsend proceeded directly to his library, and Elizabeth, who wished to select an interesting book to read, accompanied him thither. Meanwhile, Georgiana and Mrs. Townsend walked to a sitting room together. Sir Matthew went with them. Along the way, the mistress of the house rattled on about a ball they had attended on Saturday: the eldest of the Miss Beauchamps did not look well—she was steadily on her way to losing her looks, although even *she* was a beauty compared to Miss Meggott; yet, if the number of dances each had danced was anything to judge by, Miss Meggott would surely be the first of the two ladies to marry. Who could expect otherwise? What was Miss Beauchamp's paltry fortune compared to Miss Meggott's twenty thousand pounds?! ... Oh, and Lady Villiers' hair! Was it not arranged splendidly?! She must speak to her own maid and see whether Robertson could contrive something similar. On and on went Mrs. Townsend, stopping occasionally to ask her companions their opinion.

For the gentleman, time crawled during the course of the next half hour. The lady of the house showed no intention of leaving Georgiana's side in the imminent future but instead chatted incessantly on trivial subjects. It was only when the post arrived that Mrs. Townsend at last left to attend to some household business with the butler, while Georgiana stayed behind to read her correspondence. But alas! Now that the long-desired moment was finally upon him, Sir Matthew discovered that his courage had deserted him. Unable to pronounce the words he had rehearsed so carefully, the young man sat dumbly in his chair while the lady flipped through her letters to see who had sent them.

"A minute more," he told himself, "and then I will make my intentions known to her." The minute came and went, but still he could not bring himself to utter a syllable. "What cowardice is this! Speak!" thought he, but then another thought, much more appealing, followed: since Miss Darcy had already started reading her first letter, it would be inconsiderate to interrupt her. He would let her finish it, and then he would begin his speech. However, it was Georgiana who spoke first.

"I have just received word from my brother," said she, disappointment in her voice. "Fitzwilliam writes to say that business delays him once more; it will be another fortnight before he can join us. His visit at Kleistringham must of necessity be a rather short one.

"I am very sorry to hear it," replied Sir Matthew. "I had been looking forward to making Mr. Darcy's acquaintance. From all you have told me, he sounds like an excellent man."

"He is. Fitzwilliam is the best brother anyone could wish for, and he matters more to me than anyone in the whole world."

As she was saying the words, Georgiana noticed that Sir Matthew was looking at her in a very peculiar manner. He then rose from his chair and came to sit beside her on the sofa, all the while fixing his eyes on her intensely. He swallowed. Everything in his bearing indicated agitation; he looked down for a moment, then brought his gaze back up to her again. At last he said, "It is natural that Mr. Darcy should hold the first place in your affections at present, but Miss Darcy, perhaps at some future time... What I mean to say is, perhaps, Miss Darcy, that distinction may more properly belong to a husband in future, and, if it should please you to favour my suit, I will think myself the happiest of mortals to become that man."

How many times had Georgiana dreamed of hearing an avowal of the kind from Sir Matthew, but never did she expect that he would make his addresses to her so soon! One instant, she was reading her brother's letter, and the next she was hearing a proposal. Georgiana was astonished beyond words, but at the same time overwhelmed with joy. The two feelings combined rendered her quite mute. It was just as well, for the gentleman had more to say:

"Miss Darcy... Georgiana, I am sure that my eyes have already many times betrayed it, but I may as well tell you plainly: I love you... passionately and sincerely. From the very first moment I beheld you at the pianoforte, I was a lost man. You lit such a fire in my soul as cannot be quenched except with my life. No one but you can ever lay a claim on my affections. You fill my dreams at night, and during the day, I can find neither rest nor peace from thoughts of you. My enchantress, you have bewitched me, and unless you can grant a favourable answer to my fondest wishes and agree to be my wife, my existence shall become a perpetual misery."

Having thus declared his love, he looked with anxious suspense at Georgiana for an answer. The lady, overcome with shyness, emotion, and the bliss of knowing that she was beloved, hardly dared lift her eyes to meet his. Though the feelings he kindled in her were no less powerful than those Sir Matthew had confessed to himself, her sense of delicacy would not permit her to admit to being as in love with him as he was with her. The only reply Georgiana gave, therefore, was to softly, almost in whisper, say that she was grateful for his good opinion of her, and that she would be honoured to have him as her husband.

Relief and exuberance lit up Sir Matthew's countenance. "It is *I* who will be honoured," returned he. "Do not think I am for a moment insensible of what a treasure I have found, and what good fortune is mine that I will soon be able to call you my wife." His tone then softened, and in a tender accent he asked, "Miss Darcy, now that we are engaged, will you permit me to kiss you?"

As heightened as Georgiana's colour was before this proposition, her cheeks flushed to a much deeper crimson after it. She knew not where to look or how to answer. It is not that she was averse to such expressions of affection—quite the contrary, she would willingly have acceded to his wishes, but caution restrained her for once.

"Sir Matthew, I think it would be best if we waited for my brother to give his blessing to our union before we take such a step," came her tremulous reply. "Fitzwilliam has not yet been made acquainted with our love, and while I have little doubt that he will give his consent for us to marry, it would set my mind at ease to know we had his approval."

The gentleman was more than a little disappointed; thoughts of kissing Georgiana had been ever on his mind, especially since the day he taught her to waltz, when he had come close to giving her a kiss. Yet, though his desires were thwarted, he respected Miss Darcy all the more for her answer. Her female delicacy was no small part of her attractions, and after all, there would be many opportunities of kissing Georgiana in the future. With Mr. Darcy expected to arrive in Kent at the end of November, it would not be much longer to wait.

Taking her hand in his, he said, "Of course, Miss Darcy. Your wish is my law, now and always."

"There is one more thing," said she. "I would prefer it if we did not tell the Townsends or anyone else of our engagement. I should like to inform my sister-in-law and my cousin Anne, and, no doubt, you will wish to write to your sister, but otherwise I think we should keep it a secret for the present. It would not be right if everyone knew before my own brother did."

Sir Matthew agreed that this was the right course of action, and serious matters now having been discussed, the gentleman and his bride-to-be partook of more pleasant conversation. Sitting side by side on the sofa, they talked of their future together, and the time passed so quickly that they were both surprised when the hour arrived for luncheon.

As soon as there was an opportunity to speak with Elizabeth privately, Georgiana told her of Sir Matthew's proposal to her that morning, and of her acceptance. However, the news did not produce the reaction that she hoped for. When Elizabeth learned of the engagement, her expression changed to concern, and instead of the congratulations that Georgiana had expected, Mrs. Darcy had only words of caution to offer.

"Are you certain that you acted wisely?" asked she.

"You think I made a mistake in choosing Sir Matthew?"

"Well, he appears to be an amiable gentleman, and as far as fortune is concerned, it seems to be a prudent match, but it is barely above three weeks since you first met him. One can hardly ascertain a man's character after such a short acquaintance."

"But time is not all that matters," protested Georgiana. "I knew George Wickham all my life, and it was many years before I discovered his wicked character. And how about Jane and Mr. Bingley? I am sure I remember your sister mentioning that their acquaintance was a rather brief one—it was no more than six weeks, if I recall correctly, that they spent in each other's society in Hertfordshire, and then Mr. Bingley went away to London and did not see Jane again until he returned months later to make his proposals to her."

"It is not the same," said Elizabeth. "They may not have spent many weeks together in Hertfordshire, but they had months to reflect and consult their own feelings before committing themselves."

"Lizzy, I do assure you that I mean to be cautious. I will not marry unless my brother gives his consent, and of course Colonel Fitzwilliam must give his blessing too, since he is also my guardian. Until then, we will keep the engagement a secret, and in society Sir Matthew and I will behave towards each other as we did before."

Hearing these words gave Elizabeth some relief, but still she felt uneasy. Seeing her sister-in-law's countenance, Georgiana herself began to feel doubts, but these she did her best to push aside. For the rest of the day, the young lady attempted to convince herself of having made the right choice by recalling to her memory all the reasons why she and Sir Matthew were well-suited to each other, and all the proofs of his being well-qualified to make her happy. Certainly, in regard to fortune, at least, the match was very advantageous. With so many circumstances in their favour, could their union be anything but a happy one?

CHAPTER 16

After breakfast the next morning, Anne set out to visit one of the farmers on estate business. The matter was one that the land agent would ordinarily have attended to. However, a disagreement between him and Lady Catherine had seen the two part ways, and until a new land agent could be employed, Anne and her mother shared the task of addressing tenant matters. It was just as well—Rosings would be Anne's someday, and now was as good a time as any to take a more active part in managing the estate.

When she drove up to the farm, Mr. Smith, the tenant, was at that moment carrying a bucket of milk towards a young calf, which was tied to a post next to a shed. Just as the man raised his arm to Anne in greeting, the calf darted forward in greedy anticipation and began running in circles excitedly around the farmer. Each time the calf ran around, the rope wound tighter around Mr. Smith's legs, and almost before he knew what was happening, he lost his balance and fell heavily onto his side. The cord around the calf's neck having been secured only loosely, the little bull broke free and raced gleefully across the field. Mr. Smith hurried to unwind the rope that still bound his legs and then sped after the calf while shouting, "Wait! Stop! Come back!"

Hearing the commotion outside, a farm labourer emerged from the shed and joined in the pursuit of the disobedient, little bull. Before the men could get very far, however, Mr. Smith lost his footing on some uneven ground and fell forward.

"Mr. Smith! Mr. Smith! Are you hurt?" cried Anne in alarm. She descended from her carriage and moved hastily towards the farmer, who did not stir from his position on the ground.

"Mr. Smith!" Anne cried again and shook the man by the shoulder in a vain attempt to wake him. It soon became clear what had happened; the unconscious man was lying beside a tree stump—on this he must have struck his head when falling. Turning to the farm labourer, Anne said, "He needs medical assistance. Bring Mr. Brooke as quickly as you can!"

By the time the physician was found and brought to the farm, Mr. Smith had already regained consciousness. Mr. Brooke examined him and said, "Apart from a bruised knee and a bump on the forehead, I believe there is nothing else the matter. You did the right thing to use your smelling salts, Miss de Bourgh. I think you have done more for our patient than I have."

With Anne beside them, the physician helped Mr. Smith to the cottage; the farmer was still a little unsteady on his feet and limped slightly from his fall. Inside the house, the man was assisted into a chair, and with instructions to avoid exertion for several days, he was turned over to the care of his wife. Anne told Mr. Smith that she would return some other day; the business she had come to discuss could wait until he had recovered from that morning's adventures.

Afterwards, she and Mr. Brooke walked back together on the long path leading from the cottage. They did not say anything to each other at first, though the gentleman was thinking to himself that Miss de Bourgh looked truly lovely that day. Her hair, which was usually pulled back into a plain knot, was today curled and plaited in a very pretty way, and her bonnet and spencer, both made of green cloth, drew notice to her clear, grey eyes, which were shining with a particular lustre just then.

Although the lady was oblivious of Mr. Brooke's contemplations, her heightened awareness of their solitude gave a brighter colour to her complexion, thereby making her appearance all the more pleasing. Anne was at that moment feeling rather tongue-tied; conversation always seemed easier when others were present to fill any gaps in the dialogue, but now, with just the two of them walking alone together, she was at a loss of what to say or do. Fortunately, it was not long before Mr. Brooke himself said something.

"I think Mr. Smith should be quite well tomorrow," he commented.

"Yes, I hope he will."

"Miss de Bourgh, I meant to ask you, how is Mrs. Jenkinson? I hope she is feeling better?"

"Yes, much better. She was rather weak at first but is now back to her old self again."

"And your mother, I hope she is in good health?"

"Mama is perfectly well. In fact, I cannot remember the last time that she was ill."

Anne smiled at Mr. Brooke, but almost immediately, she dropped her gaze to her hands, then looked at some wild ducks flying overhead, and then at a row of poplar trees growing to one side—everywhere, it seemed, except at the gentleman beside her. Mr. Brooke felt nearly as bashful as Anne did. He searched his mind for something clever or interesting to say, but in vain.

When the silence between the pair had lasted longer than any but the most hardened soul could endure, the gentleman and young lady both suddenly spoke at once. "Miss de Bourgh, I..." and "Mr. Brooke, would you not agree..." they said simultaneously.

"I beg your pardon, Miss de Bourgh. Please continue what you wanted to say," urged he.

"Oh... it was nothing of consequence... I was just thinking of how lovely the weather is this morning. But I believe I am the one who interrupted you; what were you going to say?"

Reddening a little, Mr. Brooke answered, "I was about to remark much the same thing, that it is excellent weather for walking outdoors."

Health and the weather having been thoroughly discussed, there was another pause, but mercifully, it did not last as long as the first one, and this time, it was Anne who broke the silence. As they were approaching a weeping willow tree, she asked:

"Do you use willow much in your medical practice, Mr. Brooke?"

"No, not particularly. As a matter of fact, now that I think of it, I do not believe I have ever prescribed a medicine containing willow to a patient, though I do remember an entry in a medical botany book describing willow as being useful for lowering fevers."

Catching one of the tree branches in her hand, Anne replied, "It is also a great help for treating burns. Just last week I had the occasion to employ willow for that purpose. When our cook scalded her hand badly, I remembered something our neighbour Mrs. Collins said about having successfully used tea made from willow branches in such cases, and so I asked one of our kitchen maids to boil some willow tea; when it had cooled completely, the cook dipped her hand into the liquid repeatedly over the course of half an hour. She did the same thing the following day, and afterwards, the wounded skin healed remarkably quickly—much better than with any ointment from the apothecary."

Mr. Brooke answered with:

"Nature holds a treasure chest of medicine awaiting our discovery, and willow may well be one of those that is yet to be fully explored... Bark is to trees what skin is to animals, and I would not be surprised if there are substances in willow bark that are beneficial to the health of both types of integuments."

The gentleman then swept some fallen leaves from a bench standing beneath the willow tree, and together, he and Anne sat down upon it. Hardly conscious of the time, they spoke further, and gradually, their mutual shyness melted away. Before long, they were conversing not only on general topics but also on those of a more personal nature. Mr. Brooke told Anne about his mother and father, and about his sisters living at his childhood home in Dorsetshire. His boyhood days had been very happy ones, with summers often spent at Lyme, and memories of sea-bathing and of running atop the Cobb in the wind, while his mother below scolded him to come back down to safety. Anne, likewise, spoke a little of her own childhood, which, though not as cheerful and carefree as Mr. Brooke's, still held some happy memories. To an outsider listening in, these commonplace details of everyday life would not have held much interest, but to two people falling in love, there was no subject more interesting than each other.

CHAPTER 17

Anne returned home in an elated state of mind. She felt full of boundless energy, and every time her thoughts wandered back to Mr. Brooke, her heart gave a pleasant, little flutter. Unable to contain her exuberance, she half-skipped, half-danced across the entrance hall, but suddenly perceiving a footman, she sobered her steps and walked the rest of the way to the blue drawing room more decorously.

Upon entering the room, Anne discovered that her mother was within. Lady Catherine studied her daughter intently as she came in and then remarked, "Well, Anne, you are looking well of late. Your shoulders are pulled back, as they should be, and you move with more dignity and less awkwardness than I have seen you do before. At last you seem to have taken my instruction to heart... And your hair—I see that you have had your maid dress it in a more becoming way."

"Yes, Mama."

"Well, these are pleasing improvements indeed, and all the more so because they come at just the right time."

"The right time? For what, Mama?"

"Your marriage."

"My marriage?!" stammered Anne in astonishment. "To whom?"

"You will remember that a few weeks ago I went to London. My object in going was not merely, as I said at the time, to conduct business with the bank. The more compelling purpose of my journey was to secure your future, which, I am glad to say, I have done to my satisfaction. The man I have chosen as your husband is Mr. Cavendish, the eldest son and heir of Lord —. Mr. Cavendish owns the magnificent estate of Oisley Park in Devonshire, and he will of course inherit his father's even more extensive properties. Everything has been arranged for him to come to Rosings later today, and he is to stay with us for the next fortnight."

Anne was shaken by this news. It was just like Lady Catherine to decide on important matters pertaining to her life without consulting her, and then to wait until the last minute to make the announcement. Yet, knowing that protest would be worse than useless, her daughter did not even attempt it. Nothing was left for her to do, therefore, except await Mr. Cavendish's arrival with the greatest apprehension.

When he came, Lady Catherine received her guest with the utmost hospitality and enthusiasm. Anne observed that Mr. Cavendish was of middling height, had a slight frame, and was remarkable only for his long, thin nose and small eyes rimmed with spectacles. What hair he had left was greying, and everything about his appearance declared him to be in his forties, though perhaps closer to fifty than forty.

Feeling acutely uncomfortable, Anne spoke only when dictated by politeness, and the replies she gave were, for the most part, confined to monosyllables. Mr. Cavendish did not appear to mind, however, and seemed content to converse with Lady Catherine instead. When her lady-ship inquired about his journey, he answered that it had been dreadful— the muddy roads, the inconveniences, and the unpalatable food at the inns where he had eaten all combined to make his travels exceedingly disagree-able. Lady Catherine replied in kind, remembering her own recent trip to London. Together they enjoyed the pleasures of complaint until, before they knew it, it was time for dinner.

In the dining room, Lady Catherine and her visitor likewise found much to talk about. They had not been eating long before Mr. Cavendish remarked upon the delicious dinner. Everything on his plate, he said, was perfectly suited to facilitate digestion, but at the same time managed to be highly pleasing to the palate. This praise was very gratifying to her ladyship, who had taken great pains to ensure that the dinner would meet with his approval. Her cook had received strict instructions to omit strong sauces, roasted meats, and rough-textured or excessively rich foods, all of which tended to aggravate a weak stomach.

Lady Catherine then invited her guest to tell them more about his malady. "Come, there is no need to conceal anything from us," said she. "We are very nearly family." The gentleman needed very little urging, for he was never as miserably happy as when giving a detailed account of his ailments to sympathetic listeners. He informed the two ladies that he suffered a great deal from dyspepsia, and he enumerated as many of his digestive symptoms as could be politely mentioned at the dinner table. On account of these troubles, he was frequently obliged to consult his physician, Dr. Smart. Admittedly, the medical practitioner was privately convinced that his patient's tendency to analyse the digestibility of every mouthful and scrutinise with anxious watchfulness any signs of digestive distress following each meal was at least partly to blame for his symptoms. Even so, it was useless to reason with a man so convinced that he was gravely ill, and what complicated matters further was that despite the physician's boastedly extensive medical knowledge, Dr. Smart could not say with any degree of certainty how much of his patient's illness was imagined and how much of it was real.

When Mr. Cavendish had finished recounting his symptoms, Lady Catherine inquired into his medical care.

"Other than the pills my physician prescribes, he also frequently recommends a regimen of fasting," came the reply. "Only, neither form of treatment seems to have helped me thus far, and, if anything, the hunger pangs and rumbling occasioned by fasting are frequently worse than the illness it is intended to cure."

"I can well imagine that would be the case!" exclaimed Lady Catherine. "It is no wonder you have not recovered! Why, fasting is the worst remedy that could be prescribed for dyspepsia! Those who are ill need as much, if not more, nourishment than those who are healthy, and denying food altogether could not possibly effect a cure. I am sorry to say it, but I am afraid that Dr. Smart does not know his business," declared her ladyship. "On occasion, even *I* experience a touch of dyspepsia after a particularly celebratory meal, and whenever I do, my own physician, Mr. Wise, prescribes slippery elm. In combination with simpler, lighter fare, it never fails to make me well again. Has your physician ever mentioned slippery elm bark to you, Mr. Cavendish?"

"No Madam, he has not."

"Well, from all that you have told me of Dr. Smart, I am not surprised," returned Lady Catherine.

The gentleman was very keen to learn more about this wondrous medicine, and her ladyship was no less willing to impart her knowledge. "The slippery elm is a lofty tree indigenous to North America," said she. "The useful part is the inner bark, which, when finely ground and infused in water, forms a highly nutritious mucilage. Mr. Wise tells me that it has proven to be efficacious against all manner of digestive ailments. You must take it, Mr. Cavendish, if you ever hope to recover from your affliction."

Her guest, who had been listening with rapt attention, replied, "I thank you, Madam, for all your valuable advice, and while I am in Kent, perhaps I ought to take the opportunity of being examined by your physician. He sounds like a very good one."

"To be sure, he is. You will find none better!" answered her ladyship with alacrity, adding, "And of course, Mr. Cavendish, during your stay at Rosings, we will spare no effort to ensure that you are well looked after and comfortable. I have given orders for the eggs at tomorrow's breakfast to be soft-boiled, and when you retire to your room tonight, you will find some dyspepsia biscuits and clabbered milk by your bed."

Mr. Cavendish thanked his hostess for her attentiveness and then asked, with some concern, what sort of cow had produced the milk (for the dairy products of some breeds did not agree with his delicate digestion). "We only have Guernseys in our dairy," replied her ladyship. "I would not dream of keeping any other breed." The guest brightened at this answer. He, too, had great admiration for Guernseys and stocked his own dairy at Oisley Park with precisely the same breed. No other cow, he declared, was capable of giving such flavoursome and nutritious, golden-coloured milk. Lady Catherine was all agreement, and together she and Mr. Cavendish were united in their praise as they extolled the virtues of the breed.

After dinner, Mr. Cavendish asked Anne, "Do you like birds, Miss de Bourgh?"

"Well, I suppose so. I cannot imagine who would dislike them," was her answer. Taking this indefinite reply for more than it was, the guest said, "I am so glad that you feel that way! I myself am very fond of birds." This admission was followed by an enthusiastic description of his large aviary at Oisley Park. As he told the ladies, it was a majestic, ornate structure made of wrought iron and glass, and it housed England's largest collection of exotic species.

"What sort of birds do you keep in your aviary?" asked Lady Catherine.

"Many different kinds: songbirds, doves, macaws, and more—but of them all, the parrots are my favourite. They are the most splendid, delightful birds; you can teach parrots any word or phrase, and they repeat it faithfully. One hears back from them exactly what one wishes to hear!"

"Most agreeable birds, indeed!" remarked Lady Catherine.

"One does tire of their chatter after awhile," said Mr. Cavendish, "but when that happens, I have only to leave the aviary. Often, I order one of the servants to instead place whichever songbird pleases my fancy into a little cage, which is then brought to me at the house. I find the lovely song to be very soothing in the evenings after reading."

"Are the birds difficult to look after?" asked her ladyship.

"To some extent, yes. It takes several servants and a great deal of knowledge to tend to them properly, but all my birds are exceptionally well-fed and cared for. I would go so far as to say that if they were capable of voicing their thoughts, my birds would tell you that they are happier in their present circumstances than if they were free!"

Mr. Cavendish then went on to list all the species of birds he owned (of which there were a considerable number), and for many of them, he gave a thorough description of the colour, size, and origin of the bird, as well as of the length and shape of its beak. As he droned on and on, Anne had to fight to keep her eyes open and to prevent from yawning. She tried to look as interested as she could, but inwardly, she was thinking of how very dull the conversation was. Although she had it within her power to survive one such tedious evening, the idea of having similar ones repeated daily, for the rest of her life, was more than she could bear.

When Mr. Cavendish had tired of talking about his birds, and Lady Catherine had tired of listening, the two of them next discussed how to properly raise and educate children. Her ladyship had a great deal to say on this subject; strict discipline, she asserted, was of paramount importance, and many of society's ills could be traced back to excessive indulgence during the formative years of childhood. In fact, the revolutions in France and in the American colonies, she was sure, both had their root in parents' failure to correct their wayward sons and daughters early in life. Children accustomed to challenging the authority of their mothers and fathers inevitably grow into adults who challenge the established social order, said she, and if society did not take care, more revolutions would follow.

Mr. Cavendish concurred heartily, adding, "God, in His wisdom, placed the man at the head of the household and commanded the wife and children to obey. Sons and daughters may easily discover their duties by studying the Ten Commandments, and as for women, in Ephesians the Bible[6] tells them, 'Wives, submit yourselves unto your own husbands, as unto the Lord. For the husband is the head of the wife, even as Christ is the head of the church: and he is the Saviour of the body. Therefore as the church is subject unto Christ; so let the wives be to their own husbands in every thing.'"

While the man was speaking, Lady Catherine nodded her agreement, and, bolstered by her approval, he continued, "My mother was a shining example of all that is virtuous and dutiful. Not once did she ever contradict my father or question his judgment. She adapted her tastes and opinions to suit his and consulted him in all things, from what books she ought to read, to matters concerning domestic economy. Not a stick of furniture was ever placed in the house that had not first received his approval. To have such an excellent wife as well as obedient children is, I believe, the greatest blessing that a man could ever hope to receive from heaven."

Everything that Lady Catherine heard met with her approbation. On her marriage to (the now late) Sir Lewis de Bourgh, she had willingly vowed to love, cherish, and *obey* her husband, but truth be told, though *she* gave the promise, *he* did the obeying. As far as her daughter was concerned, however, Lady Catherine believed that the situation was very different from what her own had been. Her ladyship considered that Anne needed guidance, and she wanted to be sure that when her only child left the care of its mother and entered that of a husband, the man in question would be capable of filling the newly-vacated role of protector, instructor, and disciplinarian. To her view, Mr. Cavendish was just the man required; he had the years, wisdom, and character needed to take on the task, and Lady Catherine therefore felt reassured at the thought that her daughter would be safe in his hands.

Mr. Cavendish, too, was very well pleased with how the evening had gone. Miss de Bourgh suited him perfectly; not only was the size of her fortune beyond reproach, but also, he liked her meek, reserved manners. A life with her would be one of calm and peace, and he might come and go as he wished, or do anything else he liked, for that matter, without fears of quarrelsome scenes at home. Such liberty in the married state was a rare treasure—a pity all mothers did not bring up their daughters as well as Lady Catherine had brought up hers.

Miss de Bourgh's feelings were very different from those of either Mr. Cavendish or Lady Catherine. Even though the gentleman was not unpleasant, Anne could not agree with his views, nor could she enjoy his conversation, and neither did she believe that she could ever bring herself to love him. The thought of marrying him made her shudder. Lady Catherine, on the other hand, was clearly eager to have Mr. Cavendish for her son-in-law, and he, in turn, did not seem unwilling to oblige her in this wish. He was to remain at Rosings for a fortnight, and by the end of that time, Anne feared, he would make her an offer. The idea filled her with anxiety and trepidation, especially because, as she discovered, her heart already belonged to someone else. Had Anne's affections not been so deeply engaged, she might have been able to resign herself to a marriage in which duty took the place of love. However, the extent of her attachment to Mr. Brooke made the idea of marrying any other man insupportable.

CHAPTER 18

The next morning, Anne's mind was so far from being tranquil that she felt it necessary to take a walk outdoors to relieve her agitation. When her maid had dressed her in warm clothes suited to the chilly weather, Anne went downstairs. As she was nearing the library on her way out, a rustling sound coming from within arrested her footsteps. Who could that be?! Lady Catherine never spent mornings before breakfast in the library. The doors being a little ajar, Anne furtively leaned across just enough to see who was inside. It was as she had feared! Mr. Cavendish was seated within, engrossed in reading a newspaper, and looking very much at home.

Not able to bear the thought of seeing, much less speaking, with the gentleman, Anne removed her shoes and carefully tiptoed past the doorway. From there, she ran the rest of the way to the entrance hall and burst out of the house as if from prison.

Oh, sweet escape! Breathless from the exertion of running, Anne took a brief rest to regain her strength before slowly commencing her walk. She wanted nothing more in that moment than to be as far away from the house and its occupants as possible. In keeping with this desire, she wandered long and far through the park. Despite being no great walker, Anne did not stop until she had reached the palings that marked the boundary of the property. She was now standing in a grove, and on the other side of the fence was a lane that separated Rosings Park from the parsonage.

Miss de Bourgh stepped up to the gate and looked down the road. She perceived that there was a man coming up the lane from the parsonage-house. At first she could not distinguish his identity, but as he moved closer, with what surprise did she discover that it was Mr. Brooke! The physician had that morning been called out to treat Charlotte Collins' sick baby, and after leaving her house, he had been unable to resist taking a walk along the beautiful woods.

Mr. Brooke noticed Anne before she recognised him and eagerly came towards her. However, his joy at meeting Miss de Bourgh by such a fortunate chance soon gave way to feelings of a more sober nature. From the manner of Anne's greeting, the gentleman immediately saw that something was seriously the matter. With the tenderest concern, he inquired into the cause of her distress.

"It is my mother," said she in reply.

"Has Lady Catherine fallen ill?"

"No, no, nothing like that. I believe Mama is as strong and vigorous as ever."

"What is the matter then?"

"I hardly know how to begin... You see, Mama firmly believes that sons and daughters, whatever their age, owe a duty of strict filial obedience to their parents, and that such obedience must extend even to the most important decision in life: the choice of one's marriage partner."

"And, do you agree with her ladyship's views?"

"No, not at all, but my feelings on the subject have not stopped Mama from searching for a husband for me. Yesterday, at her invitation, the man whom she has chosen to be my husband came to Rosings and is to stay with us for the next two weeks. From his behaviour, he does not appear disinclined to become her son-in-law."

"This is very unexpected news," said Mr. Brooke, evidently disconcerted. "What will you do?"

"I do not know. My feelings are strongly opposed to my mother's plans for me, but Mama has a will of unmatched strength. If I disobey her wishes, she will make life at Rosings unbearable for me."

"Yes, I understand. This is a grave situation indeed," was the answer. A long pause followed. The gentleman looked deep in thought, then started to speak but stopped again. At last, with some hesitation, he addressed Anne with:

"A solution comes to mind, but whether you will agree... Miss de Bourgh, there is something I would like to say to you... something I would like to ask."

"Yes, Mr. Brooke?" came the eager reply.

He hesitated again, as if searching for the right words. "I never thought this moment would come so soon, or I would have prepared something decent to say," he finally uttered.

"I do not expect fine speeches," said Anne. "Simple words spoken from the heart are just as agreeable to me."

"Well, then, what I wish to say is: although we have not been acquainted for very long, I feel as if I have known you all my life, almost as if we are family. I take great pleasure in your conversation and your company, and when I am with you, I feel that I can speak on any subject without fear of sounding dull. It is like when I am with one of my sisters."

"I am like your sister?"

"Yes! ... That is, no... I hardly know what I am saying."

Hearing the nonsense coming out of his mouth, Mr. Brooke wondered whether he ought to have spoken at all. Before he could collect his thoughts and decide what to do next, a woman's voice some distance behind him called out, "Mr. Brooke... Mr. Brooke, wait!" It was Charlotte Collins. She came hastily up the lane and soon reached the couple standing at the gate. After exchanging greetings with Miss de Bourgh, she stretched out a medical instrument to the gentleman and said, "Mr. Brooke, you forgot this at the parsonage." Taking the instrument, and looking very uncomfortable, he thanked her for her trouble.

Anne, who was still standing on the other side of the fence, opened the gate and joined the other two in the lane. Mrs. Collins said a few words to Miss de Bourgh and the physician and then invited them both to come back with her for some tea. Anne accepted the invitation, but Mr. Brooke answered bashfully, "No thank you, Mrs. Collins. I must be going; I have some business to attend to." Red-faced and feeling foolish beyond words, he promptly took leave of the ladies.

While he was fleeing, Mrs. Collins remarked, "In what a hurry is Mr.

Brooke! I wonder what could be so urgent." Miss de Bourgh was at a loss to explain what had just passed even to herself. Thoroughly confused, she followed her acquaintance to the parsonage for the promised tea. Though at that moment she had not the least desire either for tea or conversation, Anne was even less eager to return to Mr. Cavendish and Lady Catherine at Rosings.

CHAPTER 19

Blissfully unaware that Sir Matthew Leigh was now betrothed to another, Priscilla Villiers was in a fairly good humour as she and her brother rode into the village on business in the afternoon. Yet, her pleasant mood did not last long, for Mr. Villiers had a talent for vexing his sister even without meaning to. Seeing that Mr. Grey's dwelling place was ahead, he said to her:

"Let us stop at Mr. Grey's home—I must return a book I borrowed from him."

"Brother, have you taken leave of your senses?! Surely you cannot be thinking that we would enter the house of a man of such low standing!"

"But Priscilla, I am already returning the book over a week later than I promised. It would be rude to keep it any longer. Besides, we need not stay long, and Mr. Grey is, after all, a gentleman."

"You use the term 'gentleman' very loosely," returned Miss Villiers impatiently.

Her brother answered, "Why, as a clergyman and a man of education, Mr. Grey is indeed a gentleman, and he comes from a good family."

"He is a curate, John. A curate may be considered a gentleman, but only just. Unlike a vicar or a rector, he has no benefice and receives no part of the tithes, nor any income from the glebe. All he is entitled to is a salary in return for his work in the parish. What little Mr. Grey does earn is insufficient to enable him to keep a manservant. I consider that a man cannot really be a gentleman if he does not have a manservant. What is more, Mr. Grey does not hold his office for life; Lady Catherine could throw him out of the pulpit tomorrow if she pleases, and then he will have to go begging on the streets."

"Priscilla, you exaggerate."

"Even if I do, you should not encourage such low connections."

"Then how shall I return the book if we are not to enter his house?"

"You can give it back to him when we go to church on Sunday."

"But that will be nearly a fortnight later than I promised!"

"He can wait."

Mr. Villiers opened his mouth to object, but his sister cut him short: "What if Miss de Bourgh, or heaven forbid, Lady Catherine should happen to drive by and see us entering Mr. Grey's house? What will they think of us? Keeping company with low acquaintances will not help your chances of making an alliance with Lady Catherine's daughter."

Mr. Villiers would have liked to say that perhaps he did not wish to marry Anne de Bourgh at all, but knowing that such words would provoke his sister to further argument, he kept silent, and so their carriage drove past Mr. Grey's residence without stopping.

Much as Priscilla Villiers disliked the idea of associating with lowly curates, she again unexpectedly found herself in Mr. Grey's society that evening at the Beauchamps' dinner party. There also were Georgiana and Mrs. Darcy, Sir Matthew Leigh, the Townsends, and a number of other guests.

The dinner passed very pleasantly, but as any young person of taste and fashion will assure you, an evening is nothing without dancing. Miss Lawson was certainly of this opinion, and when the party had assembled in the drawing room after the meal, the young lady said, sighing:

"Oh, I wish we had balls more often in the neighbourhood. It seems like an eternity since last we danced!"

"You may not have long to wait, Miss Lawson," said Mr. Meggott. "Lately, I have been thinking of hosting a dance, and Mr. Grey has convinced me to make it a charity ball. The guests will each purchase a ticket, and the money raised will be used to assist the poor of this parish."

Excitement and anticipation rippled through the room: "A ball!", "Oh, I cannot wait!", and similar expressions of delight broke forth from the company. Miss Villiers, however, was less enthusiastic.

"I am never opposed to a ball," said she, "but must it be for charity?"

"Whyever not?"

"The unpleasant association rather puts a dark cloud on an otherwise desirable event. Besides, we already pay poor rates. I should think the poor can want no more than we already give them."

Mr. Grey said, "The war has brought poverty to many families. While food prices keep climbing higher, farm labourers' wages do not, and what is collected in poor rates is proving insufficient to adequately help all those who require assistance."

"Well, there you have your trouble. The more you give to the poor, the more they want!" exclaimed Miss Villiers. "I am of the opinion that the poor find themselves in their wretched condition because they do not wish to work. Therefore, if laziness is the cause of their misery, then giving them charity would only encourage this vice and make their situation worse."

"Quite right, my child," said Sir Edward.

"There may be some who are lazy, but I believe the vast majority would rather work than go without food," said Georgiana.

"Then why do they not go to a workhouse? There is work for all who want it. Or better yet, let them be transported to Australia with the rest of the criminals," came Miss Villiers' answer.

Turning to Mr. Grey next to him, John Villiers muttered, "If only shrewish sisters could be packed off on those same ships bound for Australia, England would be paradise."

The clergyman smiled mischievously in reply.

"So then poverty and crime are one and the same in your mind, Miss Villiers?" asked Georgiana.

"In many respects, yes. I find that one often leads to the other."

"Well, would it not then be better to help those who find themselves in poverty so that they are not forced into crime?"

Sir Matthew felt himself grow restless at the turn the conversation had taken. "Ladies, what a serious topic for such a pleasant evening!" said he. "Shall we not better have some music? Miss Darcy, you play so beautifully.

Can we prevail upon you to favour us with a tune?"

Miss Villiers was left seething at this suggestion. Not only had the discussion about the poor ended with her rival having the last word, but even worse, Sir Matthew (*HER* Sir Matthew!), had chosen to ask Miss Darcy and not her to play for the company.

As Georgiana was sitting down at the pianoforte, she caught sight of Mr. Grey. He was gazing at her intently with a mixture of admiration and affection. Not wishing to encourage a passion she could not return, she quickly averted her eyes from his.

Georgiana was not the only one who noticed his tender look; Miss Villiers saw it too, and tittering inwardly, she thought to herself contemptuously, "What a fine couple they would make! The princess and the pauper!" Aloud, she said slyly:

"Mr. Grey, would you do us the honour of singing with Miss Darcy while she plays? The two of you are so well-matched for a duet!"

"Nothing would give me more pleasure," replied Mr. Grey, "but unfortunately, I have no talent for singing."

"Oh, what a pity!" said Miss Villiers with genuine disappointment.

"Sir Matthew, perhaps you would care to sing for us instead?" suggested Mrs. Townsend. Then, turning to the others, she added, "Sir Matthew has an excellent voice. He and Miss Darcy sing charmingly together at Kleistringham."

The gentleman was happy to oblige, and as he came to join Georgiana, Miss Villiers thought she would burst from vexation. Everything had turned out exactly the opposite of how she had wished, and now she must sit back in the shadows while everyone's attention, and Sir Matthew's in particular, was fixed on Miss Darcy, who was her inferior in everything! It was as incomprehensible and unjust as when the dazzling sun is eclipsed by the pale moon!

For her performance, Georgiana chose a simple Scottish air.[7] Sir Matthew's clear, melodious voice blended with her sweet one, and together they sang with joyous hearts. He directed his look at her, and his eyes held special meaning when he reached the words:

I ne'er can so much virtue find,

Nor such perfection see;
Then I'll renounce all womankind,
My Peggy, after thee.

All this Priscilla Villiers observed with envy. Resentment and fury gathered in her breast as she watched and listened until she could restrain herself no longer. At the conclusion of the song, she waited for Georgiana to rise from the pianoforte, and drawing near to her rival, Miss Villiers said, "That was lovely, Miss Darcy, really it was," and then, dropping her voice, she added, "Of course, I played that tune when I was twelve. Since then I have moved on to greater things."

Taking Georgiana's just vacated place at the pianoforte, Miss Villiers selected a composition by Ignaz Pleyel that she deemed worthy of her talents and asked, "Sir Matthew, would you be so kind as to turn the pages for me while I play?" As she spoke, she smiled at him in an inviting manner and widened her eyes coquettishly.

As the music started, tears of indignation welled up in Georgiana's eyes. Rarely did she ever feel anger towards anyone, but in the present instance, Priscilla Villiers was doing her utmost to provoke her. Why did she always find it necessary to make snide remarks aimed at injuring her, to try to outshine her in everything, and worst of all, to flirt with Sir Matthew at every opportunity?

Miss Villiers' performance was respectable, but at the same time flat and rather dull. Yet, the performer seemed to think it very fine and looked very pleased with herself while she played. Although the listeners did not find her rendition of the piece to be displeasing, neither did anyone listen with more than polite attention, and partway through, Mr. Lawson (who had been rendered torpid by overindulgence at the table) began to doze in his chair.

Hearing nothing that he considered worth listening to, Mr. Villiers took the opportunity to say a few words to the hostess:

"May I congratulate you on a most excellent dinner, Mrs. Beauchamp. The turtle soup deserves particular mention—I do not believe I have ever eaten such delicious turtle soup in my life!"

Before the good woman could answer, Lady Villiers scolded her son in a loud whisper:

"John, listen to Priscilla play!"

"In a minute, Mother. I have a question for Mrs. Beauchamp."

Turning back to the hostess, Mr. Villiers said, "I hope I am not asking too much, but might your cook write down the recipe so that ours can make the soup in exactly the same way?"

"Of course, Mr. Villiers. There is a special ingredient that gives it that additional flavour, but I will be happy to share the recipe."

John Villiers thanked her, and after receiving another admonishing look from his mother, he sighed and directed his ears back to the sound of his sister's music. After a minute or two, he looked at the clock, and with a large yawn, he thought, "Oh, how much more of this must I bear?!"

At last his sister finished playing, and as she walked past Georgiana afterwards, Miss Villiers said scornfully, "Miss Darcy, if ever you should wish for assistance in your music practice, do not hesitate to ask. I am always at your service."

Able to endure her jibes no longer, Georgiana thought to herself, "If you want a competition, Miss Villiers, I will give you one!" Her eyes flashing, she returned to the pianoforte and began to play Haydn's Sonata in C major. Oh, how Georgiana played! Her fingers flew over the keys, from which sprang cheerful notes that danced through the air, bounced off the walls, and filled the whole room with their vibrant sound. All conversation ceased, and the listeners' faces lit up with smiles; even Mr. Lawson was roused back to wakefulness. It was with the fondest pride that Sir Matthew looked upon his future bride. Mr. Grey looked also, but his expression was one of wistfulness; he was not blind to the attachment between Miss Darcy and Sir Matthew, and it pained him to see it.

When the music finished, the room broke into applause. John Villiers clapped louder than all the rest and took mischievous delight in the sight of his sister's sour countenance. Though Miss Villiers would never have admitted it to anyone, even she, in the honest depths of her heart, could not deny that Georgiana's performance had far exceeded her own. Yet, she was not one to be easily defeated. "Just you wait, Miss Darcy," she warned under her breath, "This is not the end!"

CHAPTER 20

On the following morning, Georgiana left Kleistringham House to call on her cousin at Rosings Park. Anne was overjoyed to see her and said, "I was just about to ride out and call on you, but here you are already!" Taking Miss Darcy's hands in hers, she added, "Dearest Cousin, come, sit down. I have something important to tell you."

Filled with curiosity, Georgiana went with her to the sofa and then looked expectantly at Anne. Her cousin's eyes were unusually bright, and her complexion had the joyful glow of one who has just received some wonderful news.

"What is it, Anne? I am dying to know!"

Miss de Bourgh replied with:

"This morning I had a letter... a beautiful, sincere, tender letter. It was from Mr. Brooke—he loves me and has asked me to marry him. I have accepted his offer."

This confession raised in Georgiana a confusion of thoughts and emotions; she did not know whether to be thrilled or concerned. While she had, from the very beginning, rejoiced to see that Anne had an admirer—and a very worthy one at that—her thoughts had not travelled so far forward as marriage. In many ways, Mr. Brooke and Anne were of like mind and character, but there still remained the question of Mr. Brooke's station and fortune—or lack thereof. What would be Lady Catherine's opinion of such a bridegroom? It was one thing for Mr. Darcy to defy his aunt and marry as he pleased, but for Anne to attempt the same was a completely different matter. She was Lady Catherine's daughter, her heiress, and her dependant; a quarrel with her ladyship would be of far greater significance to Anne than it had ever been to Mr. Darcy. At the same time, thought Georgiana, why should her cousin not marry whom she loved? If there was anyone in the world who deserved happiness, it was Anne.

Following these fleeting cogitations, Miss Darcy decided to view the tidings of her cousin's engagement in a favourable light. She therefore offered her wholehearted congratulations and added only, "I must admit that I had some suspicion of Mr. Brooke's inclinations, but I never dreamed he would make his proposals to you after so short a time. Had you any idea of his intentions beforehand?"

"I think he tried to declare himself to me yesterday, after I told him about Mr. Cavendish."

"Mr. Cavendish? Who is he?" asked Georgiana.

"Oh, I have not told you of Mama's guest yet, have I? I started from the end instead of the beginning. You must forgive me—I am all exuberance and agitation, so that I can scarcely think or speak rationally."

Anne recounted to her cousin the events of the past two days, this time in the proper order. She began with her mother's choice of Mr. Cavendish for her husband and ended with the written declaration of love she had received from Mr. Brooke that morning.

"He expressed his sentiments much more eloquently on paper than he did in person," said she. "When we spoke yesterday, I began to form the impression that Mr. Brooke entertained only brotherly feelings for me."

"Brotherly feelings?!" exclaimed Georgiana. "What a notion! Could you really have believed that Mr. Brooke looked upon you as a sister? His eyes and his manner clearly betrayed otherwise!"

"Well, whatever I supposed at the time," said Anne, "Mr. Brooke's letter left me in no doubt as to the nature of his attachment. My elation, when I read his words, cannot be described. I had almost given up on the possibility that any man might ever feel for me as he does."

Unaccustomed to discussing love, especially in connection with herself, Anne looked a little embarrassed while she spoke, but there was also excitement and pleasure in her countenance.

"How suddenly everything can change!" she continued. "Only yesterday, I thought myself the most miserable of humans. The man Mama selected for me closely matched her wishes, but in many respects, he was the complete opposite of mine. The idea of marrying Mr. Cavendish filled me with despair; I saw long years of joyless matrimony stretching forth before me. But then, Mr. Brooke saved me from it all."

Anne's choice of words, in combination with the circumstances she had related, brought fresh doubts into Georgiana's mind. How much thought had her cousin really put into her acceptance of Mr. Brooke's offer? Did she really love him, or was it merely that she found his attentions gratifying and saw marriage to the physician as the only means of escaping Mr. Cavendish? Might she come to regret her decision later on? Georgiana was loath to bring up such a subject, but there was too much at stake to stay silent—she would have to speak.

Steeling herself, Miss Darcy raised the uncomfortable question that had sprung up in her mind. "Anne, please be truthful with me and with yourself," said she. "Are you certain that you would still have agreed to marry Mr. Brooke had there been no threat of a loveless marriage to a husband of your mother's choosing?"

"With the most sincere conviction I can say that I would," was the answer. "Mr. Brooke has so many qualities that I respect and admire; he is honest, talented, intelligent, and uncommonly kind—but most of all, he makes me happy. I could live a whole lifetime without meeting another such as he. In short, I love him."

Georgiana's fears having been laid to rest, she replied, "In that case, Cousin, I am delighted by your news!"

Sighing, Anne said, "I wish that my mother could share your delight."

"Have you told her already?"

"No, and neither do I intend to. She would forbid the match, I am sure. If only Mr. Brooke were as wealthy as Mr. Cavendish! Not that the absence of a fortune makes any difference to me, but I know it will to Mama. I should have liked to have her blessing, but I suppose there is no alternative but to marry in secret without it."

"You are not thinking of eloping to Gretna Green?!" cried Georgiana.

"No, of course not. It would be most improper for me to travel all the way to Scotland with Mr. Brooke unchaperoned, so we must marry in this parish. Fortunately, as I am of age, it is not necessary for my mother to give her consent, but the wedding would still have to be conducted in secret. Otherwise, Mama will surely find a way to prevent it. The situation is a difficult one... Mr. Grey will have to be the officiating clergyman, but as a curate, he is wholly dependant on Mama for his livelihood. He may not agree to my wish for secrecy."

"You think he will refuse to help you?"

"I do not know. Mr. Collins, I am certain, would not even have considered such a request. Nothing on earth would have induced him to risk displeasing his patroness, but Mr. Grey is not Mr. Collins. I think there is a chance. It would certainly help if someone were to speak with him on my behalf—someone he would listen to. I was thinking of you, Georgiana."

"Me?! Why do you think Mr. Grey would listen to me?"

"He has a clear partiality in your favour. I am sure he would not refuse if you asked him."

"Oh Anne, I would rather not! Surely it would do as well if you asked him yourself, and I doubt that I have as much influence over Mr. Grey as you seem to think I do."

"There you are mistaken, Cousin. You underestimate the extent of Mr. Grey's regard for you; there is no woman in the world whose word would carry as much weight with him as yours... Please, Georgiana. Promise you will speak to Mr. Grey for me."

Though Georgiana was still reluctant, her love for her cousin would not permit her to do otherwise than give the required promise. Having made the pledge, she told Anne, "I may have an opportunity to put your request to him today. Mr. Grey is at Kleistringham now; he is out shooting with Sir Matthew and Mr. Townsend, and I might be able to speak with him on my return."

The opportunity for Georgiana to converse privately with the curate did, indeed, present itself later in the day. When her chance came, she gathered courage and addressed him with:

"Mr. Grey, I have some important business which I must discuss with you. Would you care to come with me into the library?"

He followed her in, and once they were alone together, Georgiana said, "The business I referred to concerns marriage."

This revelation startled the clergyman considerably. Had Sir Matthew proposed to Miss Darcy already? Was it her imminent wedding that she wished to discuss?

"Marriage?" he repeated, his voice barely above a whisper.

"Yes. You see, my cousin Anne de Bourgh has asked me to speak to you on her behalf. She has accepted an offer of marriage from Mr. Brooke."

Inwardly, Mr. Grey heaved a great sigh of relief as Miss Darcy continued, "They would like to marry without delay, but there is an obstacle to their plan."

"Lady Catherine?"

"Yes. I know my aunt too well to hope that she would ever consent to a union between her daughter and a country physician of modest means; but Anne and Mr. Brooke are both of age, thank goodness, which removes the requirement of parental consent. Nevertheless, the wedding would still need to proceed in secret to prevent any difficulties. That is, in fact, what I am here to ask. Mr. Grey, will you agree to conduct a clandestine ceremony without mentioning anything of it to anyone beforehand?"

The gentleman did not answer immediately. There was a long pause while he sat in silent contemplation of the situation. Lady Catherine's views on clandestine marriage were well-known to him, and therefore, he had no trouble imagining her ladyship's reaction to his assisting Miss de Bourgh with any such plan. To say that his employer would be angry was putting it mildly.

Georgiana's next words broke through his thoughts. "I realise the enormity of what I am asking, of the position in which taking such a step would place you," said she, "but I see no other way of securing my cousin's happiness. Lady Catherine is at this moment planning an alliance between her daughter and a man for whom Anne has not the least affection. It would give me great misery to see my cousin forced to marry against her inclinations when she loves another."

Mr. Grey knew there would be consequences to his actions, but at last he agreed, saying, "It will be necessary to first obtain a marriage licence, but that can be accomplished without attracting public notice, and apart from the required witnesses, no one else need know about the wedding."

This decision gave Georgiana much relief, but even so, she felt apprehension at the possibility that the scheme might be discovered. What if, despite their best efforts, Lady Catherine should still find out somehow? She was equally concerned for Mr. Grey and feared her aunt's fury. There was little chance that the clergyman would escape unpunished, and the thought made Georgiana tremble for him.

Although Mr. Grey assumed a courageous front, he trembled too; but at least he could take comfort in the knowledge that the situation was not worse—that Miss Darcy had not asked him to solemnise a marriage between Sir Matthew and herself. *That*, he was sure, his heart could not have endured.

CHAPTER 21

On the following Thursday, Mrs. Townsend's sister came to Kleistringham House for a brief visit. Her husband, Mr. Lloyd, was a respectable man who had once been prosperous but lost most of his fortune in a series of bad investments. All that he had left to his name was a cottage on a small plot of land. Fortunately, his wife was a very economical woman who possessed the great skill of being able to make the most of a small income. She immediately reduced their expenses and soon turned their little plot into a productive farm, by which means they managed to stay self-supporting. Mrs. Townsend's sister was a frequent visitor at Kleistringham House, and seldom was she allowed to return home without a large hare or some nice ham to take back with her.

"I have such news to tell!" cried Mrs. Lloyd as soon as she entered the drawing room, where Mrs. Townsend was seated with Georgiana and Elizabeth. "If not for our neighbour Mr. Wood, I could have come and told you earlier. His geese found a hole in the fence and broke through onto our land. Imagine! A whole flock of geese plucking at grass that was intended for our cow! Mr. Lloyd and I, along with our maid, spent a great deal of time chasing the geese off the pasture."

"How unfortunate!" exclaimed Mrs. Townsend.

"We have had no end of trouble from that neighbour," continued her sister. "Odious man! Another time he trapped some wild rabbits and released them onto our land. The rabbits ate all the cabbages in our garden."

"How do you know it was Mr. Wood?"

"The Johnsons' boy saw him do it. And now that Mr. Wood's geese have eaten the best of the grass, our cow will have little to eat and cannot possibly produce enough milk for our cheese and butter."

"Would you like some of our cheese?" offered Mrs. Townsend. "We have plenty of excellent, freshly-made cheese."

"Thank you. That is most generous of you. Mr. Lloyd is very fond of your fine cheeses," came Mrs. Lloyd's delighted reply.

"I will also arrange for some hay to be delivered to you so that your cow has sufficient feed," added Mrs. Townsend.

Her sister at first protested, saying it was too generous an offer, but after a little urging, she was at last prevailed upon to accept the gift. Feeling secure in the knowledge that her cow would not starve, she then began to relate the news she had come to tell:

"I heard the whole story from our neighbour Mr. Johnson, who, on his way home from the village, saw us chasing the geese and came over to help. He told us that early this morning Anne de Bourgh was seen leaving the church on the arm of Mr. Brooke, the young physician. It appears that they were married in secret."

"Impossible!" exclaimed Mrs. Townsend.

"I assure you that it is so! When Anne de Bourgh left the church, she was wearing a lace veil, and in her hand was a bouquet of flowers. What is more, Lady Catherine must have gotten wind of what happened because not long after the ceremony had taken place, she arrived in her carriage and stopped in front of Mr. Grey's house in the village. She then went inside, presumably to question the curate. The answers she received must not have been to her satisfaction because a great commotion could be heard coming from the house. Those who had gathered in the street could not make out the words, but it was clear that Lady Catherine was enraged. Mr. Johnson happened to pass by just as her ladyship emerged, looking the worse for wear and red in the face, before she stormed off in her carriage."

"Who would ever have thought it!" cried Mrs. Townsend. "Anne de Burgh always seemed so quiet, so meek, and yet here she has gone and married against her mother's wishes!"

"Yes, I can well imagine how Lady Catherine must have felt about her daughter making such a mésalliance!" remarked her sister. "It is believed that her ladyship will bring the matter before the bishop and try to get the marriage annulled, but it is very unlikely that she will succeed. As far as anyone knows, there was no legal impediment to the marriage. Anne de Burgh is now Mrs. Brooke, and there is nothing to be done about it!"

"What about Mr. Grey?" asked Georgiana with concern. "What will happen to him?"

"Ah, well, there Lady Catherine has more authority, and the curate will feel the effects of her wrath. She has dismissed him from his office."

Georgiana's heart sank; it was what she had feared would happen. How unjust that he should suffer! What had Mr. Grey done that was in the least unlawful?! Georgiana felt, also, the oppressive weight of guilt at the recollection of the part she had played in the clergyman's undoing. She was the one who had persuaded him to assist in the scheme, but he was the one paying for it, and paying dearly. It was a tormenting thought.

Mrs. Lloyd stayed a little longer and then departed to call on the Lawsons, whom she was very eager to acquaint with her news. After the woman had gone, Georgiana and Mrs. Townsend went into the village together to make some purchases. While they were pursuing their business, the ladies were detained in conversation first by Mrs. Wise and later by Mrs. Beauchamp. These acquaintances, along with everyone else from the shoemaker to the draper, could talk of nothing but the newlywed couple, Mr. and Mrs. Brooke, and the anger of Lady Catherine de Bourgh.

"I am afraid we have tarried too long in the village," said Mrs. Townsend as she and Miss Darcy were walking down the street together. "Unless we return home directly, we will be late for dinner. Do not forget that we are also attending a card party at the Hardings' tonight."

"Yes, of course, but could we make one more stop?" asked Georgiana. "I have a letter for my brother that I intended to leave at the Post Office; it should not take long."

"Very well, but let us be quick."

As they were walking past a millinery shop directly opposite the Post Office, Georgiana's companion was suddenly arrested by the sight of some items displayed in the window. Pointing to one of them, she exclaimed,

"Miss Darcy, look at that hat! Is it not darling?"

Georgiana agreed that it was, to which Mrs. Townsend replied, "Do you mind going to the Post Office by yourself while I step inside the shop? It is only across the street, and if I make haste, I should be back again by the time you have posted your letter." The young lady did not mind, and with her blessing, Mrs. Townsend disappeared into the shop to inspect the hat more closely, while Georgiana proceeded to cross the street.

After she had completed her business at the Post Office, Georgiana turned around to leave, when Mr. Grey unexpectedly entered the building. Upon perceiving her, he stopped short. She was no less surprised to see him and felt a wave of remorse mixed with sadness wash over her as he came closer.

"Mr. Grey, I heard that you are leaving Kent," said she.

"Yes, that is true."

"But... where will you go?"

"I have decided on Bath. Last week my uncle wrote to say that he is unwell, and that he has gone to Bath to take the waters. He and his wife have invited me to visit them. So you see, Miss Darcy," said the gentleman, forcing a smile, "being obliged to leave the parish has furnished me with an opportunity to see my relations."

"Mr. Grey, I cannot tell you how sorry I am that you must leave. It was not right that Lady Catherine dismissed you. Your actions, though objectionable to her, broke no law of either God or man; and, if anything, I am the most to blame, for it is I who urged you to perform the clandestine ceremony. Believe me, Mr. Grey, I feel the full extent to which I am responsible for what has happened and for your present suffering."

"Miss Darcy, I would not have you blame yourself; promise me that you will not. You have done nothing that could warrant reproach, and I was glad to help your cousin and Mr. Brooke to marry. I would not have done it if I did not think it right, and..." Here Mr. Grey paused for a moment, as if hesitating to go on. He looked away briefly, apparently wrestling with his emotions, but at last he returned his blue eyes to Georgiana and continued in a tender tone of voice, "...and I would never repent assisting those whom you love. My only regret, Miss Darcy, is that our acquaintance was so brief, and that this was the only occasion on which I was able to be of service to you. Had I my wish, it would have been the beginning rather than the end."

Feeling somewhat unsettled by this admission, the young lady replied, "Mr. Grey, I think I must tell you that Sir Matthew has made me an offer of marriage, and that I have accepted him. We have not yet made a public announcement as we must first obtain my guardians' consent, but I believe it will not be long before we are married."

Although Mr. Grey had expected to eventually receive news of this kind, and had even tried to prepare his heart for it, all that his endeavours succeeded in doing was to soften the shock, though they could not ameliorate the pain he felt from hearing Miss Darcy's disclosure. However, gathering himself, he congratulated Georgiana and expressed his wishes for her future happiness.

Just as he finished speaking, Georgiana perceived Mrs. Townsend emerging triumphantly from the milliner's with a large hat-box in her hands. The lady stopped to wait for a passing carriage and then started walking across the street.

"I see Mrs. Townsend coming," said Georgiana. "Please excuse me, Mr. Grey, but I must be going, for I would not wish to keep her waiting. She was most anxious that we should return to Kleistringham in time for dinner."

"Of course, Miss Darcy. I will not keep you."

Before they parted, Georgiana said, "From the bottom of my heart, Mr. Grey, I wish you well."

A moment longer, and she was gone. The gentleman directed his eyes at her departing figure as she hurried away with Mrs. Townsend. Soon, Miss Darcy disappeared from view, and, as he thought to himself despondently, from his life forever.

CHAPTER 22

On her return to Kleistringham, Georgiana found Sir Matthew in the drawing room. When he saw her, the gentleman smiled and sprang to his feet. He never tired of looking at Georgiana. She was always lovely, and today, after having spent the afternoon outdoors, she was especially so; her cheeks were rosier and her eyes were brighter than ever. Only her furrowed brow marred what was otherwise perfection.

"I saw Mr. Grey today at the Post Office," said Georgiana. "He told me that he is leaving the parish and plans to stay for a time with his aunt and uncle in Bath."

"I suppose it is inevitable that he should leave," answered Sir Matthew, "but I will be sorry to see him go. I like Mr. Grey—he is a fine fellow, and very brave too. He must have known that Lady Catherine would be furious about her daughter's clandestine marriage, and that he would likely lose his position as a result. To have risked his livelihood with no possible benefit to himself—not every man would have done as much."

"Would you have acted differently in his place?"

"I am not sure. I will say, however, that I am glad I was not the one faced with such a choice."

"He did a good deed, that is certain," said Georgiana, "and I will be forever grateful for the service he did to my cousin. I only wish that one person did not have to suffer so that another might be happy."

"So that is why you have had such a grave countenance all day? You are anxious about Mr. Grey's future. I assure you, Miss Darcy, that there is no need to distress yourself on that account. Mr. Grey has relations he can rely upon, and I am certain they will provide for him. Relations always do."

"Not always, surely—but that is not the only matter that has been troubling me today. I am concerned, yes, for Mr. Grey's wellbeing, especially because I feel I am partly to blame, but my pensive mood, which you haven't noticed, stems from a different source. I fear about us, about our future."

"You think that your brother will not consent to our marriage? Come, Miss Darcy, though I may not be perfect, I do not think that I am so very bad. Is it not too early to despair of Mr. Darcy's approval? He has not even met me yet."

"Oh, no—it is not that... I have no doubt that my brother will approve."

"What is it then?"

"It is... No, I am afraid you will laugh at me if I tell you."

"I promise not to laugh, but you must permit me to at least smile a little if it is something really amusing."

"I had a dream, a very distressing dream about us."

"Is that all?!"

"There, you see? You are laughing at me already. You promised not to!"

"Alright, alright. I will be serious. Now tell me about this terrifying dream. I am burning with curiosity."

Sir Matthew pressed his lips together to keep from smiling.

Georgiana admonished him:

"You may be smiling now, but I think you will not be so amused when you hear it... At least I was not when I dreamt it."

She paused for a moment before continuing:

"The dream began very pleasantly. You and I were drifting along a river together. We each had our own raft, except that they were not really rafts at all but instead giant playing cards. You were sailing on the King of Hearts, and my raft was the Queen of Diamonds. At fist the river was quiet, and all around us was peaceful and beautiful, but before long, we encountered a strong current, which pulled our rafts apart. The river swept you away so quickly that before I knew it, you were out of sight. I searched everywhere for you and called and called your name. At last, I caught a glimpse of you again; you had drifted far away from me, but now the water was somewhat calmer, and I thought I should be able to catch up to you again. Yet, no sooner did my hope return, than there was suddenly another powerful current—much stronger than the first—which swept you away, this time forever."

Sir Matthew considered her words thoughtfully and then answered:

"It may not have been the most pleasant dream, perhaps, but it was only that—a dream. It means nothing... it was not real. Our love for each other—*that* is real. You must believe it. Besides, I have no plans to go sailing anytime soon, so you can rest easy on that score."

Georgiana gave a faint smile.

"I think," he continued, "perhaps you have merely been dreading to-night's card party at the Hardings', and your mind conjured up this dream. I remember you once said that you dislike playing at cards."

"Well, I do not dislike cards, exactly. It is just that I find more enjoyment in other pastimes and am not as fond of cards as other people are. But maybe you are right. It is silly to be superstitious."

"Then shall we talk no more about it? Let us not dwell on such gloomy premonitions."

After speaking with Sir Matthew, Georgiana felt more at peace. She even found herself looking forward to the Hardings' card party, which held the promise of entertaining gossip and merry conversation. In fact, that evening's gathering brought with it the opportunity to make a new acquaintance. Among the company was a Frenchman by the name of Mr. Jonas Tardiou, who had come down from London with his wife the previous day, and whom Colonel Harding introduced to the guests as his son-in-law.

The Frenchman's presence at the party elicited the interest and curiosity that the arrival of a foreigner usually does; the gentlemen asked him what he thought about the war, and the ladies were full of questions about Paris fashions. In his charmingly French way, Monsieur Tardiou did his best to answer their queries, while reminding everyone that he had not stepped foot on French soil in over a decade, and England was his home now.

After their curiosity had been sufficiently satisfied, the ladies and gentlemen sat down at the card tables, while Georgiana took her place at the pianoforte. She had no particular inclination for whist just then and preferred instead to entertain the card players with some music. Monsieur Tardiou likewise saw little appeal in whist, and sensing a worthy opponent in Sir Matthew Leigh, he invited him to a game of écarté. Sir Matthew did not need to be asked twice; he was just as eager to play écarté.

The deck was shuffled and cut, and the deal fell to Sir Matthew. With a deft hand, the gentleman dealt the cards—five to himself, and five to his adversary. On the eleventh, he turned up a king, and marked himself a point. The Frenchman grimaced. He looked at his cards and his heart sank further—it was a bad hand. He had no choice but to propose and discarded all five of his cards for fresh ones, while Sir Matthew replaced but one of his own. Georgiana's betrothed then won four of the five tricks and scored a second point. It was not a good start for the Frenchman.

Both Sir Matthew and his opponent were impatient to continue playing—the former to make the most of his luck while it lasted, and the latter to redeem himself. However, the late arrival of the Villiers family (sans John Villiers) to the card party put a brief pause on their game. Mr. Villiers had simply forgotten about the party; the rest of his family waited for him at home as long as they could, but in the end they had no choice but to depart without him, and now Sir Edward, with his wife and daughter, were left to make their excuses to the Hardings. Colonel Harding and his wife accepted their apologies graciously and then led the newly-arrived guests to their son-in-law for an introduction.

Monsieur Tardiou occasioned much amusement in the room when, suddenly catching sight of Priscilla Villiers' hair, he cried out, "Une rousse, une rousse! Quelle chance!"

He was more than a little eager to make the young lady's acquaintance, and soon, the source of his excitement was made clear.

"In France," explained the Frenchman, "we believe that red hair brings good fortune. I wonder, therefore, Miss Villiers, whether it would be too much to ask if you could sit by my side while I play. You see, Sir Matthew has all the fortune tonight, and I am in desperate need of a little luck!"

The young woman thought that it was an excellent idea. Casting a sidelong glance at Sir Matthew, she thought to herself how there is nothing like a little jealousy to make a man's head turn back in the right direction. Smiling sweetly, she replied:

"Why, of course, Mr. Tardiou! It would be my pleasure. Only, I have a better idea; who knows how much or how little luck my sitting by your side may bring you. On the other hand, if you could actually hold a lock of my hair in your hands while playing at cards, surely you cannot fail to win!"

Monsieur Tardiou was delighted at the idea, and so a servant was sent to fetch a pair of scissors. Before long, the Frenchman was again seated at his card table with a lock of Miss Villiers' red-gold hair grasped firmly in one hand. The écarté game continued at a lively pace, while the alluring redhead by Monsieur Tardiou's side spared no effort in making herself agreeable to him.

After playing for some time on the pianoforte, Georgiana was roused by curiosity to make her way to the écarté table and see how the game was progressing. Drawing near, she was astonished at the complete transformation that Sir Matthew had undergone in her absence. At the start of the evening, he had been his usual carefree, charming self, full of good humour and easy manners, but now, before her, sat a completely different man. Sir Matthew clutched his cards with such force that every tendon in his hands protruded visibly, and in his eyes was a greedy gleam that Georgiana had never seen before. Whereas at the other card tables the players engaged in light conversation, and every so often there was laughter in response to some witty comment, at the écarté table both men sat in almost total silence and spoke only as necessary for the game. Of the two gentlemen, Sir Matthew seemed to have an especially intent look on his face. He hunched over his cards with a furrowed brow and perspiration on his forehead, and there was visible tension in his neck and shoulders. He did not lift his eyes from the card table and seemed unaware of anything else around him, including Georgiana's presence.

Miss Villiers observed the game from her position beside the Frenchman, and in contrast to the players, she seemed amused by the proceedings. A sly smile turned up the corners of her mouth, and when she looked at Georgiana, there was a mixture of mockery and challenge in the redheaded beauty's eyes. Georgiana felt uneasy and could sense that something of greater significance than simply a pleasant evening's diversion was happening before her eyes. Completely forgetting everything else, the young lady felt compelled to stay and became an unwilling spectator of the écarté game before her.

By this time in the game, Monsieur Tardiou had three points to Sir Matthew's four. The latter gentleman needed only one more point to win the game. Down came their cards, one by one, and in trick after trick, the Frenchman came up the winner. He prevailed in all five tricks and won the vole, which gave him the last two points he required for victory.

The game was over, and Monsieur Tardiou had won. He could scarcely believe how well he had played that evening and revelled in all the elation of triumph. His adversary, on the other hand, could not have looked more out of spirits. All this Priscilla Villiers noted with pleasure, which was only increased by the sight of Miss Darcy's concerned countenance. Everything was happening just as Miss Villiers had wished!

"It was a very good game, Sir Matthew," said the Frenchman. "We must play again sometime."

Then, turning to the lovely redhead beside him, he continued:

"Of course, I owe my success tonight to you, Miss Villiers."

The lady coyly disclaimed all credit, and after they had exchanged a few more polite phrases, Monsieur Tardiou excused himself from the table, saying:

"And now, I think I will go and see how Mrs. Tardiou fares at whist."

Miss Villiers accompanied him on the pretext of desiring to become better acquainted with his wife. While they were walking away together, Sir Matthew continued to sit sullenly in his chair and did not raise his eyes from the card table. Observing his dejection, Georgiana tried to console him by saying:

"Sir Matthew, it is only a game of cards. A few pounds is not worth so much misery!"

"A few pounds!" the gentleman replied, a note of sarcasm in his voice. "We played for higher stakes than that, Miss Darcy. I lost four hundred pounds."

"Four hundred pounds!" gasped Georgiana. As large as such a sum was, its loss was of course not enough to ruin a man of Sir Matthew's wealth. Still, this consideration did not ease Georgiana's distress. Had the gentleman instead lost the same amount in some sort of investment, she would have thought much better of it, but to gamble away four hundred pounds in a single evening seemed like the height of folly and irresponsibility. She had not thought Sir Matthew capable of such reckless behaviour.

"Was it necessary to play for such high stakes?" asked Georgiana. "If my brother had risked such a sum in a game of cards, I would have been very disappointed indeed."

"Fortunately, Miss Darcy, I am neither your brother nor any other relation of yours, so you need not concern yourself with how much I win or lose," came the reply.

Stunned by the cruel coldness of the gentleman's response, the young lady could make no answer but only struggled to fight back tears. She stood by the card table a few moments longer but then turned around and left without another word.

Miss Villiers, who had been observing the entire scene with interest from some distance away, saw that now was the time to strike. It has been said that a lady wields as much power with her fan and can do as much damage with it as a man can do with his sword. Priscilla Villiers was no exception to this truth; she was a true mistress of her weapon. Fluttering her ivory brisé fan coquettishly, she approached Sir Matthew, who was still sulking petulantly at his card table. He looked up to see the lady standing by his side as she fanned herself in a languid manner, sending a soft, amorous breeze in his direction with every graceful flick of her wrist.

"Mr. Tardiou had an unfair advantage," she began. "From what I saw this evening, you were the more skilled player, but your opponent had all the fortune on his side... You see, I brought him luck."

Sir Matthew gave a wry smile.

"I should perhaps have asked you for a lock of hair a long time ago, but would you have given it?" said he.

Miss Villiers slowly folded her fan partway shut.

"I may have considered your request, but my final answer would depend on whether you proved yourself worthy. A lifetime of good fortune is a precious gift indeed, and not one to be given away lightly."

Flicking her fan fully open again, Priscilla Villiers sauntered away from the table while fanning herself with slow, easy motions. Sir Matthew followed her with his eyes the entire time.

CHAPTER 23

Deeply hurt by Sir Matthew's behaviour at the card party, Georgiana slept very poorly that night. Lying in her bed, she was tormented by doubts concerning whether she had acted wisely in accepting his offer of marriage. It was bad enough that he had recklessly lost four hundred pounds at cards, but even worse were his unkind, disrespectful words afterwards. Is that how he intended to treat her once they were married? These thoughts continued to plague Georgiana as she left her room and descended the stairs the following morning.

At the foot of the stairs she found Sir Matthew, who had been waiting for her since early that morning. Seeing Georgiana come down, he immediately drew near to her and said, "Georgiana, my dearest..." She looked at him with a mixture of pain and reproach.

He tried again: "Miss Darcy, my reflections on my conduct last night fill me with more shame and remorse than I am able to express. I can only think of my actions with abhorrence. My dear angel has treated me with nothing but kindness, and all I have given in return is callousness and ill manners. My faults, I know, are many, and I have no right to expect anything but reproof, but I appeal to your compassion and tender heart for forgiveness." Sir Matthew looked truly remorseful, and Georgiana, by nature unable to harbour resentment in her heart for long, forgave him at once.

The gentleman had all this time been holding something in his hands, and he now brought the object forth, saying it was a present for her. The gift was some sheets of music, written by hand. Georgiana cast her eyes upon them with more than a little curiosity and saw that the work was a composition by Beethoven entitled *Alla ingharese quasi un capriccio*.

"I have never heard of this piece before. Is it new?" asked she.

"Well, not exactly. Beethoven wrote it a number of years ago, but as it is yet unfinished, the composition has never been published. Few other than Beethoven have ever laid eyes on it."

"However did you manage to obtain such a rarity?" inquired Miss Darcy with wonder.

"A friend of my late father travelled to Vienna some years since, and there a copy of the manuscript somehow came into his hands. As Adelaide, my sister, is very fond of music, he duplicated the piece and gave it to her as a gift not long ago. And then, after making your acquaintance, I wrote to Adelaide and asked whether she could write out the music and send it to me. It arrived in the post a few days ago, and though I had been saving it for you as a special present, I thought it best to give it to you today instead. It is uncertain whether this composition will ever be published, and so it pleases me to know that now you have it in your possession."

As Georgiana perused the music sheets, she could hear the tune of the sprightly rondo in her mind. Sir Matthew, who had been watching her reaction intently, was relieved to see that she began to smile. Looking up at him again, she exclaimed, "The music is delightful! It is such a beautiful, thoughtful gift, Sir Matthew—thank you so very much!"

The gentleman smiled radiantly in reply. "Well, what are you waiting for? Try it!" he urged her. Georgiana needed no additional encouragement. Together, she and her betrothed went to the pianoforte in the drawing room, and before long, the lively notes of the rondo chased away what remained of her hurt feelings.

Georgiana did not tell either Elizabeth or Anne about Sir Matthew's large loss at cards and the manner in which he had treated her afterwards. Indeed, she preferred to forget the incident and chose to view his behaviour as an uncharacteristic error in judgment, a mistake that would not be repeated. It was a relief to her that their quarrel was over since she could not bear to be in a state of discord for long with anyone whom she loved. For his part, Sir Matthew endeavoured to deserve Georgiana's forgiveness. During the rest of the day, he was even more attentive to her than usual, and in numerous little ways, he tried to make amends for having offended his beloved.

That same day, Charlotte Collins came to Kleistringham House to take leave of her neighbours. With her husband now dead, she was to quit the parsonage-house and return to her family in Hertfordshire. Elizabeth was sorry indeed to lose her dear friend's society, but at least the two ladies would soon see each other again in December, when the Darcys planned to make a short visit to Elizabeth's family in the same neighbourhood.

CHAPTER 24

Many a young man has arrived in Bath filled with eagerness to partake of that city's pleasures. Mr. Grey, however, could not count himself among their number. Even had the gentleman preferred city to country life, he would never willingly have come to Bath at the price of losing Georgiana's company. Yet, his wishes were one thing, and necessity another. Mr. Grey therefore had no choice but to take up residence at his aunt and uncle's house in Bath. Of course, he was glad of an opportunity to visit his relations, of whom he had seen but little in the past. Still, even their kindness and attention to him could not make Mr. Grey forget Georgiana. He missed her cheerful sweetness and her gentle, yet lively eyes.

Feeling the loss of her society particularly keenly one day, Mr. Grey sought relief for his misery in an outdoor walk. Wandering listlessly in the Crescent Fields, he thought of Georgiana and tried to remember the young lady as he had last seen her, to recall every lineament of her lovely visage, but the image that his mind presented was a slightly vague one—a mere impression of that dear face; and even that indistinct picture, he knew, would grow still fainter with time no matter how he struggled to hold on to it.

The knowledge that Miss Darcy would soon belong to another pained him to his core. Mr. Grey of course wished Georgiana every happiness, but the thought of having to tread through life without her, to be deprived of her company forever, was a bleak one indeed.

With a despondent heart, he returned to his aunt and uncle's house. There he was greeted by the butler, who brought him a letter that had arrived earlier in the day. This letter Mr. Grey opened and read with concern. Though brief, the note was full of urgency. Folding up the paper again, he addressed his aunt with:

"Lady Egerton, I must go to Trim Street directly; an old friend of mine has written to ask my urgent assistance."

"Will you return in time for dinner?"

"I cannot be sure. It is possible that I may be delayed."

The gentleman soon quitted the house and made his way to the address specified in the letter. On reaching Trim Street, he found it to be a rather dim and narrow passage. The plain buildings that rose on either side not only blocked out part of the sun but also seemed to trap the odours and noises of the street within their confines. No greenery appeared in sight to cheer the view; all around, there was only cold, hard stone.

At last Mr. Grey arrived at the right address. A maid opened the door and led him to the sitting room, where, seated on a sofa, was a very pretty young lady. She wore a simple muslin gown with no ornament to adorn her person save her light-coloured, silken hair, which was swept back into a loose knot atop her head. Her large, dramatic eyes would also have added to her beauty had they not been red and swollen from recent crying. Although the lady's demeanour was subdued at present, in her features was etched a greater than usual degree of sensibility, and her mouth, eyes, and brows were clearly all more accustomed to expressing, rather than concealing, emotion—so much so that she would have made an excellent actress had such an occupation been considered proper for ladies.

The young woman rose to receive her guest and held out her hand to him. After greeting the gentleman, she said, "Thank you, Mr. Grey, for coming so soon. I am sorry to have disturbed you, but I knew not to whom else I could appeal. Other than my sister and her husband, Mr. Clarke, I have no other acquaintance in Bath."

"There is no need to apologise, Miss Love. I should be a bad friend indeed if I did not wish to help in a time of difficulty," came the reply.

There was a pause. Miss Love seemed to be struggling with herself, as if she could not quite bring her lips to say what she knew she must. Delaying the inevitable a little longer, she remarked, motioning toward a window:

"You may have noticed how dim it is in here. The sun shines but little in this room, or indeed, in any part of the house."

"Yes."

There was another silence, or at least, what one would call silence amid the rumbling of carriages, the clicking of pattens, and other street noises that reverberated through the house. Suddenly, breaking through these other sounds came the loud, piercing cry of a baby. The source appeared to be the room directly above.

"I fear that the noise of my arrival has wakened Mrs. Clarke's baby," said Mr. Grey.

"It is not my sister's child—it is my own," was the answer.

Too stunned to make any reply, the visitor could do nothing but sit in shocked silence.

"Please excuse me for a few minutes, Mr. Grey—I must tend to the baby," said the young woman and presently left the room.

While waiting for Miss Love to return, the gentleman sat sombrely, pensively and contemplated the news he had just heard. For once, his blue eyes held no merriment. The gravity of his friend's situation struck him forcefully; for her to have a child and yet be *Miss* Love still held a significance that did not escape him. As an unwed mother, she would be a pariah wherever she went, and society would be forever closed to her.

Mr. Grey thought back to the last time he saw Miss Love. She had then been a carefree, vivacious girl living with her family on an estate in Kent. His family and hers were well-acquainted—they lived in the same neighbourhood, attended the same church, and called on each other frequently. But then, Mr. Grey left to study at Oxford and afterwards heard little of the Loves except for the occasional bit of gossip in his mother's letters. Several months before he took his degree and returned home, however, he received news that the Loves were to leave the neighbourhood. Their habitually extravagant style of living had at last compelled them to sell their estate to satisfy their debts, and soon afterwards, the eldest daughter married beneath her station in haste, while her younger sister, Miss Alexandra Love, became a governess. That was the last that Mr. Grey heard of his friend before receiving her letter in Bath.

After some minutes had passed, Miss Love returned to the sitting room. "I think you can hardly now be in doubt as to the reason for my letter," said she, "but you do not yet know how it happened—I will tell you everything without disguise.

"When I left Kent, it was to become a governess at Brelwick Park, an estate in Cheshire. I had one pupil, who was the younger sister of the master of the house, Sir Matthew Leigh. It was with a heavy heart that I began my duties as governess. I was all alone at Brelwick; my family and friends were far away, and I missed them terribly. At the house where I was employed, there frequently were parties, in which I could of course take no part, and which were a constant and painful reminder of my former life in Kent.

"Yet, gradually my feelings began to change. My position was a very good one—better than many other governesses could boast, and my pupil was a sweet-tempered, bright girl, eager to learn. The master of the house was very kind to me, and we sometimes spoke on the rare evenings he remained at home and had no company. After several weeks had passed, Sir Matthew began to frequent the schoolroom to check on his sister's progress, he said, and during his visits he paid me marked attentions.

"At first, I tried to stay on my guard, to remind myself that my situation in life was not what it had been heretofore, and that my employer's intentions towards me were unlikely to be serious. Notwithstanding, it was not long before my feelings chased away all reason. Sir Matthew told me that he was in love with me, and everything in his looks and manner confirmed his words. During those months, I was delirious with happiness; Sir Matthew was exactly the sort of man I had always dreamed of for a husband, and I often envisioned what our life together as man and wife would be like. Though he never mentioned marriage, I believed that that is what he intended.

"One night, he came to my bedchamber, and I did not send him away. His visit to my room was thereafter repeated, and several months later, I discovered that I was with child. When I told Sir Matthew, he seemed very disconcerted and asked me repeatedly whether I was quite sure. I fully expected that on that evening he would make me an offer of marriage, but no such offer came, and the very next morning, Sir Matthew departed unexpectedly for London. It was the last time I ever saw him.

"For two weeks I waited but received no word from him. At the conclusion of the fortnight, the housekeeper informed me that my services would no longer be required at the house. I protested that she could not dismiss me, that Sir Matthew would surely not wish for me to leave, but to this the housekeeper replied that she was acting on her master's orders."

Here Miss Love paused. Her large eyes filled with tears, and she was obliged to make use of her handkerchief. Finally regaining her composure to some degree, she continued in a quavering voice:

"What I felt then cannot be expressed in words. The last thing that I ever expected was to be dismissed from the household, and, as you can imagine, my mind was in agony. I was sure that there must be some misunderstanding, that if only I could speak with Sir Matthew myself, or at least write to him, everything would be right again, but I did not even know his address in London. I had no alternative but to leave. For a time, I stayed with an aunt who lives in Cheshire; I remained in the county because I still had hope that my banishment from Brelwick Park would only be temporary. During those months, I sent numerous letters addressed to Sir Matthew on his estate, but they were all returned to me unopened.

"Not wishing to impose on my aunt's generosity, I left her house three weeks ago and came to live with my sister's family in Bath, but here I feel I am unwelcome. My stay increases the household expenses, and worse, I bring shame upon the family. I know how all this must appear, how foolish and weak I must seem to you, but if only you knew Sir Matthew, you would see what sort of man he is, and why I fell in love with him."

"I am, in fact, acquainted with him to some extent," said Mr. Grey quietly.

"You are?" cried Miss Love in astonishment.

"Yes. I met him a little more than a month ago in Kent, when he came to visit his relations at Kleistringham House."

"And is he there still?"

"Yes, I believe he is."

"Oh, then I must write to him at once!" exclaimed Miss Love. "When he knows that he has a son, surely he cannot remain indifferent!"

"Miss Love, I must tell you that... well, you see... Sir Matthew is engaged to be married."

After several seconds of bewildered silence, she shook her head in disbelief and said, "No, no, it is not possible. Perhaps your source was mistaken... misinformed?"

"I wish that were so, but I heard of the engagement directly from the lady whom Sir Matthew is to marry."

"But... when did this happen? How long have they been acquainted?"

"They have known each other for several weeks. The lady came for an extended visit to Kleistringham while Sir Matthew was already staying there as a guest."

"What is her name?"

"Georgiana Darcy."

"I have never heard of her. Is she beautiful?"

"Yes, very beautiful."

"What about her fortune, her family and connections?"

"She comes from a wealthy, well-respected family, and her fortune is a large one."

"Is she accomplished?"

"Exceptionally so."

Seeing the futility of attempting to win back Sir Matthew from such a rival, Miss Love said, "I suppose there is little chance now that my son's father will recall his duty. I must look to others for support."

"What about your parents?" asked Mr. Grey. "Could they assist you in any way?"

"No, they are in no position to do so. Mama and Papa are themselves now reliant on the charity of our relations."

After a brief hush, Miss Love added, "When I first came to Bath, I applied to a clergyman of this parish for assistance, but he refused to help me. The man said that if I wished for relief, I should seek it in the parish where I was born. But how can I? There is no longer any home for me in Kent, and no place to go except the workhouse."

"Miss Love, perhaps you could try again?" suggested Mr. Grey. "Now that your child has been born in Bath, your situation is different, and it may be possible for you to receive assistance here after all."

"Maybe so, but I am loath to speak to that clergyman again. He was very unkind and took great pains to make me feel how much I am a sinner. It is for this reason that my son, who was born several days since, is still unbaptised; to face more scorn and humiliation is more than I could bear. That is why, when I heard that you were in Bath, I immediately wrote to you."

Mr. Grey replied with:

"You did the right thing, Miss Love, to turn to me. While there is little direct assistance I can give, you may count on me to do everything in my power to help you. I will be glad to speak to the parson on your behalf, and, with your permission, I can also consult Sir Philip Egerton, my uncle. It is possible that Sir Philip may be able to do something for you. And of course, I can baptise your son right here in a private ceremony, though he will still need to be brought to the church to be incorporated, and a clergyman of this parish will need to make all the necessary records. I regret that I am powerless to do more."

"You have already done more than you realise, Mr. Grey. Thank you for all your kindness to me."

Indeed, Miss Love was profoundly grateful to the gentleman. His was the only helping hand in a city of indifference and contempt. She caught herself thinking how much better a husband and father Mr. Grey would have made than the man to whom she had relinquished her virtue and honour. But what was the use of wishing? It was now too late.

That night, Mr. Grey found it impossible to sleep. His mind could turn to nothing but the sad history that Miss Love had related to him. When she first mentioned Sir Matthew, Mr. Grey's thoughts immediately went to Georgiana, and when he had heard the whole of the story, his first impulse was to write Miss Darcy a letter warning her of Sir Matthew's true character. Upon further reflection, however, he began to have second thoughts.

Mr. Grey's motive for wishing to caution Georgiana was entirely unselfish. His own chance of happiness with her, he knew, had gone forever. After losing even his modest position at Hunsford, he was in no way qualified to seek any woman's hand, especially Miss Darcy's. But what was the right course of action to shield her from grief? Concealing the truth about Sir Matthew and allowing her to marry him unawares seemed wrong, but exposing the man's conduct might do even more harm.

Since Sir Matthew had proposed marriage to Miss Darcy, at least his intentions towards her appeared to be honourable, and with her family and friends' protection, she was unlikely to suffer the same fate as Miss Love. Moreover, learning of Sir Matthew's actions with respect to the governess would undoubtedly inflict great pain on Miss Darcy. Even if she chose to forgive her betrothed and marry him regardless, her newfound misgivings about her husband's character would likely be injurious to any chance of marital happiness. If, on the other hand, she decided to end the engagement (and the betrothal may by now have already been publicly announced), there would probably be a scandal, some part of which would inevitably attach itself to Georgiana, however blameless she might be, and harm her chances of making a good match with another.

These considerations aside, had he even a right to interfere? Any attempt to warn Georgiana, far from being welcome, might instead be regarded as self-serving meddling. For several hours Mr. Grey agonised over what he ought to do, but in the end, the gentleman decided that it would be wrong for him to speak. He would not write to Miss Darcy.

CHAPTER 25

Several days later in Kent, Mr. Darcy finally arrived at Kleistringham. He had been expected in the afternoon, but because one of the horses was injured during the course of the journey, he did not come until much later in the day, when everyone was preparing to go to bed. Though disappointed that her brother would have no chance to converse with Sir Matthew that day, Georgiana was delighted to see Darcy again and felt relieved that he was safe and well.

The following morning, everyone gathered for a convivial breakfast. Sir Matthew spoke of the capital opportunities for hunting on his estate and expressed a wish to see Mr. Darcy at Brelwick Park in the future. Georgiana's brother answered that he would be glad to come and that he, in fact, had gone fox hunting at Brelwick once before during a visit to a mutual friend in Cheshire. Sir James Leigh, who was Sir Matthew's father, was still living then, and he extended an invitation to a hunt on his estate to Mr. Darcy. Sir James' son was away at Cambridge at the time, but Mr. Darcy formed a good opinion of Sir James himself, whom he remembered as a very amiable and respectable man.

While they ate, a letter arrived for Georgiana. She did not recognise the sender's name, and although curious to read the contents, she laid the letter aside until later since she was more interested to hear all her brother's news and even more eager to see how Mr. Darcy and Sir Matthew liked each other. As she nibbled on her buttered toast and apricot jam, Georgiana observed with pleasure that her betrothed seemed to be making a favourable impression. She valued her brother's opinion above anybody else's, and therefore, she was anxious that he should approve of the man who had won her heart.

When they finished the meal and everyone except her sister-in-law had dispersed, Georgiana was finally at leisure to read her letter. As she was unfolding the pages, Elizabeth asked her, "Is it from one of your friends in Derbyshire?"

"No, the letter is from Bath. It was written by a Miss Alexandra Love, although I do not recall ever having made her acquaintance."

Elizabeth thought nothing of it at first, but soon her feelings changed to alarm when she saw the effect that the letter produced on its reader. After the first few lines, Georgiana's countenance lost its tranquillity, and as she perused the pages further, she grew pale, and her eyes became very perturbed.

"Georgiana, what is it? What is the matter? Is there some bad news?" asked Elizabeth with concern.

Barely able to pronounce the words, Georgiana answered, "The letter is from a governess who worked in Sir Matthew's household. She writes to say that... no, I cannot bear to repeat what she has written. Read it for yourself."

Mrs. Darcy took the papers from Georgiana's trembling hands, and as she cast her eyes over the first page, she noticed that the words were written in a beautiful but passionate hand. In the letter, Miss Love recounted the history of her acquaintance with Sir Matthew, their illicit connection, and the living proof of that connection. As Elizabeth read, horror and disbelief crept into her face. Each paragraph brought fresh shock. The letter concluded with a plea to Miss Darcy to break off her engagement with Sir Matthew and to intercede with the gentleman on the writer's behalf—to attempt to persuade him to return to the woman and child he had abandoned.

When Elizabeth had finished reading, Georgiana exclaimed, "Oh, Lizzy! Can it be possible?! Can Sir Matthew be capable of such heartless and unprincipled behaviour?"

Her sister-in-law replied, "If what I have read is veracious, then his actions are indeed despicable beyond expression, but Georgiana, we should be cautious in giving credence to this report."

"You think that the story is untrue, then? That it was invented?"

"I have no means of knowing, but I believe it would be unwise to pass judgment until we have heard Sir Matthew's own account. We have never met this Miss Love and know nothing of her."

"But how could she have invented such a falsehood if there is nothing of truth in any portion of it?"

"Georgiana, in a similar situation, I once made the mistake of judging a man based on another's unproven assertions, and because of it, I nearly lost my chance of happiness with your brother. I would hate for you to repeat my error."

Elizabeth was referring, of course, to Mr. Wickham's slanderous falsehood about Mr. Darcy, which she had initially believed, and which had been one of her main reasons for refusing Mr. Darcy's first proposal of marriage. Remembering this history, Georgiana felt a faint ray of hope that there was similar duplicity in the present case.

"I must tell my brother about this letter. Where is Fitzwilliam? I must speak with him!" cried she.

Elizabeth tried to calm her: "He said that he intended to go to the village this morning, but not much time has passed since we finished breakfast. Perhaps he has not yet left the house."

"We must find him!"

"Georgiana, wait! You are not well. I think it would be better for you to stay here and rest awhile, and I will go after him myself. If your brother is not gone, I will tell him everything, and he will know what to do."

Elizabeth rushed out of the room in search of Mr. Darcy, and to her relief, she found him in the entrance hall as he was about to leave. She immediately proceeded to relate the contents of Alexandra Love's letter. As he listened and then read the letter himself, Mr. Darcy's countenance grew increasingly grave.

"This is a very serious matter. We must discover the truth without delay," said he.

"Sir Matthew has gone shooting with Mr. Townsend and Mr. Meggott and will not be back for hours," returned Elizabeth.

"It is possible that we may be able to learn something of this affair before then," was the answer. "On the way to Kent, I stopped at an inn where Colonel Graham, an old friend of mine, also happened to be staying. He has an estate in Cheshire not far from Sir Matthew's. When I met him at the inn, he was on his way to visit relations in Kent. They live only a few miles from here at Larsendon Hall."

"Do you think Colonel Graham may know something of this business with Miss Love?"

"Possibly, but even if he does not, he should be able to give me some illustration of Sir Matthew's general character. I shall go to Larsendon directly to see what I can discover."

Mr. Darcy left immediately to make his inquiries, while his wife and sister were left to endure a tense wait in the drawing room. Georgiana at first paced restlessly back and forth from the window, but at her sister-in-law's suggestion, she at last took up some work to help pass the time. For Georgiana's sake, Elizabeth attempted to maintain a calm exterior, but on the inside, she too was quite agitated. Seated by the window with a book in her hand, Mrs. Darcy periodically cast a discreet glance outside.

At length, Mr. Darcy returned. The moment his wife perceived him nearing the house, she rose to her feet, and saying merely that she needed to step out for a few minutes, she quitted the room and then hurried outside to meet her husband. Not wishing to unsettle Georgiana, Elizabeth thought it best to speak with him alone first.

As soon as Mr. Darcy was within hearing distance, Elizabeth asked anxiously, "What did Colonel Graham have to say?"

The gentleman dismounted from his horse before answering grimly, "I learned a great deal more than I expected to, and what I have discovered grieves me exceedingly. Sir Matthew is not at all a respectable young man, I am afraid."

"Then what Miss Love wrote in her letter is true!" Mrs. Darcy exclaimed in dismay.

"Colonel Graham does not know all the details of the story, but he is acquainted with a Miss Alexandra Love, who was employed as a governess at Brelwick Park. Sir Matthew's indiscreet conduct towards her gave rise to the gossip of servants and was much talked-of in the neighbourhood."

"Good Heavens!"

"There is more. It appears that Sir Matthew is also heavily in debt—his estate is on the brink of insolvency. After his parents died, he lived a life of extravagance. Among other things, he spent vast sums on refurnishing his house, held lavish parties, and engaged in constant and reckless gambling. Colonel Graham's nephew often played at cards with him, not only in Cheshire, but also at the West-end gambling houses of London. Sir Matthew regularly staked large sums, and on one particular occasion, he came close to losing his entire fortune at the gaming tables."

"It is almost as bad as could be imagined!" cried Elizabeth. "How could we have been so deceived in his character? ... How shall we tell Georgiana? It will break her heart!"

The possibility of there having been either a great misunderstanding or a malicious slander now appeared increasingly unlikely, and Sir Matthew's return to the house in the late afternoon put an end to any remaining doubt. When he arrived, the gentleman intended to stay only long enough to dress for dinner before departing for Belargent Hall, where he was engaged to dine with the Villiers family. Before he could go upstairs, however, the butler informed him that Mr. Darcy was in the library and wished to speak with him. The young man felt a little apprehensive at this sudden summons, but he did as requested.

Georgiana, with Elizabeth by her side, waited quietly outside. Approximately a quarter of an hour passed before the library doors finally opened. Sir Matthew came out, and catching sight of Georgiana, he stopped for a moment but said not a word, nor did he come near her. There was regret and pain in his countenance. He looked away and then swiftly went upstairs to his room.

Bewildered, and with a heart full of foreboding, Georgiana stepped into the library.

"It is not good news, is it?" asked she of her brother.

"No, I am sad to say, there is no good news."

"Then, everything that was written in that dreadful letter is true?"

"I am afraid it is. When I questioned Sir Matthew, he admitted to all of it. In his favour, he did show some remorse for his past actions, but I had no choice—I told him I could not give my consent to a marriage between my sister and a man of his character."

It was a heavy blow. Crestfallen, Georgiana replied, "Oh, Brother! You could not have done otherwise, of course, but I never thought that matters could end like this. I am so unhappy... so very unhappy."

The engagement having been broken off, an awkward situation arose. On the one hand, Mr. Darcy had only just arrived at Kleistringham, and it seemed impolite to the Townsends to suddenly leave again, but at the same time, to remain under the same roof with Sir Matthew was impossible. There was no other alternative but to leave.

It was a relief, at least, that Sir Matthew would be dining away from the house that evening, so they would not see him, and the Darcys could depart the next morning as soon as their trunks were ready. Mr. Darcy and his wife decided to go directly to Elizabeth's family in Hertfordshire. It would of course mean arriving at Longbourn a few days earlier than they were expected, but there was little other choice.

CHAPTER 26

Georgiana found no relief from her misery even in sleep, which that night was restless, fitful, and full of unpleasant dreams. The next morning, instead of her usual eagerness to start the day, she had only the disheartened feeling of having nothing to look forward to. Georgiana took breakfast in her room, in part to avoid the possibility of encountering Sir Matthew. She need not have feared, however, because he made no appearance in the breakfast room.

Following their morning meal, Georgiana and Elizabeth rested in the drawing room ahead of their journey, while servants packed the Darcys' belongings. Mrs. Townsend sat with the two ladies and busied herself with her needlework. In an effort to divert her mind from mournful thoughts, Georgiana at first tried to read but found she could make no progress with the book. Her sister-in-law, who was seated by a window with a book of her own, from time to time cast anxious glances in the young lady's direction.

After rereading the same paragraph five times, Georgiana finally tossed the tome aside and simply stared into the distance. Mrs. Darcy tried to think of something to say which might brighten Georgiana's mood. Nothing came to mind, but happening to look out the window, she saw Mrs. Townsend's sister hurrying towards the house.

"Oh, here comes Mrs. Lloyd!" cried she.

Although Mrs. Lloyd was widely regarded as the village gossip, Elizabeth found her stories amusing and never objected to hearing them. Today, she was happy as never before to see Mrs. Townsend's sister arrive, for the lady would doubtless have something entertaining to tell, which might perhaps take Georgiana's thoughts away from Sir Matthew. Yet, once the guest was seated in the drawing room and began to speak, they all wished that she had never come at all, for the very first words out of her mouth were on precisely the subject that everyone else wished to avoid.

"Have you seen Sir Matthew Leigh today?" asked Mrs. Lloyd.

Georgiana felt a stab of pain upon hearing that gentleman's name mentioned, but out of pride, she kept her composure, especially since Mrs. Lloyd knew nothing of her engagement, or that it had been broken off. Mrs. Townsend, in her turn, looked somewhat discomfited by her sister's question and hesitated before replying, "No... he dined with the Villiers yesterday at Belargent Hall. We did not see Sir Matthew at breakfast this morning, but he must have left for Belargent again to go shooting with Mr. Villiers. He mentioned something of it yesterday."

"Then I take it you have not heard the news about him!"

Immeasurably pleased at the prospect of being the first to tell them, Mrs. Lloyd opened her mouth to continue but was interrupted by Mrs. Townsend, who, being desperate to change the subject, asked the first question that came to her mind:

"How was your apple harvest this year, Sister?"

"Oh, it was excellent! The best in years! Only, the crows have been eating the apples, especially the best ones from the Ribston Pippin tree.

"The crows appear to have very refined taste!" Mrs. Darcy remarked mirthfully.

"To be sure, they are a horrible pest, but we took care of them!"

Then, remembering the main object of her visit, Mrs. Lloyd continued, "But back to Sir Matthew. Today in the village, I heard such a tale about him as I think will surprise even you, Sister!"

Mrs. Darcy marvelled to herself how quickly gossip spread through the neighbourhood. No sooner had the Darcys themselves learned of Sir Matthew's indiscretions, than here was Mrs. Lloyd, about to retell the story to them. How had she found out?

Seeing Georgiana's distress upon hearing that gentleman mentioned once more, Elizabeth hastened to ask, "What did you do about the crows in your orchard?"

"I had my husband shoot them, and then the birds were baked into a most delicious pie."

"Crow pie?!"

"Yes, why not? Even the word 'pie' comes from 'magpie', a close relative of the crow. Both crows and magpies have long been used in England for pie filling. Cooking with crow meat may have fallen out of fashion lately, but for my part, I would not dream of wasting such good meat! Waste not, want not, I always say."

Mrs. Darcy could hardly keep her countenance upon hearing such a story, but Mrs. Lloyd's next words made her serious again:

"Ladies, I have not finished telling you what I heard about Sir Matthew. I learned of it from Mr. Leech, the apothecary, who heard the report from a maid in the Villiers' household, that Sir Matthew eloped with Priscilla Villiers last night."

For a moment, everyone in the room was speechless. Mrs. Lloyd, meanwhile, inwardly congratulated herself on having delivered news of which even her sister was ignorant, despite Sir Matthew's being a guest at Kleistringham House. After recovering from the initial shock, Mrs. Townsend ventured to ask:

"He eloped with Priscilla Villiers?! Are you quite sure?"

"There is no doubt whatever. Miss Villiers left a note for her family in which she declared she was running off to the island of Guernsey with Sir Matthew to get married.

"To Guernsey?!"

"Why, yes. There are always ships at Dover ready to smuggle imprudent baggage into the land of matrimony for a fee. Sir Edward Villiers has gone in pursuit of the lovers on his fastest horse."

Georgiana could not bear to hear any more. She felt that if she stayed with the others an instant longer, she would burst into tears before them all. With as much self-possession as she could muster, Georgiana excused herself and then rushed out of the drawing room and up the stairs to her bedchamber. Once the door was closed, she gave way to a flood of tears. The young lady had not been crying long, however, when she heard a soft knock on the door, followed by:

"Georgiana, it is Elizabeth. May I come in?"

"Yes Lizzy, please do."

Mrs. Darcy entered and sat down on the bed next to her sister-in-law.

"Oh Lizzy, if he really loved me, how could he have done what he did? How could he have eloped with such a woman the moment that our engagement was ended?" asked Georgiana tearfully.

"He was in desperate need of money," returned Elizabeth. "Sir Matthew's debts were of such magnitude that unless he could retrieve himself by marriage, bankruptcy was inevitable. Miss Villiers had forty thousand pounds; that must have been sufficient inducement... Georgiana, though it must not seem that way now, I assure you that what has happened is for the best. Imagine if you had married him; sooner or later, Sir Matthew would have revealed his true nature, and think what misery would then have ensued. It is better that the truth came out now before it was too late."

"I should perhaps be grateful that I discovered his real character in time, but all I feel is pain," was Georgiana's answer.

"I know it is very difficult for you, and that you are feeling a great deal of sorrow," Elizabeth replied, "but it will not be like this forever. Time will pass, and it will be as if none of this had ever happened; you will see."

"You are right, of course, Elizabeth, and I should endeavour to forget him. Yet, even after all that he has done, I find that I still care for Sir Matthew—but for my brother's sake and for yours, I will try not to dwell on thoughts of him."

Drying her tears, Georgiana added, "I will be alright now, Lizzy. I promise."

Mrs. Darcy stayed with her a little longer and then left for her own room to see to the last of the packing. Once Georgiana was alone, she looked around her bedchamber to check whether anything had been missed. Suddenly remembering that she had left some music sheets on the pianoforte in the drawing room, she went downstairs to fetch them.

By then Mrs. Lloyd had gone home, and Georgiana found the drawing room empty when she entered. The sheets of music were still where she had left them on the pianoforte, and reaching for the papers, she caught sight of the title: *Sonata quasi una fantasia.* It was the same piece that she had played on the day when she first met Sir Matthew. Georgiana could recall the moment clearly; she remembered the joy she had felt when playing that beautiful music after the long journey from Pemberley, and she recalled, also, how startled she had been when, happening to look up, she saw a young gentleman gazing at her from the doorway with his piercing, dark eyes. How handsome he had looked, and how her heart had nearly stopped beating at the sight of him!

Georgiana sat down at the instrument and began playing the first movement, but the feelings that the music evoked in her were so different from what they had been on that magical afternoon. What she now felt was an overwhelming sadness and a sense of longing for what could never be. Georgiana thought bitterly how fitting it was that Beethoven's sonata should be titled *Quasi una fantasia*, Italian for "Almost a fantasy". What a resemblance to the events of the past month, which now seemed half dream, half reality. Sir Matthew's love had felt so genuine, so real, and yet it proved to be as lasting as morning fog. She felt like weeping, but remembering her promise to Elizabeth, Georgiana recollected herself, and gathering up the papers lying on the pianoforte, she was about to leave again when a footman suddenly came into the drawing room to announce the arrival of Mr. Villiers. That gentleman presently entered, and after greeting him, Georgiana said:

"I believe Mrs. Townsend is upstairs, but she should be down again shortly."

"Miss Darcy, I did not come to see Mrs. Townsend. I came to see you, and what I have to say cannot be said in her presence. My feelings for you..."

Georgiana looked anxiously towards the door.

"Mr. Villiers, we really ought not to be here together unchaperoned."

"Miss Darcy, I entreat you! Please allow me to speak. I assure you that my intentions are honourable!"

"Mr. Villiers, please..."

"Spare me but a few minutes of your time! I have thought of you so often! My feelings for you are so passionate! Even now, I find it difficult to put my sentiments into words. If you will permit me, I would like to recite a passage from the Bible."

"The Bible?!"

"Yes. I have memorised a portion of the Song of Solomon in the Old Testament.[8] The verses express what I feel better than I can at present."

The gentleman looked so determined that Georgiana realised any argument would be fruitless. She therefore reluctantly agreed to let him continue, whereupon Mr. Villiers straightened his shoulders, cleared his throat, and began:

How beautiful thou art! and how sweet! O my love! how...

The gentleman paused and looked deep in thought, "how... how...", then remembering, he brightened and continued:

how delightful! In respect to thy stateliness, thou hast been compared to the palm tree, and thy breasts to its clusters. I said, I will climb the palm tree—I will clasp its topmost boughs; and thy breasts shall be now like the clusters of the vine;

Georgiana's eyes widened with astonishment.

and the smell of thy nose like lemons

"No, no, that is not right. Pardon me, Miss Darcy, it was 'citrons' not 'lemons'," said he and then repeated:

and the smell of thy nose like citrons; and the roof of thy mouth like choice wine—
Which is poured out rightly for... for...

"Oh, dear! I cannot remember the rest! I tried so hard to commit the verses to memory!"

"Mr. Villiers, please do not be distressed. I think I comprehend your meaning from what you have recited thus far."

The gentleman looked disappointed at being unable to continue his rhapsodies, but determined not to spoil the beauty of the moment, he composed himself and went on to assure Georgiana of the ardour of his love for her, of the large fortune that would one day be his, and of the desirability of his family name:

"It may be true, as the great Shakespeare said, that 'a rose by any other name would smell as sweet',[9] but even so, the distinct advantage of being the next Lady Villiers is undeniable," said he.

Conscious of the courage it must have taken for Mr. Villiers to avow his feelings, Georgiana refused him as kindly and gently as she could, saying, "I am deeply honoured, Sir, by your good opinion of me, but it is not within my power to return your affections. Doubtless, the next Lady Villiers will indeed consider herself very fortunate to bear that name, but I regret to say that I cannot be that woman."

"Is there any possibility that you may reconsider your decision in the future?" the young man asked.

"No, Mr. Villiers. I am afraid not."

"Then, my fair torturer, I must bid thee:"

Farewell! thou art too dear for my possessing,
And like enough thou know'st thy estimate:
The charter of thy worth gives thee releasing[10]

John Villiers thought that if he was to be refused, he would at least give the scene as dramatic and poetic an air as possible. In fact, he had memorised these lines in advance for just such a contingency. Contrary to what might be supposed, Georgiana's rejected suitor was genuinely disappointed that his proposal had not been accepted, but his sorrow was nothing that an evening spent with a good book and a generous slice of cake could not cure. Indeed, as he was leaving Kleistringham House, he could already almost smell the delicious scent of the freshly-baked pastry.

Within an hour after he had gone, the Darcys departed for Longbourn. During the whole journey, Georgiana could think of little else other than Sir Matthew and his elopement with Priscilla Villiers. So much had happened in the space of less than two days that she could scarcely believe it was real. She wished she could forget it all as if it were nothing more than a horrible dream.

Adding diversity to these melancholy thoughts was the memory of Mr.

Villiers' proposal. Although it saddened Georgiana to think that her refusal had likely caused him pain, she could not help smiling at the recollection of his addresses to her. Never had she thought that a man would quote from Scripture while declaring his love for her, much less that she would hear verses of such a nature as Mr. Villiers had chosen. She imagined the red-haired gentleman clambering up the stately palm tree and grasping at its pendulous fruit; the idea filled her with embarrassed amusement and provided some relief against the other thoughts, entirely devoid of humour, swirling through her mind.

CHAPTER 27

At Longbourn, the Darcys were welcomed with all possible joy and hospitality. Mr. Bennet was delighted to see his favourite daughter again, and Jane Bingley, who herself had arrived with her husband and Kitty several days earlier, was no less happy to be reunited with her dear sister. Though Elizabeth was far from being her mother's favourite child, Mrs. Bennet was also pleased to see the Darcys come, for their visit would provide her with fresh opportunities to remind all her neighbours how well *her* daughter had married compared with any of *theirs*.

The first part of the following day was spent quietly. After breakfast Georgiana, Jane, and Elizabeth took a long walk, which, to some extent, succeeded in lifting Georgiana's depressed spirits. There is something about nature that quiets the mind and gladdens a wounded heart in a way that nothing else can; even the music that Georgiana loved was powerless to do as much.

In the afternoon, Charlotte Collins called on Elizabeth. Mrs. Collins had recently returned to the neighbourhood, where she was now living with her family again. Of all the pleasures that Elizabeth could have looked forward to on coming back to her childhood home, seeing her good friend Charlotte was the greatest. To both ladies sitting together in the drawing room, it felt almost like old times again, except for Charlotte's mourning clothes, which served as a reminder of just how much had happened in the past two years.

Elizabeth hoped that her friend would stay for dinner, but Mrs. Collins could not, for she was already engaged to dine with the Gouldings. Soon after she left, dinner was served at Longbourn. At the table, Mrs. Bennet began the conversation by saying:

"I had a letter from Lydia this morning. She writes to say that she is with child again. Oh, I do hope that when the baby is born, she and Wickham will bring the children to visit us at Longbourn! I long to see my grandchildren, and Lydia and Wickham too, of course. My daughter tells me that little George is more and more like his father every day, and that he will be just like him when he is grown."

Mr. Darcy's face darkened at this mention of the man whom he loathed above any other, and who had been an endless source of trouble and vexation in his life. The idea of more little Wickhams cast in the same mould as their father failed to excite the same joy in him as it did in Mrs. Bennet, and unfortunately for Darcy, his mother-in-law's next words did nothing to brighten his countenance.

"Lydia also writes that they are short of money again," said she, and looking pointedly at Mr. Darcy, continued, "Poor dears! Raising a family is so expensive these days! How much better off they would be if Wickham had a benefice, such as the living of Tadelford, which I understand has recently fallen vacant."

Before Mrs. Bennet could say any more on the subject of the church living, which was in Mr. Darcy's gift, Elizabeth remarked hastily, "It was such a pleasure to receive a visit from Charlotte this afternoon."

"Yes, we see a great deal of Mrs. Collins now that her husband is dead and she has returned to her father's house," came Mrs. Bennet's reply.

"Oh Lizzy, we forgot to tell you!" cried Kitty. "Yesterday Papa received a letter from Dr. Samuel Collins, who is the next heir of entail of Longbourn. Since his cousin Mr. Collins left no male heirs when he died, Dr. Collins will inherit the estate. In his letter, he wrote to say that he wishes to visit us at Longbourn and would like to do so in January."

"Are you acquainted with him at all, Papa?" asked Elizabeth.

"I met Dr. Collins only once, many years ago, when he was but a youth. Even then he was a rather austere, verbose young man, and from the length and unsmiling tone of his letter, I am led to believe that he is little changed.

The only other information I have of him is that he is a recently-widowed clergyman who teaches Divinity at Cambridge."

Mary Bennet, the middle sister, did not give voice to her thoughts, but in her opinion, this description of Dr. Collins painted him as a very sensible, worthy gentleman—the sort of man whom a woman would be proud to call her husband.

"Has he any children?" asked Elizabeth.

"None at all!" rejoiced her mother. "Therefore, if he should decide to marry either Kitty or Mary, one of my own grandchildren will inherit Longbourn!"

Feeling no enthusiasm at the prospect of being wedded to a widower nearly twice her age, Kitty asked, "What if Dr. Collins does not want to marry again?"

"Nonsense, child! A man who is to inherit an estate would not wish to remain alone, especially at his age, and nothing would give more relief to my poor nerves than having another daughter married!"

After a slight pause, Mrs. Bennet continued, "God be praised that Mr. Collins did not father a son. I could not bear to have Mrs. Collins and the Lucases constantly crowing over us in their hearts and congratulating themselves that Longbourn would be theirs someday."

"Poor Charlotte," said Jane. "It must have been difficult to lose not only a husband but also all hope of a secure future."

"There is no need to feel sorry for her! Sir William Lucas is perfectly capable of providing for his daughter. The whole family has always been frugal enough that they should have plenty saved up by now! For my part, I am relieved that there is no longer any possibility that Mrs. Collins will ever turn me out of my own house!" cried Mrs. Bennet.

"Unless, of course, Dr. Collins happens to take a fancy to Mr. Collins' widow, and then she might just come to live at Longbourn after all," remarked her husband.

"Oh Mr. Bennet, how can you say such things! How could Dr. Collins possibly prefer an ordinary-looking widow with a child to one of our own daughters?! No, Mary or Kitty will get him, you may be sure."

Mary, who was far from objecting to becoming Dr. Collins' wife, found moral grounds to justify why Mrs. Collins should not wed a second time. In her most sermonising tone of voice, she said:

"For a woman to marry a second time is not the same as for a man. Chastity and female delicacy, which are and ought to be a woman's crowning glory, are called into question by a willingness to once more endure that surrender to which only the most ardent love for her husband could induce a virtuous female to submit the first time."

Mr. Darcy sat silently and bore the prattling of his mother-in-law and her daughter as best he could, but at least he had comfort in the idea that such dinners would not often be repeated since both of his own estates were far from Hertfordshire. If he thought the conversation would end there, however, he was greatly mistaken, because after a brief silence Mrs. Bennet continued:

"All things considered, I would prefer it if Dr. Collins chose Mary. With Kitty's pretty face and the numerous advantages she receives from living mainly with her two wealthy sisters, she ought to be able to marry three, four, or maybe even five thousand pounds a year. If my two eldest daughters succeeded in making good matches, why cannot Kitty? Dr. Collins will do very well for Mary, though."

Mr. Bingley looked rather uncomfortable, while Mr. Darcy raised his eyes to the ceiling. "Mama, please!" admonished Mrs. Darcy and gave her mother a meaningful look, but in vain—Mrs. Bennet would not be restrained.

"We are all *family* here, Elizabeth. Why should I not speak my mind? ... And now that we are on the subject of marriage, there is something I would like to say concerning Miss Darcy. It is important to get her married while she is still young and beautiful. You do not want to wait until the bloom has gone. Otherwise, she will not be able to marry half so well. And what is this silliness I hear about spending the season on a country estate in Scotland? How is she ever to catch a husband unless she goes somewhere like London or Bath, or perhaps Brighton?"

Jane replied with: "Mama, did I not tell you? Miss Darcy is to stay for a time with Charles and me in Bath, and in January she will join her brother and Lizzy in London on their return from Scotland."

"What a clever idea!" exclaimed Mrs. Bennet. "Why, with such a plan, instead of seeing only half the rich, young men in England, Miss Darcy will see them all! Or, most of them, at least. Only, it would have been better for her to go to London first and then to Bath. The best selection of young men is to be found in London, whereas Bath tends to attract many of the nouveau riche sort. Even at the city's peak, that was the case, and Bath is not what it once was."

"Mama, there *are* things to do in Bath besides catch husbands," protested Elizabeth.

"Oh, yes," agreed Mr. Bennet. "Such as going to the theatre and concerts, and taking the waters. Yet, I find it remarkable how many mothers and fathers develop a taste for these enjoyments at just the time when their daughters reach marriageable age."

"A fortunate coincidence, indeed," smiled Elizabeth.

Georgiana, meanwhile, felt torn between amusement at Mrs. Bennet's absurdly improper discourse and dejection at having been reminded of how very unmarried she still was. Since the wounds of her heart were still fresh, dejection eventually won. Georgiana became increasingly subdued as the dinner progressed, a change that her sister-in-law did not fail to notice. Seeing the young lady's doleful face, and knowing that her mother's careless talk was the cause, Elizabeth felt the most acute concern. Her heart was wrung on Georgiana's account.

Not long after everyone had retired for the night, Miss Darcy heard a knock on her door, and presently Elizabeth entered. "I just wanted to look in on you and make sure that you are alright," said she. "I am sorry that you had to sit through such dinner conversation tonight."

"I do not blame them; they have no knowledge of what happened with Sir Matthew," replied Georgiana. "And I am certain Mrs. Bennet meant well. Perhaps she is even right—I ought to be considering my future and trying to find a good husband, but the very thought of marriage makes me want to weep. After all that has passed, I am not sure I can open my heart to anyone again. And so, the bloom will wilt, and I will become an old maid."

"Oh Georgiana, you are the last young lady in England who is in danger of becoming an old maid!"

"It is kind of you to say so, Lizzy, but regardless of whether I am destined for that fate, I feel so utterly miserable, and it is no comfort to know that I am to blame for my own suffering."

"To blame?! Georgiana, whatever do you mean? As far as I can see, all the blame lies with Sir Matthew."

"I cannot acquit myself as easily as you do, Lizzy. I did a great deal of thinking on the way here from Kent, and I see now that it was very foolish of me to accept Sir Matthew's proposal so hastily. I should have heeded your advice to take care before giving away my heart. Instead, I impetuously consented to be his wife before I fully knew his character. His passionate, lively, charming disposition was all I saw, and not once did I stop to consider whether these traits were enough to make him a good husband. Was he a principled man? Did he have a strong sense of honour and prudence? Of whether he possessed these qualities I knew nothing, though I could easily have discerned Sir Matthew's faults had I not allowed my fancy for him to blind me and to hurry away my reason. I should have recognised that his attachment to pleasure and freedom made him careless of the future and of the pain that his selfish actions inflicted on others. My mind acknowledges these truths and the certainty that Sir Matthew could never have made me happy—and yet, I cannot seem to shake off this melancholy and sense of loss that have gripped me."

"Georgiana, give it time; it is natural that you should feel some sorrow at first. And there is no need to think of marriage at present. You are still young."

"Then, must I spend the winter in Bath and London? Making a good match is the object of my going, is it not?"

Elizabeth sighed. "You do not have to go if you do not want to, but I think the change of scene will do you good. New people and new places encourage diversity of thought, which is not as easy to find in the quiet of the country. Just enjoy both cities for what they are without trying to make anything come of your stay in town. That is my advice."

Georgiana knew that there was sense in what her sister-in-law said, and after some further thought, she resolved to follow her suggestion. It was certainly better than sitting at home and grieving. Yet, what was there for her in Bath and London? Only shops she did not care to visit, dinner parties she did not wish to attend, and balls that were rendered all the more disagreeable by the requirement of dancing.

CHAPTER 28

Georgiana had hoped for fine weather on the journey into Bath, but for most of the way, there was rain, which did not ease even as the Bingleys' carriage rolled into the city. The rain was not a heavy downpour, but a steady, dreary rain, made worse by the disagreeable, smoke-filled air. Since the day was damp and cold, nearly every chimney in Bath did its duty in belching out grey smoke, which enveloped the drab yellow buildings in a gloomy haze. Georgiana had, of course, been used to thicker smoke during the time she lived in London, and there had been no shortage of rain in that city either, but somehow, London rain did not have the same cheerless quality to it that Bath rain seemed to possess. Everything around her now was grey, and yellow, and dismal.

At last, the carriage stopped in front of the Paragon building, and after alighting, the passengers hurried indoors. Not long afterwards, they sat down to dinner. While they ate, Mr. Bingley spoke of all the wonderful things to see and do in Bath. Listening to his lively description, Georgiana tried to feel some enthusiasm, but still being weary from the journey, she found herself wishing for nothing more than to rest in her room. Soon after dinner, therefore, Georgiana retired early to her bed.

On the following morning, after the refreshment of a night's sleep, Jane Bingley and her husband eagerly discussed the possibility of dancing that evening at the Upper Assembly Rooms, where there was to be a ball.

However, Georgiana, who descended the stairs some time later, expressed reluctance at the idea. She still felt tired after the long journey, she said, and could not bear the thought of dancing. Could they not spend the evening quietly at home and instead get their exercise from a morning walk outside? Strolling in the fresh air and quietude of nature seemed much more appealing. Although Mr. and Mrs. Bingley were both a little disappointed at the loss of an opportunity to dance at the ball, they did not want to press their friend to partake of an amusement for which she clearly had no heart, and so a walk outdoors it was to be.

Meanwhile, not half a mile away from the Paragon, sitting in the drawing room of a house in Queen Square, was a young gentleman. He was quite handsome, and though only of middling height, his person was finely proportioned. He, too, had only recently arrived in Bath.

Since his mother and sister were upstairs, there was no one in the room to disturb him. The gentleman sat motionless as he directed his luminous, though rather narrow, hazel eyes towards the fire without really seeing the flames that danced before him. At length, he sighed, and turning to his right, he picked up a copy of *A Master-key to the Rich Ladies Treasury* (the latest edition), which was lying on the table beside him. The pages were well-worn from the frequency with which they had been lovingly read. This book he studied more than any other; it was one that gave him immense pleasure. Opening the volume to a random page, he read the first three lines to himself:

Miss Aynsworth	*Duke Street, Ldn.*	*30,000 £*
Miss Beauclerk	*Grosvenor Square, Ldn.*	*10,000 £*
Miss Blake	*St. James's Street, Ldn.*	*20,000 £*

Many an hour of his life had the handsome gentleman spent in perusal of this excellent and useful publication; time always seemed to fly while he contemplated the lists of ladies, their reputed fortunes, and their places of abode. On this particular day, he scanned the lists carefully and took note of all the ladies residing in Bath. Though not averse to reading the section on spinsters, he preferred the one on widows. A woman of large fortune, he reasoned, who had failed to find a single man who wished to marry her must surely have some intolerable defect—bad teeth, a shrewish temper, a shapeless figure, or perhaps all three at once. On the other hand, a rich, young widow who unexpectedly lost her husband, perhaps in a riding accident or some sudden illness, might still be beautiful and desirable. If worst came to worst, however, even a plain spinster would do so long as her fortune was large enough. One could always keep a mistress, and provided that everything was conducted very discreetly, a gentleman need have no difficulty in preserving his honour.

After he had finished looking through the book, the young man knelt to the floor, and for a quarter of an hour he prayed earnestly and solemnly to God to help him win the heart of one of the ladies in the book. His devotions complete, he then rose, and after putting on his coat and hat, the gentleman left the house for his morning walk.

By that time, Georgiana and her friends had already reached the Royal Crescent. Looking up at the edifice in wonder, the young lady said, "What a magnificent building! It is like the Roman Colosseum, but turned inside out."

"Yes, it is very picturesque," agreed Jane. "In fact, if I had my choice of any place in Bath, I would live right here. The Paragon will always be considered a respectable address, of course, and I have no complaint to make in that regard, but it is situated in a much less pleasant part of town than the Crescent. You have, no doubt, observed how dim and uninviting are the front rooms of our house, and how much noise travels from the street; while here, everything is green and spacious, with private gardens in the back and pleasant views out front. But, as the Crescent is the most fashionable and desirable address in Bath, there was little hope of our securing a house here for the winter, especially since business affairs made Mr. Bingley late in coming to Bath to engage lodgings for us. By then, there was little left to choose from other than the Paragon."

"Still, I would say that your house in the Paragon is a very comfortable one," said Georgiana.

"So it is," replied Jane, "and since we will be spending the greater part of our time enjoying the city, the lack of a fine prospect from the windows is of little matter."

After admiring the building, they walked for a time in the Crescent

Fields and then continued on to the gravel walk. Almost as soon as they entered that path, in the distance there appeared, coming towards them, the figure of a young gentleman approximately Mr. Bingley's age. Georgiana hardly noticed him at first, but as he drew nearer, she could clearly perceive that his eyes were fixed directly upon her. She lowered her own eyes to the ground modestly but could still feel his burning gaze surveying her person with interest. A short space of time passed, and now the stranger was nearly close enough to speak to them. Looking up again, Georgiana saw that his eyes had not left their target, but suddenly, he shifted his look away from her and instead turned his attention to Mr. Bingley. To Georgiana's surprise, the unknown gentleman greeted her friend and claimed him as an acquaintance.

At first, Mr. Bingley could not remember where he had met the man, but just in time to avoid the embarrassment of admitting it, Mr. Bingley recalled that they had studied together at Oxford. He introduced him to the ladies as Mr. Michael Brydges. When the latter heard that the young lady who had caught his notice was named Miss Darcy, and that she was the sister of Fitzwilliam Darcy, he viewed her with redoubled interest. Although Mr. Brydges was not acquainted with Miss Darcy's brother, he had heard of him and knew that not only was the gentleman Mr. Bingley's oldest friend, but also that he was a man of great wealth and consequence. His enchanting sister must surely, therefore, have a large fortune!

Observing the new acquaintance before her, Georgiana could not decide whether she liked his looks. Mr. Brydges was certainly handsome, but his eyes, which formed two narrow slits in his chiselled face, seemed somewhat tense and watchful. Additionally, his smile lacked warmth. In fact, his features seemed less accustomed to smiling than to a more serious, slightly morose expression. On the other hand, his manners were gentlemanly and polished, and his conversation was agreeable.

Mr. Brydges told the Bingleys and Miss Darcy that after taking his degree at Oxford, he went into the law and was now a barrister of Lincoln's Inn. Mr. Bingley inquired what had brought him from London, to which the gentleman replied that he was visiting his mother and sister, who lived in Bath. The conversation continued for a little while longer, and then they parted cordially. When the man had gone, Georgiana asked:

"Was Mr. Brydges well-liked among the students at Oxford?"

"No, I cannot say that he was. He had somewhat of a reputation for being a tuft-hunter," answered Mr. Bingley.

"A tuft-hunter! I do not believe I have ever heard that term before. What does it mean?"

"You have never heard of tuft-hunters?" said he smilingly. "The name has to do with the tassels, or tufts, on the students' caps. Some students wear golden tufts, and others have plain, black ones. A tuft-hunter is a man who seeks the company of those with golden tufts and often behaves in a fawning, sycophantic manner towards them."

Georgiana asked, "Who gets to wear the golden tufts, and why are they so highly sought-after?"

"Depending on their station, the students at Oxford wear different attire," replied Mr. Bingley. "At the highest level are the noblemen, who have magnificent, coloured silk gowns ornamented with a decorative trim and golden tassels on their velvet caps. Below the noblemen are the gentlemen-commoners. These students are wealthy but have no title, and accordingly, they wear only a black tassel on their caps and have somewhat less splendid, black silk gowns. The lower-ranking independent students— the commoners and the batelers—also have black tufts on their caps, but their academic gowns are of a simpler design and are made of a coarser material. And then, at the very bottom are the students called servitors, who have no tuft at all on account of their subservient status."

"Servitors—that almost sounds like 'servants'," said Georgiana. "Is it the same thing?"

"No, not quite, but almost. The servitors form the lowest rank of students because they have not the means to attend Oxford at their own expense. They therefore are obliged to perform menial tasks such as serving meals in the dining hall in return for their education."

"It must not be an easy life for them."

"No, I imagine it is not... and yet, the education they receive, hard-won though it is, opens doors of opportunity to them that would otherwise be shut. I think they must have been very conscious of it because the servitors did more studying than almost anybody else at Oxford."

The discussion then returned to the ladies' new acquaintance:

"Mr. Brydges appears to be a mannerly, serious gentleman," said Jane.

"Yes—although I am not *very* well-acquainted with him, I have no reason to think ill of him. As I recall from our time together at Oxford, Mr. Brydges was a respectable, studious young man."

"Perhaps he was unjustly called a tuft-hunter," continued Mrs. Bingley. "It may be that he was merely eager to make new acquaintances at the university, and his overtures of friendship were misinterpreted and regarded with suspicion by some of the wealthier students."

"That is certainly possible."

"Maybe we should invite him to dinner?"

"Yes, I think we should. He seems to be an agreeable gentleman, and it has been some time since I have seen any of my fellow students from Oxford. I would be glad to become better acquainted with Mr. Brydges."

The man whom they were discussing was at that moment walking with sprightly step as he contemplated the providential nature of his chance meeting with an old acquaintance from Oxford under such advantageous circumstances. That Miss Darcy had been with the Bingleys was surely no accident! Without a doubt, this must be a sign from God! Could there be any other explanation for the good fortune of encountering such a wealthy, beautiful, well-born young woman so soon after praying to God for help? With a grateful heart, Mr. Brydges sent a silent message of thanks up to heaven as he continued on his walk.

CHAPTER 29

The Bingleys had a much more compelling reason for spending the season in Bath than merely to enjoy the city's attractions. It was Jane Bingley's dearest wish to have a child, but God had not yet blessed her with such felicity. Consequently, on the advice of her physician, and the good example of Mary of Modena, Jane decided to take the cure in Bath. It was hoped that the health-giving waters that had aided Queen Mary in begetting a son would do likewise for Jane. After their morning walk, therefore, Mr. Bingley led the ladies to the pump-room for their dose of nature's medicine.

Along the way, the gentleman spoke of the pump-room music gallery, where an excellent orchestra—as fine as any to be found in London—performed every day for the visitors. Georgiana had not heard a good orchestra in months, and at the thought of hearing the musicians play, she felt her spirits rise a little.

When they entered the pump-room, they discovered that a sizeable queue of people eager to partake of the celebrated water had already gathered in front of the pumper, so Mr. Bingley suggested instead taking a turn about the room a few times. Accordingly, while waiting for the queue to decrease in length, Georgiana and her friends joined the parade of people walking round and round the grand room. There was indeed a fine orchestra playing, but the ceaseless hum of voices from the crowd was as loud as in a marketplace and partially drowned out the music. The combined noise of the throng and the musicians began to give Georgiana a headache, and it was not long before she found herself yearning to return to their house in the Paragon. Out of consideration for her kind hosts, however, the young lady did her best to appear as if she were enjoying herself.

Georgiana looked with longing eyes at the entrance doors, which they were now approaching, when suddenly, a gentleman walked in whom she remembered well. Seeing Miss Darcy approach, the young man stopped abruptly and then slowly tipped his hat to her.

"Mr. Grey! It is you!"

"Miss Darcy! It... it is still Miss Darcy, is it not?" he asked hesitantly.

"Yes, it is still Miss Darcy," came the somewhat subdued answer.

The gentleman was not alone. With him were his uncle and aunt, whom he introduced as Sir Philip and Lady Egerton. Georgiana liked them both at once. Sir Philip was the personification of good breeding and dignity, but without any accompanying hauteur, while his wife possessed a gracious, gentle, yet self-assured manner and spoke with ease and affability.

Following the introductions, there was no awkwardness, and the conversation flowed freely. Sir Philip had come to Bath, he said, on account of his health and hoped that the waters would effect a cure for his ailments. For the present, unfortunately, there was no possibility of obtaining a cup of the renowned water, for the queue extending from the pumper was as long as ever. He and his family therefore joined Miss Darcy and the Bingleys in taking a turn about the room.

Walking a little behind the rest of the party, Mr. Grey and Georgiana availed themselves of the opportunity to speak privately.

"I understand that Miss Alexandra Love is staying in Bath," Georgiana began cautiously. "Ever since I received her letter, I have been most concerned for her welfare."

"Miss Love sent you a letter?!"

"Yes. A little over a week ago, when I was still in Kent, I received a letter from her in which she explained her situation. My family and I left Kleistringham the very next day."

"I see."

After a pause, Mr. Grey continued:

"Miss Love and her son, I am happy to report, are now living in more comfortable circumstances. I acquainted my uncle with her predicament, and Sir Philip was very kind and generous in offering his assistance... Miss Darcy, I am sorry that you had to discover the truth in such a way. I wanted to write to you myself many times, but I feared that any word from me would cause more harm than if I were to keep silent. I regret that you had to read anything that caused you pain."

"The letter was indeed very distressing," said Georgiana quietly, "but after much reflection, I arrived at the conviction that it was for the best. If that letter had not come, I would have committed a great error—the greatest of my life."

Overwhelmed with emotion, the gentleman and young lady walked side by side for some moments with neither speaking until Mr. Grey finally broke the silence by asking:

"Will you be staying long in Bath, Miss Darcy?"

"I am to leave in January. Mr. and Mrs. Bingley plan to remain in town longer—until late February, but I will be spending the rest of the season with my brother and his wife in London."

Having hoped that Georgiana would be in Bath for the whole season, Mr. Grey could not entirely hide the disappointment in his voice as he said:

"Yet, that is not too short a time to discover all that Bath has to offer. We—that is, *you* have over a month."

"Yes."

"Have you visited any part of Bath other than the pump-room, Miss Darcy?"

"Only the Royal Crescent. My friends and I went walking there this morning."

"The Crescent! But that is where I am lodging with my aunt and uncle."

"You live in the Crescent?!"

"I do. To think, today you walked beneath our very windows, and I did not know it. We must have just missed each other on the way to the pump-room... Did you like the Crescent?"

"Yes, very much. It is like a half-Colosseum, and the windows are like theatre-boxes, from which the spectators can see everything: the people promenading below, the green fields beyond, and even the city of Bath itself on a sort of stage before them."

"And has the audience not found a most willing and obliging group of actors?" asked Mr. Grey in a lively tone of voice. "Bath's most fashionable and wealthy parade there often, especially of a Sunday, and come to see and be seen as they walk along the Crescent. They play not only to the spectators above but to each other."

"You are quite right," said Georgiana with as much mirth in her voice. "I think that if Mr. Villiers were with us now, he would surely not miss the opportunity to quote Shakespeare in saying:"

All the world's a stage,
And all the men and women merely players[11]

"Without a doubt," she added, smiling, "the Crescent is serving its intended purpose well."

Since the crowd in front of the pumper had by then largely dispersed, Sir Philip led the way to the counter, where the woman serving the water handed him and his companions their cups. Seeing that Georgiana eyed her own cup with some suspicion, Mr. Grey remarked:

"It has been said that 'Bath water is better than Bath wine'. What is your opinion of it, Miss Darcy?"

Georgiana gingerly took a sip of the malodorous contents of her cup and answered, "Whoever said that must have drunk some rather foul-tasting wine. The water is excessively warm and has a pronounced mineral taste. It is difficult to describe it exactly, but it reminds me of what water must taste like after eggs have been boiling in it for a long time. Whence does the water come?"

"The spring is in the middle of the King's Bath," came the reply.

"But do people not bathe in the King's Bath?!"

"They do, indeed," said Mr. Grey with a mischievous twinkle in his eyes, "and when they are finished bathing, the same water then flows directly into the pump-room fountain for the visitors to drink. That way, nothing goes to waste."

For half an instant, Georgiana believed him and looked down in horror at her cup. At the sight of her countenance, the Bingleys, Egertons, and Mr.

Grey himself, could none of them contain their laughter, which was interrupted only by Mr. Bingley's mirthful reprimand:

"You must not say such things, Mr. Grey, or Miss Darcy will never drink the water again!"

Sir Philip then went on to explain in his calm, dignified way, that although the spring really was to be found in the centre of the King's Bath, it was housed in a large cistern at the bottom, from where the water flowed through a pipe straight into the pump-room fountain.

While they were sipping their water, Mr. Grey ventured to ask:

"Miss Darcy, there is a ball at the Upper Rooms tonight. Will I have the pleasure of seeing you there?"

"I... yes," said she, directing her look tentatively at her hosts. "If Mr. and Mrs. Bingley are not opposed, I would very much like to go. They mentioned something of the ball this morning."

Mr. Bingley and his wife exchanged a knowing smile.

"We would be delighted to attend the ball, Miss Darcy—that is, if you feel that you are sufficiently recovered after our journey to take part in dancing," said Jane.

The maiden assured them that she was.

After leaving the pump-room, everything in Bath seemed to Georgiana to be as if in a different light. The buildings, which she had heretofore thought of as 'drab yellow', became a warm, honey colour. The crowds of people, which had previously been a source of tumult and confusion, now gave the city a lively, vibrant aspect. Even the city trees, brown and naked of their leaves in winter, looked beautiful. Gone was Georgiana's headache, gone were her fatigue and listlessness, and she looked forward to the ball at the Upper Rooms with as much—no, with *more* enthusiasm than she had ever done to any dance before.

Observing Georgiana's bright and sunny countenance, Mr. Bingley noted with a significant smile:

"What a remarkable recovery you have made, Miss Darcy! Only this morning, you thought that you would be too unwell to dance, and now you are all eagerness to go to the ball!"

"Oh, ... it must be the Bath mineral water," came Georgiana's sheepish answer. "It had a very reinvigorating effect."

"Oh, yes! Undoubtedly, it was the water," returned Mr. Bingley laughingly. Georgiana coloured a little but made no reply.

CHAPTER 30

Following his return home from the pump-room that morning, Mr. Grey found that time moved exceptionally slowly, which frequently happens when one impatiently watches the clock all day long; but at last, evening came, and with it, the ball. As he was entering the Upper Rooms, the young man still could scarcely believe that Georgiana was now in Bath, and that he might dance with her tonight.

Soon after he came to the Upper Rooms, so did she, and how divinely beautiful she looked! Her gown was a gauze dress over white silk, with delicate sprigs embossed in silver threads on the net. The bodice, in contrast, was of an olive shade and featured embroidery of the same silver as in the skirt, while the short, puffed sleeves accented Georgiana's graceful arms. A silver and pearl comb adorned her hair, which was pulled back smoothly on the sides; terminated in soft, shiny curls at the back; and framed her face in pretty ringlets at the front. Georgiana was exquisite, and in Mr. Grey's eyes, she was the handsomest lady in the ball room, and perhaps in all England.

Their eyes met across the room when she entered, and hardly a minute later, he was beside her. After completing the customary civilities, Mr. Grey inquired about her cousin and Mr. Brooke.

"He and Anne are as happy as can be," replied Georgiana. "The only shadow on their felicity is the disagreement that continues between them and Anne's mother."

"Lady Catherine is still angry, then?"

"Yes, very much so. She is not used to being contradicted or disobeyed, especially by her own daughter. Anne's secret marriage to Mr. Brooke came as a great shock to her."

"I remember Lady Catherine's reaction well," said Mr. Grey. "Her ladyship paid me a visit not long after the wedding took place."

"Oh yes, I heard something of that. I am sorry you had to bear the full force of my aunt's wrath... and that her anger had lasting consequences for you."

"I would not have you feel sorry for me, Miss Darcy. As you see, I am still alive and well after that encounter, and perhaps it is even better that things turned out as they did. Being obliged to leave Hunsford parish gave me a chance to visit my aunt and uncle, which the duties of a curate would have left little time to do."

Mr. Grey also thought to himself that if circumstances had not compelled him to come to Bath, he would not now have the happiness of standing before Georgiana. Be that as it may, he did not give voice to the idea. What he said to her instead was:

"In fact, Miss Darcy, I am soon to have new employment. You see, my uncle has a church living in his gift, which he wishes to give to me at the next presentation of it. A Mr. Hill currently holds the living, but he is to remove to London in March on account of his advanced age and declining health. He wants to live in town, where he can be near to the best physicians, and when Mr. Hill leaves, he will put in a curate. It is my good fortune that the curacy has been offered to me, and of course I have accepted the office.

"That is wonderful news!" exclaimed Georgiana.

The gentleman further told her that he was to have the use of the parsonage-house, which was as comfortable a home and as charmingly situated as any clergyman could wish for. He did not enter into pecuniary particulars with the lady, but the living his uncle had promised him was a good one, 800*l.* a year in fact. Until such time as the living fell vacant, however, the young man's salary as a curate would admittedly be much smaller: 70*l.* per annum was to be his income. This very modest sum he intended to supplement by taking on several pupils.

Mr. Grey was not the only one overjoyed to see Georgiana at the ball. Michael Brydges had also come to the Upper Rooms that evening in hopes that Miss Darcy would be there. When she arrived, he had been dancing, but seeing her now, he eagerly moved through the crowd in her direction. Alas, suddenly noticing an unknown (and concerningly handsome) gentleman who was deeply engaged in conversation with Georgiana, Mr. Brydges paused. He then turned and went towards his sister, who was nearby, and asked her:

"Grace, who is that gentleman over there?"

"I do not know his name, but I saw him come with Sir Philip and Lady Egerton. Perhaps he is some relation of theirs?"

"He does seem very well-acquainted with Miss Darcy, does he not? We must find out who he is."

"I managed to discover the size of Miss Darcy's fortune, though," said Miss Brydges.

"And is it a large one?"

"A well-informed acquaintance tells me that she has thirty thousand pounds."

"Thirty thousand pounds! God has indeed been good to me!" exclaimed Mr. Brydges.

No less enticing than this excellent fortune was the prospect of marrying into the eminent Darcy family, which was an ancient and well-respected one of Norman origin. Furthermore, as the niece of the Earl of —, Miss Darcy could hardly have better connections. Since an earl is influential at court and has the ear of the king, reasoned the gentleman, her uncle could do much to help him advance in politics. Then, also, Miss Darcy's beauty and charm were such that Mr. Brydges should be proud to introduce her to all his acquaintances; he relished the thought that every one of them would admire his choice of wife and think the more highly of him for it, and perhaps even envy him. Almost as much as he enjoyed being envied, the gentleman liked possessing beautiful things, and what a pleasure it would be to feast his eyes on such a glorious wife every day! She would adorn even the finest house that he might hope to acquire.

While Mr. Brydges was absorbed in these enjoyable contemplations, Mr.

Bingley happened to pass by. On perceiving each other, the two men exchanged greetings. Mr. Brydges then introduced Bingley to his sister, and as soon as the opportunity arose, he asked with feigned unconcern:

"That gentleman speaking with Miss Darcy, is it by any chance her brother, Fitzwilliam Darcy?"

"No, that is Mr. Grey. I can introduce the two of you if you like."

"I would be delighted to make his acquaintance."

However, there was less delight than suspicion in Michael Brydges' countenance during the introduction. He immediately disliked his rival; Mr. Grey was just the sort of man a woman could easily fall in love with— handsome, intelligent, amiable, and lively. Mr. Brydges was impatient to learn more about him but even more impatient to dance with Georgiana, and therefore, instead of spending much time on conversation with his new acquaintance, he seized the opportunity to solicit Miss Darcy's hand for the next dance. She had no choice but to accept; yet, as Georgiana was walking away with him, for a brief moment she turned her head to look back at Mr. Grey. He, meanwhile, was inwardly kicking himself for having missed the chance to stand up with Miss Darcy. Why on earth had he not asked her to dance?!

Grace Brydges stayed behind with Mr. Grey, and after they had been chatting together a few minutes, she suddenly had an idea. Seeing a pretty but rather silly, young acquaintance of hers nearby, she addressed her with:

"Miss Pheasant, how lovely to see you here this evening! Come, there is someone I would like you to meet!"

After Miss Brydges had introduced Mr. Grey to the young lady, she asked her, "Have you danced yet this evening, Miss Pheasant?"

"No, Miss Brydges, not yet."

"But you are very fond of dancing?"

"Oh yes, I love it above any other amusement!" cried Miss Pheasant, beaming radiantly at Mr. Grey.

In light of such an obvious hint, the young man did his duty in asking Miss Pheasant to be his partner for the next dance. No sooner had he done so, than Miss Fanny Pheasant came towards them in search of her elder sister. To this young lady Mr. Grey was promptly introduced as well, and before he knew it, he was engaged for not one but both of the next two dances. The poor gentleman could only hope that the Miss Pheasants had no other sisters.

Mr. Brydges, meanwhile, was dancing with Georgiana and endeavouring to learn as much as possible about his rival at the same time.

"Have you known Mr. Grey for long, Miss Darcy?" asked he.

"I made his acquaintance this October in Kent."

"He is a clergyman, I think he said?"

"Yes."

"Is the estate of Mr. Grey's father in Kent?"

"His father is dead."

"And the estate descended to Mr. Grey?" asked Mr. Brydges with suspended breath.

"No, Mr. Grey did not inherit an estate."

"Ah, I see," he brightened. "The estate went to an elder brother, and Mr. Grey had to make do with a church living—an all-too-common fate for younger sons, unfortunately—sentenced to life as a parson."

"No, no, Mr. Brydges. You misunderstand. He has no brothers—he is the only son, and there is no estate."

"So then Mr. Grey only has a church living?"

"He does not yet have a living. Mr. Grey is a curate."

"Now I understand," said Mr. Brydges, though in truth, he did not understand at all. How could Miss Darcy show so much apparent interest in conversing with a man who was nothing more than a country curate?

Although to some extent relieved to learn that Mr. Grey had such meagre prospects as to put him at a significant disadvantage in making a good match, Mr. Brydges was at the same time far from being lulled into a sense of complacence. The level of Georgiana's regard for Mr. Grey was not yet clear, and it would be prudent to keep a watchful eye on the clergyman. For instance, what was his design in coming to Bath? Was it really only to visit his aunt and uncle?

As soon as Georgiana and her partner had finished dancing together, the young man's sister joined them. Miss Brydges had not come to the ball uninformed; in the course of her reconnaissance into Georgiana's life, she discovered from a mutual acquaintance that Miss Darcy was particularly fond of music. Armed with this knowledge, Grace Brydges brought up the subject at the first opportunity. As she expected, Georgiana's countenance lit up at this mention of her favourite pursuit, and having found common ground, she exaggerated her own interest in music. "I cannot imagine my life without it," said Miss Brydges. "One often hears that the responsibilities of married life leave little time for practicing on the pianoforte, but I am determined never to give up my music, not even after I marry."

That day, as Miss Brydges informed Georgiana, was not far off. She was engaged to marry a Mr. Spencer, who owned a large estate in Northamptonshire. Georgiana, in fact, had an opportunity to meet him and his mother later that evening. She noticed that Mr. Spencer had a rather blank, expressionless face and very pale, lustreless eyes. The man did not seem to be particularly interested in anything around him, and after having been introduced to Georgiana, he mumbled something about the weather and shortly afterwards disappeared into the card room. His mother, on the other hand, remained to chat with the ladies.

Meanwhile, Mr. Grey had just finished a dance with the younger of the Miss Pheasants, who had hinted her way into being asked to stand up with him a second time. But at last he was free, and now Mr. Grey came to ask Miss Darcy's hand for the following dance. As he was approaching Georgiana and the ladies standing with her, he overheard Mrs. Spencer lamenting, with a disdainful nod in the direction of the dancers footing it beneath the grand chandeliers, "I remember a time when dancing was elegant and tasteful; these days, young people merely romp about and call it a dance. The minuet—such a dignified, noble, graceful dance—is now all but out of fashion, and everyone instead scampers about hither and thither in the manner of a rowdy peasant. Oh, what is the world coming to!"

Mr. Grey and Georgiana shared a look of amusement, and then he asked her, "May I have the pleasure of the next dance, Miss Darcy?" Lowering his voice a little, he added with a mischievous smile, "That is, if you can bear to take part in such an uncivilised romp!"

"I think we should try to make what we can of it," answered Georgiana with a laugh. "But I have seen you dance, Mr. Grey, and if you continue to do it as well as you have been until now, I think you may yet add some elegance to an otherwise uncouth evening. I am sure even Mrs. Spencer could not find fault with your dancing!"

As the music began, Mr. Grey caught sight of Mr. Brydges a few couples down. He was partnered with Miss Spencer, his future sister-in-law; and clearly displeased to see the curate stand up with Miss Darcy, he was glowering at him. Mr. Grey smiled a little at the comical sight of the gentleman's scowling countenance. Perceiving his amusement but not knowing the cause, Georgiana inquired, "What is so humorous?"

Her partner recollected himself and answered, "I was just thinking, Miss Darcy, that although we have been acquainted since October, this is the first time that I have had the opportunity of dancing with you."

"You never had a chance to do so before?" asked Georgiana teasingly. "Perhaps my eyes deceived me, but I believe you danced with more than one lady this evening before you ever asked me."

"You are right, of course," replied Mr. Grey, "and there is little I can offer in my defence except to say that some of your friends were tonight most eager that I should increase my circle of acquaintance. They meant well, I am sure, but I find that the efforts of such well-wishers can make it difficult to dance with her with whom one really wishes to dance."

Colouring a little, Georgiana smiled shyly and then changed the subject. The rest of the evening passed very enjoyably. Mr. Grey was a most agreeable partner, not only because he was one of the best dancers in the room, but also because of his cheerful, lively, and interesting conversation. Georgiana found herself constantly smiling in his company and wondering how it was that he had failed to make any impression on her heart before she came to Bath.

CHAPTER 31

So sure was Mr. Brydges of his destiny that he had looked forward to winning Georgiana's heart with little effort. When, contrary to his expectations, he received his first indication at the ball that Miss Darcy would not be an easy conquest, doubts began to creep into his mind. These concerns Mr. Brydges shared with his sister as they sat together in their drawing room late in the afternoon on the day following the ball.

"Miss Darcy is certainly very polite to me, but I fear that her feelings for me do not extend beyond civility," lamented Mr. Brydges. "She seems more interested in talking to that curate, Mr. Grey."

"You must be patient, Michael," his sister reassured him. "Too many men concede defeat when the battle has hardly begun. I tell you that *any* woman can be cajoled into falling in love. Even if she is made of stone, persistent attentions will wear down the hard exterior until the heart is reached. You must not be so hasty in retreating from the battlefield."

"Even so, there is another circumstance that concerns me," said Mr. Brydges. "Regardless of what Miss Darcy's feelings for me may become in the future, there is still the matter of her brother; Mr. Darcy is her guardian, and he could very well forbid the match. No doubt, he wishes his sister to marry title and fortune, neither of which I can supply."

"A fortune you do not yet possess, perhaps, but a title is not so wholly beyond your grasp, is it?"

"You are not thinking that I ought to make a second attempt at the Chandos barony?!"

"Well, why not?"

"Sister, you know that nothing would please me more than to become a baron, but you cannot have forgotten that my first claim was unsuccessful; the case was adjourned *sine die* due to insufficient evidence that there is any connection between my own family and the Brydges, Lords Chandos. A second attempt would likely meet with the same fate as the first."

"Ah, but what if the required evidence were to be supplied?" suggested Miss Brydges. "An original parish record would, I am sure, be sufficiently convincing proof that your ancestors are indeed the descendants of John Brydges, the first Baron Chandos of Sudeley, and therefore, that you have a rightful claim to the barony after all."

Then, lowering her voice (even though there was no one present who could possibly overhear them), she continued:

"After the passage of many decades, the ink in parish registers is already half-faded. With a little effort, an entry could be obliterated altogether, and a new, more suitable one made in its place."

A smile spread slowly across Mr. Brydges' face. "Yes, I believe you are right! What an excellent idea!" he exclaimed. "Why did I not think of it before? Only, ... there is one consideration that gives me pause: in order to alter the parish register, it will be necessary for me to travel to Sussex, which I am reluctant to do. If I am to secure Miss Darcy's affections, I must remain in Bath and make the most of the limited time we have together."

"Yes, I see what you mean," said Miss Brydges thoughtfully.

After some further discussion, Mr. Brydges and his sister thought of a different way: they would write to their younger brother and ask him to arrange everything in relation to the parish register. As he owed Mr. Brydges a favour, he was likely to agree. In the meantime, the elder brother would stay on in Bath and woo Miss Darcy. Once the necessary evidence was ready, Michael Brydges could make a claim for the barony once more, and this time, it was hoped, he would succeed.

Wishing to put their plan into action without delay, Mr. Brydges immediately took up his pen and began to write the letter. Dusk was gathering, and although it was still light enough to see outside, it was too dim indoors for letter-writing, so his sister lit a candle. He then bent over the page, while she walked back and forth across the room and dictated. Several minutes elapsed in this manner. The letter was nearing completion, when, as Miss Brydges passed a window, she happened to see a carriage stop not far from their house, and a few seconds later, Mr. Bingley stepped out.

"Brother!" cried she. "Mr. Bingley is outside. He has come to call on us!"

Looking up from his letter with an alarmed countenance, Mr. Brydges called out:

"Make haste! Make haste! Hide the tallow candle!"

Dashing about in panic, they lit several wax candles and extinguished the tallow one, but there still remained one problem.

"We must do something about the smell! One whiff of the air, and Mr. Bingley will know that we have been burning a tallow candle!" cried Mr. Brydges.

They hastily opened the windows, and then bother and sister both fanned the air desperately, madly—he with a newspaper and she with her shawl.

After the offensive odour had cleared tolerably, Miss Brydges and her brother seated themselves decorously and waited for some sound to indicate that Mr. Bingley had entered their house and was being led up to the drawing room by a servant. Strangely, there was no such sound, nor any other sign of Mr. Bingley. Soon the reason became clear—when Mr. Bingley stopped in Queen Square, it had not been to call on the Brydges but to see a friend in one of the neighbouring houses.

Amid discontented sighs, Mr. Brydges and his sister retrieved the tallow candle and lit it once more, while the costly wax candles were extinguished. All that frantic activity had been for nothing! Even so, it was not long to wait before a real opportunity of conversing with Mr. Bingley presented itself, for the very next day, Mr. Brydges received an invitation to dine with the Bingleys.

CHAPTER 32

M ichael Brydges was the son of a pious clergyman. As a boy, young Michael spent many an evening listening to his father read aloud from either the Bible or some other religious text, especially works by Richard Baxter. Not infrequently, the lad heard wise words such as:

Choose that employment or calling... in which you may be most serviceable to God. Choose not that in which you may be most rich or honourable in the world; but that in which you may do most good, and best escape sinning.[12]

Michael Brydges gave much thought to these devout words and came to the conclusion that God wished for him to become a barrister. That the law, more than any other profession, was the surest path to riches and distinction was purely coincidental, as far as he was concerned. To Oxford, then, went Mr. Brydges to study the law, and at that fine institution he learned a great number of useful things, not the least of which was the art of dress. Early on he discovered the importance of choosing attire in line with the life he aspired to have rather than the one he actually possessed. He believed that to dress like beggars on the street makes one fit for their society alone, while to dress like a king opens possibilities to reach the very heights to which one might aspire. To his toilette, therefore, Mr. Brydges devoted a considerable amount of time and attention to ensure that every-thing from the knot in his cravat to the shine of his boots was absolutely perfect.

When dressing for dinner with the Bingleys and Miss Darcy, he took even greater pains with his appearance than usual. Conscious of the need to impress Georgiana and make the most of his God-given opportunity, the gentleman selected his most elegant coat for the occasion, and to his hair he applied his best pomatum. When the time came to arrange his cravat, he tied and retied it several times before he was satisfied, but just when he had succeeded in knotting the cravat properly, Mr. Brydges decided on a more elaborate knot and had to begin all over again. After some struggle, he finally arranged the cravat to his satisfaction, and pleased overall with his ensemble, he next reached for a bottle of eau de Cologne.

As with everything relating to his appearance and the impression he made on others, Michael Brydges put great care into his choice of eau de Cologne. When an Oxford student, he had worn 'Freshman', a popular scent among the more fashionable of his fellow students. After Mr. Brydges' university days were over, he decided it was time for a new eau de Cologne. Accordingly, he sniffed all the fragrances on offer at a shop in London's St. James's Street and narrowed his choices down to two: 'Mayfair' and 'Albany'. The former scent was named after the desirable part of London, where, as the reader may remember, the Villiers family owned a house. The second eau de Cologne, 'Albany', had been named after an exclusive London residential building that offered apartments mainly to single, wealthy gentlemen—no ladies or children allowed. After much deliberation, Mr. Brydges selected 'Mayfair'. It must be admitted that he preferred the smell of 'Albany', but he rejected it on the following grounds: first, he wished to live in Mayfair himself someday, and second (even more importantly), Albany's association with bachelorhood made the eau de Cologne with the same name a somewhat hazardous choice. It could very well bring bad luck and cause him to remain a bachelor forever! Mr. Brydges entertained fond hopes of marrying a lady of large fortune, and choosing 'Albany', he feared, would serve only to tempt fate.

After completing his toilette, Mr. Brydges made his way to the Paragon Buildings, and in Mr. Bingley's house he was received with kind politeness.

At dinner, the gentleman proved himself a most agreeable and adulatory guest, complimenting the Bingleys on everything from their tasteful furnishings, to the splendid dinner, to the china from which they ate. When Mr. Bingley happened to mention Mr. Darcy, Michael Brydges was very eager to hear more about him and was especially pleased to learn that Lady Catherine de Bourgh was his aunt. He knew something of her ladyship; he had seen her in church on one of her visits to London, and an acquaintance told him of her grand estate in Kent. Lady Catherine de Bourgh was clearly a woman of immense wealth and importance, and that Miss Darcy should have such an illustrious aunt could not help but add to the young lady's attractions.

At the table, Mr. Brydges spoke a good deal of his ambitions for the future, and in particular, his belief that he would be the next Baron Chandos of Sudeley; but, he said, as he had yet to bring his case before Parliament, for the present his thoughts were mainly occupied by his profession as a barrister, in which position he hoped to achieve distinction. Naturally, he also expected to advance to King's Counsel.

What the gentleman neglected to tell the Bingleys and Miss Darcy was that since being called to the bar, he had not yet received a single brief nor once appeared before a court; in consequence, he had made nothing at all in fees. Things might have been different had Mr. Brydges aimed a little lower. As a solicitor, for example, he would have had plenty of work. The trouble was that solicitors were obliged to accept money directly from clients—a degradation that placed them not much higher than common merchants. By becoming a barrister, he managed to avoid the ignominy of being in trade, and new doors of opportunity flew open before him; he might become anybody and attain the highest rank for which noble birth was not a prerequisite. Moreover, his future wife and any daughters could be presented at court—an honour of which solicitors could not boast.

The only disadvantage of his present circumstances was that as a barrister, his services could not be engaged directly, so Mr. Brydges had no choice but to wait until some solicitor brought him a brief. He therefore spent most of his days at Westminster Hall and looked on with a jealous eye as other barristers cut a fine figure at the bar or swaggered about with briefs tucked under their arms, while he himself had nothing better to do than waste good shoe leather walking to and from Westminster each day—either that or read Blackstone's *An Analysis of the Laws of England* (dry, horrid stuff!) in chambers. One might starve to death in the interim.

Fortunately, Mr. Brydges was a master at living frugally and had laid by enough money on which to subsist until such time as he might receive his first brief. The avenues for economy were many: from lighting only one candle in the evenings, to doing without entertainments such as concerts and plays, to borrowing books from the circulating library or from acquaintances rather than buying his own. Paper was dear, so Mr. Brydges kept his business correspondence as short and concise as possible. The longer letters to his family were always crossed; after filling a page with his news, he would rotate the paper and write the rest across what he had already written. As to wine, he drank an inexpensive kind but kept a much better bottle on hand should an important visitor happen to call.

Although in general he practiced the strictest frugality, one area in which Mr. Brydges allowed himself greater liberty was his toilette. It was his firm conviction that saving on personal appearance was false economy since the rank of one's social connections usually decreased in proportion to the cheapness of one's garments. In consequence, every article of his clothing was of the latest fashion and the highest quality regardless of the tailor's bill. As to his hair, Mr. Brydges entrusted it to be cut at no other place but Truefitt's in London. If King George III and Beau Brummell thought the establishment worthy of their patronage, it must be the best!

Mr. Brydges' refined taste did not go unnoticed; Georgiana considered both his hair and his attire to be very elegant and worthy of admiration. Notwithstanding, the Bingleys' dinner guest would have made a better impression on her if he had dressed with less meticulous perfection, for Georgiana was of the opinion that excessive attention to the details of dress often signalled a shallowness of mind and a preoccupation with oneself to the exclusion of more worthwhile cares and pursuits.

After dinner, Georgiana played Mozart for the party, and Mr. Brydges listened with rapt attention. At the conclusion of her performance, he cried, "Miss Darcy, it was a pleasure—nay, an honour to hear such fine music, produced, if I may say so, by your fair hands!" The gentleman continued with similar exclamations of praise, and when on the next tune Georgiana played *and* sang, he could scarcely find the words to adequately express his ecstasy. A more chivalrous and gallant wooer never was seen, and when Michael Brydges left the Bingleys' house, he felt very pleased with himself, confident that he had made a favourable impression. Mr. Bingley and his wife indeed could not dispute that their guest's conversation had been agreeable, and they had nothing in the way of criticism to say against him, but at the same time, they were uncertain whether they would like to invite him to dinner often in the future.

CHAPTER 33

Having been invited to dine at Sir Philip and Lady Egerton's house one afternoon, Georgiana and the Bingleys set out for the Crescent in advance of the appointed hour. As their carriage navigated through the streets, Mr. Bingley remarked that three o'clock was rather early to be having dinner, especially in town. "Not that I mind an early dinner," said he. "Though I have fallen into the habit of dining on the late side, as is the custom in London, it seems to me that unless one eats a fairly substantial meal at midday, one is famished by the time dinner comes around."

"And, it is not so very early, is it?" asked Jane. "My grandfather and grandmother Bennet usually dined at three or half past in order to make the most of the daylight hours."

Her husband replied, "Come to think of it, so did my parents when I was a boy. I do believe the established dinner hour creeps a little later every decade."

The Royal Crescent, in all its Rome-like glory, soon presented itself to their view. Before long, the carriage came to a stop, and the party alighted into the heart of the half-amphitheatre. Georgiana and her companions walked the short distance to the door, which was answered by a consummately dignified, yet very pleasant butler. He led the guests up to the drawing room, where Sir Philip and his wife received them very cordially. However, no one was more pleased to see the visitors than Mr. Grey, who had been looking out impatiently for their arrival during the last quarter of an hour.

When the company sat down to dinner, Sir Philip observed, "I am afraid we keep somewhat unfashionable hours, but I find that it is so much more pleasant to dine by daylight than to wait until it is almost dark. Candles never provide sufficient illumination unless one lights a great many."

Fashionable or unfashionable, Georgiana liked everything very much. Bright, cheerful sunlight streamed in through the windows, and the room had an atmosphere of warmth and comfort. There was nothing stiff or formal, nothing ostentatious about the dinner party. No elaborate epergnes adorned the table to block the view of fellow diners seated opposite, and the china, like the Egertons' dress and manners, was simple and elegant. The food that was served had clearly been chosen for its flavour rather than its costliness or rarity; the relatively inexpensive John Dory fish was favoured over the costlier (but less tasty) turbot; and instead of exotic dainties, the footmen carried in desserts created from beautifully ripe, though common-place, English fruit.

After dinner, the ladies had not long to wait before the men rejoined them. Mr. Grey chose a chair beside Miss Darcy in the drawing room, and then the pair talked a little of the music and theatre on offer in Bath. He ventured to recommend an opera he had attended recently in which the singers, in his opinion, were of the highest calibre.

"There is no shortage of amusements in Bath," the gentleman added, "but I must confess that I already feel myself growing a little restless in town. The peace of the country holds a greater appeal to me, and I miss doing duty in a parish. Though the work of a clergyman is not what one might call exciting, perhaps, there is a certain joy in occupying one's time in something useful and worthwhile that I do not find in fashionable entertainments."

"Mr. Grey, how did you come to choose the church as your profession rather than, say, the army or the law?" asked Georgiana.

"I am no warrior, so of all the possible vocations, the army was the least suitable for me. There was a time when I considered going into the law, or at least, that was my father's wish for me."

"Was the law his own profession?"

"No, he was a clergyman, but he wanted a different life for me. My father felt that if I went into the law, I would never want for anything and would live in comfort and prosperity."

"But you decided that comfort and prosperity were not to your liking," returned Georgiana with a playful smile.

"Not exactly," laughed Mr. Grey, "but I made up my mind in favour of the church after visiting a friend who was then studying the law. He showed me his books, and looking through them, I found the reading so dry and unpalatable that it became obvious I had no natural inclination for the law; I knew that if I were to enter that profession, I would be miserable for life. From that day, my path was clear. I chose to pursue Divinity at Oxford, and the more I progressed with my studies, the more convinced I became that the church is indeed my calling."

There was a momentary quiet, and then the gentleman suddenly said, "Miss Darcy, you may have noticed Lady Egerton's harp in the room. I have heard it mentioned that you are skilled at playing the instrument. Would you play something for us on the harp?"

"Oh yes, please do," urged Lady Egerton. "Mr. Grey has been telling us of your talent for music, and we are all eager to hear you play."

"Certainly—I will be glad to, although I am not such a master of the harp as I would like to be," returned Georgiana. "Do you play it much yourself, Lady Egerton?"

"I do sometimes, but not as often as in my youth. I prefer the pianoforte."

Mr. Grey added, "The harp is in great need of exercise. So far, I have only heard Miss Fellowes play it a little, and she is still learning."

"Miss Fellowes?"

"My niece," explained Lady Egerton. "She left us this morning to visit a friend, but perhaps she may return in time for you to meet her."

A little shyly, Georgiana went to the harp. Seating herself, she rested the instrument lightly on her shoulder and began to pluck its strings. The piece she chose was a slow, delicate tune that was very soothing to the ears of the listeners. Watching her play, Mr. Grey thought to himself that in her white muslin dress, and with her hair framing her face in soft ringlets, Miss Darcy truly looked like an angel from heaven at the harp. With maidenly timidity,

Georgiana's eyes met his from time to time while she played. Mr. Grey found it very endearing. As he directed his gaze at her, he was convinced that she was the sweetest, loveliest young lady of his acquaintance.

Simple though the pleasures of that evening were, Georgiana would not have exchanged them for the merriest ball or the most glittering party. In her estimation, nothing was more perfect than this tranquil moment, in which she was playing the music she loved in the company of wonderful, kind people... and, if she must admit it to herself, she was especially happy to be in the society of Mr. Grey, of whom she found herself thinking more and more with each passing day.

Yet, like all such interludes of perfect happiness, it was destined to come to an end, and all too soon. Not five minutes after Miss Darcy had finished the tune, a young lady approximately her own age unexpectedly entered the room. She was introduced to Georgiana as Miss Fellowes, the Egertons' niece. The newcomer seemed to be an amiable sort of girl with a genial countenance, and, as she informed Georgiana, she too was very interested in music. "Miss Fellowes has an extraordinary voice," added Mr. Grey, and at his urging, she agreed to sing for the company.

As Georgiana listened, she saw that Mr. Grey had not exaggerated; Miss Fellowes had an uncommonly beautiful voice. Her divine soprano was one of the best she had ever heard, and though Miss Darcy rarely experienced jealousy, the emotion awoke from its slumber with surprising force on this occasion. If Georgiana had instead heard that same young lady perform at the opera, she would have listened to her with awe and admiration, but the thought that Mr. Grey had heard that enchanting, melodious voice over the course of numerous evenings was strangely distressing to her.

Georgiana found herself wishing that if Miss Fellowes was to be so very accomplished, she would at least also be very plain, and perhaps also dull with a disagreeable temperament. Alas, quite the opposite was true. Miss Fellowes was unfortunately rather pretty, with large, brown eyes and a winning smile. Her conversation was interesting, and her manners affable and pleasing.

When Georgiana danced with Mr. Grey at the Upper Rooms several days previously, she thought that he seemed to be paying her particular attentions, but now she was no longer sure. Perhaps his affections were already engaged by another. Having stayed for some time in the same house as Miss Fellowes, could he have resisted the charms of such a songbird?

In her mind, Georgiana could envision with alarming clarity in what manner recent evenings at the Egertons' home must have passed: the beguiling nightingale luring Mr. Grey with her sweet songs of love, and he, in turn, gazing upon her with dreamy admiration. The image was too disheartening for words! The more Miss Darcy imagined the scene, the more miserable she became.

Miss Fellowes was much applauded when she finished her song. Notwithstanding that Georgiana was by then quite dispirited, she tried not to betray her feelings but instead smiled and made the proper replies when necessary. Yet, her eyes could not hide their sadness, and while the others chatted with Miss Fellowes, Georgiana grew very quiet. This change in her demeanour went largely unnoticed since everyone's attention had shifted to the talented songstress.

As Georgiana was rising to leave for home with Jane and Mr. Bingley, Mr. Grey invited her for a walk the following day. "Miss Fellowes and I had planned to take a stroll in the Sydney Gardens tomorrow, and if you are able to join us, we would both greatly enjoy your company," said he.

"Join you and Miss Fellowes?" repeated Georgiana in a doleful tone of voice.

"Yes, that is, if you are not otherwise engaged."

It was with surprise that Mr. Grey observed Miss Darcy's apparent dismay at his invitation. At first he was at a loss to imagine what might have provoked this reaction, but suddenly fathoming a possible explanation for her cheerlessness, the gentleman added, "I should mention that there is one more person who will be accompanying us on our walk. His name is Mr. Amherst. He is a good friend of mine and is more than that to Miss Fellowes—he is her intended."

"Then, Miss Fellowes is engaged?!"

"Yes. The two of them grew up together in the same house. Miss Fellowes is the ward of Mr. Amherst's father. Even as children, she and the younger Mr. Amherst were very attached to each other, and now they are to be married."

Georgiana could not have been happier for Miss Fellowes than if she had been a bosom friend, or even her own sister. What a change did the news of her betrothal produce in Miss Darcy's countenance, and how wholeheartedly did she wish the Egertons' niece joy in marriage! Far from objecting to an outing with Mr. Grey and Miss Fellowes, Georgiana was now delighted to accompany them.

CHAPTER 34

It snowed overnight. Georgiana awoke to a city painted in white; everything, it seemed, was veiled in copious layers of soft, pale gossamer, each snowflake a miracle of icy lacework. While admiring the scene from a window, she marvelled at the transformative effect that nature had produced on even the relatively uninteresting, stone fortress-like part of town in which she and her hosts were lodging.

Georgiana's thoughts soon turned to the walk that was fixed on for that day. Would the cold weather and the snow prevent it? She hoped not. It would take more than a few snowflakes to deter *her* from keeping the engagement! She need not have feared, however, for nothing short of a snowstorm would have induced Mr. Grey to give up an opportunity of meeting with Miss Darcy; and Miss Fellowes, in her turn, was very curious to learn more of the lady whom she suspected of having conquered the young man's heart.

With everyone so eager, they all came for the outing in spite of the weather. Mr. Amherst, who was one of the party as promised, was a very amiable gentleman. He and his betrothed appeared to be well-suited, and from their manner it was evident that they were very fond of each other.

Of the four of them, Georgiana was the only one who had never been to the Sydney Gardens before. Mr. Grey therefore suggested that they first go to the most interesting part of the park: the labyrinth. No one being opposed, they all proceeded thither.

The maze was a splendid creation full of serpentine twists and turns, and as the young people were entering its green corridors, Mr. Grey asked Georgiana how she liked it.

"Oh, very much!" came her enthusiastic answer. "It looks almost like something out of a fairy tale. I would not be surprised if the labyrinth that King Henry II built for Rosamund Clifford, so that she could hide in it if the jealous queen should come searching for her, looked much like this one. Of course, whether that labyrinth even existed, or whether it was merely a legend, no one knows for sure, but it is nevertheless a beautiful story. Even if there was no labyrinth, I think King Henry must have loved Rosamund dearly."

"Perhaps he loved his wife too when he first married her," remarked Miss Fellowes.

"Do you really think so?" Georgiana queried. "I am not suggesting that Henry II disliked her, but maybe he married Queen Eleanor more out of state interest and duty than love."

Miss Fellowes replied, "Eleanor of Aquitaine is said to have been a great beauty and also very accomplished and charming. She had no shortage of admirers, and if King Henry was like most men, his queen must have had at least some claim on his affections at the start of their marriage."

"He may have admired her beauty and her talents, but perhaps he never really loved anyone until he met Rosamund," suggested Georgiana.

"Possibly, but if that were the case, why was he not faithful to his dear Rosamund? It is widely known that Henry II had many mistresses."

This observation silenced Georgiana. She could not dispute that a man cannot really be said to love a woman if he is not constant to her.

"I do not mean to sound cynical," continued Miss Fellowes, "only, how often do we see such scenes repeated, and not just among kings and queens?! How many enter into marriage hoping to capture marital bliss, and how few actually find it! To wed is to plunge into the unknown. All too frequently, couples leap headfirst into matrimony only to afterwards wish they had remained on the shore!"

"You sound almost as if you are beginning to regret our engagement," teased Mr. Amherst.

"No, not in the least," replied his betrothed. "I hardly think that it is possible for us to become indifferent to each other if we have not yet done so after this many years together. I was merely speaking of other people and of marriage in general."

"Do you think that we are really so very different from other couples?" asked the gentleman.

"Well, yes. You and I grew up in the same house; we shaped one another's tastes and opinions and had ample time to discover all each other's little faults as well as to become convinced of the merits. An attachment of this nature is firm and lasting. How many other couples instead hasten to the altar after scarcely a few weeks' acquaintance! Spurred on by a burning passion, they are barely more than strangers when they marry, and within several months of the wedding, their ardour degenerates into indifference or even dislike."

"What a bleak picture you have painted!" exclaimed Mr. Amherst. "And is it fair to compare everyone else with ourselves, who have known each other for nearly two decades?! Is such a lengthy acquaintance before marriage truly necessary? Surely a much shorter period of time will suffice provided that the task of selecting a husband or wife is approached cautiously and prudently, with proper consideration given to whether the prospective spouse possesses the qualities desired in a helpmate."

Remembering her own carelessness and foolish haste in agreeing to marry Sir Matthew, Georgiana felt quite chastened. Her countenance grew clouded at the memory of that unpleasant history. Perceiving her grave looks, Mr. Grey inquired whether all was well.

"Oh yes, perfectly," answered Georgiana, recollecting herself, "but to what Mr. Amherst has said, I would add that just as one cannot be too assiduous in detecting the faults of a prospective partner before marriage, it is better to cast a rather lenient and uncritical eye on one's companion afterwards. All too often, people do just the opposite; they see only perfections before the wedding, and nothing but faults and shortcomings in the years that follow. Yet, what man or woman on earth can ever hope to live up to the extraordinary ideal that each initially imagined of the other? Would it not be better for husbands and wives to lay aside the habit of fault-finding and instead notice the virtues rather than the defects?"

Mr. Grey replied, "That would indeed be a much wiser course of action, but I believe it is equally important for married persons to endeavour to deserve each other's love and each day to strive to be worthy of the affection and esteem of their chosen companion, and likewise, not to forget to continue those agreeable attentions that helped win the other's love in the days of courtship."

For a minute or two, the company walked silently, each of them contemplating both the sweets and the difficulties of the married state. Close by in the labyrinth, they could hear the muffled sound of voices, where two young ladies were apparently strolling in a neighbouring corridor. Their conversation was not very audible at first, and only occasionally could a word such as 'dancing' or 'ball' be faintly made out; but as Georgiana and the rest walked on, the volume of the speech became sufficiently high that the party could hear the ladies' dialogue quite clearly.

"How handsome is Mr. Grey!" exclaimed one of them.

"Such melting, blue eyes, such a fine form, and so amusing too!" agreed the other. "I do not think I have ever met a man whose manners or person I liked more, which makes me all the more determined to have him for my husband!"

"What makes you think that he will choose you over me?" came the indignant reply.

"Well, for one thing, he danced twice with me at the ball and only once with you," was the answer.

Georgiana could scarcely restrain herself from laughing. Glancing at Mr. Grey, she was highly amused to see that he looked somewhat discomfited. What she heard next, however, sobered her countenance considerably.

"Do not buy your wedding clothes just yet, Fanny," said one of the ladies. "If I were you, I would instead give some thought to Miss Darcy, with whom Mr. Grey seemed quite taken at last Thursday's ball. He appeared to prefer her society to either yours or mine, and if you ask me, she seemed far from objecting to his attentions. If we do not act quickly, *she* will become Mrs. Grey before you or I do."

Her confidante asked, "What do you propose we do?"

The first one answered, "For a start, Mama must invite Mr. Grey to dinner. Unless we see more of him, how is he to fall in love with one of us?"

Although Mr. Grey was not in the habit of blushing, in general, on this occasion his face was the shade of a raspberry, and Georgiana was coloured to match. They both faced straight forward and did not once dare look at each other. Perceiving their mortification, Mr. Amherst suggested that they all leave the labyrinth to explore some other part of the gardens. This proposal being eagerly agreed to, the company turned around to go back the way they had come. They rounded one corner, then another, and when they were approaching the third, suddenly those same chattering voices rang out again, but this time they were quite near—just on the other side of the wall of green, in fact. Instead of moving further away from those face-less damsels, as was intended, they had meandered directly towards them! It was too late to do anything about it now, unfortunately. A moment later, the talkative pair appeared from behind the shrubs.

The unknown speakers were thus unmasked; they were the Miss Pheasants, the same two girls whom Miss Brydges had taken the trouble of bringing to Mr. Grey's notice at the ball in the Upper Rooms. The sisters' embarrassed astonishment was beyond description. They stared, they gaped and looked as if they wished to disappear. The clipped hedge all around had given the sisters a false sense of invisibility and solitude, but seeing Mr. Grey and his fellow walkers now, they realised that the footsteps they had heard while discussing the gentleman must have belonged to him and his friends.

No dignified means of escape being possible, the Miss Pheasants were obliged to acknowledge their acquaintances and say a few polite words, but afterwards they hurried away deeper into the labyrinth as quickly as their feet could carry them. For a considerable length of time after that awkward encounter and the conversation that had preceded it, Georgiana could not gather sufficient courage to utter more than a few syllables. How mortify-ing it was to have had herself and her suitor discussed so explicitly, and in others' hearing too! What must Mr. Grey be thinking at this moment? The idea was too agonising for contemplation.

Despite his own feelings, the young man, and Mr. Amherst and Miss Fellowes too, took pains to behave as if nothing out of the ordinary had just happened. They instead directed their attention to the interesting scenes before them: waterfalls, groves, a grotto, and various other delightful features. Georgiana made some attempt to join in their chat, but memories of that other, much more memorable conversation, still reverberated in her ears. Yet, after a time, she began to think how silly it was to allow others' ideas and opinions ruin the lovely outing. She could not prevent people from thinking or speaking, and moreover, neither she nor Mr. Grey had done anything to be ashamed of, which was all that mattered. Rather than dwelling on what she could not change, how much more sensible it was to enjoy the scenic stroll, the entertaining remarks of her comrades, and, if she must own it to herself, the pleasures of Mr. Grey's society.

After looking at some picturesque mock castle ruins inside the gardens, the ladies and gentlemen came to a bridge over a canal that cut through the park. By now, the late morning sun had gathered enough strength to begin thawing the snow in earnest, and as its feeble rays touched the earth, the soft, white blanket that covered everything began to turn into a wet slush. Nevertheless, this change did little to diminish the pleasantness of the walk for Georgiana, whose mind was very agreeably occupied with thoughts of Mr. Grey.

While they were crossing the bridge, she admired the Chinese-style, cast iron balustrade and then looked out at the water stretching beyond, though she should perhaps instead have been watching beneath her feet. There was a price to pay for this inattention. All of a sudden, just as the company had passed the midway point of the bridge, Georgiana slipped on the half-melted snow. She struggled for balance, fought to regain her footing, but alas! The force of gravity proved too much, and the next thing she felt was the sickening awareness of falling backwards.

An instant before she hit the hard surface, Mr. Grey caught her in his arms. The young lady felt the pace of her heart quicken, but whether the cause was the momentary terror of having nearly fallen, or whether it was the gentleman's proximity to herself as he assisted her to her feet, she could not tell. Having raised Georgiana back up, Mr. Grey's arm lingered about her shoulders a moment longer than was strictly necessary; the sensation thrilled her frame and brought a brighter tint to her cheeks. She could not, however, help feeling mightily foolish and clumsy. What a sight she must have been, with her limbs flailing in all directions before her narrowly-missed tumble! It was about as much embarrassment as a lady could endure in one day!

During the rest of the walk, the gentleman offered her his arm whenever there was even the slightest danger of falling on an icy patch or on sloping ground. To Georgiana's view, he was perhaps being a little overly cautious, but his attentions and concern for her safety were far from being unwelcome to her, and truth be told, on further reflection she did not in the least regret having ventured out that morning on paths still covered with snow.

CHAPTER 35

On Christmas Eve, there was to be a dinner party at the Bingleys'. Among the many invitations that Jane sent, there was one for Michael Brydges and his family. The gentleman felt very pleased to have been invited, and filled with a renewed sense of purpose and belief in his destiny, Mr. Brydges set out for the Paragon on the appointed day. Along the way, he carefully rehearsed what he would say and how he would behave to-wards Miss Darcy. Afterwards, he indulged in a little day-dream, in which he was Baron Chandos of Sudeley, and by his side at the altar, on the day of his wedding, was Miss Darcy. Smiling, he turned to look at the wedding guests, among whom were Mr. Darcy and his wife, of course, as well as Lady Catherine de Bourgh and her daughter, and all his future friends from the House of Lords.

These pleasant thoughts were interrupted only by the chance sight of his reflection in a window, which caught his eye just as he almost reached Mr. Bingley's house. Stopping to examine his reflection more closely, Mr. Brydges turned his head first in one direction, then slowly in the other. He ran his hands through his hair several times to arrange it better, and pleased with the improvements, he finally walked on with a self-satisfied smile.

Assembled in the Bingleys' drawing room were a good deal more guests than Mr. Brydges had expected; the gentleman had envisioned a small, intimate dinner party, but here were so many people that he wondered how they would all fit around the dining table. He was received very politely by the host and hostess but was disappointed to find that there was no possibility of saying anything of consequence to Miss Darcy, who was at that moment surrounded by a circle of young men, all vying for her attention. Mr. Brydges therefore spoke for a time on indifferent subjects with a few of the other guests and afterwards chatted a little with Mr. Bingley. The latter inquired after the health of Mr. Brydges' mother and sister, to which his guest replied that both ladies were in excellent health but regretted having been unable to attend the dinner party on account of a prior engagement. Then, nodding in the direction of Jane Bingley and Georgiana, both of whom were engaged in conversation with Mr. Grey, he remarked, "I see that Mr. Grey is often with you of late."

"Yes, he has become a good friend," said Mr. Bingley, and then added, "I have discovered that he is an Oxford man. Mr. Grey was a student at our university at approximately the same time that we were."

"Was he indeed?" exclaimed Mr. Brydges, making a great effort to conceal his distaste for the clergyman. "What a pity we never chanced to make his acquaintance until recently."

With a nod of agreement, Mr. Bingley returned, "Yes, he is an excellent fellow. Do you know, after his father's death, it was not in his family's power to pay for his education at Oxford, but Mr. Grey's determination and strength of will were so great that he managed it on his own without any assistance from his relations."

"Do you mean to say that Sir Philip Egerton did not support his nephew at Oxford?"

"No, he did not. In fact, I understand that for many years, Sir Philip and Mr. Grey's father were not on speaking terms on account of some family dispute. It is only lately that the two families have been able to reconcile."

Mr. Brydges was exceedingly surprised by this intelligence; he took the news silently but thought gleefully to himself that with no financial support from his family, Mr. Grey must surely have been a servitor at Oxford. During his own time at that university, Mr. Brydges had been a batteler— the lowest rank of the independent students—a painful fact that he preferred to forget. How he had chafed at having to wear a woollen robe and subsist on bread and cheese from the buttery, when what he longed for the most was to wear a fine silk robe and partake of meat, vegetables, and sweets at the same table as the noblemen! At least, however, he had been spared the humiliation of being a servitor, who had no choice but to live off the scraps from the wealthy man's table and pay for his education by serving meals in the dining hall.

While Mr. Brydges was thus ruminating, a servant came to announce that dinner was served, and as the ladies and gentlemen proceeded down the stairs to the dining room, Mr. Brydges imagined how Mr. Grey must have looked when carrying trays of food from the university kitchen. The thought gave him great pleasure, and his mind returned to it often during the dinner.

At the table, Georgiana was seated with Mr. Grey on her left and Mr. Brydges on her right. No sooner had they taken their seats, than the latter gentleman said to her:

"Miss Darcy, I have some news regarding my claim to the barony of Chandos. My case is now being reviewed by the Committee for Privileges in Parliament."

"That is excellent, Mr. Brydges. I wish you every success."

Then turning away to Mr. Grey, Georgiana began telling him about some amusing incident she had witnessed at the Duke of Kingston baths.

Mr. Brydges thought it strange that Miss Darcy did not seem at all interested in his glittering prospects. Perhaps she had not grasped the significance of what he had said? He decided to try again. At the next pause in Georgiana's conversation with the clergyman, Mr. Brydges addressed her with:

"It is almost certain that the Chandos peerage case will be decided in my favour. I will therefore soon take my rightful place in the House of Lords, and I look forward to the opportunity of doing great things for this nation."

"I have no doubt that you will, Mr. Brydges," replied Georgiana before again turning to the gentleman sitting on her left.

During the course of the whole dinner, the young lady said hardly more than a few polite phrases to Mr. Brydges. Watching Miss Darcy talking and laughing merrily with his rival, he felt his resentment towards the clergyman mounting by the minute.

After dinner, the ladies withdrew to the drawing room, while the gentlemen remained to drink their port. During this interval, Mr. Grey observed that Mr. Brydges seemed to be in an ill humour, and he noticed, also, that the gentleman was barely civil to him. Yet, brooding on the slights of others was foreign to Mr. Grey's good-natured spirit, and so he gave the matter little thought.

When the time came for the men to rejoin the ladies in the drawing room, Mr. Brydges could contain himself no longer. Approaching his rival, he lowered his voice and said to him snidely:

"How pleasant it must be to eat fine food and have servants attend you for a change after years of serving others at Oxford, is it not, Mr. Grey?"

"I beg your pardon?"

"Do not be afraid to admit it, Mr. Grey. Your secret is safe with me."

"I do not understand what you mean, Mr. Brydges."

"You were a servitor at Oxford, were you not?" asked the gentleman, his voice full of contempt.

Mr. Grey was struck by the man's impertinence but answered calmly, "No, I was not. I received a scholarship, but even if I had been a servitor, what difference would it make? Though some may consider the nobleman to be far above the servitor, the only nobility that interests me is nobility of the mind."

He then turned and went up the stairs, while Mr. Brydges, looking somewhat displeased, followed behind.

In the drawing room, as the ladies and gentlemen sipped their tea, General Wilkinson entertained the company with his thoughts on the army:

"There is a sad lack of discipline," said he, looking pointedly at the redcoats in the room. "More than a few of my officers take a greater interest in balls, parties, and the society of young ladies than in their army duties. Recently, I even caught one of my lieutenants reading *A Master-key to the Rich Ladies Treasury*."

"A Master-key to what?" asked Mrs. Tufton in disbelief.

"The Rich Ladies Treasury, Ma'am."

"It almost sounds like some sort of bank."

"There you are not far off from the truth, Mrs. Tufton, at least in the way that the book's readers see it. This volume, which is also sometimes called *The Widower and Bachelor's Directory*, contains alphabetical lists of wealthy old maids and widows, their reported fortunes, and their places of residence."

"And do you mean to tell us that there is a reputable publishing house in existence that has agreed to print something so improper?" asked Mrs. Parker.

"Indeed, there is. Hellyer & Sons is the publisher, and I understand that updated editions of the book are printed regularly."

Mr. Brydges was somewhat disconcerted by this conversation. He thought of all the times he had carelessly left his own copy of the book in plain view at home, where an unexpected caller might chance to see it. In the future, thought he to himself, it would be prudent to keep the book well out of sight, far away from prying eyes. The gentleman's musings were interrupted by Mrs. Elwood, who remarked:

"Perhaps the ladies should retaliate and publish a book with lists of known fortune-hunters."

"Such a book, if published, would be too large and heavy for a lady to lift without assistance," came the reply.

"Surely not! What makes you take such a cynical view of men, Mr. Luxford?"

"I have encountered enough scoundrels to convince me of it, Madam," the gentleman answered. "Only the other day, I heard a story about a young army officer, a very handsome fellow, who paid attentions to an older, maiden lady. She owned a very large and fine estate, but the years had not been kind to her, and she looked even older than her forty years. Nevertheless, this circumstance did not prevent the rake from courting her. Flattered by the gentleman's attentions, she at first gave credence to his utterances. Yet, as time went on, his compliments grew more extravagant and his blandishments became increasingly preposterous, until the lady began to doubt his sincerity and his motives. By then, however, the officer had determined to ask for her hand in marriage. With this purpose in mind, he called on the lady and found her walking outside in her meadow not far from the house. In his usual manner, the young officer began extolling her matchless beauty and charms, to which she replied, 'Sir, unless you are blinded by love, I can hardly believe that you mean what you say. Even in my youth, my looking glass gave me proof that I am no beauty, and the many years that have passed since then have done nothing to improve my features. I cannot believe that a young, handsome man such as yourself could truly be passionately in love with me.' The officer protested that he was indeed in love, saying: 'My feelings for you are such that *I worship the ground on which you walk.*' She answered, laughingly: '*That,* I can believe. I have long suspected that not I but my land has been your muse in creating such fine speeches, and I am now resolved, Sir, that neither my land nor my person shall fall into your possession.'"

At the conclusion of the story, the room filled with the sound of soft, elegant laughter. Everyone seemed to enjoy the tale—everyone, that is, except Mr. Brydges, who saw little humour in it.

CHAPTER 36

Several days later, Georgiana and Jane went together to buy a twelfth-cake for their Twelfth Night celebrations. The countless dinner parties and balls they had attended during the past weeks had seemed animating at first, but after awhile, these diversions became somewhat tiring, and both the ladies and Mr. Bingley were rather looking forward to spending the holiday quietly at home in the Paragon, where their merrymaking would consist of little more than enjoying a slice of the traditional cake together.

Georgiana and Jane commenced their search for a twelfth-cake by visiting a confectioner in Lilliput Alley, where they stopped to look at the tempting assortment of gateaux on display in the shop. Afterwards, they went to another confectioner in Milsom Street and found that the cakes there, if possible, were even more splendid than those in the first one. They had only just begun examining the sweet creations on offer when Mr. Grey unexpectedly entered the shop.

It was a most agreeable surprise to him to discover Miss Darcy and her friend within. His business at the confectioner's was the same as theirs: to choose a twelfth-cake for his family. The Egertons had entrusted him with the task as Sir Philip was indisposed, and his wife wished to stay home and care for him. Georgiana and Jane both expressed their concern for the old gentleman's health and hoped that his condition was not serious. Mr. Grey replied that he expected his uncle would feel better within a few days; the tumult of the festive season had proved somewhat taxing to his strength, and some rest by the fire in the comfort of his own home was perhaps all he needed to feel well again.

The cakes in the shop were not the only delicious things to feast one's eyes upon; there were numerous trays laden with all sorts of delectable sweetmeats, and pastries of every description were laid out everywhere in enticing displays. Georgiana stopped in front of one such tray, which held an assortment of sugary confections shaped like different fruits: cherries, strawberries, and even little pineapples. Mr. Grey called her attention to a different tray, which held bonbons in the form of musical instruments. "Look, Miss Darcy," said he. "Here are some that I think will interest you", and he motioned to a collection of sweets in the shape of delicate, little harps.

After admiring the bonbons, they next turned their attention to the twelfth-cakes, of which there was a great variety to choose from. There were cakes decorated with crowns, white swans, Greek and Roman-style friezes, and countless other figures which fantasy was capable of creating from gum paste. Georgiana paused to look at a cake that was ornamented with knights on horseback.

"A penny for your thoughts, Miss Darcy," said Mr. Grey. The lady smiled and answered, "I was just thinking of the bygone days of chivalry and courtly love. It was such a romantic time! Brave knights performed heroic deeds in honour of their chosen ladies and wrote them poems."

"It may have been a romantic time for some but not for others," returned Mr. Grey. "Clergymen were not permitted to marry for a sizeable part of the middle ages, you know."

"And how would you have liked to be a clergyman in those days?" asked Georgiana mischievously.

"Would you have me go through life as a celibate priest, Miss Darcy? I can see that the idea gives you much amusement!" exclaimed Mr. Grey with feigned reproach, adding, "What a fine prospect!—courtiers falling at your feet, troubadours immortalising you in verse, knights riding out to fight crusades in your honour... and poor, lonely me, sentenced to the life of a monk with no hope of ever having a wife—have you no pity, Miss Darcy?"

"You must not make me out to be so cruel, Mr. Grey. I think perhaps the present is a better time after all."

She smiled as she said the words, but unable to hold his gaze any longer, she then cast down her eyes.

When it came time to choose, Mrs. Bingley and Georgiana finally settled on a rose-coloured cake adorned on top with figures of a king and queen. Parading around them along the cake's outer edge were various Twelfth Night characters: a harlequin, Cupid, Robin Hood, and several others.

One of the most elaborate twelfth-cakes in the shop was made to look like the Garden of Eden, complete with flowers, birds, and a Tree of Knowledge loaded with scarlet fruit. Mr. Grey thought to himself mirthfully that the serpent, with its almond-shaped, green eyes, bore a striking resemblance to Michael Brydges. The clergyman liked the cake and could not resist buying it.

While admiring Mr. Grey's cake, Georgiana said to him, "Where are Adam and Eve? I only see the serpent!"

"Maybe they are hiding among the trees in the garden," came the reply. "Remember the part in Genesis, where, after eating from the Tree of Knowledge, they tried to conceal themselves from God?"

"Perhaps you are right," said Georgiana, and then continued with a laugh, "although I think the more likely explanation for their absence is that the confectioner thought it improper to display an unclothed Adam and Eve in his shop window."

Then, a little wistfully, she added, "I like that in the Garden of Eden, there was no idea of rich and poor; there were just Adam and Eve, happy together in paradise."

Mr. Grey searched Georgiana's eyes to discern her meaning. Was it only the first man and woman of God's creation to whom she was referring, or was there a deeper significance to what she had just said? He could not tell. The gentleman broke the momentary quiet that followed by remarking, "And although life in heaven was not without toil, the work was pleasant, and Adam laboured cheerfully, knowing that with the fruits of his labour, he was providing for Eve."

"But then, the serpent came and ruined everything," returned Georgiana. "If only Eve had not listened to its flattering tongue!"

The young man turned his gaze back to the cake he had chosen for himself, and especially looked at the green-eyed, slithering creature that had entwined itself enticingly around the Tree of Knowledge. Sly fiend! What trouble it had stirred in paradise! Once more Michael Brydges came to mind. For an instant, Mr. Grey almost regretted having selected that particular cake, but then he shook off the thought—he ought not to indulge such foolish, superstitious comparisons.

Georgiana interrupted his meditations to tell him some news of a letter she received from her brother earlier. Mr. Darcy had written to say that business kept him and his wife in Scotland, and that they would therefore be unable to go to London that season. On learning of this change of plans in the morning, Mr. and Mrs. Bingley invited Georgiana to stay out the rest of the winter with them in Bath, to which she gladly agreed.

Mr. Grey was delighted to hear of these developments. Miss Darcy would not be leaving soon after all! What better news could there be than that? An invitation to dinner from Mrs. Bingley completed his happiness, and with such pleasing thoughts to occupy him, all traces of Mr. Brydges vanished from his mind.

CHAPTER 37

Michael Brydges and his sister considered that going to the theatre was an extravagance, and one to be avoided. Yet, they would also be the first to admit that sometimes it is necessary to spend money in order to reap much larger rewards later on. Since dinner invitations from the Bingleys were not forthcoming; and whenever they invited Miss Darcy for an outing, more often than not she already had some engagement or other elsewhere; Grace Brydges and her brother decided to take matters into their own hands. They happened to discover through a mutual acquaintance that Georgiana had plans to attend the theatre on a Tuesday in late January, and they therefore determined to go there themselves and meet Miss Darcy as if by chance.

When reflecting on his previous conversations with Georgiana, Mr. Brydges felt that perhaps he had spoken too much of his future plans to enter Parliament, and consequently, that the impression he had made on her may have been less than favourable. Being seen at the theatre would allow him to show himself as a man of refined taste, elevated ideas, and cultured mind rather than as just an ambitious barrister, and after the play, there would likely be an opportunity of conversing with Miss Darcy. Unlike at a dance, there would be no throng of eager suitors, all vying for Miss Darcy's attention, to compete with.

Mr. Brydges had managed to procure a private box at the theatre. As he and his sister were settling into their seats, Miss Brydges looked about her with pleasure, admired the elaborate gilt lattice enclosing their box, and in general, felt very grand. Her brother, meanwhile, was wincing at the thought of what it had all cost. However, he took comfort in the idea that the prize he desired was worth the pecuniary sacrifice. Miss Darcy, he reasoned, would likely be enjoying the play from a private box herself, and if he hoped to rise in her esteem, he must have a box as well. Sitting with the masses was out of the question.

Soon after the two of them had made themselves comfortable, Georgiana arrived. She and the Bingleys came with Mr. Grey's relations, which vexed her envious suitor greatly, but at least Mr. Grey himself appeared to be nowhere in sight. Another fortunate circumstance was that the Egertons' box was situated close by, within full view of their own.

"It is a good thing that I remembered to bring this," remarked Miss Brydges and produced what appeared to be an opera glass. "Now we can watch them more closely."

Her brother protested that much as he would like to have a magnified view of their neighbours, they could not just point the opera glass directly at Miss Darcy and her friends—it would be very rude.

"We are not going to point it at them but at the stage," was the answer.

Now Mr. Brydges was really perplexed. His sister laughed at his bewildered expression and then explained that the instrument she had just brought out was not a real opera glass at all but instead a lovely, little invention called a jealousy glass. Rather than magnifying objects situated in front of the viewing tube, it presented an enlarged image of whatever a curious observer wished to see to his side. This was accomplished by means of an opening on the side of the tube, which, in concert with a mirror set at an angle inside, allowed one to discreetly watch others without their knowledge. There was no twisting and turning in one's seat, no craning the neck to see fellow theatregoers (and making a spectacle of oneself in the process). In short, the jealousy glass lent a certain decorum to one's espionage!

Mr. Brydges was delighted and pronounced it to be an ingenious, clever device. He put it to use immediately, but for the present, at least, there was little to see. The newly-arrived party were merely seating themselves and talking a little. Still, the two who were secretly spying on them kept a close watch over all that went on to be sure of missing nothing.

When the play was almost about to begin, Grace Brydges brought the jealousy glass to her eye for one last look at Miss Darcy and her companions and was dismayed by what she saw.

"Michael, look there!" she cried in whisper. Even without the aid of the optical device, her brother could plainly see that which he would have preferred not to—Mr. Grey had just entered the Egertons' box and was sitting down beside Miss Darcy. Mr. Brydges did, however, use the implement to observe their behaviour towards one another more closely and noted, with more than a little resentment, that they seemed to look at each other with something like particular regard.

Throughout the play, and especially during the intermissions, the gentleman made much use of the jealousy glass and stared into it until his eyes were overstrained and his head ached. With grim determination, he from time to time took a moment to refocus his eyes and then only squinted harder into the magnification device. Not one look or gesture that passed between Mr. Grey and Georgiana escaped his notice or his scrutiny. So concentrated was Mr. Brydges on the task that he scarcely paid any attention to the play. All he could think of, and all his mind could dwell on, was the man who stood between him and Georgiana.

During the final intermission, Mr. Grey happened to look over at the Brydges' private box for what was perhaps the second or third time, and chuckling to himself, he said, "Miss Darcy, observe Mr. Brydges over there. I believe he has been staring at the theatre curtain through his opera glass for several minutes, now. I wonder what he finds so fascinating."

An instant after Georgiana directed her eyes to the goings-on in the neighbouring box, Miss Brydges took the jealousy glass away from her brother and peered into it herself. "Now there is Miss Brydges taking her turn to stare at the curtain," remarked Georgiana with a smile, her eyes twinkling.

Suddenly realising that she had been noticed, Grace Brydges snatched the jealousy glass away from her face as if it were a hot cinder.

"I believe that Miss Darcy and Mr. Grey saw us," said she to her brother.

"Do you suppose they know that we have been watching them?"

"I do not think so, but we had better not use the device any more this evening, or they will surely guess."

After the theatre performance, Mr. Brydges and his sister put themselves in Georgiana's path at the earliest opportunity. Some small talk ensued. Mr. Grey asked the two who had accosted his party how they liked the play. "Exceedingly well," was his rival's reply. "Richard III is by far my favourite of all of Shakespeare's works—I know it almost by heart."

Indeed, to Michael Brydges this famous play was very inspiring, as it had always been to his mother. In fact, Mrs. Brydges had wanted to name her eldest son 'Richard', which may perhaps have been the more proper name for him, but in the end, his father chose 'Michael', after St. Michael the Archangel.

"I truly believe that without theatre, life is not worth living," continued Mr. Brydges.

"Michael is a great admirer of the arts," added his sister.

While the others continued talking, Grace Brydges said to Georgiana:

"I am afraid, Miss Darcy, that you have quite forgotten my brother and me, though you are often in our thoughts."

"I do assure you that I have not, Miss Brydges, and I would have returned your last call by now had there not been so many other claims on my time. As a matter of fact, I had been meaning to call on you sometime next week, and you are always welcome to come and see me at our house in the Paragon."

"Then, Miss Darcy, may I call on you this Thursday?"

"Yes, of course, if you wish."

They parted soon afterwards, and when Miss Brydges and her brother left the theatre, it was with the feeling that they had succeeded in advancing their cause.

CHAPTER 38

Having a request to make of her brother, Miss Brydges waited the next day for an opportune moment, when he was in a good humour, before saying to him:

"Michael, as you know my wedding is next week, and I have been thinking what a fine thing it would be to have a necklace, and perhaps some earrings, for the occasion. Only, unfortunately the cost of my wedding clothes was considerably higher than I expected, and I have nothing left for the jewellery."

She took a sip of her tea and then continued cautiously, "Brother, can I persuade you to part with a small sum so that I might buy something suitable?"

Putting down his teacup, Mr. Brydges answered, "It is an unnecessary expense. We cannot afford it."

"It may be unnecessary for you, Michael, but a woman only gets married once in her life. Surely we can afford to spend a little on jewellery just this once."

"Grace, our father always economised during his lifetime, and his prudence is the sole reason why after his death, you and Mother are able to live in a comfortable house in Queen Square rather than having to depend on the charity of relations as so many others do. Father did not save such a large sum by wasting his money on trinkets."

"And yet, he was not so parsimonious as you are!" retorted Miss Brydges. "Besides, it seems that you only economise on what others need but spare little expense on your own attire."

"My tailor's bill is not unreasonable; I spend exactly what is needed and not a farthing more. You know as well as I do that Miss Darcy is not accustomed to mixing with paupers. The gentlemen in her circle are all wealthy, well-dressed men, and if I am to succeed with her, I must dress at least as well as they do. Everything I spend on my clothes is an investment in the future—our future. If I manage to marry Miss Darcy, it will be the beginning of a new life for all of us. Such an advantageous match cannot fail to raise the standing and respectability of our whole family."

"I suppose you are right," sighed Miss Brydges. "But Michael, I cannot help wanting to look beautiful on my wedding day. Could we not think of something?"

"If you wish to wear fine jewellery to your wedding, why not ask to borrow something from Miss Darcy when you call on her tomorrow?"

"Borrow from Miss Darcy?! Have you gone mad?"

"Not at all, I assure you; I am completely in earnest. For some time I have been toying with the idea in my mind, and the more I think about it, the more convinced I become that borrowing something from her is a sound course of action."

More than a little incredulous, Miss Bridges said:

"Pray tell me how borrowing anything from Miss Darcy could possibly help your suit. I am all ears."

"The idea is very simple," the gentleman replied. "I have often observed that when one shows kindness or gives assistance to another, good feelings arise not only in the heart of the recipient but also in that of the giver. In other words, when a person helps someone, he or she becomes more disposed to like the one who benefits from that assistance. If Miss Darcy helps you in some meaningful way, she will begin to have stronger feelings of friendship towards you, and if the two of you become good friends, I will have more opportunities to court her. Then, with skilful manoeuvring and a little patience, we will lay the paving stones on the path that will, in time, lead to the altar."

"It is all very well to say so," remarked Miss Brydges, "but Brother, are you sure there is no flaw in your logic? I see what you mean about kindness and friendship being interrelated, but I have always thought that it is necessary to like someone first, and then kindness to that person naturally follows. You seem to view the relationship between cause and effect backwards."

"There is nothing wrong with my logic," Mr. Brydges insisted. "As I see it, the action can precede the sentiment, and there are numerous examples from daily life to support my notion. Consider, for example, how the ordinary English family acquires a house cat. Oftentimes, it is the children's idea—they ask their mother whether they can have a kitten; but being a sensible woman, she refuses. Why would she want the beast? To her, it is another mouth to feed, a burden, an unwelcome responsibility. Still, the children whine and plead until she capitulates and assents to their wishes. The cat is brought home, and the children enjoy playing with it, but of course they do not take care of the animal, whatever they might have promised their mother before. The task of caring for it naturally falls on the poor woman. What happens then? ... She feeds the cat, she gives it water and a nice, warm bed—she starts to *like* the cat! Its purring, which the woman scarcely noticed earlier, begins to sound like sweet music to her ears. She grows so attached to the animal, in fact, that she is loath to part from it even after her children grow up and leave home. In the same way, by prompting Miss Darcy to do us a kindness, we can make her grow fond of us."

"And yet, Michael, I am not sure that asking Miss Darcy to lend me an item of high value is entirely proper. If we were old friends, I would not hesitate, but as Miss Darcy and I are fairly recent acquaintances, such a request from me may be viewed as impertinence."

"She will not think you impertinent if you take care to choose your words in such a way as to make her think that lending you the jewellery was her idea. With her kind soul, she will feel compelled to offer you the jewellery herself if she believes you have a need for it."

Although still somewhat reluctant, Miss Brydges nevertheless agreed, saying, "Well, since our efforts with Miss Darcy have so far failed to produce the desired result, perhaps it is indeed time to try something new."

During her visit to Georgiana the following day, Grace Brydges brought up the subject of her upcoming nuptials as soon as the opportunity presented itself. "It will be a very small wedding," said she. "Only Mr. Spencer's family and mine will be there; but although the occasion will not be as grand as I would have liked, you cannot conceive how long I have dreamed of this day! When I was a child, I used to imagine how I would look at my wedding, and then I would draw pictures of myself dressed in all those lovely things."

"Do your wedding clothes look anything like in the drawings?" asked Georgiana.

"Well, not quite. For one thing, fashions have changed a great deal since I was a little girl, but the gown I will be wearing is just what I want; it is a very delicate, embroidered muslin of a light pink shade. If only I had a necklace to go with it—something like the one you wore to the theatre on Tuesday—then it would be perfect. But you see, my father never allowed me to buy jewellery and permitted me to wear nothing except a simple cross on a chain. He was very strong in his faith and believed that wearing ornaments encourages vanity. Papa is no longer alive to forbid it, of course, but spending the money he saved so carefully on items of which he would have sternly disapproved somehow seems disrespectful to his memory."

"But it is your wedding! Surely it is permissible to wear jewels on such an important day!" replied Georgiana.

"Yes, I think so too, but still I cannot bring myself to defy my father's wishes... It would be different, I suppose, if instead of buying the jewellery, I were to borrow something from one of my cousins—only they all live far from Bath, and my wedding is in several days."

Being of a generous nature, Georgiana immediately offered to resolve the difficulty by lending Miss Brydges a piece from her own collection, and after making the requisite protestations of being reluctant to inconvenience Georgiana, Miss Brydges eagerly accepted.

The jewellery box was fetched, and soon the two young ladies were examining its contents. Georgiana invited her acquaintance to select anything she liked and ventured to suggest one of her favourite pieces as a possible choice:

"Here is a pearl necklace I am very fond of. Pearls always look pretty with pink fabrics, and here are the earrings to match."

Miss Brydges held the necklace up to her neck:

"I am not sure... it is very fine, but perhaps the length will not suit my gown. Do you have anything shorter? Maybe something that sits closer to the neck?"

The lady tried on a number of pieces from the box, and though each was magnificent in its own way, none was quite what she was looking for.

"Do you have anything else I might try?"

"No, this is all I brought with me from Pemberley... No, wait! I do have one more thing."

Georgiana went back to her room and soon returned with another, much smaller box from her dressing table.

"This is new," said she. "My brother gave it to me as a special gift just before I left for Bath."

Inside the box was a gold necklace with a matching pair of pendant earrings. The necklace was made up of twelve segments, each one being a delicate scroll of gold ribbon and garland with topaz stones. In the centre of each scrolled link was a small letter G, which was most cleverly integrated into the overall design.

Miss Brydges' eyes lit up when she saw the jewellery, and lifting the necklace carefully, she exclaimed, "I think this one is perfect! The colour of the gemstones is exactly the same shade as my wedding gown!"

As the lady put on the ornaments and then turned this way and that to admire her reflection in the looking glass, Georgiana told her that Mr. Darcy had ordered the set made especially for her, and that the letter G in the centre of each gold segment had been chosen to represent the first initial of her name.

"How fortunate that our names should both start with G!" exclaimed Miss Brydges. If I had been an Arabella or a Margaret, what would everyone think of me for wearing a necklace with the wrong initial? I would have had to choose something else!"

Georgiana was a little hesitant to lend her brother's gift, which was very dear to her, but despite her reservations, she put the box into Miss Brydges' hands and asked only that she return it before Monday, the fourteenth of February, since Georgiana had planned to wear the necklace and earrings for the first time to Mrs. Parker's Valentine's Day dinner. Miss Brydges promised that she would and thanked her friend profusely for her generosity.

Back at home in Queen Square, Grace Brydges could not contain her exuberance as she showed the jewellery to her brother. "Is it not the loveliest thing you have ever seen?!" cried she and then went on to tell him about the design that Mr. Darcy had put so much thought into creating for his sister.

"The necklace and earrings are so beautiful," added she, "I wish I could keep them forever, but I must return everything before the fourteenth, for Miss Darcy is to wear the set to Mrs. Parker's Valentine's Day dinner."

"To Mrs. Parker's dinner, did you say?"

"Yes, the same one that we will be attending. Mr. Grey will be there too, unfortunately, but there is nothing we can do to keep him away."

"All this gives me an idea," said Michael Brydges slowly. "Grace, will you lend me the jewellery for one day?"

"Oh no, Michael. I could not! I *dare* not! What if you were to lose it, or something else were to happen to the set? How could I face Miss Darcy again, much less repay the value of it? Besides, what could you possibly want with the jewellery?"

"Sister, do not make yourself uneasy. I assure you that I will guard it with my life. If you will only listen, I will tell you what I have in mind."

At first his sister was dubious, but as she listened to his scheme, her eyes began to sparkle with surprise and delight, and it was not long before he convinced her to aid him with his plan.

CHAPTER 39

On the Sunday after his sister's wedding, Michael Brydges set out for church, only instead of proceeding to the Bath Abbey, as was his custom, he went to the Octagon Chapel in Milsom Street. There he hoped to see Mr. Grey, who regularly attended services at that chapel.

Sure enough, Mr. Grey was one of the congregation, and as soon as the church service had ended, Mr. Brydges came towards him.

"What a surprise to see you here, Mr. Brydges. I thought that you prefer the Bath Abbey."

"Indeed, I do. I find that the majestic architecture is very conducive to thoughts and reflections of a religious nature. However, today I desired a change of scene and found myself longing for the cosier atmosphere of a small chapel."

As the gentleman spoke, Mr. Grey's eyes fell on the jewellery box that his acquaintance was holding conspicuously. Seeing that he noticed it, Mr. Brydges said:

"There is a matter on which I would like to consult you, Mr. Grey. I do not know whether you are aware, but I have a high regard for your taste. It is therefore most fortunate that I should have happened to meet you here at just the moment when I needed your opinion."

With these words, he opened the box.

"What do you think of this jewellery? Will she like it, do you think?"

"It is exquisite! The present is for your sister, I presume?"

"For Grace? Oh, no! It is for my intended bride," Mr. Brydges declared triumphantly.

"You are to be married?"

"Yes—I wish I could tell you her name, but you see, we would like to keep the engagement a secret. I would be grateful, therefore, if you would avoid mentioning it to anyone."

"Of course. You can count on my silence."

Mr. Brydges slitted his eyes, and his lips curved into a devious smile as he said:

"But being such a perceptive man, you can hardly be in doubt as to the identity of my betrothed. In the past two months, I have made my preference abundantly clear. Perhaps I should have been more guarded in my conduct, but I am hopeless at the art of dissembling."

Noting with pleasure the sudden concern that overspread his rival's countenance, Mr. Brydges continued, "I am so glad that you approve of the necklace and earrings, especially considering how much effort went into creating them. The jewellery is of a unique design; I had it made especially for her. You see the little letter G in the middle of each link? It is the first initial of her name."

Mr. Grey said nothing in reply, but his perturbation was clearly evident. Satisfied of having created the desired impression in his rival's mind, Mr. Brydges said only a few more words and then departed. Mr. Grey could not even remember the last of what he said; all he could think of was Miss Darcy. For some weeks now, he had believed that she was not indifferent to him. Was it possible that such a perception had been no more than a fanciful supposition conjured up by his own vanity? Could it be that he had mistaken Miss Darcy's amiable manner for something more than it was, and that she had in fact been in love with Mr. Brydges the entire time? Such a thought was too terrible for contemplation, and he refused to indulge it, preferring instead to surmise that perhaps the jewellery was not intended for Miss Darcy after all. Perhaps the gift was meant for some other young lady, whose name also began with the letter G; but if that was the case, why then had Mr. Brydges gone to the trouble of showing the jewellery to him? Mr. Grey had no illusions that the gentleman had such a very high regard for his opinion as he claimed to. There must be an ulterior motive, and most likely it had to do with Miss Darcy. Was it possible that Michael Brydges had gained her love?

Although Mr. Grey did not like to think ill of anyone, he had more than once observed Mr. Brydges' hollowness and wily nature, and he felt that such a man could not possibly appeal to a lady of Georgiana's merit. The only remaining explanation, and one to which Mr. Grey clung with the most fervent hope, was that the jewellery did indeed belong to Miss Brydges, or was intended as a gift for her, and that her brother had purposely flaunted it before him in order to detach him from Miss Darcy.

CHAPTER 40

For Georgiana, the weeks in Bath had flown by all too quickly. Before she knew it, more than a third of February was gone, and the end of the month was all too clearly in sight. She had never been so blissfully happy, so full of joy as during those precious weeks. If only there were a way to suspend time, to delay indefinitely that day in late February when she was to depart for Pemberley.

Much as Georgiana longed to see her family again, there was one in Bath from whom she could not bear to part, but with each passing day, the moment of that dreaded farewell crept closer. Must they part at all? There was but one way to avoid it, but that was not a subject for a lady to broach. For now, at least, she had no reason to suppose that the end of February would bring with it anything but farewell.

With these meditations, Georgiana sat at breakfast one morning. The letters arrived while she and the Bingleys were eating, and one of them was for her. Thinking the letter might be from Anne or Elizabeth, or perhaps from her brother, she took it up eagerly, but it was not a message from any of them. What she found inside the envelope instead was a valentine! It was the last thing that Georgiana had expected to receive, not only because she had completely forgotten about Valentine's Day, but also because the holiday was not until Monday, and today was only Friday.

The valentine was not signed, but it did not need to be; from what was drawn on the front, Georgiana guessed immediately who had sent it. The illustration was of a bride and groom standing before a church, but not just any church! The drawing was a faithful reproduction of the little, grey, flint building—part Saxon, part Norman in its construction—where she had attended services during her stay in Kent with the Townsends, and where Mr. Grey had delivered his sermons each Sunday.

Almost holding her breath, Georgiana opened the valentine and read the verses inside. They were as follows:

No troubadour am I
but poetry I will attempt
for a chance to win your heart

No knight am I
but gladly will I join the tilt
for I've been struck by Cupid's dart

With lances pointed at my breast
the jousting knights advance
hope of your love will be my shield
in this deadly dance

No king am I
with castles thee to tempt
and yet with hope I'm loath to part

To work and diligence I therefore turn
my bread and your esteem to earn
in hopes one day you will be mine
as my bride and not just Valentine

Georgiana's heart soared as she read the poem, and when she had finished, she pressed the valentine to her lips. The rest of the day passed as if in a dream. She kept the valentine with her and looked at it often, and read and reread the poem written inside so frequently that soon she had it memorised by heart. Georgiana felt that nothing could vex her—not the beating rain outside, nor dining with the Pheasants that evening and having to listen to Mrs. Pheasant's untiring tongue, nor even getting her gown soaked when Mr. Pheasant accidentally knocked his glass into her lap. No, the day was perfect as it was.

That night before bed, Georgiana was reluctant to blow out her candle. Once more she read her valentine and thought of him who had written the verses. She looked again at the drawing on the front and pictured herself standing by Mr. Grey's side before the church. At last, unable to resist her drowsiness any longer, Georgiana gently placed the valentine on the little table beside her bed, and after extinguishing her candle, she lay back down onto her pillow and finally permitted sleep to close her eyelids.

CHAPTER 41

Monday being Valentine's Day, the postman delivered several more valentines from Georgiana's admirers. The billets were decorated with the usual hearts, doves, and Cupids and contained charming, though forgettable, verses. Yet, no female heart is immune to the enjoyment of reading such amorous declarations, and Georgiana, like so many other young ladies, took pleasure in looking at her newly-arrived valentines. Even so, when she had finished admiring them, the billets were tied together and put away in a box, only to afterwards be forgotten altogether. Mr. Grey's valentine, on the other hand, continued to stand prominently where she could easily see it on the dressing table in her room.

That evening, Georgiana was to attend a dinner party at the Parkers'. Knowing that Mr. Grey would be there, she chose her gown with special care, and for her jewellery, she selected her brother's topaz necklace and matching earrings, which Mr. Brydges had taken the opportunity of returning to her himself, on his sister's behalf, the previous day.

Georgiana and the Bingleys arrived at the dinner party near the proper hour, and a few minutes later came Mr. Grey. On entering the drawing room, he perceived that Miss Darcy was conversing with the Miss Pheasants, and after being welcomed by the host and hostess and exchanging a few words with them, Mr. Grey advanced towards Georgiana. As he drew near, she turned around, and the first thing that greeted his eyes was her gold and topaz jewellery, the same which Mr. Brydges had showed off to him on Sunday. The gentleman's lips parted, and for several seconds he was powerless to speak. Finally, hardly conscious of what he said, he mumbled some polite, vague pleasantry. Mr. Brydges, who joined them presently, was only too willing to supply the deficiency in Mr. Grey's conversation. Pleased to see his rival's discomposure, he addressed him with a greater than usual degree of civility. For the rest of the time until dinner, Mr. Brydges stayed determinedly by Georgiana's side and engaged her in conversation, while the Miss Pheasants chatted incessantly to Mr. Grey.

At dinner, it was not long before the guests turned to the subject of Valentine's Day. To Mrs. Wilkinson, the holiday held special significance since, as she told the party, it was on that very day fifteen years previously that she first met her husband. Smiling fondly at his wife, General Wilkinson said, "It was at Almack's that I first set eyes on her. She was the prettiest young lady in the room. I asked her to dance, and within three months, we were married."

"What a romantic story," sighed Miss Pheasant and directed her eyes wistfully at Mr. Grey.

"When I was young, the fourteenth of February was my favourite day of the year," said the girl's mother. "I received ever so many valentines from my admirers. The one I liked best was a puzzle purse. The square of paper was folded into an intricate shape, and as I unfolded the panels one by one, on each leaf I found a message of love, or a picture of a heart or a rose. It was the sweetest little love note—only, once I opened the puzzle purse, I never could seem to fold it back the right way again!"

"Times have changed since your youth, Mrs. Pheasant. Nowadays, the verses commonly found in valentines are often copied out of *The Valentine Writer* or some other such book and are not worth the paper on which they are written," remarked Mr. Parker.

"Not everyone copies the words out of a book," returned Mrs. Bingley, "and it takes a great deal of time and care to make a valentine by hand." Remembering her own treasured valentine, Georgiana glanced down the table at its maker, but when she caught Mr. Grey's eye, he seemed to look away.

"I feel sure that postmen must take particular pleasure in performing their duties on Valentine's Day considering that it is not only letters they are delivering but also happiness to so many hearts," said Miss Pheasant dreamily.

"I doubt whether postmen are as fond of Valentine's Day as you believe them to be, Miss Pheasant. It would not surprise me if they curse the holiday and view all those valentines they must carry as nothing more than an additional source of work and trouble."

"How unromantic of you, Mr. Parker!"

"Unromantic, perhaps, but pragmatic. Then, also, there is the issue of expense. The recipient pays the cost of the postage for what is arguably a very useless missive."

"Oh, fie, Mr. Parker! Young men pour their souls into those valentines, and all you think of is the expense!" cried his wife.

Mr. Brydges made no contribution to the conversation, but he thought the question of cost a valuable consideration. If a man sends an unsigned valentine to his chosen lady, how is she to know who sent it? She might mistakenly attribute the epistle to some other suitor. On the other hand, if the sender were to sign his name to the valentine, why send it by post at all? A gentleman could just as easily make the same declarations to the lady in person, and at no expense on paper and ink.

"Well, I think that valentines should be forbidden altogether!" Mr. Luxford suddenly exclaimed.

"Forbidden?! Surely you do not mean that, Mr. Luxford. Valentine's Day is the only day of the year on which a gentleman may with propriety send anything of a romantic nature to a lady by post. Surely you would not deny lovers their only chance all year," protested Jane Bingley.

"I would, and gladly!"

"On what grounds do you take such a drastic step against love, Mr. Luxford?" asked Mrs. Wilkinson.

"Only this, Madam. Valentines are a malevolent means of corrupting our youth, and just this morning I had proof of it. Shortly after breakfast, some letters arrived for my family; one letter was addressed to me, the second was for my wife, and the third was a valentine for my daughter. She opened the valentine and found that it contained only some lines of verse and no signature. Assuming that the poem was much like the ones commonly found in books, I thought no more of it and retired to my study, as I had several pressing matters of business to attend to. Some time later, my daughter came to ask me the meaning of a word that she had never previously seen before. It was a vulgar word, which I could not repeat in polite society, especially in the presence of ladies. Naturally, the word was not one that either I or anyone in my family had ever used, and I asked where she had heard it uttered. My daughter replied that she saw it written in her valentine. I demanded to see the valentine, of course, and was horrified to discover that it contained a poem of a grossly indecent nature. Fortunately, my daughter's upbringing and education had been such as to preserve her innocence and sense of female delicacy, so she had been unable to make out the meaning in those lines of verse. All the same, I felt more than a little discomfited when attempting to answer her questions about the poem."

General Wilkinson declared that in his opinion, the best way to prevent such mischief was for the Post Office to refuse to deliver any letter suspected of being a valentine. Others sitting at the table argued that such radical measures were unnecessary—would it not be better for mothers and fathers simply to inspect all letters received on Valentine's Day before handing the missives to their daughters? The issue of how best to protect young, innocent minds from pollution was hotly debated, but no consensus could be reached, and at length the discussion was abandoned in favour of other subjects.

After dinner, when the gentlemen had finished their port, the guests assembled in the drawing room to play games. The first one chosen was Move-All. Since different versions of the game existed, the rules for the present one were clarified. Chairs were to be arranged in a large circle, with there being one chair fewer than the number of players. Standing in the centre of the circle of chairs, the crier would call out, "Move all!" A lively tune on the pianoforte would accompany the command. At this signal, the players must rise from their seats and promenade along the chairs until the music suddenly stopped, and then everyone must attempt to sit down in a chair. In the ensuing scramble, one player would be left standing and must leave the game. One after another, they would be thus eliminated, with the winner having the honour of choosing the next game for the company to play.

Mr. Parker appointed himself the crier, while his wife provided the accompanying music on the pianoforte. Mr. Brydges, meanwhile, took possession of a chair closest to Georgiana, but Mr. Grey—to her disappointment—chose one much farther off. At the command of "Move all," the players began what on the surface appeared to be a leisurely stroll. Yet, beneath the smiling, breezy exterior, each of the guests, with muscles tensed, was ready to pounce on the nearest chair with the suddenness of a panther.

"No, Mr. Brydges—you must not hover near that chair," called out Mr. Parker. "Everyone must keep moving!" A few seconds later, the music stopped abruptly, and a mad dash followed. The game proceeded at a swift pace, and the guests, with the exception of Mr. Grey, played with great spirit. Georgiana did not fail to observe that the latter gentleman seemed to take little pleasure in the frolic; he was one of the first to lose his chair, and afterwards he watched gloomily as the others played. At the sight of his downcast countenance, Georgiana became increasingly concerned, and the game in which she had at first taken part with much enjoyment soon lost its appeal to her.

Mr. Bingley won the contest, and as it was his privilege to choose the next amusement, he proposed a game of Musical Magic. Some knew how to play, and some did not, so he explained the rules. One of the guests would be required to leave the room, said he, while the rest were to decide on some object—say, a deck of cards—that the player must attempt to find on his return, and with which he ought to perform some predetermined task, such as to shuffle the deck, for example. To aid him in his search, someone would be playing on the pianoforte. If the music grew softer, it meant that he was coming closer to the required item, while if he walked in the wrong direction or touched an incorrect object, the increasing loudness of the music would declare his error. When at last he found it, the music would cease altogether as a signal of his success. But then, said Mr. Bingley, the player must discover what to do with the item that he has correctly chosen. The music commences once more, and as he tries to guess what office he must perform, the melody increases in loudness if he errs and comes to a final stop when he guesses correctly and carries out the assigned task, which is to shuffle the deck of cards in the example case.

With the rules now clear to all, the game began. Mr. Pheasant was the first to take a turn, and Mr. Brydges' recently-married sister, Grace Spencer, stationed herself at the pianoforte. Seeing an opportunity, Michael Brydges supplied the object that Mr. Pheasant was to search for: his own pocket watch. Of this item Mr. Brydges was immensely proud; it was his prized possession. The gold-coloured case of the watch was fashioned from elaborate filigree studded with rubies on the border, while the face was edged with a floral decoration of white, rose, and yellow gold. An ornate pair of hands showed the minutes and hours. It was indeed a splendid-looking piece.

Of course, what was not obvious to the unsuspecting eye was that the watch was merely plated with a thin layer of gold, and the 'rubies' were nothing more than Vauxhall glass. The timepiece was a lower-quality imitation of one worn by an English nobleman, but even though it was only a counterfeit, its price had still been uncomfortably high. Had the piece been authentic, Mr. Brydges would have been unable to afford it at all. Yet, whether real or counterfeit, how was anyone to know the difference? Reassured by this thought, the gentleman took every opportunity of showing off his beloved watch in public (on the pretext of needing to know the time), and all the while he imagined how everyone around him must be eyeing it with admiration and suppressing sighs of envy.

After taking care to ensure that all the guests had had a good look at his watch, Mr. Brydges placed it on a table, and Mr. Pheasant was called in. The music successfully guided the latter to the location of the item, but afterwards he picked up every object lying atop the table except the one that was required; he lifted first a vase, then a candle, then Mrs. Parker's embroidery, and even poked at it a few times with the needle, but to no avail—on each attempt, the music signalled to him that he was incorrect. Watching the man fumbling about confusedly, Mr. Brydges could hardly contain his impatience. How could Mr. Pheasant fail to immediately see the magnificent timepiece before him? He must surely be either blind or a fool! At length, Mr. Pheasant noticed the watch, and after opening it, he told everyone the time.

Mr. Brydges was the next to take a turn at the game. When he had quitted the room, his sister said to the party, "Let Michael find my wedding ring, and his task shall be to return it to me." This suggestion being agreed upon, Grace Spencer took off her ring, and after placing it on the mantelpiece, she went back to the pianoforte.

On his return to the room, her brother found the right object quickly, and being an astute gentleman, he instantly understood what he was expected to do with it. Taking the ring in his hand, he started to move in Mrs. Spencer's direction, but to his surprise, the music grew louder. He shared a look with his sister and then immediately turned around and walked towards Georgiana, the music decreasing in volume with each step. The tune ceased altogether once Mr. Brydges reached his target. Before the young lady had time to think, he took her hand and slipped the ring onto her finger. Georgiana blushed and started to remove the ring while saying that it should be returned to its rightful owner, but Mr. Brydges stayed her hand, and leaning closer to Miss Darcy, he said softly, "It is true that the ring is the wrong size, but perhaps a different one of the correct circumference might be more pleasing?" Georgiana was most discomfited and hardly knew how to reply, but at last she gave a slight smile and, lowering her voice to just above a whisper, answered, "You must not say such things! It is not right."

Mr. Grey could not hear the words that passed between the pair. All he was able to observe was that the gentleman and the lady conversed quietly, almost secretly. After witnessing such a spectacle, could there be any remaining doubt that there was an understanding between them? Words could not describe what Mr. Grey felt, but he was powerless to do anything except look on in pain and humiliation.

Not content to let the matter rest there, Mr. Brydges said to his rival, "Mr. Grey, why do you not take a turn at the game?"

"Oh no, I could not. Perhaps someone else might go instead," came the reply.

"Come, Mr. Grey. It is only a bit of amusement—or do you object to a clergyman's taking part in Valentine's Day festivities?"

"No, I have no objection on that account."

"Then oblige us this once, if you please."

Though Mr. Grey had no desire to play, he agreed and then left the room so that the others could prepare what was needed for the next round of the game. During his absence, Mr. Brydges took it upon himself to arrange everything. "I will choose something easy. The task is one that Mr. Grey should be quite familiar with," said he to the party. As he spoke, Mr. Brydges took a Bible from the bookcase, and after writing something on a piece of paper, he slipped it into the book and placed the Bible on the pianoforte. It was time to call the clergyman back in.

On re-entering the drawing room, Mr. Grey had no difficulty in following the music to the pianoforte. Perceiving the book that was lying on top, he opened it to the marked page, but when he saw what was written on the slip of paper, his face turned to stone. The gentleman swallowed and did not speak at first, but only shot a look at Mr. Brydges, who had a sly smirk on his visage.

"I see that I am to read this," said Mr. Grey. Finally regaining his composure, he relieved the curiosity of the entire room by reading the words aloud:

"But I say unto you, That whosoever looketh upon a woman to lust after her, hath already committed adultery with her in his heart."[13]

"What a strange choice of Bible verse!" thought Georgiana. What did Mr. Brydges mean by it? Somewhat surprising, too, was the violence of Mr. Grey's reaction to the passage. It was all very puzzling, but Georgiana could not quite account for what had just happened.

Looking pensive, Mr. Grey started to close the book, then paused, and said, "As I already have the Bible before me, I would like to read a different passage. It is from Corinthians."

He turned the pages until he found the right place and began to read, his voice full of tenderness and emotion:

"Love suffereth long and is kind; love envieth not; love acteth not rashly, is not puffed up: Doth not behave indecently, seeketh not her own, is not provoked, thinketh no evil; Rejoiceth not at iniquity, but rejoiceth in the truth: Covereth all things..."

Here, Mr. Grey looked up from the page at Georgiana.

"...hopeth all things, believeth all things, endureth all things."[14]

In that moment, Georgiana felt that Mr. Grey was not merely a clergyman reading the Bible aloud, but rather, that it was as if his soul was speaking directly to hers. Overwhelmed by the beauty of the words and the powerful feeling with which he spoke them, Georgiana could not bear to meet his gaze any longer and lowered her eyelashes so that he could not see the crystal droplets that glistened at the corners. The other guests were likewise not insensitive to the clergyman's speech. They, too, were moved by his heartfelt words—so much so that some of the ladies in the room were obliged to dab their eyes with their white handkerchiefs. Mr. Brydges, in contrast, sat looking morose and somewhat displeased.

As the evening drew to a close and the guests prepared to return to their homes, Georgiana hoped that Mr. Grey might wish to speak with her before he departed, but he did not. To the Bingleys and Miss Darcy, he said only a brief, formal farewell and then left directly.

Feeling uneasy, Georgiana found an opportunity to talk to Mr. Brydges' sister privately and said to her:

"Mrs. Spencer, I wish you had not done what you did during the game of Musical Magic; your brother ought to have returned the ring to you as was intended—he should not have placed it on my finger."

"Miss Darcy, there is no reason to be so concerned. It was only a game; a little amusement in the spirit of Valentine's Day never harmed anybody."

"Still, Mrs. Spencer, that sort of thing may be misconstrued by others and might create the wrong impression in people's minds."

Although Georgiana spoke of the guests' opinions in general, she thought only of Mr. Grey and of his face as it had looked when Mr. Brydges slipped Mrs. Spencer's ring onto her finger. It struck her now that from a distance, it may have appeared as if she were encouraging Mr. Brydges' attentions. Of this suspicion she had some confirmation in Mr. Grey's aloof manner towards her during their parting.

Though of course, in all propriety, Georgiana could not speak of the incident with the ring to Mr. Grey, she still wanted to find some way of clearing away any misunderstanding and hoped to do so at Tuesday night's ball, which he had previously mentioned he planned on attending. To her disappointment, the gentleman did not come to the ball at the Lower Rooms on Tuesday, and neither had he appeared in the pump-room that morning, as was his frequent custom.

On the morrow, Mr. Bingley chanced to meet Mr. Grey while leaving the bank at the corner of Milsom Street. The former invited his friend to come to dinner at his home that evening. However, Mr. Grey declined, saying that he would not be at liberty to dine with them that day. On learning of this conversation, Georgiana became even more disquieted. Was Mr. Grey avoiding her? What was in his mind? Did he really believe that she cared anything for Mr. Brydges? Or maybe she was being needlessly anxious. Perhaps Mr. Grey was not, in fact, offended at her, and she had merely misinterpreted the whole situation.

There was to be another ball at the Upper Rooms on Thursday, and Georgiana had every hope that Mr. Grey would be there. Until then, she would try not to give way to distressing fears.

CHAPTER 42

At the ball on Thursday evening, Georgiana again looked out for Mr. Grey. As she weaved through the crowd and exchanged nods and greetings with passing acquaintances, her eyes searched for him. Instead of the gentleman she sought, however, Mr. Amherst and Miss Fellowes soon came into view. They had just finished a dance, and, breathless and smiling, they promptly moved towards their friend. Dying of suspense, Georgiana swallowed her pride and inquired after Mr. Grey. Had he come to the ball? Mr. Amherst and Miss Fellowes exchanged a glance, after which the lady replied that no, he had not come.

"I hope he is in good health?" asked Miss Darcy hesitantly.

"Yes, he appeared to me to be in excellent health, although perhaps not in the best of spirits. He hardly spoke a word to anyone all day today," answered Miss Fellowes. "Now that I think about it, I believe he has been that way since Monday night."

Georgiana's heart fell. Mr. Grey really *was* angry with her then. Even more dispiriting than this realisation was the knowledge that, though his resentment was groundless, she could do nothing to correct the situation. Oppressed by these thoughts, Georgiana lost all interest in dancing. Still, in order to prevent drawing attention to her misery and prompting concerned questions from Jane and Mr. Bingley, she did her best to carry on as usual and half-heartedly danced with all who asked her.

The first to seek her hand was a gentleman whom the Master of Ceremonies introduced as Mr. Cunningham. Miss Darcy accepted his invitation, and as she and her partner were walking away to join the other couples, Grace Spencer, who had just arrived at the Upper Rooms with her husband's family and Mr. Brydges, addressed her brother with:

"It is a pity, Michael, that you found it necessary to spend three hours dressing for the ball. You could have danced with Miss Darcy instead, but look, there is Mr. Cunningham with her now."

"It was not three hours, surely," came the indignant reply. "Two and three-quarters at most, but certainly not three."

"What difference does it make? The result is still the same!"

Mr. Brydges sighed, and having nothing better to do, he asked one of the Miss Pheasants to dance.

Mr. Cunningham was a rather handsome, dashing fellow, and as he and his partner footed it through the mazes of a country dance, he flirted with Georgiana a great deal. She took no pleasure in his attentions and, in fact, felt somewhat uncomfortable in his society. It was a relief, therefore, when the dance came to an end. Grace Spencer joined her presently, and although there were few people whom Miss Darcy would less rather have seen, she forced a smile and returned her greeting.

"Do you know with whom you just danced?" asked Mrs. Spencer.

"That was Mr. Cunningham."

"Yes, I know his name. What I meant is, do you know what kind of man he is?"

Georgiana had no idea, and so her acquaintance informed her of his character at once.

"He is an avaricious, unprincipled man," said she. "Last year he married a wealthy young lady for her fortune."

"He is married?!" exclaimed Georgiana. "He did not at all behave as if he were married... Where is his wife?"

"Mrs. Cunningham rarely goes into society anymore," was the answer. "Would you believe, he proposed marriage to her six times before she accepted him. Undeterred by her refusals, he only pursued her more tenaciously until at last she capitulated. Their marriage is a very unhappy one, I hear. Mr. Cunningham neglects his wife and spends her fortune, all while keeping mistresses and flirting with every pretty woman he sees."

"Oh, how awful!" said Georgiana, to which Mrs. Spencer replied, "I can assure you that my brother's character is nothing like that of the fortune-hunting scoundrels one frequently encounters in Bath. Our father instilled in him principles of virtue and honour from an early age, and as to wealth, Michael cares nothing for it. Since coming to Bath, my brother has talked and thought of but one lady. Would you like to guess whom he holds in such high esteem?"

"I would not venture to presume what is in Mr. Brydges' mind," returned Georgiana.

"Then I will not press you further, Miss Darcy, and neither would Michael wish for me to discomfit you, but what I *will* say is that I hope you will think kindly of him."

Georgiana was saved from having to make a reply by Mrs. Bosomworth and Mrs. Pheasant, both of whom came to warn her about Mr. Cunningham. "I would advise you to be on your guard with him, Miss Darcy," said Mrs. Bosomworth. "It would be best to shun his society altogether," added Mrs. Pheasant. "I hear that while his poor wife remains at home, he stays out until late to enjoy bacchanalian revels and wild parties, where he dances the waltz with other women."

"The waltz?! How shocking!" exclaimed Mrs. Bosomworth. "I consider it a most scandalous dance that none but husband and wife should ever attempt."

"Oh yes," agreed Mrs. Pheasant. "The partners hold their bodies in such close proximity, and the motion is of such a nature as to make it the height of indecency! I think it is not so much a dance as an improper intertwining of the limbs! You will not see the waltz at Almack's, nor at any other respectable place. No master of ceremonies would permit it!"

Georgiana's cheeks crimsoned deeply. With mortification she remembered the time at Kleistringham when she herself had danced the waltz with Sir Matthew Leigh and had nearly let him kiss her. This behaviour, she knew, had been immodest and imprudent. As Georgiana recalled, it was not the first time that she had allowed her feelings for a man to overpower her own better judgment and to lead her into indecorous conduct, of which she herself, in a clearer state of mind, would have disapproved. That other occasion on which Miss Darcy reflected with remorse was her near-elopement with George Wickham at fifteen years old. Believing herself to be in love with the man, she had agreed to run away with him to be married, and only by the chance arrival of her brother shortly beforehand had the scheme been prevented from coming to fruition. Georgiana now shuddered to think how narrowly she had escaped an indissoluble union with an unworthy man who wished to wed her fortune rather than her person. Struck as never before by the danger and folly of allowing others to lead her so easily into reprehensible conduct, she resolved to act more thoughtfully and prudently in the future.

While the young lady was thus absorbed in contemplation, Mr. Brydges drew near. He had only just succeeded in extricating himself from conversation with a very determined Miss Fanny Pheasant. Relieved by his escape, he now came to ask Miss Darcy to dance the next set with him. Georgiana would have liked to refuse but in that instant could think of no polite excuse, and so she agreed.

As the gentleman was leading his partner away, Mrs. Pheasant remarked, nodding in their direction:

"*There* is one couple who will soon be waltzing together as husband and wife."

"Mr. Brydges and Miss Darcy?! No, surely not! I always thought she had a partiality for Mr. Grey," replied Mrs. Bosomworth.

"Pooh, pooh! Mr. Grey, indeed! On Valentine's Day, I went to a dinner party at which he and Miss Darcy scarcely spoke a word to each other, but at that same gathering, Mr. Brydges showered Miss Darcy with attentions. After dinner, we played games, and during one particular game, Mr. Brydges took advantage of an opportunity to put a wedding ring on Miss Darcy's finger. From where I sat, it appeared that she gave him very positive encouragement. Mark my words, if they are not yet engaged, they soon will be!"

It was not long before Mrs. Pheasant had persuaded Mrs. Bosomworth that the two young people would be married in the near future. So well did she succeed in the task that Mrs. Bosomworth became even more convinced of it than Mrs. Pheasant was herself. The latter wagered that they would be married by Whitsuntide, while the former insisted that the wedding would surely take place sooner—perhaps even next month.

CHAPTER 43

The time was fast approaching when Georgiana and her hosts were to leave Bath. Only a few days remained in which to enjoy the city, and on the Wednesday before the date set for their departure, they decided to spend the evening at a concert in the Upper Rooms. With a heavy heart, Georgiana dressed for the event. Ever since that unfortunate Valentine's Day dinner party, she had taken no pleasure in the amusements of Bath, and tonight was no exception. It was impossible to derive enjoyment even from music when Mr. Grey clearly had no wish to see her.

For her personal ornaments that evening, Georgiana again chose her brother's gold and topaz jewellery. As her maid was placing the necklace around Miss Darcy's neck, the young lady thought back to the unhappy occasion on which she had last worn it. Mrs. Parker's Valentine's Day dinner, to which she had looked forward with eager anticipation, could hardly have ended in a worse way; owing to the imprudent behaviour of Mr. Brydges and his sister, Mr. Grey had turned away from her, and now, with very little time left before Georgiana was to leave Bath, she doubted whether the man who had come to mean so much to her would even wish to say goodbye.

Made miserable by these thoughts and recollections, she asked the maid to remove the necklace and give her a different one to wear, but then Georgiana thought better of it—why should she not wear the jewellery to the concert? After all, it was her dear brother's gift, a sign of his affection for her, and regardless of what had happened on Valentine's Day, she should not allow the unpleasant association to diminish the happiness that her brother's gift ought to bring. Thus resolved, Georgiana asked the maid to refasten the necklace, while she put on the matching earrings.

To Miss Darcy's surprise, Mr. Grey was at the Upper Rooms when she and the Bingleys arrived at the concert. Accompanying the gentleman were the Egertons and Miss Fellowes. On seeing him so unexpectedly, Georgiana initially felt a surge of joy, but this sentiment was immediately followed by apprehension, sadness, and confusion. How would he behave towards her? Would he speak to her?

Mr. Grey observed Georgiana's entrance and almost immediately also perceived the infamous jewellery, which served to forcefully remind him (if indeed he had in the least forgotten) that Miss Darcy would never be his, and that he must endeavour to forget her. In keeping with this resolution, he directed his gaze away from Georgiana—an action which she did not fail to notice.

When, in all politeness, it could no longer be avoided, Mr. Grey greeted Georgiana and her companions, but his manner towards her was cool and distant; to the lady's feelings, such a greeting was worse than none at all. The gentleman then spoke very briefly with Mr. Bingley and his wife but said not a word to Miss Darcy. All this neglect she felt very keenly, and when everyone sat down to listen to the concert, Georgiana found that she had no desire to hear the music.

Positioned some distance away from Georgiana was Mrs. Bosomworth, who, having just finished a very animated conversation with Mrs. Pheasant, rose from her chair but was obliged to sit back down again by the commencement of the concert. She bit her lip with impatience and furrowed her brow, all the while looking intently in the direction of Georgiana's party. Leaning out of her chair and craning her neck, Mrs. Bosomworth appeared almost as if she was about to jump out of the seat. Clearly, she had something to tell, but whatever the source of her ill-contained excitement, it would have to wait until after the concert.

"Observe Mrs. Bosomworth," whispered Mr. Bingley, smiling. "I think she must have some new gossip she wishes to share." Georgiana, however, took no pleasure in the comical sight, and neither did she feel any curiosity to hear the dear lady's gossip. All she could think of was Mr. Grey.

The orchestra was playing Mozart's Piano Concerto 23 in A major. During the first movement of the composition, Georgiana kept command of her feelings tolerably, but at the start of the second movement, she could bear the agony of her heart no longer. As the melodious adagio began, quiet tears slid slowly down her cheeks. Those seated near Miss Darcy supposed that she was merely moved by the beautiful music, but while the plaintive, heart-rending quality of the melody did heighten her emotions, Georgiana's tears were not for Mozart; they were all for Mr. Grey. Oh, why must they have this senseless quarrel?! In material terms, nothing had changed since the day he sent her a valentine. Yet, here she and Mr. Grey were, both despondent, when there was no real reason why they could not be as happy as they had been before. How foolish it all was!

From their relative placement in the room, Mr. Grey had a clear view of Georgiana, and despite himself, he found his eyes returning to her often, though she was oblivious to his furtive glances. How his heart ached at their estrangement! But what could he do now except long for her from a distance? So there they sat, two miserable humans, each yearning to be near the other, yet feeling as if they were miles apart.

No sooner had the concert ended, than Mrs. Bosomworth, her eyes sparkling with excitement, hurried towards Georgiana and her friends.

"Have you heard the news concerning Mr. Brydges?" cried she upon reaching them.

"News? I have not heard any news about him," said Mr. Bingley.

"Nor I," seconded his wife.

Thrilled at the prospect of being the first to communicate what she knew to the company, Mrs. Bosomworth wasted no time in beginning her story:

"Mrs. Pheasant, whose son-in-law has a seat in Parliament, has just told me the whole of the tale. Mr. Brydges, the same who has all this time been boasting that he is to be the next Baron Chandos of Sudeley, has been declared a fraud by Parliament! The House of Lords has at last made a decision in his peerage case and has found that not only is there no connection whatsoever between him and the Chandos family, but also that the evidence he provided to support his case was fabricated."

"I cannot believe such a thing of Mr. Brydges. Are you sure that there has not been some mistake?" exclaimed Mrs. Bingley.

"There is little chance of that," was the answer. "The parish record he submitted as proof of his descent was found to have been tampered with; the entry in question was written in fresh ink and in a different hand than those on the rest of the page. According to Parliament, the forgery was so evident, in fact, that one wonders at Mr. Brydges' not being ashamed to present the document as evidence. There is to be an investigation to discover who made the spurious entry in the parish register, but I, for one, have little doubt as to his identity—Mr. Brydges was the only one who had anything to gain from such a falsehood, and I have often perceived that there was something cunning in his countenance!"

Mrs. Bosomworth was particularly interested to see what effect this intelligence would produce on Georgiana since there was every reason to believe that the young lady might be engaged to the miscreant. The teller of the tale hoped to witness scenes of shock and inconsolable grief, which would enable her to augment and improve future retellings of the story she had heard from Mrs. Pheasant. However, to Mrs. Bosomworth's dissatisfaction, Miss Darcy showed no signs of anguish. Mr. Grey, who had heard the whole conversation, also observed that although Georgiana seemed a little surprised by the news, she did not at all appear to be distressed by it. The calmness of her reaction puzzled him exceedingly.

Not satisfied until she heard Georgiana's opinion one way or the other, Mrs. Bosomworth inquired, "Miss Darcy, what do *you* think of all this business with Mr. Brydges?"

"It is rather unfortunate, but I am not sufficiently well-acquainted with Mr. Brydges to know whether he is capable of such deception," returned Georgiana. "Yet, I think it is not right to condemn him until the investigation is complete. Would you not agree?"

"Well... I... Yes, I suppose so," came the stammered reply. Mrs. Bosomworth felt somewhat ashamed at having merited Georgiana's reproof, which she knew was just. Wishing to change the subject, she said the first thing that came into her mind:

"I do not believe I have ever seen you wear that jewellery before, Miss

Darcy. Is it new?"

"Yes, it is a present from my brother. He gave it to me shortly before I came to Bath."

Mr. Grey changed countenance. With astonishment in his voice, he exclaimed, "Your brother?! Then it is not... I beg your pardon, Miss Darcy. I am not sure I heard you correctly; you said it was your *brother* who gave you the jewellery?"

"Yes, my brother—Fitzwilliam Darcy."

"Why do you look so shocked, Mr. Grey?" asked Lady Egerton. "Surely there is nothing strange in a brother's giving his sister a fine gift."

"No, I did not mean to imply that there was. I merely... I do not know what came over me."

While the others turned to a new topic of conversation, Mr. Grey said to Georgiana privately, "Miss Darcy, I feel that I owe you an apology for my behaviour of late. I wish that I could give you some sort of justifiable explanation for my conduct, but all I can say is that I have been foolish in giving credence to malicious tongues and then imagining the worst. Most sincerely do I now beg your pardon. Can you forgive me?"

Notwithstanding that she had been deeply hurt by Mr. Grey's aloofness towards her, Georgiana gave him her forgiveness ungrudgingly. Still, she could not help wondering whose were the malicious tongues to which the gentleman had alluded. Could he have Mr. Brydges or his sister in mind? And why had Mr. Grey been so amazed to discover that her necklace and earrings were a gift from her brother? Despite still being rather mystified by what she had heard, Georgiana chose not to dwell on these questions. It was far better to enjoy the time that she and Mr. Grey had left together.

Meanwhile, the culprit behind all their former misery was at that moment in a crowded stagecoach on his way to London. Mr. Brydges had resolved on quitting Bath as soon as he received word that his claim to the barony of Chandos had been rejected. After all, why stay when nothing remained for him in the city except to face the mocking eyes of others? As the carriage jolted along, he furiously pencilled a rough draft of a letter that he intended to submit to a prominent London newspaper for publication. In the missive, he enumerated all the wrongs that had been committed against him and bemoaned the injustice of Parliament's decision in his peerage case. Every minute that he wrote, the gentleman grew increasingly incensed and indignant at the way he had been treated by the House of Lords. One might wonder at his impudence, but the explanation is very simple: after having kept up the pretence of being the next heir to the title for so long, he had very nearly begun to believe it himself.

CHAPTER 44

Friday was to be Georgiana's final day in Bath before her planned departure for home with Mr. and Mrs. Bingley early the next morning. They spent a considerable part of that last day taking leave of their many friends in the city, chief among them being the Egertons and Mr. Grey. Ahead of that final meeting, it occurred to Georgiana that Mr. Grey might perhaps make her an offer of marriage before she quitted Bath. After all, there would be no more opportunities for them to speak to each other in the foreseeable future. But would he ask her? If he did, she knew what her reply would be.

When the company arrived at the Royal Crescent, Lady Egerton received them without her husband. Sir Philip was ill in bed, she told the visitors. However, after hearing who had come, the old gentleman soon appeared in the sitting room. He looked a little feeble but was clearly determined not to let his friends leave without bidding them farewell and wishing them a safe journey.

During the visit, Mr. Grey spoke comparatively little, though there was much he wished to say. Miss Darcy's impending departure weighed heavily on his mind, and he felt acutely aware that opportunity was slipping away, but still he took no action. All too soon, the time came for the guests to leave. Lady Egerton, Miss Fellowes, and he walked out with them, and after exchanging a few more phrases, the gentleman handed Mrs. Bingley and

Miss Darcy into the carriage. As he was helping Georgiana in, Mr. Grey held her hand a second or two longer than was perhaps needed, and when he looked at her, his eyes spoke what his lips would not. Yet, all he said aloud was, "Goodbye, Miss Darcy." Nothing more.

Mr. Grey remained outside to watch the carriage drive off; it was with a sinking heart that Georgiana felt the vehicle's motion taking her farther and farther away from him. Back at the Paragon, she waited hopefully in case a message might arrive from him, but in vain, and when the next morning she entered the chaise that would take her and the Bingleys home, she felt the bitterest disappointment—Mr. Grey had neither said nor written that which she most wished to hear; he had not asked her to become his wife.

Now that they had parted for an indefinite length of time, how would they refer to one another in the future? As former acquaintances? It was a cold, harsh term considering what he meant to her, and what Georgiana believed she meant to him, but what else could they be to each other now? She was to return to Derbyshire, and he would shortly be leaving with his aunt and uncle for Somersetshire—the Egertons to their estate, and Mr. Grey to his parish. Henceforth, the young man and Georgiana would be separated by many miles with no reason to suppose that they would ever see each other again.

Georgiana was very quiet on the journey home to Pemberley. Her thoughts were entirely occupied with the gentleman whom she had left behind in Bath. Having some notion of what had brought on their friend's pensive mood, Jane and Bingley did not inquire into the cause of her reticence, nor did they press her for conversation. Instead, their behaviour towards her was marked by kind understanding, for which Miss Darcy was grateful.

After a seemingly endless duration of travel, the carriage at last brought Georgiana to her brother's estate. Mr. Darcy and his wife had by then returned from Scotland, and they were both outside to welcome her home when she stepped out of the chaise. It warmed Georgiana's heart to be reunited with her family, and all the more so when Elizabeth informed her that she was with child! The idea of having a little niece or nephew in several months' time gave Miss Darcy some much-needed joy and for a time raised her low spirits. All the same, once the effect of the unexpected news subsided, Elizabeth observed that Georgiana seemed subdued, though having no knowledge of the cause, she attributed it to fatigue from the long journey. Soon, Mrs. Darcy's attention was absorbed by another source: her father and Kitty arrived from Hertfordshire two days later, and in all the excitement, Georgiana's melancholy quietness did not draw as much notice as it would otherwise have done.

Catherine Bennet was extremely happy to be back. During the months she had spent away, she had not forgotten the handsome Mr. Morgan. In her estimation, he was infinitely superior to even the best of the fellows in Hertfordshire with whom she had danced, and now that she was in Derbyshire again, Kitty felt most anxious to renew their acquaintance. She was impatient to attend church on Sunday, not from any uncharacteristic urge to hear a sermon, but because she knew Mr. Morgan would be in the congregation. In the intervening time, Kitty busied herself with trying to decide which of her gowns the gentleman might like best, and which of her bonnets she should wear. When Elizabeth and Georgiana went into Lambton to make some purchases, Miss Bennet insisted on coming with them in hopes that she might encounter Mr. Morgan there.

As the Pemberley ladies were pursing their business in the little town, Kitty entertained Mrs. Darcy and Georgiana with an account of Dr. Collins' visit to Longbourn. When asked how she had liked the man, Kitty made a face and said she found him to be awfully dull and tiresome; he frequently quoted from Scripture in conversation, and in the evenings, he always read aloud to the family from the Bible. "It was worse than that time his cousin Mr. Collins read to us from *Fordyce's Sermons*," she complained. "At least Mr. Collins was so ridiculous as to be amusing. Dr. Collins, on the other hand, is purely a bore. I do not know how his parishioners can stand him! Mama seems to like him—but then again, she would approve of any heir to Longbourn who might wish to marry one of her daughters."

"Has he made an offer to either you or Mary, then?" laughed Elizabeth.

"No, not yet, but I suspect he will make one to Mary before long. She seems to have made a very good impression on Dr. Collins."

"And does Mary like him?"

"Oh, yes—even more than he likes her, I believe, but how anyone could like that stiff, old prig, I cannot imagine!"

"Perhaps they are well-suited to each other," suggested Georgiana. "Mary always struck me as someone who might enjoy discussing religious subjects with her husband."

"Well, then she had better take him, for it is unlikely that anyone else will ever wish to marry her," answered Kitty scornfully. "As for myself, I hope to do much better."

On quitting one of the shops they visited, Miss Bennet suddenly caught sight of Mr. Morgan, who was standing a short distance ahead with Mr. Owens, the parson, and his daughter. Noticing the ladies, Mr. Morgan tipped his hat to them, and before Elizabeth could stop her, Kitty hurried up to him. After scarcely acknowledging the two who had been conversing with the gentleman, she launched into lively chatter. Kitty simpered, and flirted, and acted as foolishly as she had ever done, completely forgetting (or choosing not to remember) all that her elder sisters had ever taught her about proper behaviour.

Mr. Morgan listened to Miss Bennet for a little while with an amused countenance and then informed her that he also had some news to share: he had recently been united in marriage with Miss Owens, the clergyman's daughter standing beside him. Kitty did not answer at first and only stared in astonishment, but at last she croaked out a half-hearted congratulation. Elizabeth and Georgiana offered their own congratulations with greater spirit and more sincerity, and after making a few polite inquiries and remarks, Mrs. Darcy took leave of Mr. Morgan and his family and led her sister and Georgiana away.

As soon as the ladies were no longer within hearing distance of their acquaintances, Kitty burst out, "I cannot believe that Mr. Morgan chose to marry that... that bluestocking!"

"I would not call her a bluestocking," protested Elizabeth. "She is a well-educated, sensible young woman, yes, but not excessively bookish, and I always thought she had a comely face and pleasant manners."

"Comely?! Well, you may call her that if you wish, but to me she will always be an uninteresting prude!"

"Perhaps, like most gentlemen, Mr. Morgan prefers ladies who conduct themselves properly," observed Elizabeth.

This last remark silenced Kitty, and though she pouted and sulked during the entire way home (and for a considerable length of time afterwards), her face at the same time wore a thoughtful expression. For several hours she reflected on what she had heard and the way in which she had acted. How silly and undignified she must have appeared when running up to Mr. Morgan and then chattering away in the manner she had done, when his wife was right there beside him! During these past months, while she had been longing to see the gentleman again and daydreaming of marrying him, he had in the meantime been courting Miss Owens, a lady whose only charms were the sort her elder sisters considered praiseworthy. These same charms, however, had succeeded where her own had failed. Could it be that Lizzy was right? Oh, horrible thought! Kitty banished it from her mind at once, but then the idea returned again... and again. She remembered, also, that Elizabeth and Jane had both married very well without resorting to coquetry, and that of all her sisters, she was the only one who had neither a husband nor any reason to expect the acquisition of one in the near future.

Her sister Lydia, it was true, had managed to catch a husband using the sorts of allurements that she herself was in the habit of employing, but at the same time, Kitty recalled, it was only with strong persuasion and substantial pecuniary incentive that the man with whom Lydia had eloped had finally been prevailed upon to marry her. Without this intervention, Mr. Wickham would almost certainly have jilted Lydia, and she would have been ruined forever. These were unpleasant contemplations, indeed, but at the end of them, Kitty started to question the wisdom of her own behaviour. The defection of a favourite beau at last began to convince her, in a way that none of her elder sisters' admonishments had ever done, that modesty and decorum, as well as education and good sense, have some value after all.

Several months wore on. After leaving Bath, Georgiana had retained a small hope that Mr. Grey might send her a letter proposing marriage, but no such communication ever came, and as March and April passed, and May gave way to June, it appeared increasingly unlikely that she would ever hear from the gentleman. Georgiana at length confided in her sister-in-law and disclosed the source of her misery. Elizabeth, who had always held Mr. Grey in high regard, sympathised and did her best to offer solace, but what can one possibly say that can compensate for the loss of a worthy love? Mrs. Darcy did, however, encourage Georgiana to attempt to divert her mind from regretful thoughts by pouring her efforts into music and painting.

As she was walking towards the music room one morning, Elizabeth heard Georgiana practicing Bach's Prelude and Fugue in C-sharp minor.[15] It was a slow, melancholy melody, and in its poignant notes, she could hear all the longing and all the quiet sadness of Georgiana's heart. Elizabeth listened to the music silently for some moments and then entered the room. As she drew near to the pianoforte, Georgiana stopped playing and addressed her with:

"Oh Lizzy, it is no use; I cannot forget him. I miss Mr. Grey so very much, but I am beginning to think that perhaps he did not really love me. Otherwise, would he not have expressed a wish to marry me before we parted?"

Mrs. Darcy sighed and sat down in a chair beside her. "I remember the way in which Mr. Grey used to look at you in Kent," said she. "He was clearly in love with you, and given what you have told me of your time together in Bath, I cannot believe that he no longer cares for you. It is more probable that Mr. Grey did not propose marriage because he does not yet have the means to adequately support a family."

"Oh, but if that is the case, I wish he had spoken!" exclaimed Georgiana. "I cannot bear to have him gone from my life and not to know whether our paths will ever cross again. There are so many things about him that I love and respect—the goodness of his soul, his integrity, the matchless endowments of his mind. As well as these admirable qualities, he possesses good humour and a cheerful liveliness that always made me forget how the hours passed whenever I was in his company. With no one else have I ever been so happy as I was with him."

Elizabeth thought for a moment about what Georgiana had said before replying, "While I agree with you that Mr. Grey is an exceptionally worthy young man—still, consider, even if he had made you an offer, would it have been entirely prudent to accept him? Though money is not everything, neither is it a completely immaterial consideration. I do not think your brother would have given his blessing to a marriage under such circumstances."

"I suppose you are right, Lizzy," sighed Georgiana, "but what kind of world is it in which a capable, intelligent, talented man, who is not afraid of work, does not earn enough from his labours to enable him to marry?"

CHAPTER 45

After their wedding, Sir Matthew Leigh and his bride proceeded directly to the gentleman's estate in Cheshire. The lady wrote to her family to acquaint them with the news of her marriage, but in reply she received a letter marked by such a degree of incivility from her father that for some time afterwards no further correspondence passed between them. While Lady Villiers was distressed and grieved that her husband refused to receive the run-away couple at Belargent, John Villiers did not mind in the least. Quite the opposite, he was rather enjoying the peace and quiet he had experienced at home ever since his sister's elopement.

Yet, the passage of time somewhat cooled Sir Edward Villiers' anger, and as the months went by, he grew increasingly concerned at the thought of his son-in-law's financial affairs. Sir Matthew's extravagance and ignorance of how to manage his money were such that unless he intervened, and soon, financial ruin for the Leighs was inevitable. Priscilla might finish in a workhouse! Neither fatherly affection nor family pride could endure such an outcome, and therefore, Sir Edward at last wrote his daughter a letter in June to invite (or rather, to summon) the young married couple to Belargent Hall.

Although affronted by the gruff tone of her father's letter, Lady Leigh chose to overlook it, for she saw that there was more to gain from a reconciliation than from prolonged hostilities. Having thus made up her mind, she wrote to accept her father's invitation and afterwards informed her husband of how she had decided to act in the matter.

On the day appointed for the visitors' arrival, the Villiers family were assembled in their drawing room, where the discussion inevitably gravitated to the elopement. "That was a devious trick they played to send a decoy carriage to Dover while they fled to Gretna Green in another!" began Sir Edward. "If I had not mistakenly first gone to Dover, I would surely have caught up with them before they reached Scotland. The idea was undoubtedly Priscilla's; it is just like her to contrive such a scheme, the sly thing!"

His daughter actually had a very good reason for choosing Gretna Green over the Island of Guernsey. Notwithstanding that the young people could have married sooner if they had sailed to Guernsey from Dover, the stomach-turning thought of voyaging on rough waters did not appeal to the bride. In her opinion, the resulting journey would have been anything but romantic. She preferred a quiet and pleasant, if somewhat lengthier, trip to Scotland.

"It was extremely foolish of Priscilla to consent to an elopement," continued Sir Edward. "In addition to tarnishing her reputation, her conduct has placed her in a precarious financial position; as there was no marriage settlement, no provision whatsoever has been made either for her or for any future children."

"Not even pin money has been provided for!" lamented his wife.

"There is nothing to concern yourselves with," their son assured them. "If I know Priscilla, she will make her husband give her exactly as much pin money as she wishes for regardless of whether there is any marriage settlement."

This observation gave Lady Villiers a great deal of comfort, for she knew that there was much truth in it. After a brief silence, she rejoiced, "Only think, everyone now addresses my daughter as Lady Leigh! I always wanted her to marry a baronet. And Sir Matthew's estate is such an enviable piece of land!"

"What estate?!" returned her husband crossly. "He has mortgaged it so deeply that it can hardly be called his anymore. A little longer, and Sir Matthew will be crushed under the weight of his debts."

"But perhaps you can help him, my dear."

"I will not give one farthing to that scoundrel! To think that I should have such a spendthrift, a gambler, and a near-bankrupt for a son-in-law!"

John Villiers replied with: "'Neither a borrower nor a lender be,'[16] said the great Shakespeare. Wise words, wise words."

"If I had listened to Shakespeare, I would never have been able to raise the capital needed to expand my business, and we might all still be living in Cheapside," retorted Sir Edward.

"Do not mention that dreadful place, I pray you!" cried his wife. Then, catching sight of the Leighs' carriage driving towards the house, she exclaimed, "Here they come! Let us go down to receive them."

"We will do no such thing!" declared Sir Edward angrily. "Considering how they have behaved, they ought to be grateful that I allowed them to come at all! We shall not stir from our places!" With some reluctance, Lady Villiers sat back down.

The errant couple soon entered. Sir Matthew came in hesitantly, penitently, as if highly conscious of his past misdeeds and unsure of how he would be received. His wife, in contrast, did not appear to be in the least contrite, and, if anything, she looked even bolder and more self-assured than ever. Lady Villiers rose to receive them and welcomed them both with undiminished affection. Sir Edward, who was still feeling very resentful, troubled himself only so far as to greet his daughter curtly and barely acknowledged his son-in-law. On the whole, it was a fairly awkward meeting, though John Villiers found the scene highly amusing.

They talked for a little while, with Sir Edward and Sir Matthew largely abstaining from the conversation. Then a walk was proposed. This suggestion was readily agreed upon, for staying indoors with nothing to look at but each other was beginning to be trying on everyone's nerves.

Soon the whole party was strolling through the gardens. Walking a little apart from the others, Mr. Villiers inquired of his sister, "Priscilla, there is something I have been meaning to ask you. Why did you have to go all the way to Gretna Green and get married over the anvil? Why not have done it properly and wedded here?"

"Brother, you ask rather too many questions!"

"Was it a case of 'strike while the iron is hot', eh Priscilla?"

"Really, John, you speak like a common farmer! And I will have you know that we were married not by a blacksmith but by David Lang, or 'Bishop Lang', to be exact, at The King's Head inn."

"*Bishop* Lang?" chuckled Mr. Villiers. "Is he a real clergyman, per-chance?"

"Whether he is or is not makes no difference. The marriage is valid in Scotland, and therefore it is so in England as well! Besides, now that Sir Matthew and I have reconciled with Papa, we intend to solemnise our marriage in England with my father's consent. And another thing, now that I am *married*, I am no longer 'Priscilla' to you but 'Lady Leigh'. You must address me properly."

"Well, if I am to call you 'Lady Leigh', you must call me 'Mr. Villiers'."

"Fair enough," conceded the young woman.

Meanwhile, Sir Matthew was making an effort to mend relations with his father-in-law. Trying to find some neutral subject of mutual interest, he remarked, "You have some very fine grounds here, Sir Edward. Have you ever considered making use of them to go fox hunting?"

"Fox hunting?! We have never engaged in that sport here and are not about to start now."

"Why, what is wrong with it?"

"It is a waste of money! When one takes into account the cost of hounds, horses, whippers-in, and so forth, the funeral expenses of each fox killed come to no less than fifty pounds, I am sure. Even the wealthy ought to be economical in their pleasures, Sir Matthew. A man of true intelligence strives to create the appearance of wealth while spending as little as possible."

"But I do not hunt to appear rich; I do it because I enjoy the sport."

"Then you ought to employ your time better!" came the growled reply.

"How would you have me spend my time instead?"

"Securing a prosperous future for yourself and your family, of course!" answered Sir Edward with a scowl. "Since we are members of the higher orders of society, Sir Matthew, we do not work, but that does not mean we should become complacent about money. Every day I read the newspapers and contemplate where best to invest and how to accumulate even more possessions than I already have. From what I see and read, factories are beginning to replace land as the chief source of wealth. If we are to maintain our position in the world, we must act early and invest our money where the profits are. Otherwise, we will be left behind as others overtake us."

When they came into the rose garden, Lady Leigh exclaimed, "What beautiful flowers you have here, Mama! The roses are even lovelier than I remember them!"

"That is because some of them are new. In autumn the gardeners planted several excellent varieties that are just now coming into bloom," replied Lady Villiers. Delighted by the fragrant flowers, her daughter declared that she would like for one of the gardeners to cut some for the bedroom she shared with her husband.

"I love a room full of flowers!" said she enthusiastically.

"Are you sure that is wise, my dear?" asked Sir Matthew. "That time when you filled our bedchamber with magnolia blossoms at home, I got a terrible headache from their strongly perfumed scent."

"What an idea, Sir Matthew!" answered his wife. "Blaming the poor flowers for your headache! Like as not, you only imagined it, or even more probably, your headache was the effect of drinking too much port. I am glad to say that at least we have gone some way towards curing you of that habit!"

Sir Matthew made no more protest about the roses, and his wife then proceeded to direct a gardener as to which flowers he should cut and in what quantity. Sir Edward took advantage of the intermission to rest his aching joints. He reclined on a bench, covering most of its length as he did so. Trying to take up as little room as possible, his son-in-law perched uncomfortably next to him on the far end, while Lady Villiers and her son settled on the opposite bench.

Once enough roses had been cut to fill at least a dozen vases, Lady Leigh expressed a wish to carry a few of the flowers in her hand so that she might smell them from time to time during the walk. Her family was therefore obliged to wait some more while the gardener stripped the roses of their thorns in order that the young lady could carry them without fear of being pricked.

When at last the bouquet was ready, Lady Leigh asked sweetly, "Sir Matthew, would you be so kind as to carry my parasol over my face while we walk? I cannot hold both the flowers and the parasol."

"Yes, dear."

With great reluctance, the gentleman rose from the bench to do his wife's bidding. As he was passing John Villiers, who had by then risen from his own bench, the latter said to him gleefully, "Now that you have caught the firebird by the tail, do not complain that it scorches your hands!"

"What was that about firebirds, Brother?" called the red-haired young lady from the rose bushes.

"Nothing of consequence, Priscilla... I mean, *your ladyship*," came the slightly mocking answer. "I was just telling Sir Matthew about the Baltimore oriolus, a species that the North American natives call the firebird on account of its brilliant, fire-like plumage. I read about it in *The British Encyclopedia*."

"Argh, playing the scholar again!" thought his sister and inquired no further. And so they walked on, with Sir Matthew's arm trembling and feeling a little numb from the effort of keeping it outstretched awkwardly to hold the parasol over his wife's head.

At dinner, Lady Leigh had much to talk about. She spoke of the improvements she had already made on her husband's estate and of those that had yet to be accomplished. "Some of the rooms must be redecorated," said she, "and of course, my portrait will need to be added to the gallery. I will commission none but Thomas Lawrence to paint it, for he is the best portraitist in Europe. And then, there are the gardens to consider. I want both a pinery and an orangery established at Brelwick Park; I love a good orange, and pineapples always look so impressive on the table when guests come to dinner!"

"Is it not too cold to grow pineapples and oranges in Cheshire?" asked her brother.

"The climate does present some challenge, but with the help of England's leading gardeners, I am sure it can be done. There is a magnificent pinery at Dunmore in Scotland after which I want to model our own, and surely if pineapples succeed in Scotland, they can in the North of England as well."

"How do you intend to pay for all these improvements?" demanded Sir Edward.

"I assure you, Papa, that I am very mindful of the expense. Savings will simply have to be made elsewhere to cover the cost of all my plans. One of the first things I did when I came to Brelwick was to change the house-keeper. The new one is a sharp-eyed, clever woman who permits neither scarcity nor waste. I have set her the task of improving the efficiency of the household so that the same amount of work can be done by fewer servants, and when Sir Matthew and I return home, I will see to reducing the servants' wages."

The time soon came for the ladies to withdraw to the drawing room. As she was leaving, Lady Leigh told her husband privately, "Papa and John will keep drinking their port forever if given the chance. I am relying on you to bring them to the drawing room at a reasonable hour. The last thing I want is to have to come and fetch all of you myself." Sir Matthew promised her that he would do as she asked.

When the ladies were alone together, mother and daughter continued the conversation on the latter's new life at Brelwick Park. Lady Leigh was exceedingly pleased with everything. The mansion and grounds were both splendid, and just as satisfying, she was much admired by Sir Matthew's friends. She had made many new and useful connections among his ac-quaintances, and it was not infrequently that she and her husband dined with Lord —, who would undoubtedly be a great help to Sir Matthew in procuring a seat in the House of Commons."

"Sir Matthew wishes to enter Parliament?" asked Lady Villiers with surprise.

"Well, he does now. I will admit, he was very reluctant even to consider the idea at first, but in time I helped him to see reason," returned her daughter.

"To have a son-in-law in Parliament—what a fine thing that would be!"

"Yes, but Mama, I do not intend to stop there. My ultimate aim is for Sir Matthew to be made a peer."

"Do you think it is possible?"

"Yes, why not? Many men have been elevated to the peerage as a reward for loyal service while in government, and if *they* can, so can my husband. Although Sir Matthew already has a title, he is only a baronet. It is better than nothing, I suppose, but what I really wish is for him to become a member of the nobility."

"To be sure, 'Lord' does have a better sound to it than 'Sir'," agreed Lady Villiers.

"I am determined that we should succeed," declared her daughter. "That is why I had Sir Matthew change the way his hair is cut ahead of the elections."

"Why, what was the matter with the way in which his hair was cut previously? I thought he looked very handsome even before the alterations."

"He did, indeed, and I must confess that my husband was most unwilling to make the changes, but I persuaded him; he must have the hair of a statesman if he is to be taken seriously."

The conversation then turned to John Villiers, for whom his sister had already chosen a suitable prospective bride from among her new acquaintances. The young lady in question, a Miss Fitzgerald, had a fortune of fifty thousand pounds (in addition to further expectations) and came from a very prominent family too! Her fortune was, admittedly, not the equal of the property that Lady Catherine's daughter would inherit, but perhaps it was just as well that match had never come about. Anne de Bourgh, now Mrs. Brooke, had shown exceptionally poor judgment in marrying so far beneath her; such a lack of sense was not to be desired in a wife. Besides, with her sickly constitution, who knew whether she was even capable of producing an heir? Thus consoled, the ladies busied themselves with planning how best to bring about a marriage between John Villiers and Miss Fitzgerald.

While the ladies were scheming, the gentlemen were talking of business.

"If you are ever to become solvent again, it is imperative that you raise the rents on your estate as soon as possible," said Sir Edward to his son-in-law.

"I would, only the rents are already quite high; my late father increased them the last time that he renewed the leases."

"It is of no consequence. Raise them again."

"I would not wish to completely impoverish my tenants."

"You must consider your own interests first," insisted Sir Edward.

"Yes, but at the same time I am not eager to increase the rents to an unfair level."

"My dear Sir Matthew, what is fair or unfair is very much a matter of personal opinion. Moreover, it is not only a question of fairness but also of social order. It is my view that excessive prosperity among the lower classes undermines the order that holds society together. If the world is to function properly, masters must maintain the upper hand, and I believe that the best way for them to do so is for the working man to eat today what he earns tomorrow."

This discussion John Villiers found to be extremely tedious. Why must his father always be talking of money and business? What an ungentlemanly use of one's time! Still, being very fond of his port, Mr. Villiers was in no hurry to rejoin the ladies. In the last several months, he and his father had grown accustomed to being rather free with the bottle, and he therefore found it very disagreeable to be presently hastened to the drawing room by Sir Matthew. The latter gentleman would himself have preferred to linger at the wine a little longer, but remembering his promise to his wife, he decided that it would be unwise to tarry. Anything was preferable to hearing another scolding from her.

John Villiers voiced his displeasure to his sister privately as soon as he entered the drawing room. "We would never have returned so soon if not for your husband's urging," he complained. "Of all the times Sir Matthew dined with us at Belargent, he never showed such haste before. What have you done to him during these past months?!"

"Only what every good wife ought to do," came the breezy reply.

"It is like *The Taming of the Shrew*, only I think in this case, the shrew is doing all the taming," continued Mr. Villiers incredulously. "I believe I would rather be a bachelor my whole life rather than have my wife telling me what to do from morning till night!"

"Nonsense, Brother! Sir Matthew's life has improved in countless ways since our wedding."

"Really? How?!"

"Well, for one thing, the finances at Brelwick Park used to be in disarray, whereas now that I have taken charge of the household, there is economy and prudence. The expenses no longer exceed the estate's income, and yet we do not lack anything that is needed to preserve our rank and dignity in society. Additionally, consideration has been given to my young sister-in-law's education. She has been sent away to school, so now there will be no more governesses."

Mr. Villiers laughed inwardly at the thought that the latter accomplishment was perhaps of greater benefit to Lady Leigh herself than to either her sister-in-law or her husband.

"In fact, Sir Matthew has become a changed man since our marriage," the young lady continued. "He drinks wine only in strict moderation, and he no longer bets high when playing at cards. What is more, I have spoken to Papa about my husband's debts and have arranged everything. Now Sir Matthew can be sure of receiving loans and any other assistance required as long as he continues his exemplary conduct. So you see, Brother," Lady Leigh said with a slight smile, "though my husband may not fully realise it yet, he is much happier as a married man than he was as a bachelor."

The Leighs stayed a week at Belargent Hall, and during that time, Sir Edward took every opportunity to instruct his son-in-law, in minute detail, as to how he must manage his money and run his estate. He desired Sir Matthew to write to him regularly and give an account of his progress with putting the directions into practice. Sir Edward forewarned, also, that he would be sure to visit him and his wife at Brelwick Park later on in the year to inspect the state of things himself.

The hour of departure for home could not come soon enough for the poor, young gentleman; and when he and his wife at last set off for Cheshire, Sir Matthew let out a long-held sigh of relief. Watching their chaise leave, Sir Edward grumbled with a gloomy shake of the head, "That I should have such a son-in-law! Who could have foreseen such an affliction?"

"Father, do not despair," said John Villiers. "You forget what sort of woman is now his wife. Rest assured that Priscilla will whip him into respectability and affluence!"

CHAPTER 46

Elizabeth's baby was born in the first week of July. The child was a healthy, vigorous boy, whom his parents named George after Mr. Darcy's late father. That same month, Jane Bingley discovered that she, too, was with child. Whether or not taking the waters in Bath had played any part in bringing about this long-awaited result, Jane could not be sure, but what did it matter? She would soon have a little son or daughter of her own!

As if all this wonderful news were not enough, Mr. Darcy announced that he planned to take his family to London for the fashionable season, and this time, his young sister-in-law was to come with them. Kitty could hardly contain her happiness. At last she would have a season in London! Considering her history of improper behaviour, one might wonder at the wisdom of allowing Kitty out into society at all, but in fact, Catherine Bennet had improved greatly of late, which factored significantly in Mr. and Mrs. Darcy's decision to bring her with them to town.

Ever since that horrible day when Miss Bennet learned that her affections for Mr. Morgan were not returned, her manners underwent a marked transformation. When in company, she no longer behaved towards men with that levity of manner which Mrs. Darcy had always found objectionable, and even when Elizabeth was not looking, her younger sister refrained from her habit of throwing flirtatious glances at handsome gentlemen.

Kitty also began to take her education more seriously. Whereas in the past the girl found every excuse to avoid reading anything except novels, Elizabeth was astonished to discover her sister reading Morell and Goldsmith's *The History of England* in the Pemberley library one day. Kitty made light of it, but she was found reading the same book again on the morrow, and thereafter she devoted half an hour of each day to serious reading. She also began practicing a little on the pianoforte almost daily, which she endured by telling herself that she would never touch the instrument again once she was married; and while her efforts paled in comparison with Georgiana's, she practiced more than she had ever done before in her life. What, might one ask, was the cause of Miss Bennet's sudden metamorphosis? Let it be sufficient to say that the desire to marry well is a powerful inducement.

After dinner one evening, when Kitty had just finished playing a simple tune for the family, Mrs. Darcy recalled some news, which she then proceeded to share with the others. Mrs. Newnham had called earlier in the day and told her that Tillesby Hall a few miles off would soon have a new occupant. While Mrs. Newnham knew none of the particulars, she could say with certainty that the house was to be let to a Sir Thomas Grey-Egerton.

"I know the gentleman!" exclaimed Mr. Darcy. "He was a friend of my father. Only, Mrs. Newnham is mistaken as to his title; he was indeed styled Sir Thomas Grey-Egerton until the end of his parliamentary career in the House of Commons, but then he was elevated to the peerage and is now known as Lord Wilton."

"I do not recall ever having met him," said Georgiana.

"Lord Wilton has not visited Pemberley for many years; you were quite young when I last saw him," replied her brother, adding, "I shall be glad to renew the acquaintance, although I am surprised to hear that he travels much these days. Lord Wilton must be over sixty years of age now, and last I heard, he was not at all in good health."

As the Pemberley ladies were walking upstairs together for the night with their candles, Georgiana asked Mrs. Darcy, "Lizzy, do you think this new neighbour of ours might be a near relation of Mr. Grey?"

"It is possible, I suppose, but perhaps not especially likely. There are a number of different branches of the Grey and Egerton families scattered throughout England; Lord Wilton could be from any one of them."

On Sunday, Elizabeth and Kitty went to church by themselves. Mr. Darcy had gone to London, where business was to detain him for several days, while Georgiana stayed at home with a cold. As the two ladies were getting into the carriage, Kitty remarked, "Whoever heard of catching cold in July, in the heat of summer?!" Elizabeth replied, "She must have chilled her throat with all those ices she ate yesterday."

Georgiana spent her morning alone quietly. First she did a little reading, and then she answered some letters, including one from Anne. Her cousin had written that she was expecting a baby, which filled Georgiana with tremendous joy when she first learned the news, but now, as she was rereading Anne's letter, she also felt a twinge of sadness. Would she herself ever have a family of her own? Everyone around her, it seemed, was having children or expecting one soon—either that, or getting married. Would her day ever come? She was beginning to think that perhaps it was not God's will that she should marry. Georgiana still kept Mr. Grey's valentine and looked at it sometimes, though ever since leaving Bath, it gave her more sorrow than happiness to see it. The dearest wish of her heart—to marry Mr. Grey—now appeared as if it would never happen.

After she had been musing in this way for some time, the sound of Kitty's complaining voice and Elizabeth's more cheerful one answering it signalled the ladies' return home. Sighing a little, Georgiana put away her letters, and a short while later Mrs. Darcy and her sister entered the room. Perceiving her friend seated on the sofa, Kitty forgot what she had just been whining about, and with a much brighter countenance announced, "We met the new neighbour in church today—you know, the one Lizzy was telling us about."

"Oh?" said Georgiana with curiosity. "What was he like?"

"Old, *very* old. What would you say, Lizzy?—did he look closer to seventy or eighty?"

"I thought my brother said he is not much more than sixty," recalled Georgiana, looking puzzled.

"Oh, but he looks *much* older!" Catherine assured her. "His hair is completely white."

"That is quite enough, Kitty," said Elizabeth with a reproving look; yet, there was also amusement in her countenance.

Undeterred, Catherine continued, "He is so aged that he can scarcely walk, and then only with the aid of a cane, and also he has a large hump in his back!"

"Really, Kitty, that is going too far," Elizabeth chided her sister. "You must not talk so. Besides, Georgiana will see for herself when our neighbour comes to dine with us tomorrow."

"What did you think of him? Was he a pleasant man?" inquired Georgiana.

"It is not easy to say... He was missing several of his teeth, which made it difficult to understand him when he spoke," replied Catherine and then burst into laughter.

"Kitty!" cried Elizabeth, but Miss Bennet only laughed harder and danced out of the room, beyond the reach of her sister's admonishments.

"What has come over her all of a sudden?" asked Georgiana when Catherine was gone. Elizabeth answered that she had no idea but looked as if she might know more than she was telling. Unflattering though Kitty's description of the gentleman had been, Georgiana was very desirous of making his acquaintance; the possibility of a family connection between him and Mr. Grey evoked more interest in meeting the man than was normally the case for her when newcomers settled in the neighbourhood.

Shortly before the appointed dinner hour the next day, Georgiana came down to the drawing room, and soon thereafter, Elizabeth and Kitty joined her. They had not been there long when the butler, with his usual solemn dignity, announced the arrival of Sir Thomas Grey-Egerton. To Georgiana's astonishment, not the elderly man she was expecting but Mr. Grey walked into the room. For some seconds, the lady could do nothing other than stare in disbelief; she knew not whether to doubt her eyes or her ears, for one or the other sense was clearly deceiving her.

"Mr. Grey!" she finally uttered in a voice hardly louder than a whisper, and after another pause she added, "It is a wonderful surprise to see you again, ... but where is Sir Thomas Grey-Egerton? ... Or was it Lord Wilton, I thought?" She turned to look at Elizabeth and Kitty for answers; the younger sister was grinning from ear to ear, and Mrs. Darcy, who was also smiling, said, "Sir Thomas Grey-Egerton is standing right here before you."

Georgiana shook her head in bewilderment. "I do not understand."

The gentleman soon explained everything. After Georgiana left Bath, Sir Philip Egerton's illness progressed rapidly, and in April, he breathed his last. In his will, he left his estate in Somersetshire to Mr. Grey on condition that his nephew take the additional name of Egerton. Since Sir Philip died childless, the young man also succeeded to his uncle's baronetcy by special remainder.

When Sir Thomas finished speaking, Georgiana protested, "But I distinctly remember my brother saying that our new neighbour was a gentleman over sixty years of age who had served in Parliament, and whose name is Thomas Grey-Egerton."

Mrs. Darcy replied, "Such a man is, indeed, living, but he holds a different baronetcy—that of Egerton and Oulton. In addition, he is the Earl of Wilton, and the Viscount and Baron Grey de Wilton."

Sir Thomas added, "Now that I have appended my uncle's name to my own, Lord Wilton and I are namesakes, though I have never met the gentleman. He is a distant kinsman of mine."

Georgiana felt an unsettling mixture of emotions. She was, of course, inexpressibly happy to again be near the man who had won her love, but her joy was marred by sadness over Sir Philip's death. She had come to like the old gentleman very much, and it grieved her that she would never see him again.

The butler presently announced that dinner was served, whereupon the party proceeded to the dining room. Several times during the repast, Georgiana had to catch herself from addressing Sir Thomas incorrectly, but in spite of her best efforts, she forgot once or twice and called him Mr. Grey. The young man, however, did not much care what she called him; all that mattered to him was that he had at last been reunited with Miss Darcy.

While they were finishing dessert, Elizabeth suggested that Georgiana show their guest her paintings.

"Yes, of course," replied her sister-in-law. "That is, if you are interested to see them, Sir Thomas."

The gentleman assured her that he would be delighted; he had heard her play and sing in the past but had never yet seen any pieces of art done by her hand, and it would give him great pleasure to do so.

After dinner, therefore, the whole party went upstairs to Georgiana's favourite sitting room, where her most recent pieces were to be found. As they were ascending the staircase, Mrs. Darcy said, "Georgiana, if you and Sir Thomas will go on without us, Kitty and I must first get our shawls, but we will join you shortly."

"I do not need a shawl! I am perfectly warm as I am," protested Kitty.

Turning so that their guest could not see her face, Elizabeth gave her sister a meaningful look and answered, "Nevertheless, I think it would be wise to follow Georgiana's good example and put on something warmer. The air is somewhat cooler than usual tonight—you might catch cold."

Suddenly understanding her sister's intent, Kitty replied, "Ah... yes... now that you mention it, the air does feel a little chilly this evening. I think perhaps we ought to get our shawls after all."

As Elizabeth and Catherine afterwards continued on to their rooms, neither lady looking to be in any particular hurry, Georgiana blushed to the tips of her ears. She guessed their true motive for wishing to leave herself and Sir Thomas alone, but determined not to show her embarrassment, she composed herself and led him to the sitting room. Yet, while they were walking, she could feel her pulse throbbing and an electric sensation flowing in every limb as hope and fear coursed through her body. The gentleman had been given an opportunity; would he take it? Making an effort to calm herself, Georgiana steadied her voice and said, "Let me again express how sorry I am about your uncle. Sir Philip was an excellent man, and a very kind one."

"Yes he was," replied Sir Thomas. "During the last months of his life, he became almost like a father to me. I only wish I could have had more time with him. You see, for many years there was a disagreement between him and my father, which prevented me from seeing my uncle and his wife until just this past year. I regret that our families were not able to reconcile sooner."

"How *is* Lady Egerton?" asked Georgiana.

"As well as can be expected; she was very attached to her husband and is deeply mourning his death."

After a brief pause, Sir Thomas continued, "Although Sir Philip provided well for her in his will, I sometimes feel that perhaps it would have been more proper for my aunt, rather than myself, to have inherited the estate. At the same time, it is not for me to question my uncle's wishes, or to be anything but profoundly grateful to him, for my inheritance has given me the opportunity to come here and ask you that which I would otherwise have had no right to do."

They had just entered the sitting room, and as Georgiana heard these last words, understood their meaning, she halted her footsteps. Tremulously, she turned to face Sir Thomas. He came a little closer. There was ardour in his looks when he said, "Miss Darcy, had it been in my power, I would have voiced my intentions earlier, but being conscious of the difference in our relative situations, I dared not declare my feelings for you openly until Providence had placed me in a position to express the sentiments of my heart in a manner consistent with honour. Now that my changed circumstances finally permit me to speak, I cannot go another day without confessing what I feel for you.

"Permit me then, Miss Darcy, to tell you how deeply and devotedly I love you. You have captivated me with your loveliness and charm, the sweetness of your character, and the beauty of your mind. I can imagine no greater happiness than to be with you all the days of my life—to hear your voice, to see your cheerful smile, to laugh with you. So long as my heart beats, it will be forever yours. I offer it to you with the promise that the chief object of my hopes and endeavours will always be your happiness."

Georgiana had scarcely drawn breath while listening to Sir Thomas' tender words. Trembling visibly, the young lady then ventured to reply. She gave him to understand, as well as she modestly could, that his love was returned, and that his wishes for the future were the same as her own.

With tears in his eyes, he took both of her hands in his and brought them to his lips. "My darling," said he, "If only you knew how I longed for you during these months that we were apart, and what I suffered when you quitted Bath, and I had to let you go without saying a word; how I feared that sooner or later, you would become someone else's wife, and that I would lose you forever. Can it be possible that you have agreed to be mine?"

They stood together quietly in a moment of complete joy, both conscious only of each other's presence, and feeling extraordinarily fortunate that fate had brought them back together; but finally remembering their original purpose for coming into the sitting room, Sir Thomas asked his beloved about the pictures she had promised to show him.

"Not only am I eager to see your work," said he, "but it might be rather awkward when Mrs. Darcy and Miss Bennet return to discover that I *still* have not seen any of them. How will we explain ourselves?"

"I had quite forgotten about the pictures!" answered Georgiana. "There are several of mine hanging in this room, but before we look at them, let me show you some that I painted during my time in Bath. I have never shown them to anyone; you will be the first to view them."

She opened a drawer and took out several paintings, done in watercolours. "Here is a scene that I think you may find familiar," said she, directing his attention to one that showed the Royal Crescent. Sir Philip and Lady Egerton were illustrated looking out curiously from one of the windows at the elegant ladies and gentlemen parading below, Georgiana along with Mr. and Mrs. Bingley among them. The painting was designed using bright, cheerful colours and had a great deal of character and charm.

The next one, which Sir Thomas viewed with much amusement, depicted bathers bobbing about in the King's Bath, from which an imaginary pipe, also illustrated, carried the spent bath water up to the fountain in the pump-room. Standing around the fountain were a number of unsuspecting men and women, who quaffed the water from their cups with gusto. There was an inscription at the bottom of the picture: "Bath water is better than Bath wine."

"I see that you have not forgotten the little joke I played on you," remarked Sir Thomas.

"Neither forgotten, nor forgiven!" returned Georgiana with playful indignation. She then showed him another painting, this one depicting their walk in the Sydney Gardens—specifically, the moment when she slipped on the icy bridge and came close to falling. With arms flung out to the sides and one foot raised precariously in the air, Georgiana tottered on the other. Painted nearby was her faithful suitor, rushing gallantly to her rescue, while a little farther off Miss Fellowes and Mr. Amherst looked on with alarmed countenances.

Smiling with enjoyment, Sir Thomas admired the rest of Georgiana's

Bath paintings. Each one was lovingly done and chronicled some little moment or experience that the two of them had shared together in town; and as he perused the scenes before him, he recalled to mind the memories captured in those pictures.

At long last, Mrs. Darcy and her sister returned wearing their shawls. When they entered, Georgiana put away the watercolour drawings she had just been showing to her betrothed, and seeing that the ladies looked at her with a mixture of interest and expectation, she relieved their curiosity and admitted, rather bashfully, that she and Sir Thomas were now engaged. Elizabeth and Kitty were delighted; they both thought she had chosen very well.

"I wish Fitzwilliam were here so that we could ask his blessing," said Georgiana, and then asked, "You have never seen my brother, have you, Sir Thomas?—there is a portrait of him in the gallery if you would like to view it." The gentleman readily agreed. He was eager to see the face of Mr. Darcy, of whom he had heard much from the family, and in whose hands lay the power to either secure or dash all his hopes of future happiness.

In the gallery, while they were passing one fine work of art after another, Sir Thomas suddenly caught sight of a painting of Georgiana. He stopped to look at it more closely, and as he was admiring the graceful form of his fair one, rendered masterfully on the canvas, Elizabeth told him that the picture, as well as a portrait of herself close by, were both recent additions; Mr. Darcy had commissioned the paintings of his wife and sister shortly after his wedding.

Sir Thomas turned his gaze in the direction Elizabeth was motioning, and in doing so, he could not help noticing another picture right beside Mrs. Darcy's own. The subject was a handsome gentleman, very dignified, and with a noble mien. In his features, there was a strong resemblance to Georgiana. Upon inquiry, Sir Thomas learned that the face was indeed Mr. Darcy's, as he had suspected.

The young man directed his eyes back to the portrait. It seemed to frown at him. Observing the slightly awed and almost startled expression of Sir Thomas' countenance, Georgiana asked whether there was anything the matter.

"Nothing," said he, "except perhaps an overly active imagination... You see, when a man intends to ask him who sat for the painting for his sister's hand in marriage, the face depicted on the canvas seems to acquire a certain severity, a sternness, a formidable quality, even, that did not seem to exist there before."

The lady answered mischievously, "If my brother's likeness can inspire so much fear, I wonder what effect the original will produce?"

CHAPTER 47

Shortly after midday on Wednesday, Sir Thomas came to Pemberley. Georgiana was in the garden when he arrived, but no one informed her of his coming, for it was chiefly Mr. Darcy whom he was there to see. After introducing the two gentlemen, Elizabeth left them alone in the library for what proved to be a rather lengthy interview; but at last Sir Thomas emerged.

As he walked out of the house and into the afternoon sunshine, he relished the feeling of a pleasant breeze cooling the anxious perspiration that moistened his brow. The trial was over! Suddenly noticing some tightness that had gathered in his neck during the private conversation with Mr. Darcy, he shrugged his shoulders a few times to loosen the tension. A servant showed him the way to the walled garden, where the gentleman had been told he would find Georgiana.

Sir Thomas discovered her seated on some soft straw covering the ground of a large strawberry bed; being partially turned away, the lady did not see him approach. He walked slowly, taking the opportunity to admire her lovely figure. Having drawn quite near, and still unobserved, he watched in amazement as she plucked a pale-coloured berry and popped it into her mouth. Then, without so much as a grimace, she reached for another, no redder than the first.

Unable to suppress a laugh, he exclaimed, "You must be very hungry for strawberries, Miss Darcy! I see you are not even waiting for the berries to ripen before eating them!"

Georgiana turned around with a startled expression, which quickly transformed into an impish smile as she answered, "Unripe though they may be, I like them very well. Love makes everything taste sweeter! Here, try one and see whether you do not agree."

She stretched out a hand and offered him one of the milky-white fruits studded with scarlet seeds. Noticing that he was unwilling, she urged in a beguiling manner, "Taste, taste!"

Sighing, he took the proffered strawberry and remarked, "What a man will not do for his beloved!" With great reluctance, he took a bite of the fruit. An instant later his countenance was a picture of delighted astonishment, and in an incredulous tone of voice he declared, "I must be in love to an uncommon degree! This strawberry tastes sweeter than a red one!"

Georgiana dissolved into laughter, and when she was sufficiently recovered, she cried, "There, I have fooled you for once, Sir Thomas! That is for the time you played a trick on me in Bath and made me think I was drinking the water that other people had bathed in."

"Fair enough, Miss Darcy; but how did you manage such a ruse with the strawberries? Did you sprinkle them with sugar? Or perhaps with some of your magic fairy dust?"

"Neither, Sir Thomas. These are South American white strawberries. They never turn red, not even when they ripen. I received some plants as a gift from my cousin Anne. She had them growing at Rosings."

The gentleman's countenance then became more serious as he told Georgiana that he had spoken to her brother that afternoon of their desire to marry.

"What did he say?" asked Georgiana breathlessly.

"The answer I received was not the one I had hoped for, but at least it was not a refusal. Mr. Darcy would like to become better acquainted with me before giving his consent to our union."

Georgiana's face fell a little at this news, but Sir Thomas reassured her: "It is no worse than what I expected to hear from a cautious and affectionate brother. In fact, I would likely have done the same in his place. In the meantime, Miss Darcy, he has given me permission to address you as a suitor, and for this evening, I have an invitation to dine at Pemberley. It is as great a sign of his approbation as I could have hoped to receive so early in my acquaintance with him."

Patience was not one of Georgiana's virtues, but patient she would have to be. Were it her decision to make, she would gladly have wedded Sir Thomas on the morrow. Unfortunately, until she came of age, the power to decide when, or even *if*, she could marry him rested with her guardians. Still, there was ample cause for cheerfulness; only a few days earlier, Georgiana thought she would never see her dear one again, and yet here he was by her side.

That evening's dinner at Pemberley passed very pleasantly. Sir Thomas succeeded in making a favourable impression on Mr. Darcy, who, in the course of observing his dinner guest's looks and manner, ascertained that the gentleman was truly in love with his sister. Before many months had passed, the suitor's superior merits convinced both Georgiana's brother and Colonel Fitzwilliam that the maiden under their guardianship would not find a better husband. The young people were soon thereafter married and began the first of many happy years together on Sir Thomas' estate in Somersetshire.

Lady Catherine de Bourgh was beside herself with anger when she received news of the wedding. Was it not enough that her favourite nephew, and worse, her own daughter, had both made deplorable matches? For her niece to then marry the villain who had helped to bring one of them about was too much! Could anyone have imagined a more vexing set of marriages?! What had she ever done to deserve such punishment from God?!

In some measure, it helped to console her ladyship that the alliance between Georgiana and Sir Thomas Grey-Egerton was at least the most prudent of the three. The gentleman's family and connections were very respectable, and the fortune he had inherited was a large one. This circumstance, in time, helped to calm Lady Catherine's outrage, as did her eventual reconciliation with Anne and Mr. Brooke.

It was the birth of Anne's first child that finally softened her ladyship's heart and gained the married couple an invitation to Rosings Park, which had firmly and resentfully been denied to them before. For the sake of being able to see her little grandson, Lady Catherine endeavoured, if not to like Mr. Brooke, at least to tolerate him. She managed it with some success, and the discovery that Mr. Brooke's great uncle had been a baron further helped to recommend the young man to her favour and to soothe her wounded pride. Lady Catherine later exerted her influence at court to procure a baronetcy for her son-in-law, and henceforth she felt a relative freedom from shame when introducing him as *Sir* Francis Brooke to her acquaintances.

Glad as Anne and her husband were that amicable relations had been restored, they found it necessary, after a time, to remove to a new home far beyond the reach of Lady Catherine's well-intentioned but highly meddlesome advice. Apart from their yearly visits to Rosings, the Brookes lived mainly in Lyme, where Anne flourished. The restorative power of the healthful sea air and the tranquil life in the coastal town, combined with the love and tenderness of her husband, made her stronger and healthier than she had ever been in her life.

Since the Brookes and the Grey-Egertons lived at a distance of little more than forty miles apart, the two families saw each other not infrequently. Sir Thomas and Georgiana's marriage being founded on love and mutual regard, they found lasting happiness with one another, and their years together were marked by deep and uninterrupted affection. Sir Thomas continued giving sermons in his parish church most Sundays but employed a curate to assist him with the more mundane of a clergyman's duties. With an income sufficient to free him from the common anxieties of life, he had the leisure to put his talents to best use in further deepening his knowledge of the sacred subject it was his vocation to teach to others; and with his wealth, he was able to do more good in his profession than had been possible heretofore. The kindness and generosity for which Sir Thomas and his wife became known earned them the love and esteem of their fellow parishioners.

THE END

NOTES

[1] Lennox, Charlotte. "The Art of Coquetry." *Gentleman's Magazine*, vol. 20, November 1750, pp. 518–519.

[2] Marlowe, Christopher. *The Tragical History of Doctor Faustus From the Quarto of 1604.* Edited by Alexander Dyce.

[3] Plutarch. *Plutarch's Lives.* Historical and critical notes by M. Dacier, vol. 7, printed for J. Tonson, 1727, p. 264.

[4] *The Whole Duty of Man.* Printed for John Beecroft, 1774.

[5] Homer. *The Odyssey of Homer.* Translated by William Cowper, 2nd ed., vol. 1, Bunney and Gold, 1802, pp. 235-236.

[6] *The Holy Bible.* King James Version, T. Wright & W. Gill, 1779, Eph. 5.22-5.24.

[7] "My Deary, if thou die." *The Tea-table Miscellany.* Printed for Allan Ramsay by Mr. Thomas Ruddiman, 1724, pp. 109-110.

[8] *The Holy Bible, Containing the Old and New Covenant, Commonly Called the Old and New Testament.* Translated by Charles Thomson, printed by Jane Aitken, 1808, Song of Sol. 7.6-7.9.

[9] Shakespeare, William. *Romeo and Juliet.* Bell's Edition. Printed for John Cawthorn, 1806, pg. 38.

[10] Shakespeare, William. "LXXXVII." *The Poems of William Shakespeare,* printed for Edward Jeffery by E. Blackader, 1804, pg. 164.

[11] Shakespeare, William. *As You Like It, The Plays and Poems of William Shakspeare in Ten Volumes,* vol. 3, H. Baldwin, 1790, pg. 161.

[12] Baxter, Richard. *The Practical Works of the Late Reverend and Pious Mr. Richard Baxter: in Four Volumes,* vol. 1, printed for Thomas Parkhurst, Jonathan Robinson, and John Lawrence, 1707, pg. 106.

[13] *The New Testament with an Analysis of the Several Books and Chapters.* Translated by John Wesley, 1790, Matt. 5.28.

[14] *The New Testament with an Analysis of the Several Books and Chapters.* Translated by John Wesley, 1790, 1 Cor. 13.4-13.8.

[15] Bach, Johann Sebastian. "No.4: Prelude and Fugue in C-sharp minor." *Das Wohltemperirte Clavier II.*

[16] Shakespeare, William. *Hamlet, Prince Of Denmark: a Tragedy in Five Acts*, printed for R. Sammer, 1800, pg. 31.